Carol McGrath taught History and English for many years in both the state and private sectors. She left teaching to work on a MA in Creative Writing from Queens University Belfast, then an M Phil in English at Royal Holloway, London, where she developed her expertise on the Middle Ages.

As well as the *She-Wolves Trilogy* she is the author of the acclaimed *Daughters of Hastings Trilogy* and a standalone novel, *Mistress Cromwell*.

For the latest news and exclusive content from Carol, sign up to her newsletter at: www.carolcmcgrath.co.uk

Praise for *The Silken Rose*

'Powerful, gripping and beautifully told. A historical novel that will resonate with the #MeToo generation. Carol McGrath bewitched me with her immaculate research, vivid characters and complex tale of politics, power and love. I could smell the secrets and taste the fear that stalked King Henry's court. Clever, intimate and full of intrigue, I loved it.' **Kate Furnivall**

'A very well-researched tale of a fascinating period' **Joanna Courtney**

'A gripping tale of a much-maligned queen' **Henrietta Leyser**

'*The Silken Rose* dives into 13th century England with the relish of a peregrine's stoop . . . Temptation for any fan of scheming behind the arras and swooning courtly love!' **Joanna Hickson**

'A feast for the senses and highly recommended' **Deborah Swift**

THE
DAMASK
ROSE

CAROL McGRATH

ACCENT

First published in 2021 by Headline Accent
An imprint of HEADLINE PUBLISHING GROUP

1

Cataloguing in Publication Data is available from the British Library

ISBN 978 1 7861 5769 0

Map and Family Tree illustrations by Simon Michele

Typeset in 10.5/13pt Bembo Std by Jouve (UK), Milton Keynes

Printed and bound in Great Britain by Clays Ltd, Elcograf S.p.A.

HEADLINE PUBLISHING GROUP
An Hachette UK Company
Carmelite House
50 Victoria Embankment
London
EC4Y 0DZ

www.headline.co.uk
www.hachette.co.uk

For all those who work with medicine today
and with a thought for those like the fictional
Guillaume who were doctors long ago.

Dedicated to the memory of those
who have died from COVID-19.

THE FAMILY TREE

Eleanor of Castile   m.   Edward I
1241-1290   1239-1307

And others who died young	Eleanora 1269-1298	Joan of Acre 1272-1307	Margaret 1275-1233	Mary 1279-1332	Elizabeth 1282-1316	Edward 1284-1327
Katherine	m.	m.	m.	-	m.	m.
Joan I						
John	1. Alphonso of Aragon	1. Gilbert de Clare	John, Duke of Brabant		1. John of Holland	Isabella of France
Henry						
Berengaria						
Alphonso	2. Henry, Count of Bar	2. Ralph de Monthermer			2. Humphrey de Bohun	

Map 2: Gascony

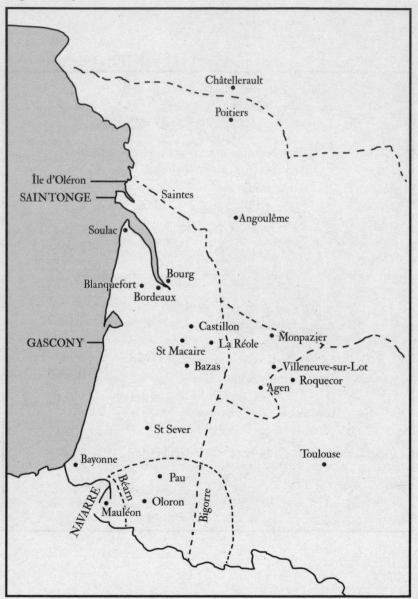

Châtellerault

Poitiers

Île d'Oléron

SAINTONGE

Saintes

Angoulême

Soulac

Bourg

Blanquefort

Bordeaux

GASCONY

Castillon

St Macaire

La Réole

Monpazier

Bazas

Villeneuve-sur-Lot

Agen

Roquecor

St Sever

Toulouse

Bayonne

Béarn

Pau

NAVARRE

Oloron

Bigorre

Mauléon

The Benedictine Hours

Matins	Between 2.30 and 3.00 in the morning
Lauds	Between 5.00 and 6.00 in the morning
Prime	Around 7.30 or shortly before daybreak
Terce	9.00 in the morning
Sext	Noon
Nones	Between 2.00 and 3.00 in the afternoon
Vespers	Late afternoon
Compline	Before 7.00, as soon after that the monks retire

Part One
England

So it fell upon a time when King Arthur said unto Merlin,
'My barons will let me have no rest, but needs I must take a
wife . . . I love Guinevere the King's daughter, Leodegrance of the
land of Cameliard, the which hidden in his house the table round
that ye told he had of my father Uther. And this damsel is the most
valiant and fairest lady I know living or yet I could ever find.'

Chapter I, Book III, *Morte D'Arthur* by Sir Thomas Malory,
published by William Caxton

Prologue

The rebel army assembled mid-afternoon on a meadow in front of Lewes Castle. Troops had streamed in from adjacent fields where they had flattened crops, created a bivouac camp, buried their dead before carrion crows ripped flesh from bones, and overnight had suffered their wounds to be tended, as well as legs and arms amputated. A gentle sun belied the horror of the previous day's battle but it could not conceal the stench of stale bodies and the metallic scent of drying blood hovering in the air.

Gilbert de Clare, only twenty-one years old and already a ruthless warlord, watched from the sidelines as his companion and leader Earl Simon de Montfort took up a position on the raised mound before the castle moat. Gilbert noted how light gleamed off the mail and scale of Earl Simon's hauberk and slanted onto his face, causing his leader to squint. They had gathered to hear Earl Simon speak of their victory over the King, now a prisoner along with his son Lord Edward and his brother the Duke of Cornwall, secured in the castle keep behind, and of the loyalist nobles whom Gilbert hoped would be exiled.

As a cloud passed over the sun Simon moved slightly into the shade of a tall sycamore tree and lifted high a tattered scroll which he waved at his troops. The excited men cheered. Three strong blasts of a trumpet followed. The crowd hushed and waited.

What, wondered Gilbert, his mouth sliding into a cynical smile, would his leader say now they had the King in their power and mastery of the land. Gilbert drew a deep breath and considered the territorial gains he might add to his vast territories on the Welsh Marches, especially those belonging to William of Pembroke, the King's half-brother – lands many of which were conveniently situated in Pembrokeshire – and he would at last recover his own castles of Kingston and Tonbridge, taken by King Henry five years ago when war between the King and the rebel barons had first broken out. They would rid the land of Jews too, a race that had long supported the King with money intended to bolster up his foolish reign. Gilbert smirked. He was proud that he had led the massacre of that unchristian race in Canterbury last month. Today he was even prouder, since he had commanded the centre of their army on the downs west of Lewes and led them to victory when Lord Edward had pursued their own vulnerable left wing for miles back towards London, leaving the King and Richard of Cornwall exposed and galloping towards the City. He, Gilbert de Clare, had personally accepted the surrender of Earl Richard, having trapped him in a windmill close to where they were now gathered. Yes, those who supported change in government deserved great rewards, and none more than himself.

Gilbert was a tall man and powerful physically, all muscle. As he watched Earl Simon, he drew himself up even taller as the last seven years fleeted through his vision. He thought of the realignment of loyalties, including his own, because King Henry had broken promise after promise. The barons and clergy had demanded simple changes in government. Henry had accepted the barons' council of fifteen, after years of negotiations, to help the king rule fairly the shires that made up England. A privy council was designed to advise Henry, curb his building and pageantry extravagances, his outrageous expenditure on feuding in Gascony, England's remaining territory across the Narrow Sea, and to put right his appallingly poor administration. They would advise the King on the custody of royal castles and oversee ministerial appointments.

After promising to accept these provisions, Henry had reneged, seeking the Pope's approval for his actions. He broke the agreement, claiming his hand had been forced. That had been the final straw for Gilbert, who had recently come into his earldom on his father's death. Gilbert's brow darkened as he felt a frown grow across his forehead and he considered how Henry's Lusignan stepbrothers as well as the Queen's Savoyard relatives between them had controlled England and the King. These foreigners were England's greatest archbishops, bishops, and even earls through marriages forged with their land's greatest heiresses and heirs. In fact, Gilbert mused with his lips curling with distaste, at only ten years of age he had been pushed into marriage with one of them eight years his senior. He grimaced as a picture of cold, unpleasant, proudly beautiful Alix, his wife, clouded his vision. He had heard rumours of her behaviour with Lord Edward when the King had taken his half-niece prisoner along with the garrison of Tonbridge Castle.

There had been hope of change when Earl Simon returned to England from exile in France two years previously and consolidated opposition to the King. After routs throughout the south, Simon had even attempted to settle the differences between king and barons in a fair manner, or so he had thought. When Simon asked the King of France to arbitrate and persuade Henry to accept the statutes proposed by his barons, pious Louis, like the Pope before him, sided with Henry. After all, the French king was autocratic and he was married to that proud Provençal woman, Queen Ailenor's sister Marguerite. King Louis would never gainsay his own brother-in-law.

How could they accept such a judgement? The war had begun in earnest after that.

He thought of how Queen Ailenor was in France raising troops to support the royalist cause. It was as well they had victory at Lewes. The victory was a stroke of good fortune after loyalist successes. Gilbert did not believe in God's will particularly, favouring instead Lady Fortune. At first it seemed as if Lord Edward and King Henry would trounce them since Edward had made such a brilliant cavalry charge, but he later destroyed his luck by chasing his quarry from the field, meaning Henry was left to launch an infantry attack up Offham Hill. Now Henry was their prisoner and must negotiate. And the Queen would shudder with fear when the news reached her Gascon stronghold.

5

Gilbert whispered his thanks to Lady Luck and shook his mane of startling red hair. What next? He would help Montfort rule, Lord Simon's right-hand man. His eyes widened at the thought of power, gold in his coffers and new castles, not that he did not have plenty already. After all, his sire had been England's wealthiest baron. Still, you could never have too much.

Simon was beginning to speak and another fleeting thought flew into his mind. What if he and Alix separated, now the Lusignan fortunes were on the wane? He must look into it, a legal separation; perhaps, one day, even a divorce if he could find proof of consanguinity.

Earl Simon began to speak in English. Gilbert noted that although Simon had never lost his French accent, that bothered none of the men. They, he and Simon, had led them to victory after all, victory over a foolish king and his she-wolf wife.

'Yesterday our army was victorious. When we marched from London to treat with Henry Plantagenet, he promised peace if we presented ourselves with halters around our necks, ready for hanging.' He shook the tattered scroll he was holding. 'That's what it says here.' Earl Simon's face looked as red as Gilbert's own shock of red hair. '*Now*, the third Henry is our prisoner and must agree to *our* terms.'

Seizing a brand from a brazier, Simon set the King's letter alight. The parchment was slow to take flame at first but he kept torching it until it flared up. Cinders fluttered into the breeze like tattered black rags. Wax dripped from the burning words to hiss on the fire. He yelled as if he was God's own herald sounding out anger at His anointed King, 'From this day forth, a new council will rule for the King. Its members will be Englishmen. We'll take back our castles stolen as gifts for foreigners. The King's nepotism stops here, today. His Lusignan half-brothers will be exiled forthwith.

'Every shire in the realm will send knights. Every town will send two of their own townsmen to Parliament. Englishmen will seek justice for grievances through laws decided by Parliament.' He drew a long breath and, even louder, he decreed, 'Prisoners held at

Windsor Castle will be returned to us. And my own dear son.' Tears swam in his eyes as he spoke of his boy.

'I would feel the same,' Gilbert muttered to himself. Bells for Vespers rang out from the abbey. Earl Simon paused until they stopped before continuing.

'Families who have lost husbands and sons in the Battle of Lewes will receive fair and just comfort this coming winter. You have my word. Go in peace. Return to your homes knowing you fought for justice.'

Gilbert joined in the resounding cheer that arose amongst their troops. Bagpipes played. Priests offering pardons for crimes of war wandered through the crowds. Slowly, Earl Simon's army dispersed. Gilbert could smell the cooking fires' smoke mingling with the welcome aroma of roasting meat rise from the fields. The men were hungry. Tomorrow, some would return to their homes but Gilbert's own men, as Simon had requested that morning, would march north to capture Windsor Castle.

The Lady Eleanor, Lord Edward's wife, another young she-wolf, was its keeper. She would not be Windsor's custodian for much longer. He would take the castle from that haughty Spanish princess. Gilbert followed Simon back over the glassy moat trailed by his own squire. Of a sudden, Simon stopped, turned to him and said in a low voice, 'I'll travel with Henry to Canterbury and keep him there but I'm sending Edward and Richard to Wallingford under close guard. Separate them, divide and rule, is my tactic for now.'

'The other prisoners, my Lord?'

'Oh, you mean Pembroke and the others.'

Gilbert nodded. He had those Welsh lands in his sights but he would wait until Pembroke was out of the way before staking his own claims. Perhaps he would ask initially for Pembroke's Kent properties and his London houses.

Simon grinned. 'Exile.' He laughed. 'Well, frankly, I can hardly execute them. I'll strip them of their possessions and hope they go off on Crusade and stay away or die in Outremer, the pack of them.'

Gilbert thought to himself but did not say, it was more likely they would connive at a return. He felt Simon take his arm.

'Best, Gilbert, that we attend Vespers and give thanks. We may have won the war but we still have to win the peace. Pray for success. Windsor is your first call. We'll persuade Henry to ask his daughter-in-law to keep him company in Canterbury, nay, command her. I'll get him to sign a summons after he has eaten a good supper. He will comply once his ear is bent and he sees he has no option but to comply and, tomorrow, you will be on your way to Windsor with that royal summons.'

Supper was what Gilbert wanted more than prayer. The smell of cooking wafted from the kitchen building, assaulting his nostrils as he followed Simon towards the castle's chapel.

Chapter One

Windsor Castle
21 June 1264

On the feast of St John, Lady Eleanor watched the forest from the castle's lower battlements. Smoke from rebel campfires twisted above the treeline. The rebels had plundered her park, hunted stags in her forest, and cooked her venison. Occasionally a whiff drifted her way, reminding her that soon the castle would run out of food. She sighed, knowing she would have to consult with Master Thomas, her steward, as to how long they could survive without surrender, before they starved. Earl Simon's deputy, Hugh Bigod of Norfolk, had positioned his troops everywhere. They were hidden by willows hanging over the riverbanks; they were concealed in meadows and hiding within the barley growing in nearby fields; they camped even closer, amongst the beech trees in the King's deer park.

Movement on the edge of the forest! A moment later a rider emerged, galloping along the track towards the castle moat. Eleanor shaded her brow. There had been many messengers demanding she gave up the castle and she had sent them away. She edged along the battlements, peering over the parapets until she reached a point directly above the gatehouse. Something appeared very familiar about this particular horseman. A second rider, a squire perhaps, broke from the trees holding aloft a fluttering pennant. She drew breath sharply because rather than showing as usual Montfort's fork-tailed lion, this long curling flag displayed the King's leopards, gold and silver embroidery glinting in the sun. Her heart began to beat faster, pumping hard at her chest. Could he be a messenger from her husband at last?

Time stilled as if the scene below was painted inside a psalter. Eleanor's mantle billowed out and her short veil was nearly blown from her head by a sudden breeze. The castle rooks, roosting in trees, made loud mewing sounds like babies crying. Bells rang for Vespers. She peered directly below at her ladies trailing into the chapel, miniature figures with bowed heads and clasped hands. She *should* attend Vespers since it was the feast of St John today, but she remained where she was, as if mesmerised, watching the two riders clip-clopping along the path, their horses' snorts competing with the rooks' unsettling caws.

The knight slowed as he approached the moat. He halted, dismounted, and removed his helmet. Her eyes fixed upon his shock of red hair. Gilbert de Clare, the Earl of Gloucester! No other. She knew him well from the days before the barons' rebellion. And if Earl Simon was the devil, Gilbert of Gloucester, once her husband's friend, had turned his mantle and was Satan's helper. Tears of disappointment welled up behind her eyes.

Earl Gilbert tugged a scroll from his mantle and with one hand still holding his reins he held it up to the gatehouse guards. Ribbons dangled from a seal. Anger replaced disappointment. If this was a trick, she would have Simon de Montfort's son, *her* prisoner, hanged from a parapet.

She twisted her head to stare up at the range of battlements just above her head. 'Raise your bows,' she ordered the waiting archers, her Spanish accent breaking through her English speech. 'Bring Earl Simon's son out.' She pointed to the knight below. 'Gloucester is not to be trusted. Others may be hidden amongst the trees ready to attack.' A sergeant gave a sharp order and several guards raced off to fetch the prisoner, a young lad not yet twenty, also called Simon de Montfort.

Gathering her mantle close, Eleanor hurried down the stairway that spiralled through the castle and ran into the hall. She pulled a short sword from a wall bracket as she passed. After all, she had taken lessons in fighting from her brother Enrique in Castile, practising swordplay with him on sun-baked courtyards when she was growing up. Pages stared at her as she sped past them, their mouths wide open. Shocked guards by the great door fell back out of her way as they dragged it open. Not pausing for breath, she raced down the steps brandishing the sword and ran across the courtyard,

'Lower the bridge. If Gilbert de Clare carries a message from King Henry, fetch it.'

The drawbridge clanked as it was slowly lowered over the moat. A guard raced across it with her demand. Moments later he returned saying breathlessly, 'The Earl says he must deliver it himself into your own hands. He says go across yourself for it, my lady, else he will bring it over to you.'

Her captain of the guard shook his head at her. Eleanor hesitated for just a heartbeat. 'Tell Earl Gilbert he may cross but his squire remains beyond the drawbridge with their horses and weapons.'

Her guards fell back, hands on the hilts of their swords. She waited impatiently in the courtyard, trying hard to remain calm, as Red Gilbert casually walked onto the drawbridge and swaggered under the raised portcullis. After what felt long enough to say a dozen Paternosters he reached her. She did not waver but stood with Edward's short sword raised and pointing towards Gilbert's breast. The rebel looked her up and down from under fox-like eyebrows. He shook his russet hair and grinned but she kept her sword-arm steady and glared at him.

'Lady Eleanor,' he said smoothly, making a low bow. 'It is good to see you so well. Do put down that weapon.' He slowly held the scroll out in his open hands as if it were a precious glass ornament and added, 'I carry an order from King Henry. You are to relinquish his castle to us.'

Her response like his own speech was spoken in the Norman French of court. '*His* castle!' She felt her face grow hot. '*My* castle. This is a royal castle and I have sworn to my Lord Edward, the King's son, to protect it.'

'And he is a prisoner in Kenilworth Castle.'

It was true and Henry was their king, if, she knew well since Edward had complained often enough about his father, a weak one. Since Lewes a month before, Simon de Montfort had had Henry and Edward both in his power. There really was no alternative. She slowly lowered her sword and snatched the scroll from Gilbert. She unrolled the letter and read its brief message, the short sword's hilt loosening in her hand as she studied the words. It indeed bore Henry's signature. She grunted her disbelief. Henry ordered her to free young Simon de Montfort, to accompany the Earl of Gloucester, and join the King's household in Canterbury. There was no mention of her husband.

She crumpled the scroll, crumbs of sealing wax flaking onto her gown. Looking up she said, her anger seeping into her voice, 'Was King Henry forced to sign this order?'

'He signed it freely,' Gloucester said, his tone light, almost amused. *How dare he sound amused.*

'Give you Windsor and free my prisoner? I swore to my lord husband I would not and I shall not. Return to the King and tell your master I do not treat with traitors.' She felt herself glaring. 'Montfort must bring my husband to *me* before I return *his* son to him.' She waved the scroll in his face and pointed it up to the ramparts, where young Simon de Montfort now stood perilously positioned on the wall, a sword at his back. 'I give my order and he'll plummet down like a bird falling from a tree.'

'She-wolf,' hissed Gilbert, all amusement now wiped from his face. 'Call your men off. Release Earl Simon's son as your King commands.'

'Bring me my husband first. Bring Lord Edward here.' She crushed the letter in her left hand, its crimson ribbons fluttering in blood-like streamers. The sword dangled loosely by its hilt from her right hand.

That moment of angry pause was her undoing. With one agile movement, Earl Gilbert grabbed the sword from her and pulled her to him.

She hissed, 'You lay hands on a princess of the realm, Gilbert de Clare? It is treason.'

'But this princess disobeys her King. Treason indeed.'

In one smooth movement, gatehouse guards moved forward with outstretched swords. Gloucester spun her around as quickly as if he was turning a child's spinning top. A moment later, he was holding the short sword across her throat. Her guards drew back. He yelled upwards, 'Free Earl Simon's son or the lady's life is forfeit.' Holding her tighter, he said into her ear, 'If you want to see Lord Edward alive, call those dogs off.' She winced as he shouted, 'The lady accompanies me. It's the King's orders.'

'I have a daughter,' Eleanor cried out so all could hear. 'Where I go, so does my child.'

'Call your guards off,' he spat into her ear as he held her tighter against his chest. 'You'll have your daughter soon enough.'

She cursed Gilbert, 'Bastard son of a bastard mother. As God is my witness, I shall have revenge on you and your master.' She shouted up, 'Set him free,'

'I am simply obeying my king. You must do likewise. Have your prisoner brought down here. He leaves with us.' As if to emphasise his determination he knocked Eleanor's veil and circlet off her head with the sword, pricking her ear. She could feel blood slowly trickling down her neck. Her chestnut hair tumbled out of its crispinette and rippled down to her waist.

'If you won't obey King Henry, you'll heed me, Lady Eleanor,' Gilbert's voice had grown harsh. She knew he meant it.

Eleanor shouted, 'Bring Simon down.' She tried hard to wriggle from Gilbert's grasp, dropping the King's letter as she attempted to free her arm.

'Worse for you, my lady, if you struggle.' He pulled her back. When the shaking youth descended to the courtyard, Gilbert turned her roughly around towards the drawbridge and whistled to the young man holding his mount. A moment later his squire was riding over the moat, leading his master's stallion. 'Simon will ride with you, Pipkin,' Gilbert addressed the squire. 'Lady Eleanor rides with me.'

'What do you mean, I ride with you!' Eleanor felt fear tighten her chest. Keeping her voice steady she said evenly, 'My daughter is the

King's grandchild. What about my ladies?' Somehow she was facing her people again and she saw fear on their countenances.

'Arrangements have been made. They will follow and the child too.' His tone softened. 'I am not a monster. Neither is Earl Simon. We seek justice and fair rule.' Justice and fair rule? Unlikely. They were an evil pair. They were devils and both capable of great savagery. She had heard about the massacre in Canterbury that April.

Eleanor scanned the courtyard where her frightened people had begun to gather in family groups. A priest hurried through them clutching a large cross, his habit flapping in a sudden breeze. He crossed himself and shouted in a voice as clear as reliquary crystal, 'You, Gilbert of Gloucester, mark this, you are excommunicate by order of our Father, the Pope. You'll burn in Hell's fire and you'll deserve your fate.'

Earl Gilbert turned his head away from him. Pushing Eleanor forward again, he said, 'Up you go, my lady.' In a heartbeat, he had hoisted her onto his horse as if she were light as a feather, and jumped up behind her. He said into her pained ear, 'Tell them they are to obey Hugh Bigod when he enters the castle this evening. He'll arrange an escort for your ladies and household.'

'We have no choice,' she called down as she managed to wriggle an arm free from Gilbert's grip. She pointed at the crumpled scroll still lying on the earth, and shouted to her shocked steward, 'Take it. Read it to my people. Tell them the King has been forced to sign it.'

Master Thomas ran forward and scooped up the King's letter. He picked her veil up from the ground and handed it up to her.

'See the King's order is obeyed,' she said in a grudging tone as she took possession of her veil. Gilbert thrust her sword into an empty scabbard hanging from his saddle, and slowly walked his horse forward onto the drawbridge.

She could not let this seizure of her royal person go without another protest. 'Gilbert of Gloucester, I shall have my revenge on you,' she barked. 'No one treats a future queen in such a manner.' She knew she was making a formidable enemy but she didn't care. Her temper could be foul but she did not care about this either.

14

'Lady Eleanor, when you behave as a queen should, with suitable decorum, I shall treat you as a queen,' he quipped. 'Until then you are no better than a harridan.'

'Arrogant bastard,' she said under her breath as they rode into the trees, followed by the trotting horse ridden by the squire with the ridiculous name and carrying young Simon, the Devil's son.

That evening, she peered from her heavily guarded tent, incandescent, watching as Hugh Bigod, Earl of Norfolk, rode to take possession of Windsor Castle. Her child and ladies would be loaded like cattle into wagons the next day to begin the journey to Canterbury. Her close friend and lady-in-waiting, Joanna de Valance, married to King Henry's own half-brother William of Pembroke, was pregnant and she, herself, had missed her courses twice.

Chapter Two

On the fourth morning after the Feast of St John, wagons and pack horses rattled into the palace yard in Canterbury.

Helped by a groom, Eleanor slid off her white palfrey.

Robert Burnell, a tall man with a thin face and dark hair, and a close friend to her and Edward, hurried from the palace doors to greet her. 'Archbishop Boniface is still abroad. He dare not return,' he reminded her. 'I am here in his stead.'

Eleanor glared at Red Gilbert who took one look at Master Burnell, grunted a greeting, left his horse to his squire's care, and swept past her into the palace. She had made a point of complaining constantly on their journey and, thankfully, he clearly had had enough of her company. He would be off to seek out Simon de Montfort. Young Simon handed his mount to a stable hand and without a glance in her direction followed Gloucester inside. She looked down her pert nose at him as he rushed past.

'All's well here,' Burnell was saying in his gentle voice. His eyes followed Gilbert and young Simon. 'The King is in conference with Earl Simon. I expect those two intend intruding on them.' He took her hands and kissed her on both cheeks. Holding her at arms' length, he smiled at her. They were old friends. It was reassuring and the burden of strain lifted from her as if she were shedding a shroud that had tightened about her these past days. She felt herself unknotting as he said, 'Lady Eleanor, you are to have the Queen's apartment and your ladies are to be accommodated with you. It overlooks the garden and that's filled with the perfume of roses at the moment. Remember how you ordered them brought to us from Spain?'

'I do indeed, Robert. My damask roses will thrive and so shall we.'

'With God's grace. Come now, and get settled. You'll be tired after such a long journey.'

She straightened her back. 'I am never tired, as you well know. If I am, it is that despicable Gloucester who has made my life miserable since he came to Windsor and kept me as a prisoner in their camp. I had to beg for my maid and fresh linens. I missed the Feast of St John and had no option but to eat my own slaughtered deer in their vagabond camp . . . or starve.' Robert made the sign of the cross. 'I may have survived that ordeal.' She watched her ladies descend from wagons. 'But my ladies not so well. As you can see for yourself, my lady Joanna of Pembroke is about to give birth, and I believe I may be with child myself.'

'May God bless you and the child, my dear lady,' he said, laying a hand on her arm.

They watched Countess Joanna awkwardly climb down from a wagon clutching her huge belly. Coming forward, Joanna said, 'Master Burnell, is my husband with the King? Do you know? Have you seen him? Is he here?'

'Alas no, Countess. I heard the loyalist earls were facing exile and the loss of all their lands. Earl William has escaped to France.' He paused and Eleanor saw deep concern in her friend's eyes. 'For now, you will be made comfortable in St Mary's Abbey. This is no suitable place for you to have your lying-in. It is full of Montfort's supporters and if the King is to remain our third Henry we must do as they wish. We are prisoners.'

'My ladies must be accommodated with me,' Joanna said, her eyes brimming with tears.

Eleanor placed an arm about the older woman's shoulders. 'I will insist on it.'

Burnell nodded, 'Of course.'

'What do you know about Edward?' Eleanor asked as they began to walk towards the palace door, a little troop of ladies gathering behind her.

'I believe the King has a letter from him, and a gift of Edward's own psalter to comfort your prayers.'

Eleanor pondered this whilst her ladies unpacked the travelling coffers. Why would Edward give her his psalter? The thought made her sad. Throughout their ten years of marriage, they had been rarely apart as they were now. She wiped her tears away with her sleeve. They were all suffering at the hands of Earl Simon, all his prisoners. She thought of Joanna and how her husband William had fled to France along with other royalists. Montfort would take their lands, all those in Pembrokeshire as well as the castle which the rebels had in their possession already. Lord only knew what else. She'd warrant Gilbert was after Joanna's border territories – and Edward's too, and whatever he could lay his thieving hands upon. Eleanor's own hand went instinctively to her own belly. Joanna was about to give birth, alone, and without her other children, who had been living on her Oxfordshire manor ever since Pembroke Castle had been confiscated by the rebels.

The hour of Nones passed. Eleanor, preceding her troop of ladies, descended to the hall. Her nose tickled by the scent of roast beef wafting out from the kitchens, she realised she was extremely hungry. Food on the journey to Canterbury had been scant: endless sour wine, apples, cheese, and tough venison. She had been constantly nauseous on the journey but refused to complain. Her women had wrinkled their noses as they drank the unpalatable wine, nibbled stale bread, and tried to swallow rancid cheese. She could not stand its smell.

When she entered the hall, King Henry had already settled into his chair at the centre of the top table. She winced to note Earl Simon with his son, and Gilbert de Clare placed to the King's left. Looking at Gloucester so close to King Henry, she narrowed her eyes. No one should lay a hand on a princess of the realm, one who would become God's appointed queen. No one should kill, maim, throw families out of their homes, rape women – Eleanor shuddered – as she had heard Gloucester's men were capable of.

An array of knights and ladies, supporters of both the King and rebel barons, jostled for positions along the lower trestles. A group of minstrels were tuning their instruments. On seeing Eleanor approach, the King rose and indicated one of two empty seats to his right. 'Countess Joanna has asked permission to dine in her chamber,' he said in his gentle voice. 'She is enceinte, I believe, and will remove to St Mary's Abbey tomorrow. Master Robert can sit by you instead.' Robert naturally slipped willingly into his place.

Eleanor noted how her enemies, Gilbert of Gloucester and the two Simons, politely stood until she was seated. She stared hard at them until they looked away. Thanking the servant who stood behind her seat for placing a napkin over her left shoulder, she accepted a cup of Gascon wine from another servitor appointed as the king's vintner. A beaky-nosed taster stopped her lifting her glass, sipped the wine first, and nodded to the King. Only then did Eleanor take a sip of her own wine. She needed to clear her throat.

Henry placed a long, ringed finger on her hand. 'Dear Eleanor,' he began, 'I am pleased to have your company. Intelligent talk has been lacking of late; my son is no better than a prisoner. Queen Ailenor remains in France.' He glanced sideways at Montfort and Gloucester and lowered his voice, 'I miss her. My brother has been sent under guard to his castle of Wallingford, and Lord Edward has joined him there after a spell at Kenilworth. Pembroke has been exiled - William of Pembroke, my own half-brother! Poor Countess Joanna.' He lifted his hands up, palms opened, and shrugged.

How tired he looked. His beard and hair were as snowy white as the image of Winter painted on the walls of the queen's bedroom at Westminster. The conflict with the barons had exhausted him. She felt sorry for him, noting the courageous face he wore to conceal his knowledge that he was not the real authority in the land. Earl Simon was that now. Eleanor shook her head. It was wrong such a gentle man, and he a king, should be treated like a prisoner.

Henry added, 'It is no small pleasure to be reunited with you and my granddaughter,' he was saying. He drew a deep breath. 'I shall see Katherine tomorrow. Tell me, how was your journey, my dear?'

This was her opportunity to disgrace the fox-like Gilbert of Gloucester in front of King Henry's court. Seizing it by the balls, she

19

pointed at Gloucester. 'Your Grace,' she made her voice loud enough for all present to hear, 'what is the penalty for abducting a princess of the realm?' She deliberately paused to allow her words to take effect. 'I, you see, am a princess of the realm, wife of your heir. I was placed roughly upon a horse and taken to that man's evil camp.' She jabbed her finger in the direction of Montfort this time.

Eleanor had made her point. There was a gasp from the trestles placed below the dais, followed by silence. Servants bearing baskets of small loaves stood still. Musicians looked up from their instruments. She could feel the air about the dais grow icy cold.

'Is this true?' Henry, growing paler, turned to Gloucester who nodded, managing a look of feigned innocence and fake contrition.

Henry leaned forward. Gloucester was the richest baron of them all and Eleanor had a nagging suspicion Henry would attempt to persuade him back into supporting the crown. The crafty Earl would happily sit on the fence and watch how the wind blew. Red Gilbert of Gloucester would switch alliances as quickly as the King changed his jewelled silken robes for differing ceremonies. Eleanor pursed her mouth. After all, her complaints were justifiable. What a pity Gloucester's wife was not present to see this. It was common knowledge Alix de Lusignan disliked her husband. Alix was King Henry's niece and her marriage to Gilbert de Clare had been arranged years before when the pair were children, organised to suit Henry. Everyone knew it was a marriage made in hell - the same hell that owned the bullying fox-like creature, Gilbert de Clare.

Gilbert spoke up in a voice that retained a slight West Country burr despite his noble upbringing and years at court. 'I informed you this afternoon, my liege, how Lady Eleanor ignored your order.' He shook his head as if genuinely sorrowful. 'Lady Eleanor crumpled your letter, threw it down, and refused to release her prisoner or accompany me to Canterbury. She ordered Earl Simon's son brought onto the battlements ready to die and, if I recollect correctly, she said something about him plummeting to the ground like a fallen bird.' Gilbert dramatically opened his hands. 'I had no option and, as you can see, Lady Eleanor is unhurt. We cared for her with delicacy' - what an

20

exaggeration, thought Eleanor, an outrage – 'we sent for the child, Katherine, and we sent for her ladies and her baggage.' Gloucester placed his hands together in a palmer's gesture and fixed his pale blue eyes on Eleanor. 'I humbly beg your pardon, Lady Eleanor, but I was ordered to fetch you. You did not make it easy. Canterbury is a place of peace. Let us make our peace today, dear lady.'

She shook her head.

Henry placed his hand over Eleanor's and whispered in her ear. 'Excuse him. We can talk later – over a game of chess.' It was obvious he wanted her to forgive the baron.

Earl Simon had remained silent during the exchange. After she made the briefest of nods towards Gloucester to satisfy the King, Montfort spoke. His dark eyes were filled with emotion and his voice was quiet. The atmosphere in the hall grew so hushed, the air seemed to still. Earl Simon was much admired. Even she was almost seduced by his soft voice but then seduction was Satan's way.

'War is a terrible thing. Civil conflict is worse,' the Earl began. 'We won't go into the cause and aftermath tonight but, perhaps, Lady Eleanor, that opportunity will occur soon. I thank you for your care of my son, but not that you may have had him flung from the battlements of Windsor Castle like a "plummeting bird". No more of it.' He waved his hand dismissively. Young Simon, seated by his father, closed his eyes obviously at the ghastly memory. Eleanor smiled. Earl Simon ignored her and looked at Henry. 'We hope to work together for the future of the realm.' He raised his goblet. The glass facets caught sunlight filtering through painted windows set along the hall. They seemed to cast a rainbow on his face. His eyes moved to meet her own. 'Welcome back to court, Lady Eleanor.'

She said in a quiet voice, 'When do you intend releasing my husband?' How she wanted to throw curses at him! With a supreme effort she contained her temper.

Earl Simon lowered his glass. His brow wrinkled as if puzzled that she dared ask. 'Lord Edward is at Wallingford. You may, of course, write to him.'

'I expect to.' Her letters must be secret. Doubtless they would be

21

read first. Eleanor turned to Gloucester and snapped this time, 'I want my husband's short sword returned to me.'

'It will be arranged.'

'See it is.'

She had said enough. The King touched her hand again and turning to the server asked for more Gascon wine to be poured. Once again, the King insisted his taster tried it before he or Eleanor allowed it to touch their lips. Henry always guarded against poison and Eleanor hoped Edward would do likewise.

Her accusation of Gloucester had made a point, but it was not going to change anything one bit since Gloucester considered himself justified in his treatment of her. He had called her a she-wolf. He had referred to her as 'the Spaniard' when speaking to his captains within her earshot. He had refused to allow her hounds to travel with them from Windsor, remarking that he enjoyed possession of 'an obedient bitch' himself, grinning as he spoke the insult.

She had shouted at this, 'I shall have my dogs, Gloucester, you bastard. The King will demand it.'

He had smirked and turned away. Tonight he was behaving in a well-mannered way but she would never forgive, nor would she forget.

For the rest of the meal she concentrated on the beef and the blackcurrant sauce that accompanied it, and the salmon fresh from the river with a dish of buttered peas. Dining on fine food banished her nausea for now. She would have to inform Henry of her pregnancy. At the knowledge she must, she looked down at her lap. Some pregnancies never came to full term. She had experienced loss when she and Edward had lived in Gascony after their marriage. She must not hope too much. As a low hum of conversation reverberated around the hall, she was relieved to have attention drawn away from her. It was not *she* who was the wolf. Rather, it was those who thought they could thwart a king's rule.

Her anger softened as she accompanied the white-bearded King to Vespers in the Cathedral. As they bowed their heads to pray, Henry touched her arm and muttered in a hushed voice, 'Do not react, Eleanor. There are eyes and ears everywhere. I have Edward's letter and he has left you his psalter.'

Since she sensed something meaningful in the manner Henry whispered the word *psalter*, for the first time since Red Gilbert had ridden to Windsor, she felt hopeful that her dreadful misfortune could turn to good fortune. She nodded and when Henry passed the familiar book to her, she slipped the psalter below her mantle into a pocket hanging from her belt.

'Thank you,' she whispered and, withdrawing her hand and her ebony Spanish rosary, began to count the black beads, clicking them as she chanted a Pater Noster.

Chapter Three

Canterbury
July 1264

Eleanor unfolded the letter. They had played chess after supper even though she was exhausted. On this occasion she indulged Henry, allowing him the closing moves, simply to hurry the game along. Now, as she sat by her open casement with silvery moonlight streaming through the window, at last alone, she began to read. Her breath caught in her chest as she peered down at Edward's words and re-read them, feeling closer to him than she had since March.

My heart's companion,

It grieves me that we have lost to Montfort's men. I shall be held prisoner in Wallingford Castle with my cousin Henry and Uncle Richard. I am not trusted to remain with my father. By the time you receive my words, I hope you are safely with the King. Understand, you cannot hold Windsor against our enemies - she swallowed as she read these words - *Care for your safety and that of our daughter. I pray for you both daily. Read the psalter I leave in your keeping. God's word carries messages of hope. Your husband, Lord Edward.*

If only she could tell him she was nearly three months with child. She set the letter aside and opened the psalter. There must be some clue to Edward's meaning within the psalter. She stared at the first page. It contained a calendar and a litany of the saints. Nothing was particularly marked. She looked for a day that might stand out. None did. For a moment her imagination was caught up by the elaborate illustrations - the decorated initials and peculiar creatures peeping through the letters; the two miracles of loaves and fishes; the visit of the three mysterious kings from the East to a humble stable at Bethlehem. Flicking through these, she shook her head. There was no clue within any of these images. Yet, as she held the velvet-covered book and turned it over twice, then three times in her hands, she wondered if the cover's padding had shifted. She felt along the backbone of the little book. Carefully slipping a fingernail inside the top, she could feel a stiff spiral of linen no wider than a taper used for lighting candles, so cunning it seemed part of the spine itself.

Her heart began to race as carefully she teased the thin roll out and opened it. As she scanned the scrap of linen, she laughed out loud and covered her own mouth to mute the sound. She glanced across the room. Lady Margerie snored away on the truckle bed. She peered down again at the stiff rag. A list of four loyal earls was scribed on the linen and below the names was a list of locations that were scattered about the Welsh borders. It possibly could be where the four earls planned to take refuge and launch an attack. Finally, she read the words *St Guthlac's Priory*. This, she remembered, was a sprawling Benedictine House outside Hereford's city walls. But why there? She studied the list and memorised the locations. Was she meant to contact the earls, and direct them to St Guthlac's? If so, that would be difficult since she herself was a prisoner.

Footsteps approached. They paused outside the chamber. Without hesitating she lit a taper from her candle and burned the little scroll. As she did she heard the footsteps move off. No matter. She had memorised Edward's message. She was a daughter of Spain and had grown up with war. Her father, King Ferdinand, kept her and her mother in safe castles close to the battles as he reconquered Seville and other cities from the Moors. She had often listened to her father talk about strategy and courage and how a successful king should rule his people and administer his lands. Now her beloved brother Alfonso was King of Castile and showed every promise of being a wise king.

How she missed Spain, even after ten years of marriage. She longed for the great libraries in the palaces of her childhood. No library in England could compete with those of Seville and Cordova.

She missed the scent of oranges, so many littering the streets of Seville, and the beautiful palace gardens with the soothing trickling of magnificent water fountains and the growth of lush plants. She missed the hot summertime sun of her childhood, and often, with heartfelt longing, she wished to see Jeanne, her mother, again.

Henry had welcomed her when she and Edward had returned to England after their first married year in Gascony; Henry even had carpets placed on the floors of her apartments at Westminster, in the Spanish tradition. He was kind, so much kinder than Queen Ailenor who was always absorbed with her children's destinies and her own Savoyard relations. Eleanor felt her mother-in-law was dismissive of her, since her gaze was always for Edward on family occasions and at court.

In contrast to King Henry, Queen Ailenor's welcome of Eleanor into their family was filled with the expectation that there would be many, many grandchildren, and she constantly sensed Ailenor's unspoken criticism that there was only one living child after ten years of marriage. She felt her belly. 'Not for long,' she murmured into the night. 'This baby must survive.'

Eleanor bit her lip and tasted blood. Yet, she was not so abandoned then as now or as lonely as she felt since Edward had gone off to war. Her father had kept his wife and family close and safe in fortresses nearby when he fought enemies in Spain, and he visited them often. She sighed. And without doubt Queen Ailenor was courageous, a true warrior queen who was even now recruiting mercenaries in Gascony to save them all from the rebel barons. She, too, must prove herself as a warrior, a warrior princess and support Edward in every way possible.

After Eleanor returned to her bed, she lay sleepless for hours, pondering how she could possibly contact each of the four names written in Edward's letter. One of the names was William of Pembroke, Countess Joanna's husband, whom she had thought was exiled in France.

Yet, according to the scroll, Earl William's location was Aust-on-Severn. A manor house of that name belonged to Countess Joanna's

26

estate. Eleanor sat up in bed, feeling her eyes widen. So William might not be in France, not continually. If only she could get word to Roger Leyburn, he could contact the others – loyal names, Roger Mortimer, Clifford, Leyburn, and seventeen-year-old Thomas de Clare, a younger brother to her sworn enemy, Earl Gilbert. Thomas, unlike his turn-coat brother, had consistently supported Edward.

Beyond the garden the angelus bells chimed midnight. She lay down again and turned on her side, confused, but exhausted too. She needed to sleep. Her mind would be clearer in the morning.

Lady Margerie, Eleanor's damsel, gently snored on.

The King met daily with Simon de Montfort. After each encounter, he reported to Eleanor how he was being forced to agree more and more conditions that were unfair.

'They are calling their declaration *The Mise of Lewes*,' he declared angrily one afternoon after a particularly heated meeting with the hated Earl Simon. He leaned on a stick with a lion's head as he walked with Eleanor in the garden. The amber jewels winking from the lion's enormous eyes seemed to glare at her.

Henry gave a wry smile. 'More like *The Misery of Lewes*. Montfort's calling a Parliament with two knights from every shire and two burghers from the towns, all of them helping to make laws in my name. They'll make me poorer than I am already. They'll control my treasury.' He raised his voice angrily. 'It'll take time for him to organise that. By the time he does, my loyal earls in the West will retake our country from Montfort's grasping hands.' Henry spat out his next words. 'He's stealing their lands and castles and keeping most for himself as recompense.'

There was no one else in the garden but since the window shutters overlooking them were open, anyone could hear him. 'Hush, Sire,' Eleanor said in a quiet voice, as she glanced around. 'Please calm yourself, Your Grace,'

Henry lowered his tone. 'Montfort says it's recompense for all I owe him. And, just to think, he accused *me* of nepotism. I don't see the difference. I dislike signing his land ownership decrees. He is

27

stealing from us.' In a sudden fury, he lifted his stick up and shook it at the windows above. 'Traitors, the pack of you all!' There was, of course, no response. Thankfully no one had heard him and if they had they had clearly decided to let the King rant on.

Seemingly exhausted, Henry sank onto a stone bench and Eleanor gathered her skirts to sit beside him. He touched her arm. 'My dear, I am feeling old these days.' He sighed. 'And how I miss Ailenor. There's no way of getting news from France and no word of the army she is raising there.'

Eleanor, however, did not miss Queen Ailenor one bit. The one positive about being trapped here alone with Henry was she did not have to endure Ailenor's critical looks every time her own beloved dogs raced about the hall. Nor did she have to observe Ailenor's disapproving glances at her dress which, while she knew was never fashionable, was always comfortable. She was frequently irritated by Ailenor's frowns when she insisted on pursuing debates with the clergy, especially the Dominicans who were growing popular in England at last and who sought simplicity.

She took a deep breath, lowered her voice, and confided in Henry about Edward's secret communication. 'I can't think whom I can trust here,' she said after she recounted what she discovered. 'I've wondered if I could waylay a pilgrim at the shrine of St Thomas to carry a message to St Guthlac's Priory. I am sure that's what I have to do.'

'You can't,' Henry said quietly, his left eyelid drooping. 'It's the same trial for us both. We are separated from our loved ones and our supporters by that devil Montfort who wriggled his way into my family when he married my sister. We are watched all the time. Messages will be intercepted.' Henry leaned his chin on hands folded over his stick. He thought for a moment and said, 'Montfort plans to move us to London soon, for his sham Parliament. Once we are in the City there are other ways to reach to our friends, loyal traders amongst the City rabble.' He laid his hand on hers. 'Though, Eleanor, you mentioned pilgrims a moment ago.' He lowered his voice further. 'It may be difficult, but if we could disguise one of our

28

own supporters as a pilgrim returning home to the borderlands, we might get a message to Hereford after all.'

Her eyes widened. It was a feasible idea, one she could help them realise. She suspected Earl Simon did not actually know how many served them. Excited, she said, 'A female might be better than a male . . .'

'Maybe so.' Henry shook his head. 'We could watch for a pilgrim group hailing from Chester, Hereford, or Gloucester.'

Eleanor looked into Henry's blue eyes. 'Your Grace, I *do* know one who might carry messages, a herbalist. In fact, she's more than just that. She understands medicines. I sent into the town for an apothecary for Katherine the other day. Her father sent her to me with a tincture for Katherine's cough.'

'I hope my granddaughter is not ailing.' Henry's eyes had narrowed with concern.

'Just a summer cold, a chill.' Eleanor could not help the worry that crept into her voice. She loved her daughter dearly. Now eighteen months old, Katherine was walking and chattering to whoever would listen to her babbling, totally unconcerned about her change in circumstances. Should she tell Henry she was pregnant? Best not. It might be too soon, and, after all, she might be packed off to St Mary's with Joanna. Worse, she could lose yet another pregnancy before the child was full-term. She had miscarried three babies already, one when she was only thirteen in Gascony.

'We could pay this girl,' Henry was saying. He pondered for a moment, his brow frowning. 'What is she called?' He lifted up a long hand and drew his mantle closer though the day was warm.

'Olwen. Her name is Olwen. *You* might pay her, your Grace, but my own purse is empty. I cannot even pay for a doctor.'

'We could send his daughter to bring plants from St Guthlac's Priory for the herb garden at Canterbury. I know that priory has rue, rare enough in England. Yes, yes, all are aware of my love for gardens.' He was nodding his excitement. 'We must do it immediately. No time to waste. The girl will deliver your message to the Prior. He will see it gets to Mortimer wherever he's hiding out and, of course, to William. There, it is settled. I shall insist. And I shall insist on a proper doctor for Katherine too. Now, tell me, my dear, how *is* Countess Joanna? Has she settled into St Mary's?'

'She has withdrawn from company. Her chamber is darkened.'

'God willing she has a healthy child.' He patted her hand. 'We'll set Edward free yet and you'll soon be enceinte again too, my dear.'

Eleanor crossed herself and whispered a prayer. 'God willing,' she said aloud and crossed herself, again keeping quiet on the subject of babies. 'I'll see if the herbalist will travel to Hereford.'

Eleanor sent for Olwen and asked the girl to accompany her into the garden. She was a sensible young woman of around sixteen years old. What Eleanor could see of her hair under her neat linen cap was mousy brown. She was neat and slim with hazel eyes and a pleasant smile. The girl seemed a little sorrowful and Eleanor wondered the reason.

'Are you married, Olwen?' she asked.

'No, my lady.' There was a moment's hesitation before Olwen said, 'My betrothed, Dicken, died after falling from a roof and breaking his neck. I knew him since childhood. He was to inherit a glove-maker's business. That and a fine house go to his brother. Now I help my father. My lady, I may never find another such as my betrothed. I am content to make simples and medicines for my father and to grow plants for medicines in our garden. We have extensive gardens and an orchard too.' She hesitated again, as if she was frightened of Eleanor, or perhaps holding something back.

'Go on,' Eleanor said.

'Although I may not practise as an apothecary, my father is teaching me much of his knowledge so that I am useful.' She shook her head. 'My stepmother resents me and I suspect my betrothed was pushed off the roof by Earl Simon's supporters. One of them my stepmother's own brother, another glove-man. I wish I lived elsewhere.'

They walked through the roses into the herbal beds beyond.

'I see. Perhaps I can help you. I have not summoned you to bring me medicine this time. The King has sent his doctor to attend

Katherine. I want you to know how grateful I am that you gave me the tincture of hyssop. It has eased her cough.' She paused. 'I know of another way you can be useful in serving your future queen.'

'How?' Olwen's eyes had widened. The young woman's mouth opened and closed again, as if she would ask more but had decided to hear Eleanor out.

Eleanor glanced around the garden. A monk tidying a distant herbal bed was too absorbed in his weeding to pay her attention. She led Olwen towards beans that climbed tall trellises and drew the girl behind their densely packed growth. 'I would like you to make a journey to a priory in Hereford. You will bring herbs back to Canterbury from there for this garden. Rue is grown there and it's not common. Do you know the herb?'

'Valuable as an infusion. It's used in nosegays and good for cleansing the stomach if used in pottage. My father makes eyebaths with rue and water of roses. They add rue seeds to wine, so I've heard.'

'All that? I never knew,' Eleanor was impressed at the girl's expertise. She took Olwen's hand in her own and said, 'That is the perceived purpose for your journey. We certainly want rue seeds and other herbs also. However, you will also carry important messages from myself to the Prior. The mission will take you several weeks. Can you ride?'

Olwen smiled and said, 'I love animals and I am a good horsewoman. My cousin owns horses. He breeds them. Papa would never permit me to ride to Hereford though, not even for a future queen.'

This time Eleanor smiled widely. 'I also love God's creatures, especially horses and dogs. My husband, Lord Edward, loves the creatures of the air and horses too.' She pondered this a moment and said, 'After what happened to your betrothed, Olwen, you have good reason to help us. The King and I would not send you alone. We shall send a nun from St Mary's to help you procure seeds – there is one such who knows Hereford well – and you will have a squire to protect you. Neither of them will know what you bring to the Prior. You will seek out the Prior yourself and pass my secret messages to him. You will carry an open letter to him, a request for you to bring a collection of herbs and seeds from Hereford to Canterbury. It is July now. You will surely return by the week following Lamas. Master Robert, our clerk, shall request permission from your father to release you. You'll travel in company with pilgrims returning from Canterbury to Herefordshire. Master Robert tells me there's a pilgrim group in the town as we speak.' Eleanor paused to take a breath. 'I promise to reward you well. You will be helping your King, your future King, and me. King Henry will see you are well provided for in inns along the route. You will not go hungry.'

She reached out and touched the young woman's arm. Olwen never spoke. Eleanor held her breath. At last Olwen nodded.

'If Master Robert Burnell can speak with my father, I am willing to carry them messages. My father is acquainted with Master Robert and speaks well of him.' She earnestly clasped her hands. 'Papa truly loves the King, Madam.'

'So be it. I promise, only King Henry, Master Robert, and I will know of your true mission.' She drew breath. 'And it's *those* messages.'

Countess Joanna's baby was born some days later. She named her Elizabeth. The birth reminded Eleanor of just how Katherine could not shake off her chest ailment. It steadily worsened. Henry had said, 'My dear, Edward suffered likewise but grew out of it. Katherine will improve with all the medicines my doctor is providing.'

Eleanor was not so sure. This illness was Montfort's fault. Katherine should be in her nursery at Windsor, cared for by nurses and devoted servants, not taken to wherever pleased Montfort.

When news of Elizabeth's birth arrived in the Bishop's Palace, Eleanor had an excuse to visit Joanna. She urgently needed to let her friend know that her husband was in hiding on an estate near Hereford. She would take this opportunity to speak with the Abbess of St Mary's about the nun who was to accompany Olwen to the west.

After Prime, Eleanor summoned Lady Margerie to accompany her to the Abbey. She demanded an escort from Montfort. As guards waited outside the Abbey walls under the canopy of several oak trees, Eleanor and Margerie entered the Abbess's house. A servant escorted them into Abbess Beatrice's pleasant chambers.

They sat in a parlour with a plate of saffron cakes and cups of fresh cool buttermilk. At first they exchanged news then, as the atmosphere relaxed, Eleanor announced her desire to procure rare plants and seeds from St Guthlac's Priory at Hereford.

'I may not have estates of my own these days,' Eleanor said, unable to prevent bitterness creeping into her voice, 'but I shall retrieve my dower lands one day.' She shrugged. 'I am interested in gardens.'

'Hereford, you say.' Abbess Beatrice smiled, though her dark eyes looked puzzled.

'Yes, Hereford. This is delicious buttermilk, a drink I have discovered here in England and very much enjoy, and the cakes possess a hint of mint. I detect marjoram too,' Eleanor said, determined to sound knowledgeable about herbs. She sat her cup down on the side table provided and added, 'I imagine, Abbess Beatrice, the herbal garden here at St Mary's is well stocked. I am sending west for unusual seeds such as rue and rosemary.' She leaned forward. 'Sister Agnes is from Hereford. I wonder can you spare her to accompany my herbalist.'

'I see.' Abbess Beatrice wore a serene countenance. 'Hereford is a dangerous place. Has there not been recent fighting there between Montfort and the Marcher barons?'

Eleanor shook her head. She assumed the west was peaceful while the harvests were gathered in. 'Not at the moment. We have spoken with pilgrims from Hereford. A party travels back in a week's space. My herbalist will travel with them. There is safety in numbers.'

'Well if this is so, and if they are escorted safely home—'

'The girl's father is particular as to who travels with her so she will travel in a company. The King is sending a squire, Eugene, as her protector.'

The Abbess folded her hands. A smile played about her lips and her dark eyes twinkled. 'I think Sister Agnes will be pleased to see her old convent of Leominster again and, yes indeed, she is good with plants. I *do* believe we can spare her.' She stood and swept crumbs from her habit. 'Would you like to see Countess Joanna now? Her child is beautiful. If she thrives, she may be dedicated to our Abbey one day as a novice nun. Come, follow me.'

Eleanor and Margerie followed the Abbess along a passage. They reached the entrance to a spacious, pleasant chamber where the Abbess left them saying, 'I'll speak with Sister Agnes. She is busy in the still room.'

'On the appointed day we shall send for her.' Eleanor took two steps down and swept into Joanna's chamber.

Joanna sat up in bed propped by cushions and tiny Elizabeth lay in swaddling in a cradle by the Countess's side.

Joanna patted the bed, inviting Eleanor to sit with her, and said, 'She has my father's look about her, I think. I never knew my own mother and nor did I know my grandfather, William Marshal, for he died before I was born.'

'Perhaps.' Eleanor never knew Joanna's father and she did not feel maternal towards babies at all, they had a nasty habit of dying. Nor would she confide her own pregnancy yet. She could not bear the fuss. She turned away from the cradle and drew out a small package from her cloak bag. She presented Joanna with a copy of *Tristan*, bound with red and green leather.

The Countess opened it and peered at the colourful illustrations. She thanked Eleanor. 'It will bring me great enjoyment.'

'I wish to speak with you alone, Joanna,' Eleanor said. 'Perhaps your ladies could show Margerie the garden.'

Countess Joanna said, 'Go,' to her ladies and waved her hands at them in a shooing gesture. 'Leave us. Return when the bells chime for Nones.'

A nurse swept up Elizabeth and took her into an adjoining chamber whilst the ladies filed out to the abbey garden. They had a precious quarter hour to talk privately.

'Joanna, I shall be brief.' She took the Countess's hand. 'Listen well. I have had a communication from Edward.'

'Is Lord Edward well?'

34

'I think so. He left a message for me before Montfort took him away. Apparently Earl William may be in hiding at your mother's old manor near Hereford. I suspect he never reached France or if he did, he intended to return in secret. There are four of them about the borders. All are determined to overthrow Montfort's rule. William and Roger Mortimer are their leaders. They seem to have made a pact.' She paused. 'I am sending what news and encouragement I have to give west to Hereford. They must raise armies and rescue Edward, who will lead them to victory without doubt.' She wished she felt as positive as her words. Joanna needed hope.

Joanna's lovely face filled with surprise; her eyes grew as round as halos. 'But why has William not sent me word?'

'How could he send anything here? Listen, Joanna, I have found a way to reach him.' Eleanor's voice dropped to a whisper. 'You must not speak of this to anyone, the nurse, your ladies, not even the Abbess. I shall let William know you have a beautiful baby girl. Go to your children. Go to Oxfordshire. You will be quiet there and safe from harm.'

Joanna sighed. 'How I miss the children. God bless you, Eleanor, and may his angels be with you always.' Her eyes welled with tears. She smiled through them. 'Come again.'

Eleanor nodded. The bells for Nones were ringing already. Joanna's ladies were tripping in from the garden carrying posies of herbs.

Chapter Four

Hereford
August 1264

Olwen had been a guest at the priory for five days. She had delivered the letters from Lady Eleanor and Prior Adam of St Guthlac's had promised they would reach Earl William. She suspected he knew where the lords were located, or would be once they returned from France. Olwen wondered if they were already raising armies and hoped there would be no danger as they journeyed back to Canterbury.

The Prior seemed kindly. He was tall, and looked like a magus with piercing blue eyes the colour of periwinkles. Holding a basket and trowel, Olwen and the Prior walked through the Priory's herbal beds as she selected herbs to bring back to Canterbury. Rue was first on her list.

He led her straight to the plant. 'We have other herbs you might need besides rue. Rosemary, for instance, is not widely grown. Let me show you.' He pointed towards a wall.

'I've heard mention of rosemary but never seen it grown. It's so rare. I have heard say it has many qualities.' Olwen turned to him with a worried look on her face as she looked into her filling basket. 'Is it delicate? I hope it will survive the journey back.'

He glanced down at her. 'The plants will survive. We can lend you a small cart and a pony. The King has sent us a generous purse.'

When they stopped walking, she found herself staring at the bush with what looked like green needles on its thin woody branches. It possessed little blue flowers. She reached out and touched a flower.

Prior Adam smiled, displaying a full set of teeth even though he was not young. 'It's unusual to find this one growing so far away from southern countries where it grows in profusion.'

She plucked a sprig, crushed the thin leaves between her fingers, and held it to her nose. 'I like it well,' she said, surprised at enjoying the sharp aroma that assaulted her nostrils. She plucked another sprig, squeezed it again, and tasted it. 'It has oil.'

'Take cuttings,' he said. 'Rosemary has not been easy to grow from seed. It dislikes unkind, wet weather, but our bush thrives and hopefully your cuttings will too. Do not water the plant much, especially in the first year. Set it without dung.' He smiled and his eyes twinkled. 'Treat it kindly, for like rue it is a holy herb.'

She asked as she carefully snipped as he bent over the bush and showed her where was best to snip, 'How can we use it?'

He stretched his back as he stood up. 'Oh, it's beneficial. A tisane of rosemary will calm and cleanse the body from within. It's a powder to cleanse the teeth when ground. I use it to good avail.' He smiled again, showing off his fine set of white teeth.

She determined to keep a cutting for herself which she'd grow in a pot. Bees were hovering over the flowers. For a heartbeat she watched them busily glide about the flowers. 'Bees like it?' she remarked.

'It's a delightful herb.'

'Lady Eleanor will enjoy it.'

'She is from southern lands,' the Prior reminded Olwen with a smile. 'So she will recognise it.' Olwen smiled back. She thought of little Katherine when she spoke of Lady Eleanor. 'Her child ails. She has a terrible cough. I used borage in a tincture but she still ails.'

'Ah, cowslip primrose. As with lungwort, the leaves look fuzzy like the lung. It's late for the primrose but ask the infirmerer here for a root. It might relieve Katherine's symptoms if ground into a tisane with honey.' His startling eyes softened. 'And I shall add little Katherine to my prayers.'

'Thank you. I pray to St Katherine for her recovery every single day.' Her eyes filled with moisture.

The Prior touched her hand. 'It is as God wills. You may or may not save this child and if you cannot, it's not your fault.'

She smiled at the thoughtful Prior through salty tears.

Later, when Olwen went to seek out the primrose root in the infirmary, she was sure she saw Eugene approaching the Priory's back gate. Eugene was a quiet man, and they had not spoken much without Sister Agnes being present. It was clear that he was reliable and devoted to the King's service. She admired his loyalty and as they had journeyed west felt comfortable in his presence. What was he doing here now, though? He was not expected to return until the next day.

'Eugene?' she called, but the shadowy figure vanished behind an oak tree. Perhaps it was her imagination. She shrugged. The shadow could have been anyone or even a trick of the light.

After supper, Prior Adam summoned Olwen to his parlour where he poured them each a tiny amount of hippocras.

'Our own honey,' he remarked with pride. He lowered his voice. 'I have a letter for Countess Joanna. And a message for the King. It is verbal just in case, Heaven forbid, you are attacked on the return journey. No one knows Earl William is in Wales. Commit it to memory, my child.' The Prior dropped his voice further and she had to lean towards him to hear every word.

' "The leopard shall roam free. The Marches will rise." ' He sipped his wine. 'It will give King Henry hope. Not all the barons are against them. Montfort is seizing lands from those who supported the King and appropriating property for himself. It makes his supporters angry. His popularity will sour.'

'I shall remember the message,' Olwen promised as she took another sip of the delicious hippocras, wishing she could stay longer in the Priory and spend more time discovering and learning about its precious plants.

Two days later, they joined a pilgrim group travelling from Hereford to Canterbury. The travellers enjoyed fine weather and frequent rests.

Olwen had enjoyed her visit to St Guthlac's and hoped that she would return. Her farewell had been poignant. 'Come again, Mistress Olwen, you will always be welcome in our gardens,' Prior Adam had said as he gave them a cart and a pony to lead it. She smiled broadly at Eugene but said nothing about believing she'd seen him on the previous evening.

'Ready, Mistress Olwen, Sister Agnes?' Eugene said in a gentle voice. 'Sooner we depart the Priory the sooner our mission is accomplished.' Peering into the cart, he added, 'You have some precious plants here. The Canterbury monks will be pleased with them.' He helped Olwen onto her palfrey and Sister Agnes onto the cart, where the nun took possession of the reins and with a light flick of her stick on the pony's rump guided the wagon along the lane and on the road to Hereford.

It was pleasant and safer to have companions. Eugene was quiet company and she liked him, but he seemed to favour the company of a pair of Templar knights when they paused to break their fast. Even so, he was always watching her and she suspected he admired her. It pleased her to have an admirer. Surely Dicken in Heaven would understand how lonely she had been since his death. Her stepmother, Doregon, was a constant annoyance. This journey had been an escape from Doregon's jealousy of her close relationship with her father and the woman's constant nagging. For a time she could forget her suspicions, which she could never prove, concerning Dicken's death.

Church bells rang out in every town they rode through, marking the hours of service. Several days passed with stopping in inns and pausing for a few hours during the day to rest and eat. 'It's such a long journey to Canterbury,' Sister Agnes sighed, stretching her legs by a riverbank. She pushed her wimple back on her forehead. 'And too quick a visit to the Priory.'

Further along the riverbank their pilgrim companions were munching loaves of bread, drinking from ale skins, or watering thirsty horses. Olwen watched idly as Eugene unhitched their pony from the cart and led it to where his jennet and Olwen's palfrey stood amongst reeds already drinking from the river. Eugene called over his shoulder, 'Not long. Halfway home now, Sister Agnes.'

'Monasteries, inns, hedgerows,' sighed the nun. 'Since I could not stay longer in Hereford, I long for my own bed.'

'We've been fortunate to have a chamber to ourselves in the inns.'

'Clean linen has not been our good fortune,' Sister Agnes said, her dainty nose turned up as she spoke. 'Still, I liked visiting my old convent.' She looked tearful. 'I may never see them again.'

Olwen handed her companion a hunk of bread and a flask with watered beer, fresh that morning from a baker and brewer in Newbury.

'What about you, Olwen? Are you happy to return to Canterbury and your people?' Sister Agnes said.

'I'm pleased to have new plants to set.' She could not help a sigh escaping her. 'I don't relish seeing my stepmother again. I can do nothing right. This past month has been freedom for me.'

The nun patted Olwen's arm and her touch was kindly. 'Lady Eleanor favours you. Perhaps she'll take you into her household.'

'She might not be permitted to.'

'You helped her ill child. That must count for something.'

Sister Agnes leaned back against a tree trunk and began to doze.

Two Templars were resting by the waterside, their swords unbuckled. Eugene had joined them and they were talking quietly together. He was mysterious, she decided, and as she watched them for a moment, she remembered again the figure she thought she had seen by the Priory's back gate.

She started, feeling a jolting movement as two bodies seemed to fall down behind her tree. She recognised the pair of merchants' voices conversing softly on the other side of the broad sycamore but it was the mention of King Henry that really alerted her. One of the merchants whom she knew to be a chandler was saying to his companion, a Hereford draper, 'King Henry favoured his half-brothers and that caused the trouble.' There was spite in the merchant's voice.

'And that William of Lusignan got the wealthiest Marshal heiress of them all and along with the wench, Pembroke Castle.'

She wriggled further around the tree roots, determined to hear more of the conversation. The heiress they spoke of was Countess Joanna. She pressed her head to the tree trunk. A snort emerged from behind followed by a lowered voice. Olwen strained harder to hear. 'He did well, too well. God's teeth, I'm sure I saw the Earl in Hereford some days since with two knights attending him; them as carried shields with birds on them. Pembroke's livery.'

'*Where* did you see him?' The chandler's voice was filled with curiosity. Olwen sat very still, not daring to move again.

'The Church of St Peter. God's teeth, I swear by Christ's toes, Pembroke himself swept out, hood drawn up though the day was hot. But, mark ye this, I did catch a sight of his face and I knows him for Earl William because he once bought cloth I was selling. 'Twas some years ago. Came himself to my house to purchase velvet for a new gown. He said Lady Joanna had just birthed a child, a son. He was pleased as a preening peacock, he was.'

'I heard he was banished from England after the Battle of Lewes.'

'To France but he's not there, he's here, he is.'

'If Pembroke is back, I'll warrant a bundle of my best wax candles, Earl Simon's men will pay well for that information.'

'God's holy teeth, maybe as so. Things will be a-changing now Montfort's at the helm.'

''Bout time too,' the chandler grumbled. 'King Henry was a spendthrift, poseur, and a fool, and he changed his clothes five times a day, I heard say. That's *our* taxes wasted.'

'Holy St Gabriel's halo, Lord Edward swore on the gospels the King would introduce reforms. I heard the King broke faith. King don't care about complaints or wars in France or Queen's foreigners crowding into England taking the plum jobs. He has his own foreigners . . . like Pembroke. By Christ, he's one of them.'

'Ignored promises to mend his ways and share the governing with good English lords,' complained the chandler. There was a pause and crackling of bracken as the chandler, who was the heavier man, leaned back against the tree trunk. Olwen nearly jumped out of her skin as he shifted closer towards her. She heard him spit and held her breath when his throaty voice came again. 'Montfort will call a parlee-ment. They'll have townsmen on it from all the big towns. Holy Pentecost candle, we'll have them people to represent us true Englishmen, God willing.'

'Let's drink to it. Good Red Gloucester and Earl Simon in charge, and betwixt them they'll direct King Henry unto caring for God's flock. I hear the third Henry's always praying at shrines. Maybe as those saints will speak sense to him now.'

A huge spider scuttled along Olwen's arm. She resisted the urge to sweep it away and tried to ignore it as she listened again. The merchant slurped from his wineskin and she heard him pass it to his friend and say, 'Queen's in France raising troops. Marcher lords on our borders are Earl Simon's enemies.'

'Did you fight for Earl or King, chandler?'

'Neither, friend merchant. I was in Hereford minding my own business. Whoever is in charge will get greedy sooner or later, you'll see. I'll be raising the price of my candles if any of them tax us again.'

The pair rose grunting and farting. When they moved off towards their horses, Olwen nudged Sister Agnes awake, saying, 'Time to set out again.' She instinctively touched her skirts. Pembroke's letter to Countess Joanna was secure within the inside pocket she had attached to her gown.

Olwen found herself avoiding the draper and chandler after that day.

'Master Eugene,' she said as they led their horses into the stable. She gave hers an apple which the mare began to munch with ready teeth.

'What is it?' Eugene said, his eyes concerned at her voice which she knew sounded anxious.

'I don't like or trust the chandler and his companion.'

He stopped brushing down his horse's mane and looked worried. 'Have they bothered you?'

'No, but they have no love for the King.'

Eugene looked thoughtful. He laid his hand over hers. 'Stay well away from them and remember I am watching out for both yourself and Sister Agnes. I would not allow them to harm a hair on your head, be sure of this, fair Olwen.'

After that Olwen avoided the pair. Both were popular raconteurs of tales told after supper by the light of inn hearths. Instead, after a day of travel she fell into a dreamless sleep. Daily, she watered the plants she had secured in the cart and each night, Eugene paid an inn boy to guard the wagon as they slept. As dawn broke, Olwen crept down into the inn yard and examined plant leaves and roots, seeking signs of decay or damage. It hadn't rained since they set out. Thankfully, river water was plentiful in streams. She kept huge jugs filled with it wedged into the wagon bed, and with careful attention the plants were surviving the cart's shaking and bumping on the long route to Canterbury.

They passed their last night in an inn situated amongst a scattering of dwellings in a small hamlet in Surrey. As their company approached the end of their journey, they grew exhilarated. On the last morning together when they packed up bundles everyone chattered together like magpies.

Olwen hurried into the stable, thinking she would soon be safe in St Mary's. She spotted from the corner of her eye horsemen bursting noisily into the yard, their long pennants, red chevrons on gold, flying behind them.

'Fetch a blacksmith,' their leader, a young noble with red hair, shouted at the staring bystanders.

Eugene peered out of the stable door. He pulled her inside and drew back.

'What is it?' she said.

Blood had drained from his face, which in the barn's dim light looked fearful, his eyes narrowing as he looked at her.

'I know them, those three knights.' He laid a hand on Olwen's sleeve. 'I know their leader and I don't want to be seen. I'll have a word with the Templars to draw our party onwards out of their way.' He pointed towards the doorway. 'Those knights are Gilbert de Clare's men.' He held on to Olwen's arm. 'Slip up to your chamber now and warn the nun. I'll say she's unwell. We'll wait until that company and ours too have departed.' He stuck his head out of the door again and withdrew it in a jerk as if it was swivelling on a stick. 'Gilbert of Gloucester. He knows me to be King Henry's servant and if he discovers I have been to Hereford, it'll raise suspicion. Only the King knows my whereabouts.'

Olwen gasped. They were so near the end of their mission. It also occurred to her Eugene had been aware of her true mission all along and was most likely on his own business for King Henry too. She nodded to him. Another heartbeat and she took a deep breath and marched across the yard. She tried hard not to race up the outside stairway. As she glanced back she noted the red-headed knight was occupied in conversation with the blacksmith. *Good Gloucester himself*, she thought, recollecting the conversation overheard a few days earlier. The knight had an arrogant stance and he looked impatient. She disliked that. Reaching the inn gallery, she hurried through a doorway.

Sister Agnes grumbled at the delay. Olwen's excuse that they did not want to get caught up with the knightly band was feeble. She lied that Eugene had a quarrel with some of Gloucester's band of thuggish soldiers and did not want to invite trouble if he was recognised.

'Well, in that case, I hope they're on their way soon. I've been looking forward to dinner in the abbey, my dear.'

'We'll catch the company up. You are supposed to be unwell. Your flowers have fallen. It's your time of the month.'

'What!' the nun said, her hands rising to her face in horror. 'Don't speak of that, my dear, please.'

'You can say you had a stomach ailment if anyone asks.'

Some time later, Eugene tapped on their chamber door. 'It's only me.'

Cautiously, she opened it.

'The pilgrims have departed and, thankfully, the knights are on their way too.'

'They are not following the pilgrims to Canterbury, are they?'

'No, Mistress Olwen, they are on their way towards London. Apparently, King Henry and the rest of the court departed for London some days ago.'

'How do you know?'

'I heard their squires talk as I sat behind a pillar in the taproom downstairs. I am sure Lady Eleanor will have left you a message with Master Robert.'

'I hope Countess Joanna is still at St Mary's,' sighed Olwen.

'I think she will still be there,' Eugene said. Olwen was not so sure.

They caught up with the pilgrim party as they rested at midday in a glade just off the main route. No one questioned them. Olwen's head ached. Worry gripped her. She might not be able to deliver the messages. She had never been to London.

That evening, they parted with the company. Olwen decided to spend a few nights at St Mary's before returning home. She must seek out Master Robert Burnell, deliver the plants, give him the message for the King, and find out if little Katherine had made a recovery.

They did not arrive in Canterbury until nightfall. The Abbess sent for a supper of bread and cold meats.

'You know, my dear, the King and Princess were taken to London. We are close to the palace and you'll have deliveries to make. Stay here in the guest house,' she said to Olwen. 'You will want to see Countess Joanna tomorrow. The Countess has not yet moved to Oxfordshire. She has just been churched. You are in time.'

'I'll deliver the plants first,' Olwen said. 'We have seedlings for the Abbey garden here too.'

At that the Abbess smiled and said, 'A productive journey.'

Master Robert remained in the palace by the Cathedral. What a relief this was. Olwen's small frame relaxed. She lifted her cup of buttermilk and drank deeply. 'Thank you, Abbess, for your hospitality.' She turned to Sister Agnes. 'And will you accompany me tomorrow to deliver the seeds and plants?'

'I shall enjoy seeing the Princess's famous rose garden. May I accompany Olwen?' she said, turning to the Abbess.

'Indeed, and later you must see to our planting. We have missed your green fingers.'

After a breakfast of bread and eggs at the nunnery, Olwen sorted out plants for the Abbey. She arranged to speak with Countess Joanna later that day. Setting out with the wagon, Sister Agnes, skilled at driving it, manipulated the cart and Welsh pony through narrow streets that were like dim tunnels because of so many overhanging gables. Deftly, the nun manoeuvred the cart through honking geese and grunting pigs, calling to passers-by to get out of the way.

Olwen waited in the palace hall until Master Robert appeared. He hurried breathlessly towards her and drew her into a window alcove.

Olwen could hardly wait to ask, 'My lord, how are the princess and baby Katherine?'

There must have been much upheaval. The palace hall felt deserted. King Henry's courtiers had vanished with their king. Robert replied calmly to her garbled question. 'Lady Eleanor and King Henry have removed to Westminster as you now know.' He touched her hand. 'The child is ailing. Montfort and Gloucester promised the King's doctor would travel with little Katherine in a carriage – a minor concession, but something.' He shrugged his shoulders and raised his arms. 'What could I say? It was decided by my Lord King I would remain at Canterbury for news from the Queen and from Paris. Archbishop Boniface is afraid to return so I stay here in his stead. Prince Edmund remains in Paris with his mother, the Queen, and, yes, I need to see to things here.' He looked at her with quizzical eyes. 'Was your journey a success? These are difficult times, little Olwen.'

She nodded and drew a deep breath. She lowered her voice. The very walls could possess ears. 'The Earl of Pembroke is hiding in the borders. He'll contact the other lords. But . . . he has been seen in the town.' She recounted what she had heard the pilgrim merchants say and told him the message she carried to Lady Eleanor.

46

'Pembroke should have stayed away from Hereford. Foolish knight.'

'Perhaps he was collecting a message,' Olwen said, realising it was the Prior of St Guthlac's who had most likely contacted the Earl at the church in Hereford.

'A dangerous move. The town of Hereford has mixed loyalties.' He smiled down at her. 'You have done well, Olwen. Brave girl, indeed. And how about the plants?'

She glowed at his praise. 'The plants are safe, Master Robert. They're all in the wagon in the yard. Can a gardener unload it? I brought rosemary, rue, and other rare plants. Sister Agnes is there and wishes to see the gardens.'

'Of course she must. Rosemary indeed; that is pleasing.'

'I have to return to St Mary's to speak with Countess Joanna.' She paused and coughed politely. 'I am sad not to see Lady Eleanor and Katherine again.'

He reached out again and touched her arm. His face broke into a broad smile. She registered how handsome Master Robert was when he smiled. 'I was coming to this. Squire Eugene will travel on to London in a few days' space. You'll travel with him. Lady Eleanor says she has need of a herbalist. She is with child. Lord Edward was with her in March last, she says, and the child will come by Christmastide. I have spoken to your father. He is pleased to see you well settled.' His eyes looked sad. 'Your father says his house is not a happy place these days.'

She shook her head. 'My stepmother – I can never please her.' She did not say that she suspected her stepmother might even want to kill her out of jealousy, or that Doregon's brother may have been responsible for Dicken's murder. She had no proof.

'I understand, and I hope you will be happy in Lady Eleanor's household. She will be glad of your medicines.'

Olwen clasped her hands together and felt tears of gratitude fill her eyes. 'I do wish to help her,' she said. 'Thank you, Master Robert.'

'Return here with your baggage on the morrow. The cart and pony will be of use to you, though I suppose we must return both to Hereford.'

'My palfrey is stabled at St Mary's.'

'You may keep her. She is yours now. The King has left you a purse. Here, take it. You will have need of the coin.' He drew a velvet purse from his cloak.

She accepted and slipped it into her gown, then curtsied and hurried out of the hall. When she arrived by the gardens, the gardener's lads were already unloading her plants, directed by Sister Agnes who seemed to be annoyed at the boys' rough handling of the precious rue. She was flustering about and scolding them.

'Take care of those,' Olwen said with firmness to the boys. 'When I come back tomorrow I expect to see those plants in the ground without damage. Go, Sister, walk in the gardens and I'll watch them unload.'

All the way back to the nunnery, Sister Agnes praised the roses but complained about the gardener's boys. On arrival back at the Abbey, Olwen hurried towards the countess's chambers. Countess Joanna was seated outside, her baby in a wicker basket, among her ladies in a shady arbour of the garden. Olwen peered into the basket at the perfect little girl. One day she would love a little one of her own. If only her betrothed had not been taken from her . . .

She smiled through tears and quickly wiped them away. She remembered the day well when Dicken's broken body had been carried into the church in a shroud. Her tears had flowed relentlessly afterwards. It was worse that her stepmother had said in such an unfeeling manner: 'He was a no-good king's man. You are well rid of him.'

Her pragmatic father, besotted with his second wife, never contradicted her, which was unforgivable since he was loyal to Master Robert, the King's friend. He had looked away but later had folded Olwen in his arms and said, 'These are difficult times, my child. Least said . . . for now is best. Times will change again. I loved Dicken too.'

His words had been a small comfort.

'What ails you, Olwen?'

'It is nothing, my lady. I am sad not to see little Katherine, sad she is ill.' She looked up. 'I have a message for you.'

Countess Joanna called for her wet nurse and led Olwen to a small wicker gate leading into a pleasant plantation of peach trees. Out of sight of the nunnery gardeners, Olwen passed Joanna the Earl's letter. The Countess seized it with delight and secreted in her sleeve. 'I shall enjoy it later.' Her clear blue eyes were shining. 'Did you see my lord?'

Olwen shook her head. 'He's in hiding.'

'And I will be so close in Oxfordshire – yet so far from my lord too. Ah, I'll be relieved to see my children. I never want to deal with Simon de Montfort again.' Her generous mouth widened and her blue eyes smiled. 'And you, Olwen, now your mission is over, what awaits you?'

'I'm to serve Lady Eleanor in London. I've never been to the City before and I have no love for my stepmother.'

The Countess smiled again, this time a complicit smile. 'I don't like mine either. I thought I might be sent to her.'

Olwen's thoughts returned to the princess's daughter. 'Master Burnell says little Katherine remains unwell.'

Joanna's earnest blue eyes filled with concern. 'There are dangers everywhere a child dwells.' She touched Olwen's hand. 'If medicines do not cure what ails Katherine, I think it must mean God intends calling her to him. You can only do your best, Olwen. It is not your fault if Katherine dies.'

'I know, but I pray I can make her comfortable, my lady.'

'I pray so too.'

For a moment they watched a little swarm of bees descend on a row of flowering bushes. As Olwen rose to leave Countess Joanna embraced her. 'Godspeed, Mistress Olwen. Be careful in the City, my child. Westminster is a place filled with intrigues. Be on your guard – at all times. Serve Lady Eleanor well.'

Olwen said in a gentle voice, 'God bless you, Countess Joanna, and your child.' Neither spoke of the princess's pregnancy. It was as if Joanna sensed Eleanor preferred her not to discuss it.

Chapter Five

Evesham
Summer 1265

The summer roses in the garden at Westminster were in full bloom and their scent floated in the air. Eleanor could almost, but not quite, forget the penury she had endured throughout winter, her agonising childbirth early in darkest January. She had been thankful for Olwen's services and those of the midwife. The little mite had survived. She called her Joan and gave her over to a nurse. It had all eaten into the little coin she possessed.

The King lived in luxurious apartments in the Tower. Queen Ailenor remained in France, still trying to raise an army to rescue the kingdom from Montfort. Eleanor was housed in the queen's apartments in the Palace of Westminster where she had struggled to heat her rooms during the dark days between December and April. Every time she'd glanced at the striking painting of Winter painted on her bedchamber's walls she shivered even more.

She could not forget how Montfort was responsible for her poverty. He removed what little income Edward possessed, taking over her husband's lands and reducing the whole royal family to penury. Eleanor was forced to borrow coin from her custodian, Hugh Despenser, and even from her own tailor to provide food for her kitchen and wood for her chambers.

Montfort freed Lord Edward, for a short while, bringing him to the City to be with his father. Edward was forced to promise before Montfort's Parliament not to raise an army against Earl Simon's rule.

If he broke his word he would be dispossessed of his inheritance as heir to the throne.

Eleanor was exhausted and cumbersome. Before Christ's Day she went into seclusion. Olwen cared for her, her travail was long and difficult but baby Joan seemed healthy. They washed her but did not allow her sleep in a fresh night rail and on clean sheets in her bed until the afterbirth was delivered. After this Eleanor wanted to sleep for a very long time because she was so weary with everything, her pregnancy, the long birth, limitations on her freedom, never mind her poverty. She was a princess of Castile, one of the greatest kingdoms in Christendom. She longed for the comforts of the palaces of her youth, the pleasant winter air and extensive gardens through which she walked in her mind's eye. This treatment by Montfort and his warlords was unacceptable.

'Her name is Joan,' she'd found herself anxiously snapping at Olwen and her midwife. 'Now take the babe away.' Turning her head to Margerie she had added, 'You will be responsible for the christening, the wet nurses, dry nurses, and servants. Find a reliable girl to rock her cradle.'

Olwen looked at Lady Margerie for guidance. Lady Margerie simply said, 'My lady, all will be as you wish. Olwen will make you a sleeping draught. You must rest.'

'Rest, rest, rest, Margerie, that's always your advice? How can I rest? I have too many cares. Just see to the infant and let me be.'

Lady Margerie, nonetheless, ordered the sleeping potion. Eleanor sighed as she drank a few mouthfuls and pushed it away. 'Enough,' she snapped. 'I don't need it. Take it away.'

It had been a dreadful year. Eleanor blamed Gilbert of Gloucester and Simon de Montfort both for baby Katherine's death the previous September. No one could save the delicate girl. Her daughter's tiny chest had not healed despite the administrations of the King's doctor and tinctures proved by Olwen. Eleanor grieved for Katherine all winter and found herself too sad to be interested in Joan, who was small compensation. She might die as well. Best not to become attached to the child. She took one look at the infant and sent the baby, with her wet nurse, a rocker for Joan's cradle, and a maid, to the nursery. This was now another room to keep warm and more mouths to feed. She had no money.

Her grief that winter had been pervasive and her financial situation horrific. Her ladies suffered chills. Olwen worked hard to create salves and tinctures from plants growing in the Westminster gardens. For this Eleanor was grateful, just as during the previous September, she had taken heart from Olwen's report from Hereford.

Christmas had been miserable. Eleanor discovered sadly she simply could not give her heart to this child. She was too frightened of yet another lost infant. There had been so many already, not least poor Katherine whom she had loved with all her heart.

Some days later, she wrote to Edward and received a short note in return but Edward was even more a prisoner than she. He, too, grieved for Katherine. Eleanor hoped and prayed daily he would not soon be grieving for Joan.

Eleanor's misery was only slightly eased in February on Robert Burnell's return to the City. He negotiated her possession of a farm, namely Somerton, because she had no income of her own. Thanks to Robert's requests on her behalf, she acquired revenues from three further manors in the wardship of Cecily, daughter to the deceased William de Fortibus. Eleanor held the documents to her chest and swore to Margerie she would never be poor again. She smiled to herself. If harvests were collected, she could look forward to profit from the Fortibus manors and the new farm at Somerton. Land was the answer.

'I'll gather as much land and as many estates as I can. I'll safeguard my own future. I'll outmanoeuvre the wealthiest of those barons, in particular Gilbert de Clare.' She spat his name. Her ladies bent over their mending. They knew her temper.

She glanced over at Margerie who was mending a precious veil. 'Take more care with that, Margerie. You will damage it. Smaller stitches. God knows when I can afford another silk veil.'

Margerie nodded politely and complied. even though her sewing was always neater than anyone else's.

Eleanor was horrified at how Earl Simon was enriching himself. By Eastertide he had offended his apprentice Gilbert of Gloucester by denying the Earl reward for his service, but she saw how Gilbert kicked back. She laughed publicly on the occasion when the arrogant Gilbert stormed at Earl Simon during the Easter Day feast in Westminster hall in front of them all.

'You favour lowly knights and commoners. You, my Lord Simon, are greedy too. You set their needs and yours above those of us, your barons, who fought for your cause.'

'You have more than enough wealth, Gilbert de Clare,' countered Montfort as he chewed. 'It is thee who is greedy.'

Eleanor met Henry's eyes. She had begun to laugh again. Henry placed a finger over his lips and summoned the wine servitor with a wave of his hand.

'Pour my Lord Montfort a cup first. Taste it too. Would not do for there to be a sour taste at a king's table.'

Yet Gilbert de Clare was not done with his tirade. 'Distribute your own gains. You have confiscated lands belonging to Lord Edward, there –' Edward, too, was present over Easter - 'and have enriched yourself, Montfort.' Gilbert bowed to Henry and with a dramatic flurry of his crimson mantle departed the table. The meal continued in silence. Eleanor was relieved to retire to her own chamber to sit with Olwen, Margerie, and her ladies by the fire. They talked about the quarrel in hushed voices deep into the evening, when Edward came to bid her goodbye. He was returning to the Tower with his father.

Eleanor had heard the following day that Gilbert had ridden out of Westminster for his own London dwelling before any harm could come to his person. Within days the Earl took himself off to his castle on the border with Wales, followed by a posse of highly trained and armed troops. He would change sides again as she knew Henry hoped he would. Gilbert would do his best to destroy Simon de

Montfort, just as last year he tried to destroy her Edward. She disliked and mistrusted de Clare even more.

Yet, soon after Gilbert's departure, news slipped into the palace of Westminster. Exiled barons were moving into the Welsh borderlands and were raising troops. Now they had Gloucester on their side, there was a small hope they could oust Earl Simon from power. Later Eleanor had heard, from a merchant visiting her with fabrics, that Earl Simon rode with troops west to Hereford, taking Henry and Edward with him. She also received secret notes from Edward hidden in wine casks and delivered by loyal servants to her. Henry hoped to bring Red Gilbert back into his fold.

During June she had remained hopeful of an end to it all but heard nothing more and she despaired of ever hearing from Edward again. The King, long gone to Hereford, never wrote. Nor did she hear from Pembroke or Mortimer.

Eleanor sank onto a garden bench. The scent of roses and a July garden could not compensate for a life that promised endless bleakness. She would never be a queen if Edward plotted with his mother, Queen Ailenor, to raise foreign mercenaries. If such troops landed on English shores the royalist cause would be hopeless. City citizens possessed long memories. No Londoner had forgotten the French occupation half a century before. Besides, Londoners disliked Queen Ailenor. When the rebellion began some years before they had pelted the Queen's barge with rotting fruit and offal from London Bridge. Fearing for her life Queen Ailenor had had to take the Lord Mayor's protection and shelter. After that she had departed for France.

Eleanor tried hard to concentrate on her Book of Hours, staring at illustrations she never really saw, turning pages she never actually read. Glancing up, she observed Olwen who had been gathering herbs, peering over the gate, shading her brow. A basket lay on the ground spilling nettles and marigolds, splashes of yellow vivid as the sun, startling against the green plants. She snapped her book closed, laid it on the bench, scrambled to her feet and hurried towards the little gate into the courtyard. Looking back over her shoulder she saw her ladies were oblivious to anything other than their task, mending linen nearly past repair. They earnestly bent over their stitches as if nothing else mattered.

On seeing the princess, who had trusted her to keep her eye on the courtyard and warn her of anything unusual, Olwen turned and called out, her voice filled with excitement, 'My lady, it's the King's squire. It's Master Eugene. He's climbing off his jennet. He's given it to a stable boy. He's looking all about. Shall I let him in through the wicket gate?' There was a conspiratorial look in her eyes.

Eleanor's heart beat faster. 'Yes, at once.' There could be a message from Edward. This was why she used Olwen as her eyes and ears about the palace and even the City. No one would suspect her close relationship with a mere herbalist who made her and her ladies possets to cure their aches and pains. Olwen was perfect, and she was intelligent as well as loyal. Her speech had improved as well. 'Bring Eugene straight to me.' She hugged herself and paced up and down the shrubbery, not knowing whether to be worried or thankful.

She observed Eugene glance her way. The squire nodded as Olwen beckoned him and he slipped through the low gate, approached her and knelt on the grass. Her mouth became a round O as the squire withdrew a letter from his satchel. There was news at last! Pray God it was good news.

'My lady, Lord Edward is safe.' The squire had clearly determined to put her mind at ease. 'He escaped Hereford two weeks since. I managed in the confusion to get out of the castle with a message for you from the King.'

'Praise be to God.' She laid her hand on her heart. She could hardly breathe.

Moments later she was walking around trellises of clambering roses reading a crumpled message sent to her by King Henry. Eugene collapsed onto the bench, fortunately out of sight of the courtyard. Olwen raced to the nearest kitchen and fetched a cup of ale. How he had evaded guards posted on the gates of Westminster was nothing short of miraculous. The guards could not have recognised Henry's squire. He wore Montfort livery. They would assume Eugene had business with Hugh Despenser, another utterly hideous person.

The message was short. *Lord Edward has escaped from Hereford Castle and ridden out with Thomas de Clare while pretending to exercise and test out horses. He galloped away on the fastest stallion. I believe he met with Earl Mortimer in the forest. My information is that he and Gilbert of Gloucester are treating together. Let us pray for a successful outcome. Take heart.*

The letter was unsigned but Eugene assured her it came from King Henry himself, who was in good spirits and mischievously gleeful because Edward and Gloucester were giving Montfort trouble on the Severn.

'Praise God,' Eleanor said, tears wetting her cheeks, folding the brief message into her bodice. 'We may be saved yet.'

Edward was free but Henry remained a prisoner. She thought to herself, I know what I should do now.

After supper Eleanor summoned Olwen to her chamber. Eugene, whom she had briefed after sending him to her apartment up by the back stairway from the garden, was already present. She sent her servants away, bade Olwen sit on a stool opposite, and poured them all glasses of hippocras and offered wafers around. As they sipped the sweet wine, Eleanor launched into her suggestion. 'Olwen, I know you may feel this too dangerous but I shall ask of you a great favour.' She took the girl's hand. 'You may refuse.'

'My lady, what favour?'

Eleanor leaned forward. 'I am concerned for Lord Edward. I need to know where he is and what is happening. Would you travel to Hereford again, to St Guthlac's with Eugene - she glanced over at the squire - and gather information?'

The girl's face became shadowed. Eleanor looked away. She should not ask this of Olwen. She should not. The west was dangerous. Yet Eugene could protect her.

After a pause, Olwen said, 'Cannot Eugene discover all this for you, my lady?'

56

It *was* too much to ask. A sparrow fluttered by the window. Edward was free but she must know where he was and if he was safe. 'Eugene will return to the King. King Henry will be in great danger if there is a battle between Earl Simon's barons and my husband's supporters. Eugene must remain with the King.' She found herself anxiously twisting a piece of her gown between finger and thumb. 'I only want you to *find* Edward for me. It will be easier for you to discover his whereabouts. You can slip into my lord's camp with medicines for his troops. You could deliver a message to him.'

'What?' Olwen looked even more uncertain.

'I shall send a trusted boy as your servant. He will bring news back if you find my lord. Stay at St Guthlac's until it's safe to leave.'

Eleanor heard Olwen draw breath. 'I can try. There will be no pilgrim party this time to provide cover for the journey. God only knows the west is dangerous. It was dangerous last year. I fear it is worse now.' She looked thoughtful. 'Yet without others to hold us up, we could, of course, make greater haste this time.'

'You will do this for me?'

'Yes,' Olwen replied. 'As a herbalist, I might reach Lord Edward, but only if the Prior assists this quest. Lord Edward will know me. Remember how I treated his chill before he departed for Hereford.'

'Yes, indeed I do. Thank you, thank you a thousand times, Olwen. If we regain our kingdom you will be rewarded well. Could you be ready to depart in the morning?'

'Yes,' the girl replied. 'Gladly.'

'The boy will ready your palfrey for you by dawn.' Eleanor handed her a leather purse. 'Wear this under your gown. There is more than sufficient for your journey. May God's blessing go with you and keep you safe.' She nodded at Eugene. 'Guard Olwen well. Deliver her straight to the Prior of St Guthlac's. Make sure the boy watches over her.' She chuckled and grinned at the squire. 'Tonight you can conceal yourself behind the arras on a mattress in my antechamber.'

She noted he had the grace to blush.

*

The journey to St Guthlac's Priory only took the best part of a week as they rode fast, changing horses at loyal manor houses where they stopped overnight. Olwen had accompanied Eleanor on her many rides through the meadows of Thorney Island. It was exercise they both enjoyed. Whilst Eleanor's ladies would hang back, they would canter around the fields closely watched by palace guards.

Only Lady Eleanor's ladies knew of Olwen's departure and they begged her to find out about their own husbands and cousins. Olwen was also free to come and go from Westminster, so it was no surprise to the palace guards when she went into the City on an errand for the ladies. When she set out for the west that morning it simply appeared to others she was riding into the City to procure herbs from the markets, accompanied by a male servant wearing Earl Simon's own livery and a boy called Luke whom they all knew.

'So Olwen, here we are again, such comfortable old companions. It's almost as if we are an old married couple now,' Eugene said as they rode towards Worcester, Luke trailing discreetly behind. 'Into the west, you and I, travelling together on the Lady Eleanor's business.'

'And that of Lord Edward and the King too, if only we can find them.'

'Oh, we shall.' Eugene slowed his horse to a walk. 'How have you found Lady Eleanor's service this past year?'

Olwen hesitated for a heartbeat before answering. She had said goodbye to her father in Canterbury months before and left with Eugene for the City, her stepmother's anger ringing in her ears.

'Fancy this, you working for a princess! You, a mere girl, you, a lazy slut with airs and graces. I'm glad to see the back of you. You are useless, do you hear! Lady Eleanor will soon enough discover your indolent character. Go and don't darken our doorstep again.' It was as well her father had been visiting a customer when her stepmother spoke so wickedly to her.

'Master Eugene, I have been greatly honoured to serve Lady Eleanor and her ladies. I am learning so much. I enjoy the herbal garden at Westminster. The ladies have suffered a harsh year. Lady Eleanor has been distraught, is often irritable with us, and it is my greatest wish to see her happy. She cannot love her daughter as she should. She is frightened she will lose Joan just as she lost Katherine and says it is hard for her to believe that God would allow the loss of children. She throws things when she is angry.'

Eugene raised his eyebrows. 'Really. Who does she throw things at?'

Olwen shrugged. 'She throws cups, serving bowls, and glassware at the walls and curses Montfort for keeping her in poverty. She blames him for Katherine's death. She says in Spain he would be whipped to death for what he has done to us or he might be burned on a stake as a devil. When she is like this I have to brew up sleeping draughts she rarely wants to calm her while the ladies scurry into corners in the corridor beyond her chambers for fear of being in the way of her thrown dishes. They have to sweep up after her, but not until she is calm again.'

'It is sad indeed, Olwen, Lady Eleanor is suffering so. God must have his reasons. Let us hope our journey is successful. May God bless us both and our lady.' He glanced over his shoulder at the boy. 'And you, Luke, too.'

The youth grinned. All knew of the lady's irritability.

At a manor close to Worcester they discovered Lord Edward was recruiting knights loyal to the King but no one could tell them exactly where Edward was. It was likely close to Mortimer's castle of Wigmore, but it could be anywhere along the border with Wales.

The innkeeper of an hostelry in a small village in which they stopped for a brief rest at noon informed them about something else. As he served them outside, the day being warm, he remarked, 'That bastard Simon de Montfort has made a pact with Llywelyn of Wales. Can you believe it? The Welshman has pledged to help Montfort in return for full recognition of his title as Prince of Wales and the promise he'll keep all military gains inside the Welsh border.'

'How do you know this?' Eugene said as he thirstily downed a cup of watered ale. 'My lady wife here is scared of the Welsh. Are we in danger?' Eugene poured a second cup of ale from a jug into Olwen's cup, looking worried.

The innkeeper placed a pair of hairy hands on his hips and stared at them. Olwen made herself appear suitably scared. Luke, recently her shadow, moved closer with a frown on his face as if to guard her. Eugene impatiently waved him to be seated. Olwen coyly lifted her veil across her face, and only removed it aside to sip her ale. *Wife indeed,* she thought to herself. *I had best keep up the pretence. He could have said I was travelling to visit relatives in Hereford and he was escorting me.*

'*Husband,* are we truly safe?' she said, using a pleading voice.

'Your sister's manor is far from danger. Fear not, my love. We shall be there soon.' She felt him pat her arm and the little intimate gesture was not unpleasant.

Luke's eyes widened. He drank deeply from his cup and began to cough.

'An innkeeper always hears things from passing knights.' The man finally answered Eugene's question and tapped a reddened nose with his first finger on his right hand. 'As for Lord Edward, heard he's escaped Montfort and is on the move too.'

'Good to hear. Thank you for information and the ale. A pleasant brew. Our thirst is quenched,' Eugene said nonchalantly and set his cup back on the trestle table. He stood and stretched. 'We must be on our way to arrive at our sister's manor in time for Vespers. Come, lady wife. Horses please, boy.' He slapped Luke on the back. 'Bad cough. A bit of cheese gone down the wrong way?'

Luke shook his head, stopped coughing, and went to untether the horses.

'God speed,' the innkeeper said. 'You'll be in Hereford before nightfall.'

'Everything is moving so quickly,' Eugene said later that afternoon as they neared the Priory. 'We must be very careful.'

'Will I get to fight for Lord Edward?' Luke piped up.

'No, you'll remember your duty. You are Mistress Olwen's servant. You'll stay with her at all times. That is as Lady Eleanor has insisted. Remember it well.'

Luke touched the sword and scabbard he wore. He looked at Olwen through pale, earnest admiring eyes. 'I shall guard you well, Mistress Olwen.'

'Good. I hope there'll be no need.' Olwen doubted Luke would be able to fend off Montfort's soldiers or the Welsh army should it be necessary. For a moment she silently cursed herself for having accepted Lady Eleanor's mission. Lady Eleanor was fearless and, in truth, she was not. She quaked at the thought of an ambush.

When they arrived at St Guthlac's the Prior, who was clearly delighted to see her again, ushered them into his parlour.

'Welcome, dear friends. You will be in need of refreshments.' He rang a bell and a friar shuffled in carrying a tray with bread, ham, and a jug of wine.'

He smiled with benevolence at Olwen. 'You, my dear girl, must lodge in this house rather than in the priory guest house as before. Your servant and Master Eugene here can sleep on pallets in the hall. My female servants will see to your needs.'

Olwen smiled to note how Luke frowned at being sent away from her side. She then sighed at his chagrin. The boy acted as if he were already a chivalrous knight belonging to a lady of legend, keener and more possessive of her as their journey proceeded closer to Hereford. He rode beside her. He helped her to dismount her frisky palfrey at every stopping point. He groomed the palfrey and was ever watchful, his hand constantly straying to his scabbard if there was as much as a blackbird rustling in the hedgerows. He slept outside her chamber door at every inn or manor house, and she suspected he wanted this to continue. Yet if Eugene noticed Luke's fawning treatment of his 'wife', he never remarked on it.

The Prior was saying, 'It is safer no travellers know of your mission; better, too, that none know you are close to the King's family. We shall do our best to locate Prince Edward. When we do, I'll send you with our own apothecary into the camp. There being so many skirmishes with the Welsh, he'll have need of herbalists and apothecaries.' The Prior poured cups of ale and offered them seed cakes. 'However,' he continued, 'Lord Edward's camp may be miles distant. There have been battles fought up and down the River Severn all summer. Lord Edward could be camping at any point on the river.' He turned to Eugene. 'The good news is he has taken control of most of the Severn. I have a sense that both sides are camped around the valley of Evesham. What about you, Eugene? Can you ride into the camp with my apothecary and Mistress Olwen?'

'I fear for the King and must return to him at the castle. Luke here can ride with you in my stead, Mistress Olwen.'

Luke grinned from ear to ear.

The Prior stroked his chin. 'The King is not at Hereford Castle anymore. Montfort has fetched him into his camp. I am told this by my friars who are often in the town selling our honey. Even the miller who grinds our corn has claimed sight of King Henry riding with Montfort's troops this past week.'

Eugene sank onto the bench. He covered his face with his hands. Removing them he said, 'This is worrying news, Master Prior. Montfort is using the King as a hostage. I'll go to the castle nonetheless and see what I can discover. When I return, we can decide if it is safe to find out exactly where Lord Edward is and try to enter his camp.' Worry lines creased his forehead as he looked up from the Prior to Olwen. Luke, somewhat deflated by this, never spoke until the Prior addressed him.

'I believe you are here as Mistress Olwen's servant and messenger.'

'Lord Prior, I am her protector.' He reached into his surcoat and produced his short sword. 'To assist and watch over her. Lady Eleanor said so.'

'That weapon remains at my door while you are with us. I allow none in my house.'

'But I am here to protect Mistress Olwen.'

'Outside my house, yes. There will be no need here.'

He bowed his head. 'But if there is danger I must retrieve my weapon.'

'If there is danger in my Priory, your weapon will be returned to you.' He turned to Olwen. 'I'll call for a servant to show you your chamber. She'll bring you water so you may bathe. Supper follows Vespers. You may pray in my private chapel as before.' He looked at Eugene. 'May God protect you. Return safely. Sleep in the hall and use the bathhouse. We shall provide you with linens.' He rang for the servant adding, 'Within a few days we shall find Lord Edward.'

Olwen was not reassured by his confidence, but she promised Lady Eleanor they would find Lord Edward and find him they would.

At last, Eugene brought news on the third day of August. They gathered together in the chapter house away from prying ears and eyes.

He accepted ale, bread, and cheese as they sat around the roughly hewn table.

'Lord Edward's camp is hidden amongst hills close to Evesham. He has sent for men from the towns between Evesham and Hereford and further afield. Lord Edward, himself, has ridden to attack Kenilworth. Montfort's son has gathered a great army at the fortress there.'

'How do you have this intelligence?' questioned the Prior.

'Ah, there's the great advantage I had today. I knew the recruiting captain.' He slapped his knee and drank back the mug of foaming ale. 'We're riding to Lord Edward's camp with him . . . tonight.' He looked at Olwen, his eyes quizzical. 'You don't have to come, you know, Mistress Olwen. It could be dangerous. By the rood, you would be safer here. I can take the Lady Eleanor's message to her lord and bring you back the information you seek for her.'

Olwen felt afraid at the thought of entering a military camp preparing for battle. Even so, she was not going to be deterred and after all this was what she had come to do. Steeling herself, she stared at him. 'It is *my* mission. I am duty bound to fulfil Lady Eleanor's trust and see Lord Edward myself. I shall accompany you,' she said. Her firm look forbade argument.

'I'm coming too,' squeaked Luke.

Eugene's lips moved as he looked upwards at a statue of St Guthlac. 'I suppose you, St Guthlac, having fought in the army of Ethelred of Mercia hundreds of years ago, know all about battle. Lend us your protection.' He turned to Luke. 'You are coming.'

Before Matins, Olwen, Luke, and Eugene, leading ponies and accompanied by Brother Anselm the priory apothecary, made their way through the darkness of the Priory grounds. Close to the town gate, just outside St Guthlac's, they met with a band of horsemen clad in chain mail. These friends of Eugene's were riding from Hereford to the prince's camp. Their leader said, 'Simon de Montfort is riding towards the Abbey of Evesham.' He looked straight at Eugene, Luke and the apothecary. 'You three may ride with us. Safety in numbers.' He turned to Olwen, 'No camp followers.'

'I'm the herbalist,' she said, feeling peeved.

'She comes with the friars' apothecary. Mistress Olwen is trained with medicine.'

The horseman raised his forehead. 'A female apothecary?'

'Nay, just a herbalist,' Olwen said. 'I possess much knowledge of apothecary because my father treated those close to King Henry. I have learned his trade.'

'Welcome then, Mistress Olwen.'

As they rode away from Hereford, Eugene explained, 'The King is Earl Simon's hostage. He insists Henry ride with him. It's a measure of his ruthlessness that he places our King's life in such danger. Earl Simon thinks Prince Edward might not attack him if he has Edward's father riding within his own troops.'

'Earl Simon would not take King Henry onto a battlefield?' remarked Brother Anselm as they entered a wood to take a forest path.

'He would. He's ruthless,' Eugene responded with an impatient shake of his reins.

It grew dark and shadowy inside the woods. Olwen heard the

scurrying of small animals in the undergrowth. She could hear her own pounding heart and tried to think of pleasant things like making possets, gathering herbs in the garden at Westminster, and her mattress by the great arched window of the maidens' dormitory, her lavender-scented linen sheets and especially her embroidered coverlet, a gift from Lady Eleanor.

The conversation around her continued in hushed voices. 'Montfort's the Devil. He would not think twice about dragging our King into battle,' she heard Eugene reply to the previous question. 'Christ's bones, Lord Edward intends to fight Montfort regardless. Gloucester is determined to destroy Earl Simon. You'll see, they will lure him into battle.'

Olwen thought for a moment. 'Lady Eleanor does not trust Gilbert of Gloucester. She says that since the conflict with the barons began, Earl Gilbert has changed sides four times. She calls Earl Simon the Devil and Earl Gilbert his servant.' The soldiers laughed heartily at this.

She urged her mare forwards. They had left the woods now and were riding at a firm trot along field paths, away from the main route north-east, yet still leading towards Evesham. Corn awaiting the scythe and leafy hedgerows allowed them a little shelter. The moon was half-concealed by clouds. The air felt heavy. A threat of thunder haunted the heavy night air.

Just before dawn, they turned into the hills. After a shorter ride through more beech woods, the trees heavy with leaf, the party arrived at the edge of a broad meadow where they reined in and stared ahead. Olwen was astonished by her first glimpse of Lord Edward's camp. The sea of tents stretched before them for several miles. A sentry posted by the path from the woodland's edge softly called to them. Another raised his sword and whistled. Armed men emerged from the trees. They formed two lines, blocking the passage forward. Some raised bows. The leader of their own party called out his name followed by what seemed to Olwen a password.

'We bring archers to fight for Earl Gilbert of Gloucester and Lord Edward,' their leader said to the camp guards. 'We've an apothecary from Hereford and his herbalist with her servant. We also have one of King Henry's squires who wishes to speak to Lord Edward.'

Their lead horseman dismounted. The guards let them pass and two accompanied them towards the camp. As they entered it, the group of archers travelling with them filed away with another guard. Eugene turned to her. 'We are on our own now. Dismount. Lead your palfrey. The other guard will take us to Lord Edward.'

They moved into the camp's heart, through lanes filled with tents, where men were polishing swords and talking in low voices. A blacksmith was shoeing horses. Men were arming. Priests wandered about with blessings and prayers. Cooks walked along the lanes with steaming cauldrons of frumenty. Catching a whiff of the spicy scent, Olwen realised she was hungry, but she forgot her hunger when she saw a small clearing opening up before them. In the centre of this clearing stood a tent emblazoned with leopards, guarded by fierce-looking warriors.

'Lord Edward's tent,' their guide pointed to a collection of smaller tents. 'Over there is an infirmary and a makeshift kitchen. I'll leave you to explain yourselves. I have a battle to make ready for and my prayers to say.' She felt her heart thump faster. Battle was imminent.

Hands moved to sword hilts as their small group approached.

'I have come with a message for Lord Edward,' Eugene said loudly to the guards placed around Edward's tent. They were menacingly alert. 'I am the King's squire,' Eugene went on. 'I have been in London. I bring him a message from Lady Eleanor.' He gently pushed Olwen forward. 'This woman is a servant to Lady Eleanor, her herbalist.' He touched Friar Anselm's arm. 'We have an apothecary from St Guthlac's Priory in Hereford.'

The guards surveyed them with coldness in their eyes. Terrifyingly huge mastiffs barked at them. A guard picked up a bucket of entrails and threw them the creatures' way. The black animals looped off around the back of the great tent. The captain folded his arms, though how he managed to do so Olwen wondered. His chain mail looked too heavy. He announced gruffly, 'Lord Edward is resting.

Hereford, you say. You are lucky to be alive. Montfort's men will be everywhere seeking such as you.'

'We avoided the roads. I have heard Montfort has my lord, the King, with him?'

'We believe so.'

'In that case I must find King Henry. I am his squire.'

The guard scowled. 'You'll be hacked to pieces first.'

The tent opening was pushed aside and a tall young man strode out, his light brown hair long as his shoulders, stubble gracing his chin, and his eyes piercing blue, though like his father his left eyelid appeared to droop. 'Who is it?'

'It's me, my lord,' Eugene said as he fell on one knee followed by Luke and the apothecary. Olwen sank to her knees.

'What, by the rood, are you doing here, Eugene? Rise, man. Christ's Holy Blood, Why are you not with the King?'

Eugene waved a hand at Olwen. 'I was in London on King Henry's business. Lady Eleanor has sent Mistress Olwen to you because there's been no news of your whereabouts for months. When I brought her to St Guthlac's, the King had already been taken away by Earl Simon. My friends have deserted Hereford and joined your troops this very morning. Here we are and with us this apothecary.' He swept a hand in the friar's direction. 'Brother Anselm.'

'Ah, I remember you, Brother.' Lord Edward turned back to Eugene. 'I'll have need of him.' His sharp eyes lit on Olwen. 'Rise, Mistress Olwen. I remember you too. Come inside. You have a quarter hour. We are riding to Evesham within the hour. We intend finishing Montfort this day.'

Olwen bit her lip until she tasted blood. It was terrifying and at the same time exhilarating. Lord Edward lifted the tent flap and ushered them inside.

When they were seated on stools with ale, bowls of frumenty, and hunks of bread Edward said, 'Listen well. We are giving battle. I pray I shall survive. We have a strategy that cannot fail. It gives us the advantage and it will hoodwink Earl Simon, but I pray when he rides out to give battle he does not bring my father, the King, with him; that he leaves him in the Abbey.'

'Sire?' said Eugene looking up from his bowl. 'Since there's no time to find the King, I shall ride with your army.'

Edward looked at the others. 'You will remain behind the battle lines, do you hear. You,' Lord Edward nodded from Brother Anselm to Olwen, 'your boy can carry messages from our lines to the camp. We have a band of boys for that purpose. He is now one such. We have need of apothecaries and herbalists. The enemy will not need your help.' Edward grinned, showing a set of strong white teeth. 'No quarter will be given. Not only do I have a collection of Montfort's own banners from the rout at Kenilworth, to confuse him as to thinking his son has ridden with an army to rescue him, but I shall fly the dragon banners. When he sees those he will know that he has an appointment with God, though I fear God will be sending him to the Devil.'

'He is the Devil.'

'Aye, that he is, Eugene. And the Devil will take his own.'

Edward dismissed the friar and Olwen. 'Wait in the adjacent tent and pray.' He turned to Eugene and the boy. 'That lad shall stay with the baggage train behind our lines but you, Eugene, may ride with us.'

'Willingly,' Olwen heard Eugene say as she and Friar Anselm lifted the tent flap to leave.

Lord Edward called after her, 'Mistress Olwen, I shall send a letter to you for my wife and a ring. See she receives it.'

Olwen turned her head. 'Sire, I shall.' She could not help wondering if she would survive long enough to return to London. 'Godspeed,' she called to Eugene and Luke.

'God will support a just cause,' Eugene replied. The prince laughed.

By midday the sky cracked open. It was as if Hephaestus was pounding the earth in furious rage. Olwen peered out from the apothecaries' tent as rain began to lash down in sudden dense dark sheets. Thunder banged as lightning streaked the heavens. She dropped the tent flap

68

and they waited. They could hear distant horns sounding through the downpour. When she peered out later the thunderstorm had stopped and sun had burst through the sky. By afternoon, the injured were being carried to the camp on makeshift stretchers or supported by their companions. Soon she was busy assisting the camp surgeons, apothecaries, and doctors who all had gathered in the large tent that dripped water through holes in its oiled fabric. Olwen moved from injured man to injured man, laying poultices on injuries and helping surgeons to set bones. She administered draughts of poppy provided by Brother Anselm before a surgeon cut away a limb or cauterised a wound. There was so much blood and agonised cries of pain, she felt her stomach turn over and over. She wrapped a linen cloth over her skirt but soon that too was splashed with blood and guts. She had seen animals slaughtered for the Canterbury meat market, but never had she seen humans with such evidence of slaughter about their own broken bodies.

Occasionally, she asked about the battle raging only a few miles distant. Men shook their heads. 'It's a sorry pass when Englishmen kill their own brothers,' one man grunted to her as she cleaned a wound on his head and wound a bandage about it.

'Were you not wearing your helmet?'

'Lost it. Knocked off my head,' he said. 'But we have the better of them. Llewelyn's men scurried from the field when they saw we out-numbered them by nigh enough double. They thought Earl Simon's son was riding to swell their numbers. Was us as carrying the banners we took when we routed his son at Kenilworth Castle night before last. We deceived the bastards. We 'ave better of the battle already. Our men are slaughtering the enemy, troop by troop. Slash, slash. Too bad many of them are good Englishmen.'

Olwen breathed more easily after that. In her belt purse she carried the brief note from Lord Edward to Lady Eleanor, delivered to her before the royalist army rode out, and a gold ring set with a gleaming sapphire from his finger. Perhaps Lord Edward would return and take it from her. He might see his lady sooner than she.

There was a shout outside the tent whilst she was tending another wounded knight. She recognised Luke's voice. 'Mistress Olwen, Mistress,' he called. 'You and Brother Anselm are to ride to Prince Edward now, this moment. They have rescued the King. They're in Evesham Abbey. I've an escort for you. Hurry!'

She grabbed a stretch of linen, plunged her hands into water, and called for the apothecary.

'You are sure?' he said.

'Lord Edward is with the King. He is terrified by the sights he has seen this day. You are to tend to him. After he is comfortable you are to return to St Guthlac's. I am riding with you and our escort,' Luke said breathlessly.

A short time passed and they were on their way escorted and guided by a small troop loyal to the King. As they rode, she heard the full story best as Luke could garble it. King Henry had been taken into the battle. He was rescued by none other than Eugene and a band of knights. The King had called out, 'I am your King. Do not harm me.' He removed his helmet. Eugene had recognised him.

Luke said excitedly, 'Mistress Olwen, England is restored to our King and our Prince. Montfort is dead.'

'Are you sure Montfort is dead?' she said as some hours later they entered the Abbey at Evesham, led by Edward's knights, who wore red crosses on their breasts to distinguish them from those of Montfort's men who had worn white crosses stitched on their surcoats.

'I saw the carnage that was Montfort's body with my own peepers.' He lowered his voice. 'They treated it badly. 'Twas wicked to destroy a body in that way.'

'Oh, how?' she said. Luke shook his head and would not elaborate. The Abbot hurried to them, followed by a troupe of monks, and at once escorted them to the King's chamber.

Night was falling. Along with Brother Anselm and the Abbey apothecary they made King Henry comfortable. She was pleased when Henry recognised her and managed a weak smile. He had aged much during the year of Montfort's rule. His hair and his beard were snowy white and his blue eyes were red-rimmed, lined, and tired. He looked like the image of Winter in Lady Eleanor's chamber. His left eye drooped more than ever. They tended his superficial bruising. After being administered a poppy drink, the King fell into a deep sleep.

As another misty dawn broke, Olwen heard what had happened to Earl Simon, and his son who had fought beside him. The Earl's head had been cut from his body to be sent to Roger Mortimer's wife, Countess Maud. His body was hideously mutilated, his manhood draped over his ears as his head was paraded around the battle field, then stuffed in his mouth. How cruel war is, she thought to herself. I never want to be part of it again. She smiled through her tears of exhaustion. Tomorrow they would begin her journey back to London rather than St Guthlac's Priory. Life could become normal again. She would plant gardens, tend herbs and gather them for tinctures and salves. What was broken would mend as seasons tumbled through the year's cycle.

On her departure with a group of soldiers, Lord Edward thanked her for her care of the King.

'If you return me what I gave you, I shall give the ring to my wife myself,' Lord Edward said with a smile on his lips. 'God has favoured us, for he has rid us of the man who was once my uncle and who now will suffer hell's fires for his sins against me.' He gave Olwen a purse of silver coin. 'This is but small recompense for the service you have given my lady and myself. I send you to London with a sizeable escort. Let us hope the next time we meet we shall be speaking of castle gardens and herbal beds.'

She sank into a deep curtsey and accepted the proffered purse. 'Thank you, my Lord Edward,' she said as her tears fell.

She knew what she would do. Her greatest wish was to one day purchase a small manor of her own, and to have gardens filled with plants.

Chapter Six

Westminster
1265

After Edward returned from Evesham, Eleanor moved from Queen Ailenor's chambers into rooms of her own. King Henry kindly ordered these hung once again with heavy tapestries after the fashion she had loved in Castile. He had carpets placed on her floors and sent her delicious expensive fruits such as oranges and figs imported from Spain. He granted her lands he confiscated from rebellious barons, but these were to be a temporary gift. Henry was already considering returning manors to their old owners as long as the dispossessed made payment for them to him and swore their loyalty to the crown.

'I shall compensate you elsewhere, Eleanor,' Henry had promised. 'You will have income from this year's harvests.'

'He had best do so,' Edward said. 'You'll need an office from which to administer your estates.' He drew her close. 'You'll never be hungry and cold again.'

'There must not be such times again, Edward. Montfort was responsible for Katherine's death. She was delicate and he forced us to live like beggars in cold draughty chambers.' She never forgot how she had to borrow to afford Katherine's funeral. She had miscarried several times and Katherine's death was another cruel blow, though Joan was a compensation because Edward adored the baby. Such a difficult pain-filled birth, she often thought but tried to forget. She could not forget she had nearly died that January. She could not love Joan in the way Edward did.

Edward drew her to the bed and began to unlace her over-gown. As her gown slid to the floor carpet, he whispered, 'There will be many more children, bonny like Joan. And, my love, we *shall* be rich. Much of our wealth should be written in your name. It is safer so. You will be the custodian of great lands. It will be our security. I won't cause the barons envy. If I die, *you* will hold our lands and pass on great estates to our children.' He pulled the pins from her hair, allowing it to tumble in a rich chestnut cascade to her waist. She stepped out of her slippers and he covered her face with kisses. He looked into her eyes. 'We are going to have many healthy children. We shall be the most important royal family in Europe. I won't be making the same mistakes my father made. If I don't have titles to great lands, I can't ever be accused of granting castles to favourites. They will remain your lands. We shall live within our means. We'll continue to hold Parliaments. The people must be content because happy subjects will remain loyal. I am already helping my father rule. The earls and the wealthy merchants of London will listen to me as they never listened to him.'

He kissed her lips and she responded, winding her arms about his neck. To her delight, they tumbled onto the bed where they indulged each other in caresses and love over and over. How she had missed him. He whispered into her hair how he had missed her too.

In September, baby Joan died. Eleanor was glad she had not allowed herself to feel any affection for the baby. Too many babies were claimed by God. There would have to be more pregnancies. None of their children had survived.

As Eleanor knelt in prayer by Joan's tomb, her tears spilled over at last. Edward reached over and clasped her hand. His own face was stricken with grief. 'Our baby Joan is with Katherine and with God who is her heavenly parent. She is watching down from Heaven. No purgatory for the innocent. There will be others, my love. We are young and healthy.' He lifted her hand to his lips and kissed it.

It came as a shock to Eleanor when before Christmas she overheard her junior ladies whisper to each other that there had been relations between Alix, Gilbert of Gloucester's wife, and Lord Edward during the uprising. How could there have been? Alix shared a grandmother with Edward, King Henry's mother Isabella who, after her husband King John died, had left England to marry Hugh de Lusignan. King Henry always favoured Alix, his niece, as did Queen Ailenor. A marriage had been negotiated for her when Earl Gilbert was only nine years old and Alix already seventeen. Alix was very beautiful. She resembled her grandmother, who had been the loveliest lady at King John's court.

Eleanor frowned. Marriage to Earl Gilbert must be torture, but to seek a relationship with Edward, her cousin, and a married man, was outrageous if true – and unforgivable. She also had two daughters with Gilbert.

Edward would never betray her. He certainly would not betray her with his cousin, even if she was the most beautiful lady at court. Eleanor dismissed her ladies and summoned the girls responsible for the rumour to her antechamber.

She drew a deep breath and stared at the two young women for enough time to make them uncomfortable. They shifted from foot to foot. At last she broke the silence. 'What is this rumour you speak of concerning my husband and Lady Alix de Lusignan, his cousin, who is married to the Earl of Gloucester?'

If they had appeared nervous before, now they seemed about to burst into tears. One reddened. The other girl began to weep.

Eleanor softened her tactic. She stood to her full height of five feet and five inches and folded her hands in front of her. She cared little for expensive gowns but on this occasion she decided to look regal. Today she wore crimson. She tried to appear cool, collected, and queenly because one day, God willing, she would be a queen.

'Well? Speak!' she said. 'You must tell me where the nonsense hails from if you wish to remain at court and not be returned to your parents' estates in disgrace. Earl Gilbert of Gloucester is a powerful man. He won't like hearing slanders concerning his wife. Lord Edward is my husband and if such a rumour comes to his ears you will lose all hope of noble husbands and –' she hesitated to allow her words to strike home - 'frankly, if you are fortunate, you will be sent into a nunnery.'

Now they were both crying. One gulped through her sobs, 'We heard it from a page who returned to court from Chester.'

The other fell to her knees. 'Lady Eleanor, we are sorry.'

Eleanor thought for a moment. 'The page's name?'

'Humphrey de Clare.'

So, a distant relative to Earl Gilbert. He had been in Edward's service for the past eighteen months, and was all of fourteen years old.

'I see. You may go. What this boy says is a foul rumour. If I hear it repeated you will be sent away to do penance for speaking untruths. Go out of my presence.'

The girls hurried away as if wings had been attached to their slippers. She knew who their families were. If she heard this rumour repeated again, their families would indeed never find noble husbands for their daughters. Humphrey de Clare! She would make an example of the arrogant little rat.

She buried her head in her hands. What if the rumour *had* substance? Alix had been Edward's prisoner briefly before the Battle of Lewes and he could have been in her company daily after he escaped from Hereford to Chester.

The story ate into Eleanor's heart, filling her thoughts with suspicion. She walked about the Palace of Westminster in a distracted manner. She kept looking in her mirror, peering at it for wrinkles. She summoned Olwen and asked her to make her a facial cream with oil of violets and egg whites. She, who rarely cared about fashion, invited her tailor to Westminster and ordered new gowns of velvet and satin in her favourite colours of red and green.

'I must look fashionable this Christmas,' she said to her ladies looking through the selection of fabrics brought to her by the tailor and his apprentices. 'It will be upon us before we know it.' She patted one of her little dogs and leaning down said, 'You, Doucement, will have a felted coat in crimson to match my best gown.'

Every time Eleanor saw Alix at prayer in the abbey, kneeling with the newly returned Queen Ailenor, she was sure the woman watched Edward. At table, she was convinced those violet eyes followed his. It was noticeable how Alix avoided Gilbert's company and was always by Queen Ailenor's side stitching some gorgeous piece of silvered embroidery.

All the new gowns, mantles, shoes, and face creams would not put her mind at ease. The only person who could was Edward himself. She had kept silence for a whole fortnight. It was unbearable. Leaving her ladies sewing, she left her new chambers and with Doucement trotting along at her heels she sped through the palace looking for Edward. She found him in his bedchamber, feeding titbits to a blackbird he kept in a wicker cage.

He looked away from the bird and said, 'Ah, my Eleanor, what brings you here in the afternoon? I thought you were with your hounds. Are you not seeing to their safe removal to Canterbury for the Christmas hunt?' He leaned down and patted Doucement.

'Not today,' she said. 'No, I come because something unpleasant has reached my ears.'

'What? Don't tell me my father has taken away another estate and returned it to an enemy.' Edward ushered her to his comfortable armed chair and took a stool.

She sat on the edge of the seat and looked him in the eye. 'No, maybe worse. Maybe an enemy to me, a personal enemy.'

He raised his brow.

'It's Alix, Earl Gilbert's wife. I have heard a rumour and it concerns you and therefore me.' She explained as best she could. She wept and then folded her arms and glared with fury at him. Edward had listened intently. 'Humphrey de Clare is responsible for this rumour spreading. That family is the most untrustworthy and despicable in humankind. They belong to the cesspits of Troy. The men steal husbands and wives and they murder children. As for Lady Alix, I simply hope and pray to the Madonna this rumour is a lie.'

She was sure he looked contrite for he bowed his head. She tugged her wimple from her head and tossed it onto the matting.

She shook out her chestnut hair and drew herself up to her full height of five feet and six. 'Am I, a daughter of Spain with my olive skin, not more beautiful than she with her pasty look?'

Edward never replied.

'It's not true, is it, Edward?' She felt her heart beat faster. Her right hand flew up and before she fully realised what she was doing she delivered a slap to his face. He turned away, one trembling hand touching his left cheek.

He turned back to face her. The imprint of her hand had marked his face with a rosy blotch. He reached out and took her hands into his own. 'Not true in the way you have heard it. Alix and I have long been friends. Her father is my father's half-brother.' He stopped, turned his head and glanced past the twittering blackbird, out of the long window that looked towards the Cathedral. She followed his gaze noticing how leaves had all fallen from the oaks and how a red-breasted robin settled on a branch outside. It was a cold day. Within a week they would move to Canterbury where they would pass Christmas. What did Edward mean by *not exactly*?

She cleared her throat. 'What do you really mean, Edward?' Her voice dropped to a whisper. 'Tell me, is it true?' She let go of his hands.

'By St Edward's bones, Eleanor, what a suspicious mind you have! We have never lain together. It would be unnatural,' he said with a horrified look on his face. His right hand touched a large cross hanging over his surcoat. 'After all,' he added, 'Alix has a second daughter born last spring.' He paused. Eleanor pursed her lips and waited.

'What difference does that make?'

'It is true she does not like Earl Gilbert. It's true we were in each other's company at Chester after I escaped from Hereford Castle, but Gilbert had been harsh to her, accusing her of infidelities. She came to me for advice.'

'What advice can a prince give to an earl's wife?' Eleanor spoke quietly.

'Plenty. I told her we were living in difficult times. Gilbert is exhausted by the war. We all are. She must be patient. She has two little girls by him. She should be happy with her daughters.'

'And *her* children live. Mine die.' It was an ungenerous comment but she could not help herself.

'How can you be like this, Eleanor? We are young. We shall have more children. Do not resent those others have.' He shook his head and she could see his displeasure in his eyes. His eyelid, so like his father's, began to droop, making him look a little sinister.

'Earl Gilbert is detestable, a worm and a devil,' Eleanor said quickly, getting to her feet. 'He took me prisoner and treated me with contempt. What have you said about this? He threw me up on his horse, a great stallion, and took me into an enemy camp. He mistreats his wife. How can such a man be your friend?'

'You, Eleanor, disobeyed my father's order. Gilbert is loyal. He saved the day at Evesham. As Christ said, "Forgive thine enemies".'

'*You* saved England at Evesham, Edward. He is a snake. In truth, I pity Alix and any other woman he pursues, for I hear he is persistently unfaithful. Just make sure his wife does not give our court any cause for gossip. It is not permitted for cousins to have relations.'

She left him as he rose from the stool. He reached for her. She deftly side-stepped him and swept off to her own chambers. She refused to share Edward's bed for two whole nights, not until he begged her on his knees and swore on the psalter she thrust at him, the same she had had in her possession since Canterbury, that he would never see his cousin Alix alone again; nor had he had intimacy with her; nor did he intend to do so.

After he made his oath she said, 'You will summon the source of this rumour into your presence and dismiss him?'

Edward rose from his knees still clutching his psalter. 'Eleanor, I love you with all my heart. This is unnecessary.'

'Humphrey de Clare is a relative of Gloucester.' She narrowed her eyes. 'I don't want him here, that slippery little worm. He slides around and listens at keyholes.'

'If I do as you ask, Earl Gilbert will know the reason his relative has been sent home. It could go badly for his wife.'

'Better he knows you do not believe such a rumour and will destroy such talk rather than permitting it to fester.'

Edward lowered his head in thought. For a moment she wondered if, despite the vow taken moments before, something *had* evolved between violet-eyed Alix and her husband. She closed her eyes. Edward took her into his arms. This time, she felt her resilience melting. She loved her husband and because of it this suspicion must never occur again. Her hand flew to the jewelled belt she wore low on her gown. Her courses had not arrived since late August.

Alix of Lusignan may have turned her eyes on Edward when she was a royalist captive a few years before Lewes. She may have confided her misery in him. Alix was probably in love with Edward. There was a way to be vigilant. From now on, where Edward travelled, she, his wife, would go also. She swept her hand over her belly again. They would, they *must*, have healthy boys to inherit the crown.

Edward was saying, 'I shall send the page into my brother Edmund's service with a reprimand. He will leave court tomorrow.'

It must be enough, she supposed. If she had control, she would send the page into service in Gascony, far, far away, and Countess Alix too if it were possible. Queen Ailenor would never agree to that. She liked Alix.

After supper Edward took her hand in front of the whole court. He dismissed her ladies and drew her from the hall. She willingly went with him, a pleased smile playing around her mouth, and from the corner of her eyes she noted a frown cross Alix's face.

'Humphrey de Clare rides tonight for Dover with a letter for Edmund,' Edward leaned down and whispered into her ear.

'Good,' she said and let the subject rest.

That night she and Edward made love again. He kissed her and held her in his arms. 'You are precious to me. It will never happen again.' He stroked her hair and kissed her again. 'When all settles in England, what do you think of going on Crusade, before my father grows too old to rule?'

He stroked her hair and she nestled closer to him. 'Yes, yes. I've always wanted to crusade.' She kissed his mouth, then drew back and added, 'You know, Edward, I do believe I am with child again.'

He rested his chin on her head. 'We'll have a nursery full yet.'

She fell asleep in his arms thinking about Jerusalem which was the centre of the world.

Chapter Seven

Christmas
1265

The court travelled in a large colourful procession to Canterbury where there would be hunts and celebrations, gift exchanging, dance and song from Christ's Day until Epiphany. Eleanor peered through glazed windows at a frosty landscape. These chambers were just as pretty as those Queen Ailenor enjoyed, the same Eleanor had used before. Edward occupied adjoining chambers, a low door linking her bedchamber to his. The period before Christmas was a time of abstinence, strictly observed in Canterbury, the holiest of cities, but she did not mind. She was with child. She would watch Edward closely.

Eleanor led her ladies in decorating the hall for the lighting of the Christmas log. Woodsmen dragged it in from the courtyard and placed it in the enormous fireplace where the fire spat and crackled. This log would burn throughout the Christmas festivities until Twelfth Night and it was so thrilling to see it lit. King Henry himself hurried into the hall to admire it. Queen Ailenor swept in with her ladies and both Ailenor's household and hers gathered around a long trestle filled with greenery and piles of ribbons that descended to the floor tiles in flowing piles. Once the log was lit, they applied themselves to creating Christmas wreaths to hang throughout the hall. Queen Ailenor called for her musicians to play for them. Servants brought them hot spiced wine and carried in trays of ginger and honey cakes warm from the oven and dishes of sugar-coated fruits.

Marzipan mice were proffered to the ladies who squealed their delight. Children begged treats from the women and tried to make their own tiny festive crosses with small nimble fingers. Eleanor's little dog, Doucement, snapped up crumbs and watched her mistress with soft brown eyes. As they worked, Eleanor occasionally observed Alix, who was seated by Queen Ailenor's side creating an attractive arrangement of holly and ivy. Ailenor began to sing a carol about the king called Wenceslas. Knowing it well, they all joined in. Ailenor followed it with a ballad about Arthur and Guinevere. The musicians caught the new tune, filling the hall with the sounds of recorders, citoles, and gitterns.

Eleanor glanced up. Olwen was carrying a new bucketful of greenery towards the trestle. The smell of the spiced wine was heady; the scent of the green branches astringent and sharp; the honey cakes melted on the tongue and the singing was joyfully tuneful. As song followed song, Eleanor forgot about Alix de Lusignan. She began to plait green withies, into which she would place holly berries. Lady Margerie fished a mistletoe branch from the pail and handed it to a servant to place above the porch doorway.

Olwen had just emptied the rest of the greenery onto their trestle when the servant, who had just placed one foot on a ladder against the wall, was knocked aside. The heavy hall door was flung open. Earl Gilbert pushed past, causing the page to fall backwards. Eleanor turned in shock from her leafy arrangement. Her ladies dropped their evergreens. The singing paused. The musicians waited for Queen Ailenor's signal to start up again, their instruments lowered. Eleanor's gaze slid to Lady Alix. Alix had turned pale. Her hand was clutching a long scarlet silken ribbon. It seemed to freeze.

Earl Gilbert approached the Queen. He bowed and said, 'I have business with my wife. I request permission to speak with her.'

Eleanor stared at Alix, for whom she felt a just little pity. She mouthed 'No' to Ailenor and shook her head. Gloucester must not be permitted to spoil their afternoon no matter her own feelings towards his wife. Ailenor reached protectively for Alix and took her hand.

But Alix said, 'I shall speak with him. Madam, I fear I must.'

Gilbert seized his wife by the arm. He bowed to Queen Ailenor and hurried from the hall dragging Alix behind him. The scarlet ribbon lay on the rushes where she had dropped it. Olwen scooped it up and placed it on the trestle. Gilbert must have heard rumours and he would wonder at Edward's removal of his young kinsman from their service. Eleanor regretted the fuss she had made, but only for a moment. Alix's adoration of Edward could not be tolerated.

She watched Alix's retreating back as Gloucester dragged his wife out of the door. Alix may have turned her violet eyes on Edward and confided her misery in him. Now, at last, Eleanor was convinced Edward would never return that woman's love. She swept her hand over her belly. Her happiness this Christmastide was complete. She would breed healthy boys to inherit the crown.

The Queen signalled for music. The musicians started up a new tune. Soon it was as if the disturbance had not happened. Smiling, Eleanor concentrated on the wreath she was weaving and joined in the songs. The incident had passed for now. Later, alone in her chamber, she could not help wondering what would happen between Earl Gilbert and Countess Alix.

The following day, Margerie told the ladies Lady Alix was departing both Canterbury and Queen Ailenor's service to be with her children in Hereford.

'Their children are ill. Earl Gilbert has decided they need their mother,' Margerie reported with a frown.

'Earl Gilbert dislikes her flirtatious behaviour,' another lady remarked. Eleanor glared at her. Obviously chastened, the lady looked away.

The yule log burned and the festivities continued. Heavy snow fell for two days. It would be a hard journey west for Alix de Lusignan. Her name was not mentioned again in the hall or in the bower. On occasion Queen Ailenor was curt with Eleanor, and Eleanor wondered if her mother-in-law blamed her for Alix's removal. King Henry though remained kindly to everyone and Edward was attentive to her throughout the festivities. There was a pleasing angle of repose between them and in front of the Christmas court Edward led her out to dance roundels each afternoon after dinner. He encouraged her to play her lute and to sing Spanish songs in her tuneful voice, as beautiful, all said, as Queen Ailenor's. She found her smiles came from deep inside her heart once again.

With the Christmas feast over, Eleanor anticipated several days of hunting. The snow had not lasted. They could ride out into the forest. Earl Gilbert, as ever, remained close to Edward, joking, recounting humorous stories, always solicitous. Sometimes he would turn his blue eyes on her and try hard to make conversation, but she only responded to his efforts at making peace with her when she absolutely had to.

A boar hunt was planned for New Year's Day. Eleanor had transported her own pack of hunting dogs to Canterbury, all of them adored by her. They were named for constellations set high in the skies. Her favourite was a handsome hound called Scorpio. Her own birth chart showed her to have been born on the cusp of Scorpio and Sagittarius. This hunter was a rich brown colour with a tiny white star on his back. He was sleek and fast and she honoured him with a gem-studded collar. Scorpio was fast, always the leader of her pack. His collar twinkled brightly as he raced over the snow.

Their foot huntsmen blew horns and those riding moved forward. As they entered the deepest part of the woods and the dogs grew excited, barking wildly as they caught a boar's scent, her ladies all drew back. Not so Eleanor. She kept pace with Edward and the huntsmen.

'We'll root the creature out yet, sweetheart. Meat for feasting to come,' Edward called to Eleanor. 'We are close now. Ride carefully, my dearest. We don't want to lose the child.'

'I always ride carefully,' she called back.

They slowed down dipping their heads below the tree branches, avoiding ruts in the forest floor. Her dogs raced on yapping and barking, scattering about the paths to either side of the riders. She was not sure when Scorpio went missing. All of the pack been within her sight; a moment later they were barking and racing after Scorpio along a left fork, plunging deeper into the forest. It was not Edward but Gilbert of Gloucester, who, bending his head to avoid the snowy branches, pursued her dogs, followed by his squire, the ridiculous, overly proud Pipkin, whose bow lay across his breast, a quiver of arrows hanging from his saddle. The barking grew a little distant. Huntsmen cantered past her into the trees, following Gilbert's tracks.

The dogs continued to bark. There was a long, deep-throated howl. 'My dogs,' cried Eleanor. 'I don't like this.'

'I dare not ride Hercules through there,' Edward said, sounding disappointed. 'It's too dense.'

'I could,' she said nosing her mare forward onto the path.

He caught her reins, impeding her movement. 'No, they should flush the boar into an open clearing first.'

'But perhaps this path leads us into one,' she reasoned.

'No, Eleanor, too dangerous.'

She grew even more anxious.

The forest stilled. She could hear no birdsong nor the scuffling of animals. The uncanny quiet was soon followed by rooks rising into the sky with infernal caws, by trees rustling, huntsmen's shouts, renewed barks, and the whinnying of horses, followed by a thunderous crash. She heard an enormous growl. She heard a loud whining. Gilbert broke out of the trees, horseless and bloodied. His face showed indescribable agony. Looking down from his face to his arms, she saw a bundle held in them and knew the worst.

'My lady, the boar tried to gore Scorpio. This brave animal got butted by the boar over and over.'

Edward looked at the huntsman behind Gilbert. He barked at him, 'Cut that animal's throat. He will never be whole again.'

A scream caught in Eleanor's throat. She began to get down from her mount. A page ran to her aid. 'No,' she managed to shout. 'He might recover.'

'No,' Gilbert repeated the word to Edward in a firm tone. 'My lord, I know of a remedy. The dog's wound looks worse than it is.' He looked at Eleanor who handed her reins to the shocked squire.

85

She hurried to Gilbert and touched Scorpio's ears. There was a very low-throated growl. The dog was still alive.

'Can you save Scorpio?' She gently touched Scorpio again and looking up at Gilbert noted genuine concern on his countenance. So, he cared for animals. She never knew.

'Yes, my lady, but we must be quick. I'll hurry back to your ladies and find your herbalist. I know who she is. We'll take Scorpio back to the palace at once. There are carts at the wood's edge. I promise you, we can save him with the right herbs and poultices.'

In that instance there was an enormous distraction. Along the path came huntsmen carrying the boar, lifting it high as if it were a great trophy. At a glance Eleanor realised it was a young creature. She felt no pity. It had hurt her dog and deserved its death. The other dogs excitedly followed. They smelled blood and knew rewards were coming to them. Edward hurried from her side to inspect the kill. Gilbert's squire arrived leading his horse. Together they wrapped Pipkin's short cloak around Scorpio. The creature was still alive but losing too much blood, moaning as it lay in Earl Gilbert's arms.

'Go,' she said to Earl Gilbert. 'Do your best. God go with you. I can't leave my other dogs. Find Olwen but please hurry.'

Her eyes were filling up with tears. They coursed along her cheeks. Earl Gilbert disappeared along the track with a flash of scarlet mantle, Pipkin following with their horses. She glanced over at Edward, who was scratching his head. 'Has Gloucester taken that wretched dog away at last?' he said.

'Yes, and he's not a wretched dog, Edward.'

'Pity the Earl does not watch over his family as well as he cares for animals,' he said and climbed on his horse. 'We're ready to go now, Eleanor. The huntsmen will bring the kill. It's been a good morning's work here.'

'Has it indeed?'

'Can he save the hound?' Edward's tone was softer.

'I hope so,' she replied.

'Then mount again and we'll see if he has.'

Gilbert had cared deeply about her dog when all Edward cared about was the kill. He had surprised her. Waving her waiting groom away, she bent down and patted each of her other dogs, saying their names one by one, finishing with Capricorn. They had all returned but they seemed subdued and she knew they missed their leader. When she allowed the groom to help her mount her mare and she followed Edward, the pack trailed behind them. From time to time she would turn her head to watch them. If dogs could manifest sullen feelings, the animals seemed downcast as they ran alongside the master of the hunt all the way back to Canterbury.

Chapter Eight

Olwen
Early 1266

Scorpio looked up at Olwen with doleful eyes. She had brought him into the dormitory and kept him in a large basket lined with a woollen blanket close to her own mattress. All the ladies made a fuss of him and Lady Eleanor came to see him daily.

A number of weeks passed and one morning when Eleanor made her visit, she sank down on the padded window seat and bade Olwen to sit on the chest beside her. Scorpio climbed out of his basket and lay by his mistress's feet.

'You have saved my favourite hound,' Eleanor said to Olwen. 'He'll be hunting again by Eastertide.'

'I am glad of it, my lady,' Olwen said. 'If Earl Gilbert had not been so quick to rescue him from the boar it would have been impossible. All I did was wash his wounds with sweet amber and give him bugloss in a syrup daily. Look, he is not so stiff now, even though I had to stitch his wounds.'

'And now I have something else to ask you, Olwen.'

'Yes?'

Eleanor folded her hands in her lap. 'Lord Edward and I intend to take the cross in the near future. It takes time to prepare for a Crusade. We won't depart for three years but when we do I shall travel with a selected group of these ladies.' She swept her hand towards the women who were busily folding fresh linen the laundress had just delivered. 'Would you consider being part of my retinue? Your skill with animals, never mind people, is valuable to us. Will you give it thought?'

Olwen took a deep breath. 'Yes,' she said. 'I don't need to think about it. I want to join the Crusade as one of your ladies and as a herbalist.' Olwen looked at Lady Eleanor. She was rosy with health. It occurred to her that the princess was glowing, perhaps with child.

'You have skill with healing, Olwen, and I shall need your help before then. I am enceinte, around four months I believe, and this time I hope nothing will endanger this child.'

Her suspicion had been correct. There would soon be another child in the royal nursery. 'I am honoured, my lady,' Olwen said, delighted at the prospect of being respected by Lady Eleanor as no less than an unofficial female apothecary. Female apothecaries were forbidden and she knew better than to tread on the territory of the princess's doctors. She would learn from them. On her return, she would purchase her own manor and her own herbal beds. She was already giving her savings to Master Robert to keep for her. If she went to the Holy Land she would fetch back plants. She heard that in the East there were doctors so talented that their ability surpassed all other medical knowledge. But three years was a long time. Anything could happen before they set out, but one thing she knew was that she would remain close to Lady Eleanor whom she admired. She would not return to her stepmother, though she knew she should visit her father to seek his advice on how she should approach her future.

'In a week we return to Westminster.' Lady Eleanor leaned down and ruffled Scorpio's ears. 'And I am glad Scorpio will be travelling with us. I shall take him into the garden this morning. Come with me, Margerie.'

Her senior lady smiled. 'What a pleasant idea. It's a gentle day.'

After Lady Eleanor left the room, Scorpio limping alongside her, followed by Margerie and two others of her ladies, Olwen made a plan to visit her father before the court moved on.

Olwen approached her father's house and allowed the knocker shaped like a large pepper-pot to fall gently against the door. A new maid answered her knock. She informed Olwen the mistress was visiting relatives and was not expected home for some days.

89

Olwen breathed more easily even though she had determined not to fear Doregon. 'I've not come to see your mistress but my father, the apothecary and spicer. I'm Olwen, his daughter. Please tell him I am here.'

The maid gave her a quizzical look and opened the door wider. 'Master is in the workshop,' she said.

'I can find my own way through the hall.' Olwen gently pushed past the girl, thinking once again what good fortune her stepmother was not at home. Her father, a man of medium build with a serious face and intense blue eyes, came hurrying from the workshop wiping his hands on his apron, saying, 'Took you long enough to visit, my girl. I had heard the Christmas court was at Canterbury.'

'Papa, I hoped you might visit the King's doctors. Some of the gentlemen had aches and pains but nothing serious,' she said and added, 'I've been busy looking after an injured hound.'

'An injured hound indeed.' He looked bemused. 'Here you are now.' He called back through the hall to the kitchen area. 'Bessie, bring us refreshments. Hot spiced ale and currant cakes. Bring them through to the workshop.' He turned to Olwen. 'How fortunate you chose today. I have you to myself. Doregon left us this morning for her brother's house. She won't return for several days. His wife is about to give birth. Doregon is helping the midwife with the medicines I have sent. You may remember the woman is choleric.' He sighed. 'They all are all choleric in that family, including my wife.'

He smiled as he ushered her through a heavy curtain at the far end of the hall and into his workplace. She glanced back at the hall's central hearth where a fire blazed and drew her mantle tighter. It would not be so warm where her papa mixed medicines.

She sat on the stool by the brazier which allowed a little warmth. Drawing his own chair close, her father said, 'And whose was the dog?'

'Lady Eleanor's favourite hunting hound. He has recovered. I used camomile, bugloss, and comfrey in a paste for his wounds.'

Her father nodded. 'Good choice.'

The maid arrived and thrust a mug of ale into her hand with a diffident smile. This Bessie must be scared out of her wits by her master's wife. She decided not to mention her stepmother to her papa since he was besotted with the woman.

Papa offered her the plate of currant cakes. Olwen bit into one and remarked, 'Did Bessie bake these? They are delicious.'

'She did. I wish Doregon appreciated her baking too. Thin as a pole, your stepmother.'

'I taste spice. What is it?'

'Nutmeg, but sugar sweetens the batter.'

'The nutmeg tastes fresh. So sugar, not honey? Expensive.'

'I had a consignment of sugar arrive and the nutmegs came in the same delivery.' She nodded. 'I have good news, Olwen,' he continued. 'I am to be a full member of the new Grocers' Guild as a Master Spicer and Master Apothecary and I am permitted to sell confectionery as well as medicines, pepper, and spices. Doregon plans to create a selection of sugared fruits and angelica for sale.'

Poor Bessie, thought Olwen. *She'll* be busy creating these goods. May the saints protect her from my stepmother's wrath if her work is lacking. She glanced around the workroom. On the rows of shelves there were several rows of pots which she knew contained powders and herbs ready to mix into medicines. Others held mortars and pestles. Shelves were lined with medicines, labelled ready for sale. A long scrubbed wooden trestle held the herbs and powders he was currently working with, all neatly set out in small pottery basins.

'Papa,' she said turning back to him, 'I have news for you too. Lady Eleanor will have a child in July. I am to provide her with tinctures, advise on her diet, and assist with the birth. Her pregnancy last time was difficult.' She felt her eyes swim with tears. 'Lady Eleanor lost her daughter, Joan, only a half year old, in September. Little Katherine died the previous year.'

'Poor lady. I am proud of you, my daughter but . . . a husband . . .'

'I am not planning to marry. I'm saving for my own business and I am to help Lady Eleanor with the choice of planting for her new

91

properties. If she and Lord Edward go on Crusade I'm to accompany them.'

Her father sat up straight, his eyes widening. 'To travel to eastern territories would be my dream. You must learn to write, daughter, so you can record all the new plants and spices you discover. The princess needs you and if her service makes you happy, I am happy. If you change your mind, your home is still here by my side learning what knowledge I have learned. Spend time with the royal infirmerer and never, ever upset the King's doctors. They dislike female apothecaries.'

'They'll never recognise female apothecaries. Yes, I shall remain humble and assist them as I did after the Battle at Evesham.'

'You were very brave, my child. A woman apothecary indeed.'

'Not exactly, but near enough.'

She thought of Lord Edward's generous purse which Master Robert had in keeping for her. He was now Lord Edward's personal treasurer and she knew her savings would be safely accounted for with Master Robert.

She rose and put her plate and cup on the table. It was time for her to return to the palace. She would see Papa again when she accompanied Lady Eleanor to Canterbury. 'I must depart now, Papa, but may God protect you,' she said brightly.

'Dear Olwen, may our good Lord protect you too for you have a great adventure ahead of you at the royal court. Come again soon.'

She saw tears fill his intelligent blue eyes and felt moisture gather in her own. It was hard to leave him to his life with her brittle stepmother but he was content enough with his spices and potions. She hugged him and tried not to look back as she climbed onto her palfrey and left him behind waving her off.

On the twenty-fourth of June, the feast of St John the Baptist, Olwen helped the midwives with the princess's lying-in. Clutching the Virgin's girdle, removed from its safe home in the Abbey, Lady Eleanor gave birth. Olwen shared Lady Eleanor's joy at having given birth to a son who was christened John. The baby was healthy but he was small. Olwen received another purse to lodge with Master Robert.

At Christmastide, King Henry presented Lady Eleanor with expensive heavy damask robes for herself and her senior ladies, matching those worn by the Queen and her ladies. Lady Eleanor seemed pleased because they were crimson and lined with ermine. Crimson was one of her favourite colours. Eleanor herself provided green wool for garments for her junior ladies who had not received such a generous gift from the King. Olwen treasured her new green woollen gown and her new pair of soft leather boots lined with fur. She kept them within sight by her narrow cot in the junior maidens' dormitory. When she awoke on frosty mornings there they were, waiting for her to pull on before she attended her mistress.

They moved to Windsor, which was healthier than London. Olwen was granted a small allowance from Lady Eleanor's wardrobe and had furnished the square chamber attached to the still room in Windsor with shelves, a table and benches and a brazier by which to warm her fingers, and heat up her crucibles. She felt comfortable amongst jars of ingredients and the smell of herbs hanging from the rafters. She was learning to write as her father had advised. Brother Gregory, a scribe employed at Windsor producing books for the princess was pleased to instruct her.

'We shall grant you a place amongst the scribes,' he told her as he held up the scraps of parchment she had quickly progressed to after practice on a slate. 'Lady Eleanor has requested this. Her own new offices are not as yet ready, otherwise you would be welcome there, she said. What do you think?'

'I am grateful,' Olwen said with excitement in her voice. It was a privilege to spend an hour daily at a vacant desk of her own in the scriptorium. There were books there too. She would ask permission to look at any that spoke of herbs and medicine even if she could not decipher Latin. She might recognise the plants.

Throughout the dark afternoons of winter, Olwen climbed a narrow winding staircase to where Master Jonathan supervised a team of scribes who copied books. Permitted a desk of her own, she made quick progress. She was granted books which Brother Gregory picked out for his pupil. The scribe helped her read the Latin names for plants and write them down in the English tongue. Delighted, she made labels for all her jars of ingredients and considered how fortunate she was to be learning to write and to be in Lady Eleanor's employ.

Her greatest joy was when on a morning in early March, heavily pregnant, Eleanor herself visited Olwen in the still room. 'I want to see where you make the delicious herbal drinks that make me feel well when I suffer refluxus.'

'My lady, it is a simple place for a princess to visit,' Olwen said, blushing with pleasure.

She felt honoured when Eleanor lifted down a jar from her shelf where all her dried herbs were labelled. The Lady lifted up and studied the marker tied onto the jar's arm. 'Rosmarinus. Rosemary. Did you write this, Olwen?' Her hazel eyes sparkled with delight.

'I did.'

'You have learned quickly, I see.'

'My Lady, we learn fast when we wish to learn. I had some sense of writing from my father but not enough. Brother Gregory has been a good tutor.'

'My investment has paid off. I like my ladies to be educated. Many read but cannot write. If only others could learn as quickly as my herbalist does then we would be a company of women whose weapon is the pen rather than the sword.'

Eleanor's eyes were earnest. In that moment Olwen loved the princess. She felt they were in a place where time paused and who they were did not matter. For a heartbeat there seemed to be a meeting of minds between a princess and a commoner.

Olwen glowed at this thought. And yes, Lady Eleanor was correct. One way to true independence for a woman who did not desire the convent was through learning. Lady Eleanor was as scholarly as any learned monk.

She curtsied as Eleanor departed. Something had shifted in the air they had shared. Now she was not just Olwen, the poor herbalist

94

who had acted as a spy for a princess. She felt accepted and this was her heart's desire, almost. There were long wintry days when she missed Dicken. There were others when her path crossed Eugene's since he served the King. If they met on the palace stairways, Eugene always had a gentle word for her.

Chapter Nine

Olwen
1267

Another year had passed. Spring came again at last when narcissi pushed their way up through the soil and herbs grew in profusion during the mild weather. Olwen delighted in making tonics for everyone to dispel the dreariness of winter, brighten their skin and make the ladies feel happier. Just before Eastertide, Lady Eleanor summoned Olwen into her antechamber.

Lady Eleanor looked well today, clad in a simple gown of fine red linen with tight sleeves. A loose linen over-gown flowed to ankles which were encased in sensible leather shoes. She had set aside her wimple. Her waving hair, the shade of chestnuts, was plaited into a neat coil at the back of her neck. Her hazel-coloured eyes always looked enormous. She was a number of years into her twenties but, despite childbearing and the sorrow of lost pregnancies and children, the princess always appeared fresh and healthy. Besides, she had a precious healthy son called John, born the previous May and now almost a year old.

Once they were comfortably seated in the window embrasure with honey cakes and cups of wine at their elbows, Eleanor said, 'I need you to help me with a garden at Ringwood. It's in the New Forest, one of my new properties. Could you advise the gardeners?'

'On planting, my lady?' Olwen drew breath. For almost a whole year she had spent her time making simples and salves in a still room close to the kitchens. Now she would help design a garden. She would be a purveyor of plants, travelling with Lady Eleanor to her manors. She did not hesitate. 'My Lady, I am happy to be of service,' she said lifting a second honey cake from a silver plate. Her heartbeat quickened at the thought of designing a garden for Lady Eleanor. She glanced out of the window down on the Windsor herbal garden. To design a garden like this would be thrilling.

Eleanor proffered the plate of delicious cakes again. 'Have another,' she said to Olwen. Olwen accepted her third cake. The princess jumped to her feet and walked over to her desk. She looked back at Olwen. 'Lord Edward has set up an administrative office for my new estates. My steward, you know him –' Olwen nodded. Walter de Kancia, the princess's steward, was a long-faced, fierce-looking man of few words, always dressed in a flowing robe, and a man of whom she felt wary. She hoped he was not accompanying them to Ringwood. Lady Eleanor continued, 'Sir Walter has chosen Master John de Ferre to oversee these properties. Sir Walter has already been to Ringwood to oversee building works. Since Ringwood lies deep inside the New Forest, we hope to hunt too.' She smiled. 'I think Scorpio will enjoy hunting there.'

Olwen often visited Scorpio in the kennels. When she entered the spacious pen where four of the hunting dogs lived, the hound always bounded towards her, his tail wagging, ready to accept any tiny treat she would bring him. She wiped her fingers on a napkin. She had eaten enough of those tempting cakes. 'Scorpio is more than ready, my lady.'

Lady Eleanor nodded and continued speaking with enthusiasm of her plans for a summer progress. 'From the great forest we intend travelling north to Leicestershire, into Norfolk, and finally to Kingsthorpe in Northampton.' She tapped what looked like a plan lying on the desk. 'We'll be at Ringwood for easily a month. That should give you time to organise a new herbal garden. Ringwood will be redecorated as a special retreat by the time we arrive. It's close to Winchester and many of our court can lodge there or at Odiham since that castle no longer belongs to the King's sister and is now mine.' She raised an elegant eyebrow.

The princess pushed the sketch she was holding into Olwen's

hands and described how she would like the garden to appear once planted and blooming. Mid-sentence, she paused and looked up, her face earnest. 'Do you wish to visit your family in Canterbury again?'

'I think not, my lady. My father is very busy and I do not enjoy my stepmother's company. I am content to remain at court.'

'I see. Well then, close up your work chamber for the summer. Pack a travelling bag. Ride your palfrey but if you tire share the long coach with Margerie and my handmaiden, Joan de Viridi.' Eleanor paused. She smiled. 'I am leaving baby John at Windsor with the Queen.' For a moment she looked thoughtful, her brow wrinkled into several creases. She was frowning. Either she had no love for the Queen or would miss her child. It was as well John stayed at Windsor because, at almost eleven months, Baby John was more delicate than he had been at birth. Olwen made a mental note to leave a jar of her salve for his chesty coughs.

The junior ladies fluttered around planning what they would take on the journey. They were speculating on which handsome household knights would protect them on the roads in the great forest.

'Will you ride with us?' Lady Anna de Fiennes said to Olwen.

'Yes,' Olwen said. She was as thrilled as the younger ladies were.

Lady Anna touched her arm, causing Olwen to turn around. She dashed over to her clothing pole. Searching under gowns and cloaks Lady Anna said, 'Olwen. I've a riding mantle I never wear. You cured me of a terrible cold last month. Would you accept a gift?' She pulled down a woollen garment.

Anna was only fourteen. She came from a junior branch of the Fiennes family. On account of being distantly related to Eleanor, she had been taken into the princess's service that year. She was not wealthy but she was kind and Lady Eleanor liked her. When the maidens had no duties to attend, Anna often sought Olwen's company because she, too, loved plants and she possessed a small herbal which they sometimes pored over together.

Olwen opened her mouth intending to refuse the cloak but could not.

'I have a cloak. Are you sure?'

'I have others. It's yours. I know your cloak. This one is lighter in weight and warmer.'

'I have a spare cloak pin,' interrupted Maudie, whose family were related to the De Clares. She had grown up in a Marcher castle. 'You must have it.' She returned to her cot and dragged a box out from under it. Opening the coffer, she drew out a cloak brooch shaped like a strange bird with tiny red garnets for eyes. 'You cured my cold too. I could have died.'

'That's an exaggeration, Maudie, but thank you.' Olwen accepted the gift, admired it, pinned it to her new cloak and dropped the garment onto her mattress. She grasped fifteen-year-old Maudie's hands, tears welling up at the girls' kindness to her. 'I thank you both with all my heart. You do not need to give me gifts.'

Olwen's heart glowed with warmth. The junior ladies liked her even though she was far below them in status.

As she put away her presents, carefully hanging the cloak amongst the three gowns on her rail, Lady Margerie entered the dormitory clapping her hands. She glanced around at the opened coffers. 'Ladies, tut, tut, what an untidy mess. We're setting out after Ascension. You've only a few days to prepare.' She laughed her tinkling laugh. 'Oh never mind, I see some of you have your chests drawn up already.'

On the nineteenth of May Lady Eleanor's court set out: her ladies, lords, a collection of servants, her cook, her steward and her gentlemen including a royal gardener, a master stonemason who would inspect the works already done and give further advice, and John de Ferre, who after all joined the lady's party. In addition, archers and guards rode in front of and behind the royal party.

Sumpter horses and wagons, two long carriages lined up, horses neighing and stamping hoofs impatient to be off. Pennants flew, red, gold, silver, green, and blue. Trumpets sounded. Olwen stared up at the red striped chevrons of the de Clare flags and the birds and blue stripes scrolled on the gold pennant of Joanna of Pembroke.

Lady Joanna had stayed away from court for nearly two years, at her castle in Pembrokeshire that had been confiscated during the *annus horribilis* of Montfort rule. It was then under Gilbert de Clare's control but had been safeguarded by him after he switched back to the loyalist side. After the Battle of Evesham, Pembroke had been returned to dear Joanna and William. It was the one thing Eleanor recognised that Gilbert had done right even if she could never bring herself to trust him. Gilbert, she mused as she sat erect on her palfrey waiting to ride out of Windsor's gates, was duplicitous, a womaniser and a ruffian. He might like animals but did the sly fox really care a Spanish fig for his neighbours' orchards, or were his own interests foremost in his mind? Poor Alix de Lusignan. Eleanor almost felt sympathy for her. She was never permitted to return to court. Alix was lingering with her little daughters in one of Gilbert's castles in the Welsh marches.

Olwen came out of her reverie as the horses grew restive. Mist, her grey palfrey, was pawing the ground, anxious to be out of the courtyard. Horns blew again. Queen Ailenor waved them off. Lord Edward trotted his dark stallion up to Eleanor's mount and kissed his wife. He spoke to Earl Gilbert, one of three lords riding with them. Olwen could not hear what he said though both men were smiling. Gilbert rode directly behind Lady Eleanor followed by the taciturn Pipkin. Olwen sat erect on Mist some way behind Eleanor, Countess Joanna, and Lady Margerie. They were moving forward at a walk. She nudged Mist's flanks. They gathered pace and trotted out of the great courtyard.

On the stops they made as they rode south she made the acquaintance of the royal gardener, Philip the Gardener. He was to be responsible for overseeing the planting of flowering plants in the newly created walled space adjoining Ringwood Manor's southern wall. It was one of several new walled-in areas, created in advance.

He sat at the long table in a monastery guest refectory and explained. 'It's to be a paradise garden with roses, lilies, herbal edging to the pathways and beds of flowers with delightful scents.'

Olwen smiled at him and sipped her cup of cider. She was to

100

design and supervise planting of herbal beds in another herbal just below Lady Eleanor's bedchamber. 'What flowers will you be planting in the Paradise Garden?' she asked, filled with curiosity. She knew about Paradise gardens. There had been one at Canterbury closed and walled, reminiscent supposedly of a Biblical paradise.

'They'll be flowery plants carried from nearby abbeys and priories. Roses and lilies, but I'm expecting deliveries of violets and gilly-flowers. I'll grow heart's ease by the wall. I'm hoping for campion, hollyhocks, woodruff, ox-eye daisies, periwinkles, and peonies. If there's enough I shall spare some plants for you to grow with your herbs, and, in return, you can provide me with herbs to scent the Paradise garden. After all, a door will lead from your herbal garden straight into the Paradise.' He winked and grinned showing a mouthful of crooked teeth, some of which were blackened. The King's gardener was an out-of-doors man, used to physical labour, muscled, squat like a goblin.

'Thank you,' she said, wondering if their gardens would please the particular Eleanor.

'It's a deal of planting to source,' Olwen said. 'I hope I can get all the herbs I require.'

'The nearby abbeys will provide all we need. They are aware of the lady's love of gardens.'

Olwen smiled. 'The court adores gardens these days, Master Philip, and I don't think I've ever seen as many orchards and gardens as I've seen in the City. I'm honoured to be making a herb and physic garden for my lady.'

'We both are. But gardens have to be built and the soil for her damask roses manured before we can plant. Let's hope, little wise woman, it's thoroughly prepared and ready for planting.' His blue eyes twinkled as he pushed his ale mug away. 'Let us hope, too, there are enough gardeners available to do planting under our direction.'

She was not sure she liked Master Philip calling her *a little wise woman* but his tone was without malice. The lined, sun-burned gnome-like gardener *was* kindly, she decided. 'I don't mind planting myself. In fact, I relish the task,' she said.

He guffawed, his gnome-like face crinkling. 'I've heard Lady Eleanor's not averse to soiling her hands either.'

Buildings the shade of butter appeared through oak trees. They were almost hidden within the ancient forest. Ringwood was a beautiful stone manor. A sandy avenue led up to its gatehouse. Once inside the walls that surrounded the manor house itself, Olwen saw that the building was not only romantic but large. A square court-yard contained stables and a buttery, a still room and a laundry. The steward informed her she was to have a room to herself. It was a privilege, he said, to have her own chamber, albeit a small closet belonging to the still room. When a servant led her to her chamber, she liked it well. The still room itself was full of the scents of dried rose petals, lilies, and herbs drying from the rafters - sage and thyme and pennyroyal. She would miss being in attendance on Lady Elea-nor with Anna and Maudie but she shrugged the feeling off. She was not here to indulge in court gossip but to work. As she unpacked her meagre possessions, folding her three gowns into a lavender-scented chest along with her linens, she determined she would labour with diligence to create a perfect herbal garden, her first commission. After all, she was achieving one of her long-held ambitions. Happi-ness tugged at her. Life was good.

Chapter Ten

Eleanor
1268–1270

Eleanor hummed a Castilian tune to herself as she meandered through the newly created Paradise Garden at Ringwood with Lord Edward by her side. They paused to admire the roses, lilies, periwinkles, and pansies edging new flower beds. They sank down onto a turfed seat, leaning back against a whitewashed wall holding hands as if they were once again young lovers.

Edward spontaneously lifted her hand and kissed it. Her fingers tingled at his touch. 'We have made a wise decision to acquire all these properties, my love,' he said. 'And one day you will own more land and manors than Gilbert of Gloucester.' He chuckled.

A smile played about the corners of her mouth at this thought. 'I was discussing him with Joanna recently. She blames him for the year she spent at Bampton and they had a terrible struggle to make ends meet there.' She paused, wondering if it was wise to mention Alix, but decided to. 'I hear he's petitioned the Pope for a formal separation from Alix.'

'He could get a dispensation should he wish. They are related. She has agreed a fair settlement with him.'

'But it would dispossess their daughters. They could be considered illegitimate.'

'That depends on how he provides for them. He is very fond of his girls.'

Alix remained a painful topic between them. 'Come,' she said, changing tack. 'The door over there leads to the herbal garden. Olwen has included rosemary, which comes from Canterbury.' She rose to her feet. 'I hope when we leave the manor the gardeners will care for it. Come.' She tugged his hand, pulling him from the comfortable seat.

'You are always restless,' Edward said, smiling down at her from his great height. The sun caught his pointed beard. Today golden lights glinted through it.

'So are you,' she said smiling back. 'We are well-matched.'

The herb garden was almost as enjoyable to wander through as the Paradise garden. Chamomile flowers growing on grassy separations between herbal beds released a pleasant aroma as they trod on them. Olwen was in the garden, kneeling by a herbal bed, picking mint and marigolds.

'Lord Edward might like to see the rosemary,' Eleanor said to her.

Olwen scrambled to her feet, dipped a curtsey to them both, and led them towards a rosy-hued brick wall where she had planted the little rosemary bush. She looked earnestly at them both. 'It's small. All the plants are tiny, but they'll grow larger as long as they are well tended.'

Eleanor said, 'Master Philip has agreed to remain here to instruct the gardeners. It's time we moved north to the other manors.' She glanced at Edward. 'Olwen will take a look at the herbal gardens on our other properties. She'll journey with us.'

'Good,' Edward said. 'It's a delightful garden. If you do half as well with the others, Olwen, we shall be pleased indeed.'

The girl smiled, showing pretty, even teeth. She curtsied again. 'Thank you, my lord. I am infusing woodruff and mint from the kitchen garden into cooling drinks. The marigold flowers are for salads.' Excusing herself, she discreetly withdrew to the still room that opened into the garden.

Eleanor would always love Ringwood. The manor house was spacious and in good repair. When she had arrived its chambers were aired and scented with angelica seeds; floors were scattered with fresh strewing herbs; a pleasantly scented pot of century had been placed by her bed. The Lady Chapel was enchanting with a painting of the Wedding at Canna adorning one wall and the

Nativity another. There was no Doom painting here to cause shudders, no figures tortured far below Heaven's lofty heights, figures dropping off a ladder into Hell's cauldrons. The Chapel bell rang out the canonical hours. Now it rang the hour of Terce.

'We'll not bother with morning service today,' Edward mused aloud, reading her thought. 'We'll attend Vespers since Robert Burnell will be officiating.' Master Robert was now a rising star within the Church; perhaps he would become a bishop as well as handling Edward's accounts. He was a pleasant officiator at services and never overly pious. 'Let's go in now, my love. I promised to ride out with Uncle William. We'll take the falcons. Do you want to join us?'

'Not today,' Eleanor said. 'Countess Joanna and the ladies are making garlands for St Barnabas' Day. The Priory sent us woodruff leaves and daisies. I prefer hunting with my dogs.'

Edward's laugh rang through the garden. 'I promise you a hunt in the forest after St Barnabas' feast.'

'Ringwood is a perfect hunting retreat. We have already brought in a stag. That's why you are enjoying venison these afternoons.'

Edward rubbed his hands together. 'The wood will be valuable. The vineyard produces verjuice and wine. That will bring us an income as well as the deer, the coneys, and the fish in the stew ponds.' There was speculation in his look as he said, 'If your other properties are as productive as your Hampshire manors you shall realise a great income.'

He was right. She could forget the year of poverty, when she was so poor she had to borrow coin from a tailor to feed her household, at last.

The year turned and Eleanor discovered she was once again enceinte. Remembering the hunt at Ringwood and all the other new properties she visited since, Eleanor longed for summer to return. Her assets excited her. Her property acquisition had begun because after the strictures she had suffered during the year of Montfort's rule, she'd determined never to be impoverished again. It had been Edward's idea that they gathered lands in her name, to keep them safe from seizure if the barons rose up again against King Henry, but now she found she enjoyed gathering up land for the sake of it and because she loved travelling around them. She would study where her manors were situated and seek others adjacent to them.

Gradually her office at Westminster expanded as she employed more lawyers and clerks to oversee enclosures. She loved the sense of independence she possessed through her land holdings, but most of all she liked to escape the court to her own manors because while she and Queen Ailenor had managed to exist pleasantly and respectfully in each other's company, Ailenor's face lighted up the moment Edward appeared and she, Edward's wife, was utterly forgotten.

'Why do you spend so much time in that land office you have created?' Ailenor asked her one day between Christmas and New Year as she joined the ladies in the bower. 'You excuse yourself because you choose to read a book or visit your greyhounds or spend time with land transactions best left to clerks. You should be in the hall entertaining our guests as Lord Edward's wife ought.' She leaned forward and lifted the embroidery she was working on, a gorgeous alms purse, glittering with golden and silver threads depicting a lady receiving a ring from her lover.

'It is beautiful,' Eleanor remarked. 'This is your talent, your Grace. Mine lies elsewhere.'

Ailenor patted her arm. It was a kindly enough gesture but Eleanor felt Edward's gracious mother would never understand her. 'You are an elegant woman, Eleanor, daughter of a beautiful woman and a clever king. Use your intelligence and your charms well. After all, one day you will be a queen.' She looked dismissively at Eleanor's gown, one she had worn on several occasions over Christmas because it was large enough to be comfortable. 'The way you dress is important. Perhaps you should consider a wardrobe of fashionable new gowns. How you converse with courtiers is very important too and if you don't circulate during the festive period you won't know what they are thinking.'

At that moment Edward entered the women's bower and immediately Ailenor's attention shifted. Eleanor seized this opportunity to flee. She said, 'Please excuse me. I intend to speak with the Castilian envoy. As you know, he has joined the court for our New Year's celebrations.' Ailenor raised an eyebrow and Eleanor holding her composure, though she seethed inside, inclined her head to mother and son, and calling to Margerie said, 'Lady Margerie, I need you in attendance.' Sweeping from the chamber, Margerie following, she went in search of the envoy who would talk to her of the delights of Castile and events in her native land.

It snowed all of February, great fluffy flakes coating courtyards with a thick white blanket. Wintry gales blew into the castle at Windsor and, despite huge fires, chambers remained chill. Eleanor read and played chess with King Henry. She occupied herself trying on gowns that needed to be loosened. As she fingered silks and woollen fabrics, her attention wandered. She was hewn of a restless nature. As soon as she was churched, she intended setting off with a small court in attendance to visit new property acquisitions in Norfolk.

'Madam, it can still be cold in May.' Joan de Viridi held up a flowing soft burgundy woollen quintise. 'This will be easy to let out.'

Eleanor called Margerie over to her bed where another selection of gowns lay waiting the seamstress's attentions. 'Which ones do I need, do *you* think? The quintises are a practical choice.'

'What about this for grander occasions?' Margerie lifted a rustling green satin gown trimmed with dark fur. A scattering of dried fennel and lavender slid from its folds. She swept the herbs to the floor with her hand. 'It may need a new panel inserted, but it's becoming.'

Eleanor took it and held it up. Her hair fell onto the bodice. 'Yes, that will do. I can wear it afterwards as well. And I'll need another for my Churching.' She pointed to the colourful pile of whispering silks, soft wools, and slippery satins. 'That purple silk quintise might be suitable. It looks queenly.' But as she lifted it from the bedcover she found herself whispering a prayer to St Katherine, the saint of all pregnant women.

'Dear St Katherine, please grant me delivery of a healthy child.'

★

Eleanor gave birth to a second boy. They called him Henry for the King. She wore a new gown of cloth of gold for her churching ceremony, not the purple quintise after all. King Henry had insisted, and since her new golden gown was a gift to her for this occasion from Queen Ailenor, she conceded. Queen Ailenor walked by her side into the Abbey at Westminster. Touching the silk approvingly, she said, 'You look very becoming today, my dear. Yes, just like a princess and the mother of kings.'

Don't I always look like a princess? Surely I possess the regal bearing. After all, my own family is more royal than Ailenor's with their Provençal heritage, she thought angrily, but knowing how much Edward loved his mother, she held her tongue. Ailenor had an irritating habit of intruding into her life with Edward, giving her advice, constantly fretting about John's health, and seeking Edward's company when King Henry was busy with his drawings and designs. She impatiently clicked her tongue against her teeth as she walked into the Abbey.

'Is anything amiss?' Ailenor whispered.

'Not at all,' she replied.

The sooner they set off on progress the better. She felt annoyed at her mother-in-law but she smiled graciously at the populace who stood outside the Abbey hoping for a glimpse of their new prince. They cheered for her and the baby. Soon enough, she knew, life in the City would return to normal, with the usual City concerns - trade, taxes, and endless complaints against King Henry. Courtiers, in turn, grumbled about the greedy London merchants and Henry's property taxation.

When Eleanor re-joined court, all their friends could talk about was crusading.

'I want to pledge myself,' she said excitedly to Edward as they walked through the gardens at Westminster. She leaned down to smell her budding red damask roses. 'How I have longed for summer, Edward.' Glancing up she added, 'I am well enough to travel to Northampton. We can stay at Kingsthorpe. We'll take gardeners with us and see what they can do by way of planting. I think Olwen could see to new herbal beds.'

Edward squeezed her hand. 'If you like.' He stopped to pluck a nosegay of herbs which he gave her. She held it to her nose and breathed in the scent.

'This garden is what I like best here.' She pointed to a bed of herbal flowers. 'Hyssop. It smells of oranges. It reminds me of Castile.' She spun around to face him, her long, loose sleeves catching on the flowers of an Alexander plant. He loosened her sleeve and swept the yellow flowers away. Lifting her free hand, he kissed it. She said, 'Dear Edward, I want to Crusade, to leave palaces and castles behind and live simply in God's Kingdom. I hear Crusaders call it *The Kingdom of Heaven*.'

For a moment his blue eyes grew serious. 'The oath-taking at Northampton will be a solemn occasion. There'll be tournaments since so many knights intend gathering to take the cross.' He rubbed his large hands with pleasure. 'Are you sure that if you come on Crusade, you won't miss John and Henry?'

'Queen Ailenor will watch over them,' she said, remembering how the Queen had only that morning looked over the sleeping Henry, John clinging to his beloved grandmother's hand. Eleanor's heart missed a beat. She had never fully recovered from losing Katherine. She was frightened to allow herself to love her own babies too much. They might die like the others. Yes, she was afraid they would love their grandmother better than their mother. And yet she could not part from Edward, not ever. 'The Queen adores them,' she said quietly.

'Do *you*, Eleanor?' Edward was saying, his brow creasing into a frown. 'Do *you* love the children as my mother loved us and still does?'

'I do.' She took hold of his hands. 'But Edward, I love you too. I want to be with you all of this summer and when we crusade. The babies are too little to travel. I need to take my Crusader oath.'

'I wonder should you come on the Crusade. Acre could be besieged like all the other cities in Outremer. So many cities have fallen to the Infidel.' Her mouth opened in an angry protest. Just in time, Edward deflected her speech before she made it. 'It will encourage others if they see you at the ceremony.' He smiled down at her from his great height. 'Of course you must come. You may accompany me on Crusade. You can take your oath too, privately.'

'You mean it would persuade Gloucester – and Pembroke, Edmund, and, possibly, your sister Beatrice and her husband.'

'And many others. It'll unite the dissenting barons, put the civil war behind us. We'll liberate God's Holy Shrines from the infidel.' He took her arm. 'I have to meet with Master Burnell. You can join us today, my love. He's to be my chancellor.' Edward looked serious. 'So he will take the cross and join us on Crusade.'

'That's good news.' Eleanor had always liked their newly appointed and very clever chancellor.

'Take up your cross and follow me.' The words from the Gospel of Matthew echoed through the Church of the Holy Sepulchre as the most important warriors of England's aristocracy gathered in North-ampton to take the cross. It was midsummer. The air was close but Eleanor did not mind. 'What a display of Christian devotion,' she whispered to her friend, Countess Joanna. Further along Queen Ailenor was waving a feathery fan over her face. King Henry's was filled with emotion. 'I think the King wishes he could crusade too.' Eleanor shook her head. 'He's just not strong enough.'

Joanna leaned towards her ear and murmured, 'No, but neither is King Louis and *he* wants to save Jerusalem.'

'And Henry always wants to do as Louis does,' Eleanor whispered back. 'Louis has the Crown of Thorns so Henry has a vial of Christ's Holy Blood. Anyway, the country needs him here. It's best Edward leads us.'

'Look, I can see my William,' Joanna said standing on tiptoe, her gentian blue eyes shining.

Eleanor whispered, 'And I can see my dear, dear lord too.'

'You can't exactly miss seeing Edward!'

True, Edward was the tallest man in the Church, taller even than Archbishop Boniface.

Eleanor glanced around the Church, proud so many barons and earls had gathered to take the cross alongside Edward and his brother Edmund. It was a magnificent occasion, one Eleanor had never witnessed before in her twenty-seven years, and one she might never again. She took a deep breath. This was truly a holy and extraordinary day and one she knew she would never forget. Over and over, her eyes strayed from the ceremony as she glanced around her: incense wafted about the pillared interior; oriel windows allowed rays of sunlight to shaft over the great altar; hundreds of candles created light and shadow throughout the circular interior.

She longed to see Jerusalem's churches for herself. The Northampton church had been built a century earlier in precise replica of the Church of Holy Sepulchre. It was exactly half the dimensions of that in Jerusalem. Like other round churches in Winchester, Cambridge, and London, it was humbling in its simplicity. She felt a deep sense of peace and hoped she could hold on to this day as a precious memory for ever. As her eyes returned to the ceremony, she sensed God's approval and felt His love.

As they had ridden to the Holy Sepulchre through Northampton in a grand procession, the populace cheered and threw flowers. A warm sun cast golden rays upon the princes, barons, earls, knights, and ladies who rode mounts with gold and silver trappings. Squires followed, holding aloft their lords' banners. Others rode with banners displaying crosses, in surplices decorated with red crosses.

Archbishop Boniface had told Edward and Eleanor, over dinner in the castle, that his sermon *de Sancta Cruce* would promote the cross as a military banner. They were the vanguard of the new crusader army raised to liberate God's holy city from infidel rulers. They were Christ's army.

After hymns were sung, the congregation was asked to take the cross. Boniface reminded them, as if they did not already know, the cross would be worn on their right shoulder. He then said a peculiar thing. *'You will not be fresh water fish fleeing the salt water of the sea.'*

Eleanor suppressed a smile at the thought of them flapping like

111

washed-up fish on a ship's deck. Of course, he was speaking about courage.

'Come; who desires the blessing of God?' Boniface continued, 'Who loves the company of angels? Who yearns for the crown incorruptible? Those who come to take the cross will obtain all these things. They avenge the injuries to God and his Holy Land. Crusade is the supreme pilgrimage. The Cross is a protection and a pledge of grace.'

The flower of England's nobility, clad in white surcoats, knelt. When Archbishop Boniface announced Lord Edward would lead them she felt important and proud. She recognised the brevis from which the Archbishop preached because she, herself, had read it. Today, it pleased everyone. Many of those present might not return from the Crusade. The Archbishop's words were comforting. Death led to life, a fate not to be feared but to be embraced. Those who died fighting for the Outremer would be martyrs who would dwell for ever in the meadows of Heaven.

'Look,' whispered Joanna, disturbing her musing. 'Red Gilbert is taking the cross.' She looked around. 'No Alix?'

'Didn't you know? They have separated. They're related in the fifth degree. I expect he *could* formally divorce her but he won't, not yet – because of the girls, I think. The King is incandescent. Alix is his niece but Gilbert has no respect for Henry whatsoever.'

'He respects Edward?' Joanna's blue eyes were amused.

'Apparently that slippery turn-mantle does. He helped him escape Hereford and Gilbert fought courageously at Evesham. Who knows! I wouldn't trust his opinion on anything except hunting hounds.' She watched Gilbert approach the altar and added in a very low voice, 'I never cared for Alix de Lusignan and I doubt she'll frequent court again.'

Joanna raised an eyebrow. 'I hope not, at least not until you and Edward both are sailing away on a Crusade ship.'

'And that will take . . . maybe years. Crusades require organisa-tion. Apparently, King Louis is hopeful we can embark in two years' time.'

'Two years *is* a long time. Still, it'll pass quickly. If I were not busy managing our estates and nearing forty years old, I would insist on taking the cross too . . . I've the children and I'm much older than you. It is best I look after our castles until William returns. We intend rebuilding Goodridge Castle.' She looked thoughtful. 'Will Queen Ailenor look after your boys?' She paused and continued with a smile, 'Maybe there'll be three babes for her to guard by the time you depart.'

'Queen Ailenor will *not* be watching over the children while I am away,' Eleanor said quickly. 'I have other plans. Hush, it's over. The bishops are processing with reliquaries. They'll be taking them outside. We must join this procession. Clergy, Crusaders, the King and Queen and –' Eleanor touched Joanna's arm – 'us too.' They turned to follow King Henry and Queen Ailenor, and she hoped her tactless remark about the Queen had not been heard other than by Joanna.

Later, along with Beatrice, Edward's sister, Eleanor wept as she, too, took her crusading oath in front of many of their nobles in the Castle's Lady Chapel.

As another Christmastide approached, Edward was accounting so they would know how much tax they needed for the Crusade from those joining the Christmas Court, particularly from barons who had taken their oath and who now, to Edward's chagrin, were saying they could not afford to Crusade after all, unless King Henry forgave them fines for taking the wrong side during the Civil War. 'They'll be paying a Crusade Tax now. Chests will be placed in parish churches for Crusade donations,' Edward said in a fury. For a moment nothing more was said and Eleanor returned to her own accounts from her ever accumulating properties. Edward glanced up from his ledger. 'At least the Pope has agreed the Church tithe of a twentieth.'

'It's not enough,' Eleanor set aside her own register of crusade accounts. She kept these as assiduously as she kept her property accounts. Her household would all be paid, though she might just persuade them otherwise in the name of God's Holy War. By helping the Crusade they would be forgiven their sins. Surely it was payment enough to be assured a place in Heaven. 'It's not enough. Your knights have to be paid, ships built and provisioned, if Outremer is to be saved.'

She felt a little hand clutch her foot. Two-year-old John was arranging wooden figures in a boat which was a precise replica of a crusading ship. John was a quiet child who was slowly beginning to speak. He was a small, dark-headed little boy, so unlike his tall father. John's brother, Henry, only six months old, was advanced and could sit up already. Eleanor liked to place him on one of her rich carpets with a set of wooden cups. These he banged about, making her laugh. Today, his nurse had kept him with her. Henry was in a fractious mood because he was teething.

Edward swept a hand though his abundant head of hair. 'We'll provide a hundred marks a year for each knight who sets sail. After Christmas, I shall request another tax from Parliament.'

Eleanor set her lists aside. 'Why don't we take up the loans made to the Jewish moneylenders by impoverished landowners and sell them at a discount to Christian investors.'

'Get their mortgages?'

'Yes, and King Louis could lend us money, though that might come at a price.' She smiled, looking down at her stomach. It remained flat. Even so, now was the time to tell him. 'It's as well, Edward, we are not departing immediately.'

He stared down at her hand. It had instinctively flown to her belly. 'You are never . . .'

'Yes, I am with child, my love. I feel it will be a girl this time.' She rose and crossed to his sloping desk. She kissed the top of his head. 'She will be born in June.' He leapt up and swirled her around. After kissing her on the mouth, he let her go. Little John was watching them. Edward scooped his son up. John shrieked. He lifted the child high and galloped around the chamber, John laughing gleefully from Edward's shoulders.

'Careful, Edward,' Eleanor said, anxiety creeping into her voice. 'He's not strong. Don't overexcite him.'

'Nonsense, he's made of the stuff of kings. I was chesty as a child too.'

Eleanor was not so sure. John was showing signs of delicacy and she even wondered if it was wise to leave him and go far away on a lengthy crusade. God would protect her children as a reward for her devotion, a devotion that would take her and Edward to the very centre of Christendom. Besides, she thought practically, it is as well to leave an heir here . . . just in case. Just in case of what? She shuddered at the thought and strode to the window. Just in case we never return. The day darkened. Snow batted against the window glass.

'Edward, bring John here. Look, it's snowing in time for Christmas. Let him see.'

She felt love for Edward all over again as she watched him show their son the white flakes falling from the sky. 'Why don't we wrap up in fur mantles and go outside to make a snow creature?'

'Bear,' John cried. 'Papa will make me a snow bear.'

Eleanor touched her belly again. She *would* have a large family of living children to create future snow bears. 'Go on,' she said. 'I'm working, but if you make a bear outside the windows below, I'll see it.'

June sunshine slid softly through the blue silken cloth covering the bedchamber window. 'She is beautiful,' Edward said holding his infant daughter awkwardly in his arms. Eleanor smiled up at them both as he hesitantly touched the baby's head. 'A dark fuzz already. Blue eyes. You are beautiful.' He kissed her tiny brow.

'Their eyes change colour you know. My lord, I think you like girls better than boys.'

'No, I like them all. But she has your look about her already.' He looked up. 'We'll call her Eleanor for her mother, for my mother, and for my great-grandmother of Aquitaine.'

'There are too many Eleanors in this family. We could call her Eleanora at home. Less confusing. Edward, I have something to ask you.'

'Today, I shall grant you anything.'

'I think that since your Uncle Richard is not accompanying us on Crusade . . . and your father's health is delicate . . . and Queen Ailenor will be Edmund's agent, I think . . .' She paused. Edward adored his mother. He might not like what she was about to suggest.

'*What* do you think, Eleanor?' Baby Eleanora began to howl. Edward handed the baby over to the wet nurse. 'Keen to get her way,' he remarked. The nurse nodded agreement and hurried Baby Eleanora away. 'Like her mother,' he added looking at Eleanor.

'And like her father. Edward, I think we should leave the children with Richard at Wallingford when we are away. They'll have their nurses and their own households to care for them. Wallingford is healthier than the City. Richard will watch over your political interests so why not ask him to care for our family as well?'

'Not my mother?'

'It's too much to ask of her. Your mother will see the children often. They adore her, I am sure, but the Queen has many responsibilities of her own.'

He thought for a moment. Slowly he said, 'Perhaps you are right, but we'll have to be tactful. Since Boniface has travelled to France and Savoy and she's not happy with us all departing England, leaving her and my father for years possibly.'

'Wait until Christmas to tell her. Anything can happen within the next six months.' She whispered a silent prayer that nothing would now stop their departure in the spring. 'How are preparations going, Edward?'

'I am sailing for France this week. You would normally accompany me to Paris but you, my love, must rest and get strong.' He smiled. 'A crusade unites princes. I am seeking that loan from Louis. He has sent word he wants one of our boys as guarantee but I've sent him back a letter declaring my word as a prince is good enough. Neither of our boys will be raised in France.'

She was sad not to accompany him to Paris. Hiding it, she said, 'Bring me back a new book from Paris, one with Crusade stories.'

'Of course, my love. Keep on making your lists. You'll need to put your office in order too. The properties are more than paying their way.' He took her hand. 'John of Brittany and Beatrice may even be here by the time I return. That will cheer you.'

116

'I'm glad of Beatrice's company. Cousin Jeanne is in my party too. Of course, there'll be Prince Philip of France's wife, Isabel of Aragon. We'll be like wolves stalking prey, watchful for each other.' Eleanor gave him a pleased smile. 'And I had a letter from Flanders. My brother, Fadrique, has written he is coming.' She smiled. 'He likes to fancy himself one of King Arthur's knights.'

'And I am King Arthur who delights in the presence of formidable she-wolf women, especially my wife.'

'Is that so? I wonder? Go now, husband. God keep you safe.'

They kissed and held hands. Within the moment it would take to blow away seeds off a dandelion stalk, Edward was gone.

King Louis lent Edward money to be repaid from the sale of Gascon wines. The promised one-twentieth tax was finally granted by Parliament. This added another thirty thousand pounds to their war chest. Edward had at last collected enough to pay one hundred marks per knight to each of the nobles who took the cross. He returned from France in time for the translation of Edward the Confessor's body into a magnificent new tomb in the transept of Westminster Abbey. The rebuilding of the Abbey and the translation of the Confessor's body had been a project spanning decades, one which King Henry considered *his* Crusade. He had created his own Jerusalem in the very latest architectural styles, bringing masons from France to guide his building works. There was yet work to be completed on the Abbey's Nave but the mosaic Cosmate pavement laid below the shrine was now complete.

'It is inlaid stone with geometric patterns,' Edward said as he and Eleanor stared in awe at the completed mosaic. They are cut into a variety of rectangles, squares, circles, triangles. Look, Eleanor, a central roundel flanked by four orbiting roundels, a quincunx made of onyx.' He strode along the length of it studying its magnificence. 'Amazing. The materials include glass of red, turquoise, blue, and a bluish-white.'

She peered down. 'It is more beautiful than any of the mosaics I've seen in Spain.'

'The Romans never used glass in their mosaics. This is unique,' Edward said, placing his palms together as if in prayer.

That October, King Henry, Edward, Edmund, Richard of Cornwall, and other noble barons put their hands to the bier and carried the saint's body to its new resting place.

'He's not here,' Eleanor said to Edward after the ceremony.

'Who?'

'You know very well who.'

The whole court, except Gilbert of Gloucester, had come to watch the ceremony unfold.

As they left the abbey, Edward turned to her and whispered, 'Eleanor, before we set off to Palestine I want to commission an abbey of our own.'

'Why, Edward? We can't afford it.'

'I want to thank the Cistercians for protecting us during the war. The order was kind to me when I was in captivity.' He tugged his beard thoughtfully. 'The abbey must be close to the Welsh borders. After Christmas we'll take a look and think about a site for it. What do you think?'

She nodded. 'I am always happy to travel.' She was thinking about the pleasure she would have enjoying a visit to her friend Joanna.

After Christmas, Eleanor and Edward visited Cheshire to choose a location for the new Cistercian monastery. They rode about the countryside in freezing winter weather and discovered Darnhill in the Forest of Delamere. Afterwards, their party rode south from Cheshire to Goodridge Castle, where William of Pembroke and Edward discussed final plans for the forthcoming Crusade. Joanna and Eleanor sat in Joanna's solar and chatted.

'I am having this solar redesigned while William is away,' Joanna said, stretching her hands towards the fire.

'It's comfortable already,' Eleanor remarked, leaning back against a cushion.

'By the time you return from the Crusade, it'll be magnificent.'

'Your favourite castle?'

118

'Always.'

As it often did, before long their conversation turned to Gilbert de Clare, who had not been at court for many months, even ignoring a summons at Christmas.

'And he never appeared at the Translation of St Edward in October. Edward thinks he'll not crusade after all,' Eleanor said, feeling a renewed sense of disappointment. Gilbert remained unreliable.

'He feels his lands are threatened again.'

'From whom this time?'

'Other barons, and the Welsh.'

'He's using it as an excuse not to crusade. I heard he thinks King Louis makes poor military decisions.'

'William thinks there's a solution. Edward's uncle Richard was here last month. He had just visited Earl Gilbert at Cardiff Castle.'

'So we heard.' Eleanor kicked off her boots and wriggled her stockinged toes at the blaze. 'As I've always said, if Montfort was the Devil, Gilbert of Gloucester is Satan's minion. In fact, Joanna, I am planning an Apocalypse illustration with both of them and their companions facing Hell's fires, and that has to be where Montfort suffers just punishment. If Gilbert reneges on his Crusade it'll be his well-deserved fate too.' She sighed. 'Of course, we'll miss his knights, money, and ships.'

'He's an able leader of men. He might be better guarding England.'

'Untrustworthy, Joanna. Never forget how he treated us five years ago.' Eleanor knew her tone was vicious but she still distrusted Gloucester.

'Never.' Joanna's mouth curved up slightly. 'You *did* say though he saved your favourite dog.'

'All he has in his favour.' Eleanor tossed another log on the fire. It hissed and crackled. The sound of it splitting reflected her mood.

Shortly after her visit to Joanna, Eleanor's maids could organise her personal chests at last. She was taking two clerks on crusade, plus her steward and valet; a group of her women including two junior maidens, and Olwen.

As Margerie folded gowns into enormous chests, layering them with dried fennel and lavender, Eleanor ticked off items on her wardrobe list. She was frowning, puzzling whether she needed an extra riding gown or a pair of male leggings and a tunic instead, when unannounced, Edward swept into her chamber. 'Leave,' he grunted at Margerie who hastily dropped the gowns, bowed to him, and withdrew. Eleanor could feel his impatience.

'It's settled,' he said. 'Gilbert will follow in six months.'

Eleanor carried on ticking off her lists. 'Do you believe him? Really?'

'I want his knights.'

'I certainly would not miss him, though I suppose the Crusade might.'

'He's important whether we like him or not.' Edward glanced around the chamber. 'I can see you have everything in order. My father gave us his blessing in Parliament today.' He seized her hands. The list fell to the floor. 'My dearest, we have a thousand souls sailing with us to Aigues-Mortes and enough ships to cross the Narrow Sea.'

She withdrew her hands from his and swept her hand around the chamber. 'As you can see, we are busy packing.'

When Edward pulled her close she laid her head against his breast.

'We'll ride for Winchester two days from now and wait for the wind.'

'At last,' she sighed into his tunic. 'At last. May God protect our ships and bring us safely there.'

'Amen,' he whispered. His voice possessed a tone of anticipation that matched her own.

Part Two
Crusade

1270–1274

Chapter Eleven

The Mediterranean
1270–1272

On arrival at the southern French port of Aigues-Mortes, Eleanor and Edward had discovered Louis had left for Tunis to give support to his brother Charles, King of Sicily, in his attack on the Tunisian Emir, who was helping Sicilian rebels in their long fight against Charles. Louis wrote, *A manoeuvre in North Africa could establish Tunis as a muster-port from which to attack unfriendly Egypt and aid the Crusaders' aim of liberating Jerusalem.*

In a fury, his eyes dark and his countenance terrifying, Edward tossed the note down. 'This is not what we sailed for. We sailed to save the Outremer states from the infidel.'

Louis's representatives purred their reasoning to Edward, who remained furious.

Eventually he calmed down. 'There may be sense in destroying the Mamluks. They are controlling Christ's Kingdom from their Egyptian headquarters.'

His own council of crusading earls reminded him, 'King Louis failed in this very objective on his previous crusade.'

Louis's ambassadors insisted, 'Join our king in Tunis. Sail there, not straight to Acre. Our king leads and commands.'

Since Louis was the nominal head of the crusade, Edward had to agree, but he did so with reluctance.

Disaster struck. When they arrived in Tunis, Louis, along with many of his army, had already died from dysentery. The sudden deaths included one of Eleanor's own cousins and Jean Tristan, Louis's son.

'We can winter in Sicily,' Charles said, trying to smooth things over. He had already made a peace treaty with the Emir of Tunis. 'Best to make further plans from the comfort of my palaces.' He looked so sad, Edward could not object. Eleanor took his hand in hers and murmured, 'Do not make a great fuss. He is heartbroken. Can't you see?'

Though it was not hot at all in the temporary camp, Charles mopped his sweating brow with a cloth. 'I must leave you, Edward, to lead the Crusade in the King's stead. I must accompany his funeral procession to Paris.'

Eleanor sighed relief when Edward agreed. She was with child again. It would be better the baby was born in the comfort of a Sicilian palace than endangered Acre.

It was not to be.

'I am unlucky,' she cried to her ladies when she lost the child that winter.

'God is angry with me because I have delayed our departure to God's Kingdom,' she cried to Edward.

'Nonsense,' he said. 'There will be other children.'

In summer 1271 they sailed to Acre where they lodged in a vast citadel larger than their own Tower of London. Sure enough, Eleanor was quickly pregnant again.

Determined not to lose another child, she rested throughout her new pregnancy. She had no desire to ride into the baking hot dusty and arid territory that lay beyond the city walls. Instead, she passed hours reading books from the extensive library and exploring the shady gardens laid out within the citadel of the Knights of St John. It was delightful. She was reminded of Spain with geometric mosaic paths, stone fountains, miniature canals, and exotic climbing plants such as softly perfumed jasmine and roses. The fortress looked out over the sea and she never tired of watching trading vessels sail in and out of the great harbour. Occasionally a new Crusader ship arrived, brandishing a red cross on its pennants, proudly coasting over the waves toward the port. This was always thrilling because ships carried news from England – until one ship brought Eleanor sad news. Their elder boy, John, had died at Wallingford Castle.

'Our prince. Our heir,' Edward wailed. Later he calmed and comforted Eleanor who was broken-hearted. 'We'll make more children,' Edward said, tears rolling down his cheeks. 'There is Henry.' They held each other and wept together.

'But, I am already with child again, Edward. Have you forgotten?' Eleanor said, smiling through her tears. 'John is with God. He will be one of His most precious angels.'

They prayed together for Prince John's soul and for the safe delivery of their child.

After John's death, Eleanor prayed daily for a new brother for Prince Henry and Princess Eleanora.

As Eleanor prayed, read and rested, Edward regularly led sorties beyond the city walls. He needed to attack Baibars, the leader of the Mamluks, who had his eyes focused on Acre. Baibars possessed a huge, efficient army whilst Edward desperately needed reinforcements. Desperate, he secretly sent ambassadors to Persia to seek help from the Mongol leader, Abhaga, a sworn enemy of Baibars. United, they could defeat the Mamluks who ruled Jerusalem and the once-powerful French crusader kingdoms.

There was no response. Edward waited and waited.

Christmas passed again as did winter. Eleanor withdrew to her apartments in April of the next year. She hoped to emerge quickly, but this birthing was agony. Why, why was she being punished? Refusing to use the birthing stool, she lay on sheets of cool cotton covering a pallet, enduring each painful contraction with stoicism. As each pain gripped her, she reasoned that if the child was fighting to enter the world, he must be a strong, male child, to cause her such terrible pain. Clutching a jasper stone between the agonising contractions, she moved her lips in prayer. A soft breeze whispered through silken curtains but she hardly felt it. A clutch of midwives hovered about her pallet, some of them Arab with dark skins and enormous dark eyes. She was unaware of them all. Bell after chapel bell rang out the hours - St Lawrence, St Breda, St Michael, and the Holy Cross. She had visited them all and had prayed in them all too. Surely her prayers would be answered. She craved relief. If only she could pass from consciousness into oblivion, but she must not because that would be death.

'Push.' The woman's accent was unfamiliar. Another bathed Eleanor's forehead and the scent of lavender tugged her back into consciousness. God would protect her. God had spared their English fleet when their sails had caught a storm as they approached Sicily when the French fleet had been destroyed. So many deaths. John had died. Her beloved Katherine had died. Her child born during winter in Sicily had died. This baby must live.

She bit down on the twisted cloth given her and looked up into the strange midwife's eyes. They were liquid brown like soft honey. The woman repeated firmly in French, 'Poussez, Madame.'

Eleanor gathered what little remaining strength she possessed and pushed hard. A moment later, the midwife was lifting up a baby. There was a cry. All the women who gathered about her bedside clutching crosses and precious stones dropped them onto the floor tiles.

'A girl. A little girl, dearest Eleanor.' The voice belonged to Beatrice, Edward's sister. Eleanor allowed a stone of jasper to slip from her hand. She permitted Beatrice to lift her head. 'A strong girl,' she whispered, looking up at Edward's sister. 'A granddaughter of Spain.'

As if from a great distance she heard Olwen say, 'Drink, my lady. It will help you.'

'Bring me my daughter first.'

She was not unhappy that the baby was a girl-child, just relieved this infant was born alive and that the long trial of giving birth was over. 'I shall call her Joan,' she said, thinking of the child who had died in Wallingford and of her friend, Joanna, whom she loved dearly. Besides, she thought with optimism, there would be another male child. 'Beloved Eleanor, you are fruitful,' Edward was wont to say, laughing as they made love.

There *would* be other children.

As she touched the child she realised the efficient midwives had already bathed the baby and swaddled it. After a few glorious moments she felt her newborn lifted by someone as she was removed from the pallet and gently bathed. She felt a fresh night rail slipping over her shoulders. She was placed on her great bed which stood in the middle of the chamber, covered with sweetly smelling fresh linen and hung with calming pale blue silken curtains. She would love this Joan and keep her safe.

'My lady, drink. Honey water and crushed chamomile flowers,' Olwen was saying, her voice distant.

'Where is Lord Edward?'

'Lord Edward is with his knights praying in the chapel. We have sent a messenger with good tidings already. We'll show him the child,' Beatrice said into her ear. 'Rest, our dear sister.'

As Eleanor eased into sleep she could hear birdsong from the cypress trees outside and smell the scent of roses drifting up from the courtyard below. She heard the tinkling of water in fountains and the soft voices of her ladies as they cleansed and prepared her chamber for Edward's visit. He would be with her soon.

Joan was christened two days later. Her godmother was to be the other Joanna, who was busily watching over affairs in Pembrokeshire. William of Pembroke stood as the child's godfather, along with Edward's brother Edmund who had sailed into Acre with reinforcements.

Joan came to be called Joan of Acre after her place of birth. After all, thought Eleanor, Joan was conceived and born in God's precious kingdom.

Within the month she was churched in the fortress's Chapel of St John at a ceremony witnessed by Edward and all his knights. As Eleanor glanced around the nave she saw her own household and a group of Venetian merchants clad in colourful silk gowns. They

127

were accompanied by wives attired even more extravagantly than her own ladies. She glanced down at her simple light rose-coloured silk gown wondering if she looked like a great princess amongst all the richly hued velvets, satins, and silks worn by the Venetians.

She looked to her own ladies. They were a vision in blue silk shot through with silver thread. Eleanor held her head high. The magical atmosphere of the ceremony in the Templars' church was only marred by Joan's grizzling. As they left the candlelit church her child drifted into a peaceful slumber.

'She snores,' Beatrice whispered to Eleanor with a smile on her lips.

'She's healthy. Her lungs are strong,' Eleanor returned.

The procession paused before the great doors into the Hall. Her women fussed and adjusted her train. Her hearing exceptionally acute, Eleanor listened to two Christian wives who had turned to each other and were conversing in French.

'My maid is of the Alawite faith. Baibars is forcing the Alawites to build mosques in their villages even though he can't force them to pray there. They use them as stables for their cattle and beasts of burden. Her father was murdered for his faith. Her family have hidden in caves to escape massacre and my maid wants my husband to bring them into the city, hidden amongst spices he bought from the Muslims.'

'He's trading with the Egyptians? Mine too. Who can blame them? We need the trade routes open.'

'We hoped when Edward of England came it would all be resolved. The English prince cannot defeat Baibars. Baibars will enter Acre and destroy our city as he did Saphet. We'll all be sold into slavery just as the women and children of Saphet were eight years ago.'

'We have no hope,' the other agreed. 'Krak fell last year. The English never saved Krak'

'But I've heard the English prince will seek a truce. He has tried twice to seek battle with Baibars but Baibars has eluded him. So says my husband.'

'This citadel is the strongest place in the city. As long as our husbands supply Baibars with metal and timber for his siege weapons. If the merchants from Genoa provide the Mamluks with slaves, we'll be saved. There'll be a truce, you'll see.'

'Let us hope you speak true, Maria. I pray for our safety daily.'

The voices faded as the women melted into a crowd waiting to gain entry to the feast. Eleanor wondered if Edward was indeed considering a truce. She gave a backwards glance. None of her ladies seemed to be paying the slightest bit of attention to the conversations of others. They were talking quietly together and fiddling with their veils. When, at last, she entered the great hall, Edward was already seated at a long table with his knights. Joan was whisked away to their apartments. Eleanor saw she would not be able to repeat this conversation to Edward until much later.

She turned her attention to the dishes of fruit placed before her, to the spiced pasties, the fresh fish from the sea, chickens stuffed with nuts, raisins, and exotic fruits, and the light red local wine that she very much enjoyed. They reminded her of her childhood and of Spain. Acrobats performed. Tumblers juggled. Dancers swirled, their arm movements sensuous. English musicians played haunting music on flutes and pipes. The music made Eleanor long for the hunt and, in particular, for her hunting dogs. That thought led her back to Gilbert of Gloucester, who had promised to follow Edward on Crusade once he had settled rebellions on his borders. But Gilbert said King Henry needed him by his side. So, slippery and wormlike as ever, Gilbert could not possibly depart from England.

On the following evening, Eleanor repeated what she had overheard on the previous afternoon.

Edward leaned against cushions and plucked a grape from a bunch. 'You have done well to overhear this talk. I have long known the Venetians and the Genoese to be treacherous to our cause. Merchants need trade but the sale of metals and wood for the infidel siege machines is a negotiation with the enemy too far. They betray

129

the God they serve and will bring about their fellow Christians' destruction. We tolerate their arrangements because their dealings keep Baibars away whilst we await the outcome of my negotiations with Abhaga of Persia. Better the Mongol shares control of Jerusalem than Baibars. But, Eleanor, I cannot ban the Italian trade, because Hugh of Cyprus has licensed it. I have tried over and over to stop it. My knights are restless. I don't know what to do. The waiting is intolerable.'

She exhaled a breath. 'I have something for you,' she said, climbing down from their bed. 'A gift. It will help you with strategy.' She crossed the floor tiles to a coffer. Reaching up to a niche in the wall above, she lifted down a small casket from which she withdrew a tiny key. Kneeling on the tiles, she opened it and lifted out a small book wrapped in linen cloth. Returning to the baffled Edward, she said, 'Master Richard has been working on its translation from Latin into French since we were in Sicily. He has completed it at last. It is your name-day gift.'

'A name-day gift that is three weeks early,' Edward reminded her as he unwrapped the linen protecting the book. Opening its stiff leather covers he laid it on the coverlet. '*De Re Militarii*. Vegetius.' He laughed. 'You are a warrior princess, my Eleanor.' She could hardly contain her excitement at his delight when he added with tears in his eyes, 'This is a wonderful book. I shall treasure it always, my love.'

Together they studied the pages of Roman military instruction, 'I thought you might have need of it sooner. Look at the drawings.' She pointed them out to him. 'See, there you are! Look at you approaching Vegetius seeking instruction. And look here.' She gently turned some pages. 'A battle at sea; you attacking Baibars' fleet last year, and here too.' She turned back some pages.

'You are clever, Eleanor. Sadly, last July's raid on Saint-Georges was not a success. My thirsty troops, so unused to the heat, drank from corrupted wells. My knights were poisoned.' He sighed. 'With help from the Mongols all that can change.'

'You *did* destroy Baibars' fleet.'

'God indeed granted us a storm.' He smiled. 'He is challenging his soldiers.'

'My brother has this same book. He always said it provided good military advice.'

'We must prove him correct.'

In July a messenger rode into the courtyard seeking Lord Edward. Edward sent his squire to summon Eleanor. He found her about to enter the chapel dedicated to St John. She shooed her ladies into the chapel's cool. Followed by Lady Margerie, she turned on her foot and hurried along a dim corridor to Edward's privy chamber. It was hot and her haste caused her to perspire relentlessly.

Edward was holding a letter, his face ashen.

'What has happened, Edward? Your father? Our Henry? Eleanora?'

'No, not our children,' He drew breath. She waited. 'They are without their guardian. Uncle Richard died of a seizure in April. The great Richard of Cornwall is dead.'

She fell to her knees and looked up at his tear-filled eyes. 'Oh, Christ's Holy Mercy, Edward. I know what he meant to you. Where will the children go now? Do your knights know?'

Edward reached for her hands and lifted her to her feet. 'Don't kneel to me, Eleanor. I must call a council meeting. I fear my uncle's death is not the end of today's dreadful news.' He breathed so deeply she heard the exit of air as he released his breath. She waited, her hands folded and her spine erect. 'What is it?' she whispered after a few moments passed and he had not spoken.

'Hugh of Cyprus has agreed a treaty with Baibars. He is doing this to protect trade and he's doing it behind my back.'

Eleanor thought it not so terrible a treaty was made with Baibars. The Mongols were not proving reliable allies. If Baibars granted rights to pilgrims approaching Jerusalem it would be better than a hopeless war to win a holy city that was long lost to the Christian world, a war that was dragging on without any success. Edward had not regained any of the Crusader Castles and Acre was in serious danger. Acre, too, could fall if a treaty was not forged.

She kept her tongue still. Now was not the right moment to reason with him.

'Shall I attend the Council meeting?' she said instead.

He nodded. 'Do, my love. First, I must speak with Edmund. Richard was his uncle too.'

By the time they convened in the knights' hall, Eleanor suspected the tragic news had already leaked out since knowledge of Richard's death showed on their knights' faces. Edward read aloud the letter from England. John de Warenne, a muscular, determined-faced young man whose yellow hair had grown long in Acre, averted his eyes to the floor. William of Valence withdrew a linen cloth and dabbed at his eyes. Thomas de Clare whispered a 'Te Deum'. She could hear him murmuring the prayer since he was seated next to her. The moment was made doubly poignant because the knights had a month earlier discovered that Henry of Almain, Richard's son, was brutally murdered on his way to Gascony. He had been attacked and stabbed in the Italian city of Viterbo by the de Montforts, Simon the younger and Guy. Edward had sworn revenge. Many of his knights determined that when Jerusalem was freed from the infidel they would hunt the Montfort brothers down. The brothers were protected by Charles of Anjou, who employed them.

Eleanor had wept for Henry of Almain. She should have ordered young Simon hanged on that unforgettable day at Windsor when Gilbert of Gloucester had taken her castle. Apparently, when Henry of Almain begged mercy, Guy de Montfort had refused, saying, 'You had no mercy on my father and brothers that August day at Evesham.' He had taken vengeance even though Henry of Almain, as Simon de Montfort's prisoner, had not even fought at Evesham. Now Henry's father was dead too but at least, thought Eleanor, at least, Earl Richard died in his bed.

'We should return to England,' declared Edmund angrily. 'We're at a standstill and our knights are restless. This accursed land delivers nothing but broken spirits and defeat. We need more support and that's not happening. The French have deserted our cause.'

132

'Aye to that, Edmund,' said John de Vescy. 'We return.'

'No,' Roger Clifford said. 'We stay, go out and fight for the Cross. We have waited too long to launch a proper campaign.'

'I agree,' shouted Eleanor's household knight, Robert de Haustede, married to Lady Margerie.

Eleanor could not remain silent any longer. 'You will not survive. Baibars would very much like you all to ride unprepared into the desert. You would die of thirst and he'll poison the wells before you reach any significant village. Besides, his army is the greater.'

'Where is he? Where is Baibars?' Edmund said with impatience, waving his arms dramatically about. 'He's invisible, impossible to find, never mind defeat. Tell them, brother.' He repeated, 'Where is Baibars? Where are our allies?'

John de Vescy mumbled, 'Another sound reason not to go looking for shadows. We don't know where to look'

Edward hammered the table with his right fist. 'We shall finish building the new Tower here. We must defend the Holy Land and continue the fight. Hugh of Cyprus seeks peace but *we* never came here to make peace with Baibars. *We* came to defend Jerusalem.'

'Brother, be reasonable. We could not even take Qaqun on the road to Jerusalem, so, tell me, how can we retake Jerusalem? Surely it is better to seek an advantageous peace.'

'No!' shouted Edward. 'The Mongols have ravaged the land around Aleppo. They can help us.'

'But they have retreated beyond the Euphrates,' said Edmund in a quiet voice.

'Only to regroup.' Edward hammered his fist on the table again. 'The Crusade must go on. The path to Heaven must be regained. It is God's will.'

Eleanor felt a headache come on. She pondered for a moment what Vegetius would advise. She had no answer. What would her warrior father, Ferdinand of Castile, have done? She could not know.

She rose and gestured to Margerie who sat in a cushioned window embrasure probably listening to every word. After all, her own

133

knight was present. Margerie folded the cuff she was embroidering, tucked it into her work bag and rose to her feet.

'My lords, please excuse me,' Eleanor said, without providing any excuse and followed by Margerie swept from the columned hall leaving Edward to persuade his company to remain loyal to his crusade. She turned to Marjorie, 'Find Olwen. I want a tonic to ease my aching head.' She swirled around and pointed back at the hall. 'They will talk in circles all night and return to where they began, undecided and divided.'

Chapter Twelve

Acre
June 1272

Olwen hardly heard the maid enter her chamber. She was absorbed watching a young man gather herbs in the garden below her window. This wide opening was grilled with lattice work and as she gazed down on the young man he appeared patterned with hexagonal shapes. Even so, he was very handsome.

For fifteen months she had occupied a small chamber on the second storey of the palace guest quarters. The palace partly overlooked the vast courtyard belonging to the impenetrable fortress built by the Knights of St John. Much of it was built over the knights' halls where Lord Edward's troops slept, ate, and practised warfare, but Olwen was fortunate that her own chamber overlooked the gardens which were an oasis of fig trees, lavender bushes, and colourful flowering plants that climbed trellises. On her own explorations of the gardens she discovered lilies, honeysuckle, and climbing roses.

The young man glanced up and waved. She waved back. His name was Guillaume and he had told her he was the bastard son of a French lord and an Arab concubine. Guillaume had been given to the military priestly order to raise and train as one of their own. Instead of an interest in the military, he had developed a passion for plants and was training as an apothecary who would tend the knights inhabiting the fortress. Olwen shared his interest so when their paths had crossed in the herbal gardens a year before they had quickly developed a friendship. She understood anything more between them was impossible. The monkish knights of St John would never let him go. If only . . .

She smiled, lifted up her right hand, and showed five fingers to suggest she would meet him in the garden after the hour of Vespers.

'Lady Olwen.'

The voice made her start. Olwen spun around on her slippered foot. One of Eleanor's maids stood in the midst of sunbeams sliding in through the opened doorway. 'My lady needs a draught to help her headache.'

'I shall see to it forthwith,' Olwen replied, guiltily moving away from the window. 'Tell her I shall be with her shortly.'

The girl slipped off as silently as a cat stalking a bird in the garden below. Olwen turned back, gave the youth a final wave and leaving her chamber hurried along the outside arcade corridor to her locked still room. This was always cool on the hottest of summer days. It was opposite a high opening in the courtyard walls through which breezes fanned in from the sea beyond. She lifted a brass key attached to her girdle and unlocked the door. Once inside, she stood on tip-toe, lifted a jar from an upper shelf, and turning to the bench took a silver cup from a drawer. She poured a little of a restorative tonic, which she had distilled from lavender, cinnamon, and sandalwood, into the cup which she placed on a tray of cypress wood. Reaching for a bunch of dried lavender she clipped off a few twigs, tied them with a thread of silver silk, and placed the posy beside the cup. Finally, she arranged a small dish with crystallized strips of angelica stems. Lady Eleanor would appreciate their green delicacy and, after all, it was as important to provide a restorative to the mind as well as the body. Carefully carrying the tray, Olwen exited the still room, locking the door behind her.

Later, Olwen watched as Guillaume left the Church of St John. She never tired of looking at him amongst the choristers, clad in his belted black tunic of the Hospitallers' Order. His dark hair shone in the candlelight like a raven's wing. He was of average height but handsome, and when he smiled his face lit up and his black eyes shone like polished stones. When he sang he looked peaceful and joyful, like an angel. Today he smiled at her as she rose from prayer. Olwen felt Margerie's sharp blue eyes light on her and was sure Eleanor's chief lady noticed because she felt her tap her shoulder to draw her attention back to the Augustine Prior who was reading from the Vulgate.

She knew the passage by heart and understood what the words said in English.

'*The voice said cry. And he said, "What shall I cry? All flesh is grass, and all goodliness thereof is as the flower of the field. The grass withereth, the flower fadeth; because the spirit of the land bloweth upon it, surely the people is grass."* '

She had heard the rest of the passage often enough too. *The grass withereth, the flower fadeth, but the word of God will stand for ever.*

Was this a message of hope for a lost crusade and the death of Earl Richard who had been a great crusader himself? Lady Eleanor had said that afternoon the earls were discussing the crusade's future. They could not agree. It all had brought on her headache. Lady Eleanor was resting. Olwen could still meet with Guillaume.

Olwen had hoped to see Jerusalem with her own eyes. As she stood in the dim, incense-scented church, she found herself reflecting on her time in Acre - how she had learned new things about plants, and of course, Guillaume. She would miss Guillaume. If there was a truce they would leave Acre. Guillaume's life was here and hers was in England. He had helped her with her great project. She had carefully put together a herbal, pages and pages of drawings of plants, and now she could write words she added descriptions of plants' attributes to accompany her drawings. Guillaume aided her project's progress and promised a monk from the scriptorium would sew the pages together. He could bind the book before the royal party left Acre.

After Vespers she excused herself from supper, collected her scissors and basket, and slipped down the outside staircase into the scented garden. Guillaume was waiting by the fountain, clad in a loose linen tunic and leggings. He was not smiling as was usual. He knew everything that was spoken of amongst the knights.

When he rose to greet her, she lifted up her basket. 'I need to gather herbs. Come and help me.'

'Wait. Sit down for a moment. I have something to tell you.'

The fountain behind them bubbled. A fish splashed. The sky was the colour of lavender. A breeze rustled through a fig tree. There was concern on Guillaume's face. He knew things were about to change. Olwen sank, fainthearted, onto the stone seat.

'What is the matter?' she said when he sat by her side.

'I feel uneasy . . .' he began.

'Uneasy?' she repeated slowly. 'Why?'

'Yesterday I attended a man who came to the infirmary. I gathered he belongs to a party sent into Acre by Sultan Baibars himself. He seemed an important personage and mentioned he was here to speak with Lord Edward. I think he is a leader of an embassy carrying gifts for Lord Edward. He was accompanied by a Venetian merchant.'

'Why were you treating this man?'

'He had a wound. A goose had pecked him but I don't think he will die of it, just a scratch. I administered a salve of azob mixed with goose fat and gave him a vial of oil of thyme and hyssop.'

'Hyssop's an effective salve,' she murmured.

'Yes, indeed, but listen to me. It was peculiar. When the emissary spoke of presents for Lord Edward, I disliked his condescending laugh. Odd to laugh if you are bringing gifts into the fortress, no matter who is to receive them. To be truthful, I thought he was no ambassador. He studied my shelves with greedy eyes. He was a very strange personage.'

'You say a merchant accompanied this emissary?'

'That was odd too. They thought my back turned reaching for a salve but in the small mirror glass on my shelf I saw something. The merchant glanced at me, looked back at the emissary and placed a finger on his lip.'

'You are not supposed to hear about emissaries and gifts for Lord Edward.' She thought for a moment. 'But if we were to go into the square where the Venetians have their shops would you recognise the merchant?'

'I might. He was wealthy, dressed in a green gown trimmed with gold. His hair was black and he was almost as tall as Lord Edward himself. His face was thin. His nose was long.'

'The envoy? How did he appear?'

'Breath that smelled of cinnamon. Perfume. Musk I believe. His gown rustled. Yes, heavy yellow damask. His eyes were hooded.'

'Lord Edward has a droop to his eyelid and he does not look sinister,' she reasoned.

'Those eyes did not droop. They were hooded like the eyes of a hawk.'

They fell silent as the air whirred with the sound of cicadas. She watched a tiny salamander crawl up the fountain wall. It was the month of June with long days and it would still be hot outside. This garden was a cool and shady chamber, an oasis behind a wall, surrounded by a baking courtyard haunted by biting insects. She had coated herself with a lemony salve to deter them.

She turned to Guillaume and broke the thoughtful quiet that had fallen between them. 'Tomorrow is Lord Edward's name day and I have a morning to myself. Why don't we go to the Venetians' piazza and see what we can see. Besides, I need to purchase spices.'

Guillaume nodded. 'Yes, it is a good plan. Let me help you gather your herbs now.' They both rose, picked up her basket, and began to gather hyssop, sage, lavender, and rosemary. Occasionally he bumped against her as they bent down to seek out camomile growing along borders. The sensation was not unpleasant, and as they both rose they smiled at each other.

On the following morning, Olwen asked if she might go into the City with Guillaume to purchase spices. Permission was granted by Lady Margerie. She apparently liked the apothecary and trusted him for, after all, he was part of a monastic order.

'You say the apothecary will help you choose ingredients for your salves and potions. As long as the Hospitaller guards you I suppose you can come to no harm.'

Olwen nodded. 'Of course, my lady.'

Lady Margerie's searching blue eyes studied Olwen's face. Olwen prayed she was not blushing. Clearly she passed some degree of test for a moment later Margerie said, 'In that case permission is granted. I expect you back by supper.' Smiling, she lifted the garment she was embroidering and made another stitch. Peering over her embroidery she added, 'Otherwise I shall send Lord Edward's army to find you. Be sure to return by the seventh hour.'

The thought of Lord Edward's knights searching for her through the streets of Acre was enough to make Olwen determined they would not be late returning to the fortress.

Olwen was easily distracted by ships flying pennants bearing crosses and others with foreign banners bobbing about in the harbour. She forgot how she had suffered sea sickness on the journey to Acre. The fierce summer heat had not arrived and it was a beautiful morning, the sky the colour of wild thyme. The sea stretching far into the distance was crested with white waves. Water closer to the piers glittered in the sunlight and as they explored the harbour she watched traders unloading goods; carts noisily rattling over pavements towards the town's piazzas; dock workers shouting out in a host of varying languages; gulls squawking as they soared overhead seeking titbits from fishermen's nets piled up by the water's edge. Battles for God's Kingdom felt far away. Nothing could threaten Acre's peace whilst Arabs, Christians, and Jews worked side by side unloading silks, spices and grain from trading vessels.

Guillaume remarked, 'Yes, you are thinking of how they all work together. There are two mosques in Acre, one inside the city walls and one without. It is as it should be.'

'I am not sure Lord Edward would agree.'

'Nonetheless, Acre is a city of many peoples. God cares for them all.'

'And I hope *they* all care for God's word,' she said.

He touched her hand and she felt a shiver. 'They do as they perceive it. And hopefully, one day, peace between nations will be,' he said in a gentle voice, removing his hand. 'I have helped heal soldiers wounded in battle. I've heard of many atrocities following sieges and all because one group or another thinks their right to this country is greater than another's claim. In truth, Olwen, some leaders simply profit from war whilst others suffer. This cannot be God's will.' Glancing up she noted tears in his eyes and bowed her head.

She pondered his words as they walked on. He was right. So many wasted lives because they all sought God's Kingdom on earth.

The air felt as if it was swallowing her up as the morning grew hotter and hotter. When the Sext bells rang midday, Guillaume diverted her into the shade of a Church Nave. The cool was welcome. As they listened to the choir sing Ave Marias, he whispered, 'This is a Templar Church. Look, their monks wear Benedictine robes. There are secret Templar tunnels under the streets leading to their sea fortress.' He drew a breath and further lowered his voice. She could hardly hear him now. 'There's been competition between our orders. Now, faced with danger from Baibars, we are at peace with each other.'

'Why? You are both Christian.'

'Christians fight amongst each other until they are united in common cause.'

She thought of the war that had torn England apart and nodded agreement. 'Sadly, 'tis true.'

They exited amongst bands of pilgrims carrying bundles and crosses. Multitudes now inhabited the dusty hot streets. She smelled flowery perfumes, sweat and spices.

'It'll be impossible to find that merchant,' she said as they were pushed together. 'The City is packed with merchants and knights and pilgrims. It's too busy.'

He grasped her hand. 'Let us get to the Venetian piazza. It's not far. They should have ginger roots and I need alum for dyes. Stay close. I don't want to answer to Lady Eleanor or her dragon, Margerie, if I return without you.' He gripped her hand tighter and she felt colour rise into her face. He hissed into her ear, 'You could be kidnapped by a Venetian slave trader and sold to the Mamluks.' He

141

laughed, flashing his even white teeth. 'You would make a feisty slave.'

She laughed too. Guillaume was good company. She did not want the day to be over.

At length they discovered the shady arcades leading to the Venetian piazza. She forgot about the merchant. She forgot the strange emissary as she filled her basket with medicines, herbs and spices including ginger and saffron. The piazza was charged with thrilling sounds and exotic scents.

Shadows were lengthening when they exited the piazza. They must find a cart to take them back to the gates of the Hospitallers' palace. As they moved out of the market crowds they found themselves in a narrow street leading towards the palace. Spotting a litter near the end of the street they hurried forward hoping it was available.

A few heartbeats later Guillaume stopped short. He drew her into an ally stinking of offal. She covered her mouth with her veil. 'What are you doing?' she said, gasping for air. He grasped her arm and directed her attention along the street to the waiting litter.

'Look, the emissary. That litter is not for hire. See, look, they are putting gifts into it. This must be the merchant's house.'

She watched as servants dressed in Eastern style loaded caskets through the curtains. The man now climbing inside was just as Guillaume described. He wore a plain blue tunic, blue silk cloth wound about his head and matching loose trousers gathered into his boots.

'He may be what he claims to be.'

'Lord Edward will be with his earls. They'll protect him from any danger but I wonder what is in the caskets?' she said.

'Sweetmeats perhaps. Maybe perfume and jewelled ornaments of gold and silver.'

'The caskets looked valuable whatever lies therein.'

Two servants took up positions behind the emissary and the men bearing the litter began to walk slowly along the street towards the palace.

142

He shrugged. 'Unless we find another litter to take us, we must walk too, like his servants,' he said. 'Are you thirsty? Let us find a stall with pomegranate juice first.'

She nodded her enthusiasm.

'There was no sign of the Venetian,' she said as they sipped juice and ate spiced cakes back in the market, sitting on a fountain wall.

'Maybe he was within the house. I do find it odd that an emissary from Baibars lodges at a merchant house.' Guillaume frowned. 'Baibars is truly deceitful. Last year he sent a note purportedly from the Hospitallers' master in Tripoli to de Chevalier in Krak, telling him to surrender the castle to the Mamluks. The Hospitallers in Krak surrendered as ordered. The note was a forgery. This is the deceit we deal with here.'

'Lord Edward will not sign the peace treaty if Baibars is not to be trusted,' she said, anxious at the dark turn in their conversation. 'You know, I think we should be on our way. I feel uneasy now.'

Fortune favoured them. A cart stopped to unload melons. Guillaume spoke with the driver in Italian and offered him a coin. The trader agreed to take them back to the fortress once he had finished unloading. Guillaume hurried him along by helping.

They tried to enter the palace guest building. Guards stopped and questioned them as to where they had been. No one would tell them what was amiss. There had been trouble. A Hospitaller monk, one she knew to be a surgeon, descended the stairway from the upper floor, his dark robe flowing behind him, his face filled with horror.

'Guillaume, where have you been? Never mind. There's been an attack on Lord Edward. Come at once.' The surgeon gave no explanation.

Guillaume thrust the basket into Olwen's hands and sped up a stairway leading to the apartments inhabited by the prince and princess. She hurried after him.

Mildred, one of Eleanor's junior attendants, flew along the corridor towards her as she carried on up to the women's quarters. Her thoughts raced, churning over as if in a fast boiling cauldron. It was the emissary. It had to be. They should never have stopped for pomegranate juice.

'You must attend Lady Eleanor at once.'

'What has happened?'

'It's Lord Edward. He's been attacked,' Mildred cried. 'He killed his attacker but he was stabbed first.'

'Holy St Raphael, God protect him.' Olwen dropped her basket and crossed herself. She immediately thought again of the emissary who must have reached the palace several hours before. Picking up her basket she gave it to the maid and requested she take it to her chamber. She mounted the stairway. There was to-ing and fro-ing of many personages, most of them Edward's knights. She was known by them and none stopped her.

On entering the King's solar, she stuffed her fist into her mouth to prevent the shriek that wanted to escape. King Edward was lying in a faint on a cushioned bench with a knight cradling his arm. His face was drained of colour. On the floor lay the emissary with blood pooling around him. He had been run through with a sword and was dying. It was the man they had seen earlier that afternoon. Three caskets sat on a low table below the window. Her shocked eyes scanned the tiled floor, at blood splattered on the carpets, the tiles, the silken drapes that hung from the ceiling. Otto de Grandison was rinsing Lord Edward's mouth with water from a goblet. Lord Edward began spitting into a basin. The knight knelt and sucked at Lord Edward's arm. The Prince was pale, near to oblivion again, but even so, he pointed a shaking hand towards the emissary.

'Get the poisoner out of here. Send his head to Damascus. Baibars is responsible. Baibars sent him here,' he was croaking. 'I should never have trusted his emissary.'

Lady Eleanor sat weeping hysterically on a stool by Lord Edward's side, comforted by Lady Margerie.

Olwen was frozen as if trapped inside a winter frost. Lady Margerie glanced up and noticing her said, 'Thank heaven you've returned. We'll escort Lady Eleanor to the women's rooms now. She can do no good here.' She turned to Eleanor. 'Hush, my lady.' She looked back at Olwen. 'Go and make her a soothing potion.' As way of explanation, though Olwen needed none, she added, 'Lord Edward was stabbed. His arm. The weapon was poisoned. It is for the apothecaries to save him now.'

'The assassin . . .?'

'Lord Edward ran him through with the poisoned dagger.'

'I cannot leave my lord,' Lady Eleanor said through her tears, 'and I can't stop crying.'

John de Vescy stepped forward. 'Better, my lady, you should shed tears than all the English land should weep for loss of our prince. Please take some rest, Lady Eleanor. The apothecaries must do their best for Lord Edward now.'

He nodded at Otto who had risen from sucking the wound on Lord Edward's arm. Otto spat into a bowl. John de Vescy acknowledged Guillaume who was entering the chamber with the surgeon. 'Hurry,' was all he said.

Guillaume carried his surgeon's satchel. She recognised it, knowing it contained sharp instruments and salves.

John de Vescy said to Eleanor in a gentle voice. 'Otto has sucked away the poison. The doctors will do their best now. They must cut away flesh if the poison is to be completely purged. Come away, my lady, the girl will bring you a sleeping draught.'

Eleanor rose to her feet. For a moment her face was thunderous. Olwen thought she was about to burst into a temper as her face had darkened and she looked about to attack John de Vescy for telling her to rest. However she did not pull away as John led her through a curtained archway linking hers and Edward's rooms. Lady Margerie caught Olwen's arm in a firm grip. 'Do not discuss this with any of the servants. Master Guillaume is the best apothecary of the pack of them. Thank God he returned in time to help. Go and make our lady a potion to calm her.'

'Yes, my lady,' Olwen replied.

The curtains seemed to float and the whole incident felt as unreal as a dream. Guillaume's eyes sought her own. His held sorrow and regret. If only Guillaume had spoken of his fears for Lord Edward's safety earlier. He must speak out so the Venetian merchant was brought into the palace and questioned.

Olwen tossed restlessly that night, feeling guilt that she had not confided their suspicions to Lady Eleanor. The following morning, as she left the chapel with her head bowed in prayer, a page stepped into her path and handed her a note. She secreted it in her sleeve and waited until she returned to the still room before reading it. Guillaume wrote, *The surgeon has cut away blackened flesh from Lord Edward's arm. Meet me in the garden after Vespers.*

All day rumours circulated amongst the women in Lady Eleanor's apartments. Lord Edward might lose his arm if it did not heal well. There was another rumour that Lord Edward had already lost his arm. It was dismissed as untrue. Someone announced the emissary's head had been sent to Baibars in Damascus. Finally, news invaded the Queen's rooms that an Italian merchant was being questioned. Olwen could only guess this was the outcome of the information given to Lord Edward's earls by Guillaume and felt as if an enormous weight had been removed from her conscience.

The long anxious day was punctuated by church bells ringing the hours. She attended Sext and Vespers both, adding her prayers for Lord Edward's recovery to those of others. She made tonics and possets for Lady Eleanor but could not eat a morsel all day. She raged and snapped at them all and she was so wrought with anxiety, hunger left her. She physically pushed away a maid who carried a plate of meats to her.

Olwen waited for an hour pacing in the cool of the garden. She had brought Eleanor's dog with her, saying the creature needed exercise. Lady Margerie agreed without hesitation. Lady Eleanor was too distraught to walk today. Lady Eleanor, Olwen understood, had returned to and remained by Lord Edward's bedside.

'She is angry now but she would be pleased to know her dog has been released into the air for an hour or two,' Lady Margerie said, sadness invading her voice. 'Return by dusk and make another potion to help my lady sleep.'

Olwen nodded. 'I shall be only a few hours.'

She walked along paved paths leading the animal on a plaited cord attached to his jewelled collar. Guillaume was late. He must be occupied with the surgeon and doctors who were trying to save the prince's life. She had observed scribes led by William of Valence, Master Robert, and Prince Edmund hurrying along the corridor into Lord Edward's chamber. All was not well.

Olwen allowed the dog off his leash. The small hound bounded around the garden chasing butterflies until he grew too hot and began lapping water from the pool, splashing her as he drank. Satiated, the dog flopped down beside her.

Every day knights rode horses around the adjacent courtyard and up the broad shallow steps that led up to an arched second storey above the knights' halls. There they practised archery and sword play close to the garden wall. Even now, she could hear the clanging of weapons beyond the wall and shouts as they outmanoeuvred an opponent. At last, Guillaume appeared through an archway into the gardens.

He sank down on the rim of the pond and placed a finger on his lip. 'You must not tell anyone.' He drew a long breath. She instinctively placed a hand over his. 'Lord Edward is writing his will in case he does not survive.'

'He will survive, won't he?' She kept her hand on Guillaume's as the little hound took himself off to stalk salamanders. She felt even more guilt for her previous silence.

'I hope so, but the poison was deadly,' Guillaume said quietly. 'The master surgeon examined the dagger carefully. It was fortunate that Lord Otto sucked out most of the poison. And also fortunate he is not dead. The surgeon has cut away blackened skin on the prince's arm. We have used a salve of angelica and the wound must be treated daily. Lady Eleanor refuses to allow him to be bled. She insists it will weaken Lord Edward further.'

'Did you tell them your suspicions?'

'Yes, of course, and the Venetian merchant has been brought into the citadel already. He won't live long enough to cause more mischief. Earl John says he must be involved with a sect called the Assassins.'

'Who are they?'

'Religious leaders, who murder their enemies by stealth.'

'And King Edward is their enemy?'

'All Crusaders fear them. The Assassins are trained killers. They murder for religious purposes. Baibars will have employed them.'

'Why did a merchant get involved with them?'

'Lord Edward refused to sign Baibars' peace treaty. I suspect the Venetians and Baibars were secretly united.'

'Will Lord Edward sign the peace treaty now, do you think? Will we be returning to England?' She felt tears fill her eyes. While she longed for England again, she could not bear to be parted from Guillaume.

'I know not. What will be must be. Acre cannot sustain a siege, and if there is not peace, a siege could be the outcome. Slavery and massacres would follow. No one wants that. Merchants need trade. Pilgrims must travel the roads in safety. It's what is important now – that and saving Lord Edward's life. I gave him a potion to break his fever and it seems to have worked.'

'Lady Eleanor and Lord Edmund may insist on peace,' she said. 'I'm relieved the merchant was apprehended.' She shook her head. 'Pity it was not sooner.'

'There was no proof of anything before.' He managed a smile. 'The good news is that I am to be appointed as Lord Edward's personal apothecary because of the salves I made to cover the wound. And the potion that has broken his fever. Earl William said if Lord Edward did not keep me with him, he would take me on himself.'

Her heart sang. 'What a compliment, but I still wish we had rushed back. We might have prevented it.' She thought for a heartbeat. 'Does that mean you could come with us if we leave?'

He shrugged. 'I am unsure.' He rose. 'I must return to Lord Edward. We can talk again.'

'Yes, I can walk the little hound again.'

He looked down at the dog which was now chasing a leaf about. 'What's his name?'

'This one is Saturn.'

'A good name for a hound. Don't feel guilty, Olwen. We could not have prevented this.'

She was not entirely convinced and determined to pray hard for forgiveness. They could have acted.

Guillaume rose, touched her hand and departed. She called Saturn to her. As dusk enveloped the garden, she hurried away, to make yet another sleeping potion for Lady Eleanor.

Chapter Thirteen

Eleanor
Autumn 1272

Otto de Grandison drew himself up to his full height. He was a tall man with dark eyes and hair, and cheekbones any stonemason would enjoy chiselling. Eleanor trusted Otto and knew him to be devoted to her service. Today, they were joined in concern for Edward. 'My lady, the Venetian merchant claims to know nothing of the plot. He denies the emissary belonged to the Assassins. He is an important merchant and has been released, otherwise we anger the Venetians. We cannot try him without proof. He thought the assassin to be an emissary also.'

'And Baibars?' Eleanor said.

'He claimed ignorance, insisting the attacker was not one of his emissaries. The Sultan has sent gifts to Edward.' Otto raised his eyebrows. 'They have been returned to Damascus.'

'Good. I would have had that Venetian's head.'

'Not wise, Eleanor.'

'So we have definitely agreed to the peace?'

'Yes, the Mongols returned to Persia. Peace was agreed with Baibars. The Mongols have abandoned any possible alliance with us.'

'Maybe it is best. Perhaps God means us to save Outremer another time.' Today she felt calmer. She put her hand on his sleeve. 'I must go to Edward. Thank you, Otto. You are a dear friend to us both.' He bent down and they clasped hands. She noted the care, more than that, on his countenance: the love. The handsome Lord Otto was indeed an honourable, loyal knight.

★

Peace was agreed and signed. As they prepared to depart Acre, Eleanor did not fail to observe pleasure on Olwen's countenance when the young apothecary was installed as part of Edward's household. Guillaume's father was pleased by his son's elevation to the royal court of England and came to the fortress to thank the Hospitallers for releasing his son. He sent oranges from his orchards as a gift to Lady Eleanor and her ladies. Kneeling before Eleanor, he said,

'Dear Lady, thank you. I have other sons, and Guillaume has to make his own way in the world. May he serve you well.'

For a moment, Eleanor wondered what would happen if Acre should fall to Baibars.

As if reading her thought the French knight said, 'We have trade and are more use to Baibars alive and with connections. I think we'll survive, my lady.'

That summer, one by one, the English nobles and their armies set sail from Acre until by October only Edward and his household remained.

Edward announced, 'I am well enough to leave too. Acre will continue to stand without us, with the truce. We, at least, achieved more than the French here this time.'

'We'll start packing,' Eleanor said with firmness before he changed his mind.

She lost no time organising the sea journey to Sicily. They would be Charles of Anjou's guests. This time would allow Edward's further convalescence before continuing through Italy to France and Gascony then home to England.

Eleanor supervised the packing of silks, the dismantling of furniture, with a lighter heart than she had felt in months. In Sicily they could hunt every day. They would not suffer dust blowing from the desert or the chill, damp winter weather. They would enjoy the safety of a palace far away from the dangers they had faced in a city threatened with siege. Now the English court had broken up, they were left with only their servants, physicians, loyal Otto, and their personal knights and swordsmen to protect them. The royal apartments grew quieter; the columned halls, emptied of horses and their riders, fell silent; the vast courtyard was returned to Hospitaller monks and pilgrims.

On a sunny late October morning, Eleanor stood on the deck of the *Leopard* as Acre retreated into the distance. The ship crested the waves towards Sicily. It was a poignant goodbye to God's Kingdom because she had come to love the beautiful sea port, the bells ringing from Acre's churches, voices speaking various tongues, and the delivery of exciting goods for her perusal – books of song and poetry, ebony caskets, gleaming jewels, finely woven carpets, crisp cottons and delicate silks from as far away as India, spices, and dried herbs. They possessed coffers filled with luxury items including her collection of reliquaries containing saints' fingernails, vials of blood, and scraps of linen and even hair. If these reached England safely, they would always remind her of Christ's lands, his Kingdom of Heaven on earth and their Crusade.

Edward joined her on the deck and her women discreetly moved away. For a few moments he stared over the water. At last he said, 'There will be other Crusades.' She thought to herself, *not for us, Edward, though perhaps for others. You did what you could for God's Kingdom when other kings abandoned us.* Had Eleanor of Aquitaine, their mutual great-grandmother, known sorrow mingled with joy on leaving this strange kingdom? Despite exotic plants, luscious fruits, and chambers and halls that often took her breath away; the feasts with entertainments and dishes delicately flavoured with spices; games of chess that went on for days, and their company, whom she enjoyed challenging with her intellect, *this* Eleanor looked forward to Sicily.

They had received news that King Henry was unwell a few days before sailing from Acre. Eleanor felt a deep sadness, remembering how they had comforted each other as prisoners of Montfort during the Civil War, how together they endured penury. Henry had helped her then as best he could. He might survive until they returned. Queen Ailenor would be fussing over the children they

152

placed in her care after Earl Richard's death. Eleanor watched a fat gull swoop for a fish, snatch it up and soar high again into the sky. Queen Ailenor would not allow Henry to die.

A quiet voice was speaking to Edward. She recognised it to belong to Master Guillaume. She turned around as the apothecary said, 'Lord Edward. I am sorry to disturb you. It is time for your medicine.'

Edward placed a hand on her arm. 'Eleanor we'll go below.' He smiled at Guillaume. 'For certes, I must grow strong again.'

'Indeed, you shall, my lord,' she said.

They remained for Christmas in Sicily. The year turned into another. On the day following Epiphany, Eleanor returned from a morning's hunting to find Edward alone in their chamber, his head in his hands. A letter spilling seals attached to plaited ribbons lay on top of a pile of correspondence. She lifted it and stared at it. Earl Gilbert of Gloucester and others were proclaiming loyalty to Edward. Her husband was now King of England. She held it to her breast. She was Queen of England. Elation seized her. No longer was Ailenor the most important woman at court. She then, and only then, considered Henry's death. She moved her lips in a silent prayer for King Henry's soul. Her hand moved to rest on Edward's bent shoulder. He was sobbing, clearly unaware of her standing beside him.

'Edward,' she said, her voice gentle. 'Look at me.'

'My father has died, Eleanor. I loved him,' Edward managed to say. 'Papa was a good man and a loving father.' He was mumbling into his hands. 'Beatrice and Margaret will be broken-hearted. Mama will be inconsolable.'

She put the letter down and prised his hands from his eyes as if he was a child, forcing him to look up at her. She passed him a napkin on which to blow his nose. When he finished she held his great head against her breast and said into his sheaf of hair, bleached the colour of pale wheat by the sun, 'Edward, your father was very old and tired. He was king for most of his years. Now *you* are the King of England and we must return without delay.'

Edward looked up at her though tear-filled eyes. 'It's January. Passes through the mountains are treacherous. The messengers have advised that we wait until spring.' He pointed to other letters with important seals scattered across the table. 'Those are from barons on the council. There are several letters from my mother and one from Edmund. My father died in November. His body has already been placed beside St Edward's tomb in Westminster Abbey. England's earls have sworn loyalty to me. They insist I am King from the very day of my father's death. Our crowning will occur when we return.' He managed a smile through his tears. 'You are already Queen of England.'

'Our children. Does Ailenor speak of them?'

'Both are well and in her care. She says they are a comfort to her. We should send Joan to her.'

'No, I want to keep Joan with us.' Eleanor felt relieved at this news. Taking his hand, she said, 'What must we do?'

'We shall keep a vigil this night for Papa's soul. The whole court will pray for my father.'

Eleanor hurried to the women's quarters. Her women already knew of King Henry's death and were weeping. She determined to be a strong queen and not cry, even though she felt great sadness for the passing of the artistic, endearing and complicated man who was Edward's father. That evening, she led her ladies into the chapel where they knelt to pray for the safe passage of King Henry's soul into Heaven. Charles of Anjou arranged three days of official mourning for the dead King of England. Once the three days of mourning passed, he provided a lavish feast to celebrate Edward's and Eleanor's new roles as King and Queen.

As the void, plates of fruit and cheeses, was served up first, Edward leaned towards his cousin. 'You can do something else for me, Charles.'

The King of Sicily put down the knife with which he had begun to peel an orange. Raising a bushy grey eyebrow, he said, 'Anything, Edward, anything.'

Edward's face darkened. 'My father's soul will rest more easily if

154

you bring Guy and Simon de Montfort to justice for the murder of my uncle's son, Henry of Almain.'

Charles of Anjou had a shifty look about him. Shaking his long white curls he nodded. 'Dreadful deed. Of course the Montfort brothers must pay the ultimate price for barbarity but . . .' Charles's pale blue eyes swam with crocodile tears, 'they are held in high esteem in Italy and are excellent fighters. One is in His Holiness's employ. I feel your pain, King Edward, I truly do. I will send spies to discover their hiding places. They won't escape justice.'

Biting into a peach, Eleanor averted her look of fury. She did not believe Charles's promises. The sooner they left Sicily, the better for them all.

They hesitated for two more months. After all, Sicily had its comforts.

On the fifteenth day of March a south-westerly wind gusted, as their ships drew closer to the coast of Italy, and in breaths and snatches the notes of church bells drifted over the city walls towards the *Leopard*. They recovered from the crossing in Charles's palace in Salerno.

Master Guillaume begged leave to study medicine in the University medical school before joining them in England.

'Sire, it has long been my dream. I'll return to your court a doctor as well as an apothecary.'

Edward consulted with Eleanor.

'You are well enough now. Let him.'

She noted how Olwen seemed despondent. As she passed through the bower she overheard Lady Margerie reassuring the girl that Guillaume would return to them one day.

'One day, Lady Margerie, could be never,' she heard Olwen retort.

'You have little faith, Olwen. Besides, there are others.'

'There will never be others.'

Eleanor stopped by the arras to see Olwen rudely turn away and open the book of herbs she would consult, her head bowed into it as if it alone could cure the girl of heartsickness.

Eleanor asked Margerie quietly why Olwen was so upset.

'I hope she can concoct a potion to heal her aching heart,' Margerie whispered into Eleanor's ear. 'She's in love with the apothecary.'

'Time and a good husband will be that particular healer,' Eleanor snapped. 'And one day I'll find her one.'

Eleanor and Edward were feted in every Italian village they passed through, as they followed the route taken two years previously by King Louis's funeral procession, slowly moving mile by leisurely mile towards the high mountains and France.

They were welcomed in the Episcopal palace at Reggio on 20 May. The Pope presented Lord Edward with a golden rose in acknowledgement of his work in Christ's Land. She felt proud of Edward, who had felt himself a failure because he had not reached Jerusalem, nor had he reconquered the Outremer.

'Edward, the Pope appreciates your trying, that you protected Acre, keeping the sea port open for trade.'

'Small consolation,' he grumbled, but even so appeared pleased with the golden rose.

'Edward, I believe I am with child again.' That would cheer him. Her second Joan was always with her nurses. Eleanor found her a demanding if a very active and bright two-year-old.

He smiled a broad smile. It was more like a huge grin. He kissed her and swung her around. 'That is a great consolation. It demands celebration.'

'Not yet, my love,' she said. 'I must be sure this child is safely birthed first.' She could not bear another disappointment.

To Eleanor's delight their travelling court was also greeted enthusiastically in Milan, where citizens presented them with a dozen chargers caparisoned with scarlet trappings.

'I can't think of a better present,' Eleanor said, thrilled with the horses' ability to step high and move fast.

Everywhere they paused, King Edward was feted as a great Crusader prince and praised as a hero. They continued through mountain passes topped with snowfall until they reached the pass at Mont

Cenis where a party of English nobles and Philip, Count of Savoy joined them. They travelled on together into Savoy where Edward and Eleanor received homage in Vienne for lands inherited by the English crown a hundred years earlier.

'Nearly home,' she whispered into Edward's ear after receipt of the homage.

'Paris first and Gascony too,' Edward replied with a frown. 'We may not reach England for some time yet.'

'The children?'

'My mother has their care. She understands children.'

Eleanor's brow wrinkled. No woman could compete with Edward's mother. As for Eleanor, she really had no maternal feeling for small children at all.

After a brief pause in Paris, they rode for Gascony where Aquitaine was troubled by civil strife. They simply could not sail for England. Pedro of Aragon visited them while they remained in southern Gascony. They made a match for their daughter Eleanora with Pedro's eldest son. He was a powerful king and this was a good alliance. 'Daughters are special,' Edward said looking fondly from a castle window at Joan who was chasing about the autumnal garden with her nurse. 'They help us forge alliances.'

'Don't send them into marriages too young,' Eleanor retorted.

'I am pleased you came to me young,' he retorted with a grin.

Whilst Edward spent October and November bringing Southern Gascony to heel, Eleanor took up residence in Bayonne. On the twenty-fourth day of November she gave birth to a boy whom they called Alphonso for her brother, the King of Castile.

'Another son,' Edward said. 'Alphonso. I like it well.'

She smiled for days after that. Her dearest brother was having problems in his kingdom of Castile. Now she called on him to act as one of Alphonso's godparents. He wrote back how he felt honoured and crossed the mountain passes to visit them.

After Eleanor was churched, they rode through Gascony to Bordeaux. They settled into the Palace of Shadows with long dark

157

evenings shared with their small court. They played many games of chess and hunted. One day Edward said, bursting into her chamber, 'I have received a letter from the King of Navarre. It's welcome news. Another alliance.' His mouth widened into a broad smile.

'How came it about?' Eleanor stretched her toes towards the fire. A dry log spat sparks and she quickly edged her slippered feet out of the way.

'Good news for Gascony. The King of Navarre wants his daughter to marry Henry. This betrothal means we secure peace on our Gascon borders. And, thankfully, I have dealt with Gaston de Bearn yet again, hopefully once and for all. With allies in Navarre and Aragon as well as Castile, peace will endure. This princess will secure our ambitions.'

She lifted her cup of wine to her lips and drank deeply. Her forehead wrinkled into a frown. 'The Aragonese could make trouble for Gascony. Navarre could also.' The frown soon changed into a smile. 'Even so, my love, it bodes well to agree these future weddings.' She lifted her eyebrows in a questioning manner. 'Ah, you have other news.' She nodded at a second letter he held.

'The Crusade near crippled us. The Pope has granted us a subsidy from the Church, another twenty-two thousand marks.'

'He will expect you to lead another Crusade.'

Edward shook his head. 'I saved Acre. It is enough. A long delay. My father was excellent at just that tactic – delaying a Crusade.' He touched his long nose and smiled in a knowing way.

Eleanor sighed. When would she ever feel secure? 'Don't let us dwell on that now,' she said quickly. 'We'll celebrate Christmas in our Palace of Shadows and that is all I can think of – except – what do you think of visiting my mother in Ponthieu? I'm her heiress. We *should* visit Ponthieu. I haven't seen my mother for decades.' She crossed her arms across her breasts.

By the twinkle in his right eye and the lazy droop in the left one, she knew he would agree. He said, 'She'll enjoy seeing her grandchildren, especially her namesake. Naming Joan was your idea, my love. It was for your mother you called our daughter Joan, was it not?'

'I was thinking of our other little Joan who died and Joanna of Pembroke too.'

Edward took her hands, raised them to his lips, kissed them and said, 'You shall soon enough see Lady Joanna.' He kissed her hands again. 'So, we shall spend a month or two with your mother before we sail for England and for now we'll enjoy this Christmastide.'

Hearing horses entering the courtyard below, Eleanor pulled away from him and crossed to the window. She spun around, feeling her eyes widening in astonishment. 'Edward, we have visitors. Two pennants – the Mortimers and, I don't believe it – Earl Gilbert! We have company for Christmas.'

Edward joined her by the window. They watched as sumpter horses drew into the courtyard behind the pennants. Roger Mortimer helped his wife Maud from her palfrey. The sprightly Maud was more than fifty years old yet she still moved with energy and grace. Eleanor turned to Edward. 'I hope I emulate Maud when I'm past fifty years.' That was, if she did not die first in childbed. She shuddered at the thought and whispered, 'St Katherine, protect me.'

Edward, laughing, said, 'There's no one like Lady Maud. No woman alive, not even my mother. She's courageous. Roger adores her.' He clapped his hands. 'She's very welcome. What a surprise. Gilbert too and with a retinue.'

'What is *he* doing here, I wonder?'

Edward looked in disbelief at her vehemence. 'I thought you were over your dislike of Earl Gilbert.'

She shook her head. 'He's just as duplicitous as ever. He took vows to crusade and never realised them.'

'He guarded my kingdom.'

'*Our* kingdom.'

'Yes, Eleanor, our kingdom.' He put an arm affectionately around her shoulder and drew her closer. He said quietly, 'Doubtless they have both come from the Council to plan our coronation. Gilbert will be directing it, or at very least organising the organisers.'

'Finger in many bakers' pies, as ever,' she said warily. She would not argue over Gilbert now but instead choose her battle and win this renewed war. 'I had better *organise* chambers for them. As well we have barracks in the courtyards for their retinues.'

Edward peered down again at the busy yard. 'Not a great number of retainers. Indeed, lucky *they* won't be sleeping in a hay barn, though I imagine Maud would not bat an eyelid if they had to.' He laughed and rubbed his hands together gleefully. She frowned at him. 'This is going to be a merry Christmastide with Maud and Gilbert in the same company,' he said with a loud guffaw.

It was true. Maud would take no nonsense from Gilbert de Clare who had long been her neighbour in the Welsh Marches. Thank goodness, she mused, we don't have Alix. Odd that since they are legally separated Gilbert does not seek remarriage. Perhaps the Pope would refuse permission whilst Alix lives. Perhaps he enjoys the freedom to lay his head wherever he wishes to.

Aloud she said, determined not to prod that sore either, 'I'll order Joan de Valle and Margerie de Haustede to prepare chambers for them all. Edward, you had best greet our surprise guests.' The evening bells for Vespers began to chime. 'They are just in time for supper.'

With those words, Eleanor left his side and hurried up the staircase to the solar above calling for Margerie. 'We have visitors from England,' she said with excitement in her voice. 'Our guests can have the Raven Tower. Margerie, it's only a matter of setting and lighting fires there, fresh linen for beds and water for bath tubs and basins.'

Within a half hour, Margerie had everything under way and a bevy of servants hurried to do her bidding.

Other Christmastide guests arrived on the following day, Beatrice and John sailed down the coast from Brittany. They were followed within the week by Edmund and Aveline, his wife, who was only fourteen years old.

'Do they share a chamber, do you think? She is so young.'

160

Eleanor whispered to Edward as they broke their fast on Christmas Eve along with their other guests. Maud heard her words. That woman had acute hearing.

'And so were you, by all accounts, Eleanor,' Maud said and lowered her voice, 'Can't you simply place them in adjacent chambers?'

'Yes, I can.'

Maud nodded her approval. 'Her maid can share her bed.'

Unlike Maud, Aveline appeared exhausted after the sea journey. She withdrew to her chamber without saying a word other than a repeated 'thank you'. Eleanor sent her water for a hot bath, and Olwen to ensure she had restful herbs to place in her bath.

'We shall remain here with you some time, Edward,' Edmund said after Aveline had been swept away by Margerie and her own maid, who looked as green about the gills as her mistress.

'You will be very welcome to stay, brother. Your wife can't make that sea crossing again anytime soon.' They withdrew to a window alcove together to discuss the Pope's Crusade grant. Eleanor overheard Edmund saying, 'Some of that money is due to me, Edward. I had enormous expenses. I still am in debt.'

The crown was impoverished. Edmund would have to wait. She would insist on it.

It was their first Christmas as Queen and King. They celebrated Christ's birth with prayers followed by a gathering of their friends and retainers in the great hall for the Christmas feast.

'If only the children were here and my mother too.'

'Next year,' Eleanor said quietly, glad Ailenor was not with them. 'God willing.'

Later the musicians struck up a lively tune, and led by Eleanor and Edward, couples moved into the large space in the hall's centre.

Edward remarked, 'Edmund should never have brought Aveline with him. She's too fragile.'

'Maud has taken her under her wing but I don't like the way Gilbert looks at her. He's been making eyes at Olwen too.' Eleanor wrinkled her nose as if there was a bad smell near her.

'I don't think your herbalist has eyes for any other than the apothecary we left behind in Salerno.'

'I wonder when he will return to us.'

'I've paid Master Guillaume's fees and for his raiment as well as a horse. He'll be well trained by the time he returns.'

'By which time he'll have forgotten my herbalist.'

Edward's eyes followed the dancers as they circled and created arches and the music grew faster. 'By the saints, you are right,' he said with disbelief. 'Gilbert is wooing your herbalist. He's leading her in the dance. They have reached the arch.'

'And since he is far above her in status, no good will come of it so I had best find her a husband before Gilbert ruins her reputation.'

Eleanor cornered Gilbert behind a pillar but Saturn chose that moment to follow her, sniffing around his mistress's damask skirts. Recognising Gilbert as a lover of dogs, he scampered from Eleanor and jumped around Gilbert's legs.

Gilbert leaned down and patted his animal friend. 'The dog deserves a Crusader Cross embroidered on his coat.'

She drew herself up to her full height knowing she looked every inch a queen. 'More deserving of that than yourself, Earl Gilbert. You never fulfilled your oath.'

He looked nonplussed as he patted the dog's head. 'I had more pressing duties serving on King Henry's Council.' He held her hazel eyes with his own pale blue ones which looked bemused. It was as if they were back in that courtyard at Windsor ten years earlier. 'And now on King Edward's Council, helping Master Burnell organise a coronation. Burnell only stayed a few months in Acre, as I recollect, before *he* returned to England.'

'You were *never* loyal to Henry, Master Burnell was,' she accused.

Fox-like eyebrows shot up. 'I *am* loyal to Edward, as he knows well. And Edward will be a great king.' He took a long drink from his goblet. 'He will be less influenced by his queen, I'll warrant.' His smile was challenging.

Eleanor ignored the rise and swallowed her anger. She noticed his eyes stray towards Olwen who was seated with one of Eleanor's ladies.

'Both comely, don't you think?' Gilbert remarked.

'I have a marriage in mind for my herbalist. See you do not ruin her chances. If I discover you have, you will lose all favour.'

'*All*, my lady?'

'All.' She turned on her heel and wound her way around the dancers to Lady Margerie. 'See that Gilbert de Clare does not approach my herbalist again. In fact, keep watch over Olwen and an eye on Aveline too.'

Margerie looked over at Gilbert with distaste. She was immediately complicit. 'Olwen shall share the demoiselles' chamber for the rest of Christmas. There'll be guards on the stairways.

'Give Olwen's chamber to two of Aveline's maidservants.'

When Eleanor turned her attention to the dancers again, Gilbert was nowhere to be seen. Doubtless he had slid off like a fox to seek out the kitchen maids or, with luck, the privy.

After Epiphany, guests prepared to depart. Decisions were made as to when their coronation would occur. Edward suggested they return to England in August. 'Meanwhile,' he said to Roger Mortimer, 'I shall continue taking homage in Gascony.' He leaned across the table and took Eleanor's hand. 'We'll visit Jeanne of Ponthieu before our return. Eleanor is her heir.'

'So be it, Sire,' said Roger.

'Aye,' agreed Gilbert. 'God be with you both, your Grace.' He had not, to Eleanor's relief, looked at her ladies since Christmas night. He played the charming courtier, was witty, and Edward clearly enjoyed his company. She bested Gilbert at chess though, and he constantly complained about that, saying he would look forward to snapping up her queen on another occasion, his fox-like smile meaningful. He was like a cat stalking prey. All her dislike came flooding back and she hoped once they were crowned, the Welsh would keep Gilbert too busy protecting his own lands to be at their court.

January was mild and a good season for hunts. Late in the month, when ships sailed easily across the Narrow Sea, Gilbert and the Mortimers prepared to return to England. On the afternoon before Roger and Maud departed, Maud drew Eleanor aside.

'Let us walk in the garden, Eleanor, I need air.'

As they wandered through beech trees devoid of leaves, dripping with the morning's soft drizzle, Maud gave Eleanor a word of warning. 'Eleanor, I wish to speak of Queen Ailenor.'

'Are the children unhappy, Maud?'

'They are content. Having lost King Henry, your two children are a comfort to her.' Maud drew a deep breath. She touched droplets on a spider's web as she took Eleanor's arm. 'You may have to be tolerant towards Queen Ailenor. She won't relinquish her title and I doubt she'll be happy to be called Dowager Queen either. England will, in effect, have two queens.'

Eleanor nodded. 'We have little in common, but Ailenor is a devoted grandmother.' She sighed. 'Life will be much changed for her. Edward adores his mother. I must proceed gently, Maud.'

Maud nodded and squeezed her hand. 'You, dear Eleanor, are going to be a great queen.'

Eleanor squeezed Maud's hand back. 'I mean to support Edward in every way I can.'

Part Three
Eleanor, Queen of England

Chapter Fourteen

Summer
1274

Eleanor and the Dowager Queen, though she still signed her letters as 'Queen Ailenor', bowed cordially to each other in the hall of Leeds Castle. Eleanor had taken pains to dress beautifully in a pale green silk gown edged with golden roses and darker green tendrils. The silk had travelled with her from Acre and had been stitched in Ponthieu by her mother's seamstress. It was light enough for the hot August day and elegant enough to gain her mother-in-law's admiration. Her chestnut hair was caught in an elegant crispinette at the nape of her neck. A veil thin as a dragonfly's wing fluttered about her face. Ailenor smiled her approval and said, 'Eleanor, you look beautiful, a true Queen of England.'

Eleanor could not help remembering, after three and more years away from England and Ailenor, her first meeting with the King and Queen when she had come to England a year after her marriage to Edward. She had arrived feeling forlorn and fragile, without Edward and without clothing the Queen considered suitable for a princess of Castile and a future queen. Henry and Ailenor had provided her with a choice of palfreys to ride and they had paid for a new wardrobe.

After their initial meeting years before, Ailenor had said, 'Dear child, you cannot be seen by Londoners until you are suitably attired. This will not do.' She had looked down her pretty nose at her new daughter. 'We have decided that a stay in Dover Castle will be restful for you and when all is ready, new clothing and understanding of

167

what we expect in an English princess, our friend Reginald of Dover will escort you to Canterbury for St Edward's Day and later to the City where we shall receive you.'

Eleanor was dismissed with a cool smile and did not see her new family again until St Edward's Feast in October. For a whole month in a draughty castle with sour-faced people tending to her needs, she missed Edward with all her heart. There had been a child, a little girl who was stillborn in Gascony, and she was sad the whole time. She missed Seville and the castles of Castile and she longed for Edward. She was only approaching her fourteenth name day when the child was born and when she saw London a year later for the first time it rained and she thought she could never get used to this watery place with houses so close together and disgusting odours of offal and sweating people. As time passed she learned to build up a carapace of reserve and learned how to enjoy pursuits beyond the City walls. The City was nothing like Cordova or Seville. There was no running water, though plenty of marshes around London harbouring biting insects. It was a smelly and uncivilised dirty city.

As years passed, she tolerated Westminster, and came to like Windsor because she could hunt in the park, but most of all she enjoyed the countryside manors and castles far away from unpleasantness and stinking airs. When Edward had joined her by Christmastide that first year they resumed intimacy. He made her happy but she endured more miscarriages, Queen Ailenor's sympathy and offers of advice concerning pregnancy intrusive, until little Katherine was born and taken from her. And Joan who also died, John who died, and Henry and Eleanor who were thriving.

Now *she* was Queen and Ailenor relegated to Dowager. She would live as she wished. No one would look at her with critical eyes. She would purchase more lands, castles and manors and travel between them as often as was possible. In fact she would spend as little time in the Tower and Westminster as was possible. Eleanor smiled as she graciously said, 'Thank you, Ailenor, and here today we have our family too.' For a moment she felt tearful but refused to give into emotion.

Henry, Eleanora, and the two Breton cousins, John and another little Henry, stood at Dowager Queen Ailenor's side. A nurse trailed behind the troop carrying the new addition, the baby Alphonso, who had been sent ahead to England into Ailenor's care from Gascony.

They enjoyed a rare private family dinner that afternoon, an occasion orchestrated by the Dowager. Eleanor felt she did not know the children she left behind four years previously. Five-year-old Eleanora showed signs of great beauty. She had her mother's enormous brown eyes and brown hair tinged with chestnut like Eleanor's own, kept neat by a thin golden band placed on her head.

'Where is Joanna?' the Dowager asked as she arranged her blue gown gracefully within her armed chair. 'She's not unwell, I hope?'

Four pairs of children's huge questioning eyes leaned forward to look up at the adults.

'Eleanor will explain, Mama,' Edward said.

Eleanor moved a vase of pretty pansies aside, accepted a glass of wine, and was watchful as the servitor moved along the table to serve others. 'Not for the children,' she said to the servitor, asserting herself. 'Small beer only.' Another servant advanced with a pottery jug.

She answered Ailenor's question after they were served. 'Joan is very well, thank you. She remains with her grandmamma in Montreuil-sur-Mer.' She decided not to say that it might be some time before they called Joan back to England. Her mother had fallen in love with the little girl, and likewise Joan adored Jeanne, always watching out for her to enter her nursery, which was often. She and Edward loved Joan, but when it was apparent Joan wanted to be with her grandmother Eleanor thought, this time *my* mother has a role to play in our lives. After all, I am now her heir. To ensure Ailenor's goodwill she added, 'Thank you, madam, for your care for our children. They are clearly fond of you.'

169

'And of you, my lady mother,' Eleanora said with studied preco-cious five-year-old diplomacy.

'Well, sweeting, we have gifts for all four of you children, so eat your dinner and when your grandmother, Aunt Beatrice, and your Papa are all walking in the garden together, we'll play with them this afternoon.' She did not much like this distasteful idea, playing with children, but she ought to give them a little attention. She, after all, was their mother, not Ailenor.

The decorum displayed by the children broke down after that. They could hardly conceal their excitement as they sampled morsels of pigeon pie, nibbled at meats and salads, and heartily enjoyed help-ings of gooseberry tart with cream. Eleanor summoned their nurses and her ladies. Together, they climbed the stairs to the solar above the hall, little Eleanora clinging to her brother Henry's hand.

Later, Edward and Eleanor retired to the bedchamber overlooking the rose garden. Eleanor slipped off her nightrobe, climbing into the high bed using a step. She watched Edward shake off his robe. She never tired of watching him disrobe. His body was muscular and, at thirty-five years old, he was still very handsome.'

'It was a successful afternoon,' he said, smiling down at her.

She leaned against the pillows. 'Little children are exhausting. I prefer them older, but they did love their gifts.'

'I am glad we chose well.'

'Eleanora said her poppet had to be called Aveline for her aunt. Henry lined all his knights up in front of his castle. The drawbridge really works and the ballista fires pebbles!'

Edward laughed. 'As long as he fires at his castle and not his attendants!' He peered around the chamber. 'What's in that cup-board? I hope they've refreshed it.' He crossed to a lattice-doored cupboard and pulled it open. 'There's night supplies indeed, by Christos. A little something in bed.' He turned his head and grinned wickedly at her.

'Why not. Bring out napkins too.'

Dextrous as a page, he carried over goblets, napkins, and a jug of wine covered with a lid and set it all out on the side table. 'And Beatrice's boys. Did they like their gifts?' He poured wine into the goblets and passed her one.

'Of course, the Noah's Ark and the Crusader ship.'

'I hope the boys shared,' Edward said, placing a napkin on the bed cover. He cut the cheese into morsels and broke the loaf. Eleanor bit into the bread and sipped her wine. It was soft on her tongue and slid down her throat. She felt a warm glow. 'They did. They insisted I played at crusaders with them. I did. Eleanora joined in.'

'I hope you had better fortune with Baibars than I.'

'Destroyed him, utterly. How did you find your mother?'

'In good health.' He paused, poured his own goblet of wine and, looking up, frowned. 'She fears for Henry. He is too delicate.'

'Really. I pray it is just her anxiety.' She turned to him. 'Do you think we should order prayers said and candles lit in shrines?' Worry snatched at her very core. Henry was their heir. 'Pray God does not take another of our children.' She stopped eating, her eyes widening with fear as she remembered something odd. 'Henry did tire quickly today.'

'We'll have candles lit and prayers said but it may be an undue concern,' Edward said. 'Allow your King space, or he may decide to keep to his own chambers in future.'

She edged along the huge bed and smiled into the candlelight. 'You *must* from tonight, Edward, until after the coronation. Your queen should not despoil you, my lord.'

'Or I thee.'

'I think you may have done that already.' She pointedly touched her belly. 'I hope I can fit into my coronation gown.'

Edward stopped chewing. 'When?'

'March, I believe.'

'Only two months with child.' He glanced down. 'You don't show it at all. I am sure the seamstress at the Tower will make sure your gowns fit.'

'Hopefully.'

'Beatrice says they will stay with us until October. You will be glad of her company. Mama will expect to spend time with her too. Margaret and Alexander should be at Westminster already, all the way from Edinburgh. Mama will be happy. Both her girls together. A family reunited.'

Eleanor recollected how they had spent time together in the early years of their marriage. She had enjoyed Margaret's company. 'What a pity Edmund is not joining us in London.'

'Aveline is with child, unwell, and cannot travel. But I fear there are two other reasons.'

'What are those?' She was sitting right up now. For Edmund not to attend a coronation was an insult. Edward would not forgive this slight.

'He wants half of the Pope's Crusade money and I can't afford to give it to him. We have empty coffers, Eleanor.'

'Then we must set about acquiring the lands your father gave away. They should revert to the crown. And my dower. That must be settled. Your mother has twice the size of mine.' She flashed her angry dark eyes at him.

'Don't give me that angry look tonight, Eleanor. All in good time.'

'And the other reason for Edmund's withdrawal?'

'Gilbert insists on carrying the ceremonial sword.'

'Why should Gilbert de Clare take precedence over the King's brother, a prince of the realm, tell me that, Edward?'

'Because Gilbert organised and contributed some of his own wealth for the coronation. Because we are penniless.'

She gulped down her wine. It was true and must be corrected. They were poor. He moved the remains of their night feast away and brushed off the crumbs. She slid down into the bed and he protectively drew her into the crook of his arm.

'Edward, we cannot be poor,' she said with firmness. 'I intend to set up a more efficient land office. You'll help me.' It was a command, not a request.

'Yes, my love.' He kissed her hair and a moment later began to snore softly. She slipped from under his arm.

She could not sleep. As her thoughts turned over and over, her head filled up with plans. She would map out those properties she already possessed. She would look at properties bordering them. Her lands might be increased throughout the realm where she was already owner of many small manors. She would be the greatest landowner England had ever known and own more properties than even Gilbert de Clare. A smile of satisfaction hovered on her lips. After all, she was Queen. No one would gainsay her will.

It was a shame they had to ride to Canterbury tomorrow. The castle was enchanting. Her mind raced. It was possible, of course, that she could acquire it. Henry had seized it after the barons' insurrection. Young Robert Crevequer, its owner, had backed Montfort. Foolish young man. He had to buy his land back now and tonight she had heard at supper how he had huge debts. Their friend Roger Mortimer had owned the magical castle, but he had died on the Crusade. She would get hold of Roger's debts and Robert's too. She would see their families were compensated elsewhere but in return she would take over the barony with its pretty castle and create luxurious rooms within the donjon – and out there, under the moon, new gardens as splendid as those in the Sicilian palace of La Ziza which both she and Edward admired. She would name it Gloriette.

An owl hooted far out in the darkness. The moon cast thin beams through the shutters. The perfume of roses drifted in from the garden. A moment later, she drifted into a contented sleep.

On the eighteenth day of August, Eleanor and Edward rode opulently bridled horses as they crossed the bridge into the City. The roar of crowds made it impossible to hear each other speak so they remained silent. Heralds rode before them, their trumpets so loud they could be heard from the Tower to St Paul's Cathedral. Hundreds of knights rode behind them. Pennants with the royal leopards flew above them, unfurling in the summer breeze. She glanced back at the carriages rolling along behind pulled by white palfreys with plaited, ribboned manes. She caught sight of the children peering out from the litters. Their nurses fished them back. Ignoring them,

Eleanora and Henry pushed their heads out of their carriage, waving and smiling at the crowds as they passed. What a magnificent day.

Golden puffs of clouds and blue skies created a heavenly canopy above the King and Queen's procession all the way from the Tower of London to Westminster. She noted how the Cheapside conduit ran with red and white wine for Londoners to drink. Windows and doors were adorned with silk hangings and cloths of gold. Tableaux were established at St Paul's and again at the City gate leading onto Fleet Street. Crowds cheered as they rode out of Aldgate and along the Strand.

As they approached Westminster, Eleanor remarked on the cleanliness of the streets. 'So many have come to see the procession.'

Edward managed to say above the cheering. 'The palace is filled with noblemen and women from every part of our kingdom.'

'Edward,' she managed to say as she controlled her horse which was stepping extremely high, 'No king has ever enjoyed such a welcome. It is good to be home.'

His beautiful blue eyes filled with moisture.

Many hours later, after dining, Eleanor withdrew to the Queen's chambers at Westminster. Edward removed to the Painted Chamber where he would observe a vigil below a painting of the *Coronation of Saint Edward the Confessor*. Eleanor fell into an exhausted slumber with the painting of gnarled old Winter watching over *her*.

In the morning, dressed in a simple white gown, her long chestnut hair loose under a plain gold band, Eleanor stepped onto a blue ray silken carpet, glimpsing up as she and Edward entered the Abbey. She heard the clatter of the greatest knights of the realm on horseback following them but paused with Edward to make offerings of filled purses at the shrine to his namesake St Edward. They walked to a giant wooden stage so high the jangling knights following could ride their horses underneath it. Censors swung back and forth. Incense rose up towards the vaulted ceiling, reaching her, making her want to sneeze. She glanced around, awed. Torches and candles illuminated hanging banners, picking out golden threads on lions, griffins, leopards of England, rose hearts, lilies and stars on others, causing them to gleam and glitter with colourful richness.

The air hushed. Horses seemed to stop breathing. In a clear voice, Edward made three promises: to protect the Church, do good justice, and suppress evil laws. You could cut the air with a dagger as he paused. He made a fourth promise, the one he had discussed with her many times. The crown would never again be threatened. *He vowed to protect the rights of the crown.*

After his declaration, Edward descended from the stage to the altar. He disrobed to his silken undershirt and the anointing began. The choir sang the 'Unexant for Solomon'. The holiest of oils, the chrism, was poured over his head. He was dressed in apparel so decorated with jewels Eleanor wondered how he could bear its weight. Now there came another surprise, one for which she was patiently waiting to hear. Edward removed his crown, set it aside, and announced, 'I shall not take up this crown again until I have recovered all the lands given away by my father to the earls, barons, and knights of England.'

Edward intended to recover what had been lost during the Civil War. Great men would not again shut out the King's agents, his bailiffs, justices and chosen sheriffs. She found a smile hovering about her lips. Evil barons must not be able to create private fiefdoms. When Edward spoke these words her eyes sought those of Gilbert of Gloucester. *You too,* they warned.

Eleanor's own coronation followed. It was no less magnificent. Like Edward she was dressed simply. After a short ceremony and sermon during which the Archbishop of Canterbury spoke of loyal Judith in the Old Testament, a crown of golden lilies was placed on her head. She held her sceptre in silence and bowed to Edward, honouring his majesty with all her heart. She would honour him all her days.

A sumptuous feast followed their coronation. Extra kitchens had been built for the occasion. Cooks roasted sides of beef, swans, and peacocks; broiled lampreys, pikes, salmon; baked pies and concocted sauces with rich creams and spices; they served thousands of salads and created a magnificent subtlety, a gigantic pastry concoction resembling the Cathedral – a fantasy church, a dream, the dead King's dream.

Eleanor changed into a gown of crimson silk and cloth of gold and now a crowned queen, she was happier than she had ever been in her thirty-three years. She glanced around the vast hall. Margaret of Scotland was present with Alexander her husband. Edmund had clearly recovered from his fit of pique over who carried the ceremonial sword during the coronation. He'd left his sick wife to attend the coronation feast.

Eleanor and Joanna of Pembroke sought each other's company after the void of fruit and cheese was served and actors began presentations of small plays. Guests had exchanged places to gossip with those they had not seen for years.

'You look radiant today, Joanna,' Eleanor said embracing her friend. 'Blue is becoming on you. It matches your eyes.'

Joanna smiled back. 'And you, Eleanor. You are lovelier as the years pass.'

'Thank you. Will you come with us to Kempton? We'll spend a few days celebrating, hunting, feasting, and dancing before we join the children at Windsor.'

'We would not miss it for a world of riches.' Joanna hugged Eleanor and held her back, scrutinising her face.

Eleanor had drunk a cup or two more than she ought. She hiccupped and said, 'We'll have more time to talk then. And later, Windsor? You'll come to Windsor as well?'

'If William agrees,' Joanna said.

'Edward will ask him.' As she spoke, a great thundering noise was gathering pace beyond the opened palace doors. Without any warning an army of knights trotted into the hall, scattering the musicians, actors and acrobats in all directions. Servitors dived for shelter as trays were knocked to the ground. Wine jugs crashed from tables. Cheeses rolled across the floor tiles. Guests retreated to huddle against walls and hide behind pillars, knocking over goblets of wine in their haste. Ignoring the clamour, Edward rose to his feet, laughing and calling for calm.

The players had taken refuge under trestles. 'I don't believe it. Horses wrecking the banqueting hall!' Eleanor pointed at a rider with a crimson cloak edged with gold. 'By Holy Marion, it's Margaret's Alexander – King of Scotland. Edward knew all along.'

The thunder of at least one hundred knights trotting around the enormous hall, in and out of pillars, grew deafening; the smell was pungent. Alexander rode straight up to Edward, leapt from his horse, and knelt, followed by the host of knights. They all let loose their mounts. Alexander and Edward exchanged a few words. Alexander spun around and shouted at the courtiers, who were aghast, 'Catch a mount and it's yours!'

Edward and Earl Gilbert raced each other to catch Alexander's magnificent white Abyssinian stallion. Edward won the race. Gilbert claimed a handsome black charger and tried to get himself a second. He called for his own knights to catch the cantering horses.

Eleanor clutched Joanna. 'What chaos! Trust him to compete.' She pointed at Gilbert and looked with meaning into her friend's blue eyes. 'The smell of horse and sweat makes me nauseous. We'll retire into the garden.' She signalled to the Dowager Queen, Beatrice, and Margaret, who with looks of horror were drawing back from the high table as far as the hanging wall tapestries. She frantically waved to her attendants and beckoned them to her. She tugged at Joanna's arm. 'I am not staying here another moment.'

'Nor I.'

Eleanor led her along the wall to a side door. She lifted an arras covering it and withdrew a tiny key hanging on a thin golden chain around her neck. Once she inserted it into the lock, it was stiff and would not give. She tried again. At last, after more gentle twists of the key the padlock dropped to the floor. Throwing the door open she gulped great draughts of fresh air.

'There are steps down,' she managed to say between gasps. 'Into the lily garden.'

'The monks will be busy scribing this feast's account for years to come,' Joanna said laughing.

'I hope they remember our glorious coronation too.'

'No doubt about that.'

Eleanor lifted the arras again and peered back into the hall. Led by the tall Dowager, the royal women, followed by their ladies, arms covered with hanging embroidered sleeves opened like colourful wings, were edging their way around the walls. Horses cantered again around the pillars, reins trailing the tiles. Eleanor and Joanna waited for the women to dodge the chaos and reach the door.

Joanna held the arras back as the ladies joined them. She summoned a page who was lolling against the wall. 'Have cakes and hippocras served in the garden. Ensure the guards allow no man through it.'

When the boy scurried off to do her bidding, she turned to Eleanor. 'I should have said, "And no horse either."' She shrugged. 'I doubt man or horse could manage the stairway. They are all blind drunk.'

'And I don't want my lilies trampled.' Eleanor hiccupped again. 'I think I am a little drunk too.' As they stepped into the garden, the women began to laugh again at the absurdity of Alexander's prank. They fell laughing onto turf seating around a lily pond.

'They'll be chasing those horses all evening,' the Dowager remarked.

'For ever,' Beatrice said.

Beyond the garden, the Abbey bells began ringing for Vespers.

'There won't be too many Westminster monks at their prayer this evening but I am sure God will forgive them,' the Dowager added with a smile on her lips. 'Do you know, I believe Henry watches it all.' She pointed to the heavens and sank onto a bench where she arranged her silvery gown neatly and accepted a tiny cup of hippocras offered by one of the pages who had arrived with a tray, cups, and sugar-coated almond cakes. 'What a glorious day for my son.'

'And your son's queen,' Beatrice said quickly.

Eleanor gave them a controlled smile. 'Pass around the cakes,' she said and politely lifted one herself. She would not spoil Ailenor's reunion with her daughters by showing petulance now.

The following week was a holiday. They relaxed in the company of friends as they rode beyond Windsor Castle, falcons and sparrowhawks on their wrists. Eleanor admired how Countess Joanna sat so elegantly, straight-backed on her palfrey, her sparrow-hawk poised on her wrist. Joanna's hair was still bright despite her years, almost burnished gold as the sunlight caught wisps of it escaping from her crispinette after the gallop through the park.

As their gallop turned into a canter and slowed to a trot, Eleanor turned to Joanna. 'Edward says William is to go to Gascony soon. Do you think you will join him?'

'I have our estates to manage and the children are growing up. I need to be here for my girls.'

Eleanor swallowed. She tried hard but, no matter how hard she tried to feel a mother's love, she simply could not feel maternal in the same manner as Joanna and the Dowager. She constantly feared loss. Children died.

For a heartbeat they watched as Edward's hawk swooped up and brought down a pheasant. The bird was so fast it was over before it had begun. 'There will be a surfeit of game for days,' she said. 'It's William's turn now.' For a moment they followed William's hawk as it brought a small bird down.

'I can't make out his kill,' Joanna said, screwing up her eyes 'It's the sun. Too harsh! I expect it's a thrush, or a blackbird perhaps.' Joanna averted her eyes and adjusted her little hat and veil with one hand; her hawk sat still on her other wrist and her horse stood still. 'Goodridge Castle needs my attention, Eleanor. The building work is underway at last.'

'It's a lovely castle. I remember it glowing red and golden in the morning sun.' She would tell Joanna about the castle she had fallen for. She took a breath. Edward was approving. She could say. 'On our way to London we stayed at the Leeds Donjon before Canterbury and I'm going to purchase it and create gardens there with an aviary, fountains, and a courtyard in the centre with a pool. I might even create a large bathroom.'

Joanna smiled. 'A lovely idea, Eleanor. A bath with piped water. I'm planning a new solar in a tower for my ladies and myself. There'll be water basins with spouts and sprockets. We'll pipe water in. The garderobes won't smell. And . . .' Joanna leaned towards Eleanor. 'And I have to be there to curate such work.' She sighed. 'Our son can remain with William in Gascony as he did on Crusade. He has much to learn before he is granted his knighthood. I'll miss them both.'

'So you would not join our travelling court?' Eleanor felt a sense of disappointment.

'No, but thank you for asking. I have Agnes to worry about again. She is twice widowed now. Maurice and Hugh both gone, two husbands within five years. We've decided to allow her to choose her next husband herself. Aymer and Joan are still in the nursery and there's Margaret to see off to the nunnery in France. Elizabeth and Isabel will need husbands soon. John will help me with the estates. There are endless disputes over our inherited estates. We have a bevy of lawyers working on those arguments. I doubt they'll all ever be solved. Too many claimants all squabbling over my grandfather's manors.'

Joanna was everything Eleanor wanted to be. She admired beautiful objects. She was thrifty, and she was organised; Joanna was very astute when dealing with her land problems. 'You were the perfect Seneschal of Winchester Castle while William was on the Crusade.' Eleanor reached over and patted the older woman's hand. 'Now you must look to your own properties.'

Joanna nodded. 'Aye to that. And you, Eleanor. What are your plans?'

'I am taking an inventory of all I possess. My scribes will map out my properties and look for others to purchase adjacent to those I already own. Manors are the way to wealth, great estates with forests full of timber, fields fat with grain, and uplands for grazing sheep. I shall be a greater landowner than *him*.' With a nod she cast her eyes in the direction of Gilbert de Clare who was showing off as usual, allowing his newly captured horse to prance as he set off his hawk.

Joanna smiled back. 'A vain man but a clever one. As long as my own properties are safe from your gathering of lands, I shall be very pleased if you acquire control of his. I shall never forget how he coveted our lands during the civil war.' They lowered their voices in case their ladies heard. Gilbert was flirtatious, attractive, and in his prime: available and wealthy. Anyone might carry tales.

'The only reason he turned from Montfort was because our lands were given elsewhere.' Joanna shuddered visibly. 'That year after I left you in Canterbury, I had to live on what I could produce on Bampton and Moreton. I learned to eat simply and mend clothing. I even learned how to brew and bake bread. Those were valuable lessons. I still love Bampton and Moreton. They are productive and comfortable. You will enjoy manor houses as well as castles, Eleanor.'

'We are visiting manors in East Anglia and Leicestershire this autumn. I have purchases in mind there too. My stewards are already investigating for me.' She glanced up at the sky. 'I hope the weather holds. You remember Olwen, my herbalist. She will accompany us. She has brought seeds all the way from Palestine. We intend to plant them.'

'She's still unmarried?' Joan said with surprise in her voice.

'I am thinking of finding her a husband. There was someone she liked but he is studying medicine in Salerno. We don't know if he will ever return to us.'

'Do you have someone in mind?'

'Perhaps. It should be a man of middling rank, maybe the steward of one of my manors, one who cares about gardens.'

'I never put you down as a matchmaker, though I imagine whoever you choose will be kind and sensible. Olwen has a gentle manner and pretty green eyes like sea glass. Just don't give her to an aged widower.'

'No, someone closer to her own age.' She stared over at Edward, catching his eye. 'Look, they are waving to us. We can fly our hawks at last.' Eleanor gave her palfrey a gentle kick and she was off.

'Is that Eugene, the young squire Henry had with him, the squire who helped us in Canterbury and saved Henry at Evesham? I remember both Eugene and Olwen as very brave then. Is he married?'

'It is Eugene. There was someone. He's a widower now.'

'Well?'

'Maybe.'

Gilbert's hawk swooped and snatched another bird.

Chapter Fifteen

Guildford
1274–1275

Olwen watched from the window of the maidens' chamber as after the week following the coronation came to a close and the earls departed for their own estates. Her eyes were drawn to Gilbert de Clare. She was sure he glanced up and winked at her. Surely Gilbert was not as terrible and dangerous as Lady Margerie said. Since she had first glimpsed him nearly ten years previously he had matured and was now a handsome and kindly lord. He had, after all, saved the Queen's dog. Now, unbeknown to all, Gilbert had made a habit of seeking her out in the garden at Windsor as she gathered plants and herbs for potions. He had sat on a turfed seat watching her and he asked her advice as to what potion she would suggest for a sorrowful heart.

'My lord, the plant they call heartsease. It has petals shaped like a heart and we have it here in the garden. I can make you a potion and send it to you.'

'Ah, if only the lovely Olwen could deliver such a potion herself it might ease my pain.'

'It would be unseemly.'

'Ah well, indeed. Send a page. My thanks to you.' He looked a little peeved.

Smiling to herself, she had continued to fill her basket with herbs including late-flowering pansies for his complaint. A little later she glanced up and he was gone. The days of the Barons' War were long past and Earl Gilbert was high in the King's favour, yet she was aware how the Queen disliked him. Her own heart was sad these days and she wondered if the Earl was sorrowful because he missed Lady Alix, the wife he'd separated from; was this the reason for his tortured heart.

After she sent him a potion, his squire delivered a silken pouch to her. Opening it, she discovered a brooch. She concealed the pouch amongst her clothing. She would wear it with delight, for it was shaped like a rose, enamelled crimson with a golden centre and green leaves. It was, she knew, a damask rose.

Guillaume of Acre had not returned, nor had he written to her. He had vanished from her world.

Later that week, there was a bustle of preparation for further departures. The Queen and King were to set out on a court progress to Northampton and Fotheringay. They intended a visit to the Merciful Mary, a little-known shrine in the region, to pray for Prince Henry's health. Olwen thought she, too, would accompany the progress until Queen Eleanor called her.

The Queen asked her to sit on a stool by her writing desk and Olwen wondered if she had heard about Earl Gilbert speaking with her in the garden. Her heart beat faster.

For a moment or two she waited, her sweating hands folded as the Queen continued signing her name on letters. Eventually Queen Eleanor looked up from her pile of correspondence. 'Olwen, I know the fig trees you sent on the ship from Acre to England have survived, one at Windsor and another at Winchester, all thanks to your instructions for their care, transport, and replanting. And the roses you sent back to England from Acre are thriving in the garden at Westminster.' The Queen stood up, circled the chamber and returned to the desk again. 'Do you have healthy seeds? It has been more than two years since you acquired them.'

'Your Grace, I have cumin, wheat seeds known as salamoni, coriander, and pistachio seeds. They have all been kept cool and dry in the still room at Westminster.'

'I want you to fetch them and join the children's nursery and the

Dowager Queen in Guildford. Henry is ailing. Do what you can to make him comfortable. Plant your seeds there.'

'I am sorry Henry is unwell, your Grace.'

Eleanor straightened her back and sighed. 'We shall pray for his recovery. Care for him. See if the seeds will grow into plants.'

'I can experiment as long as I can protect them from frost. I shall try to grow a few in a box on my window ledge if I have a window at Guildford. It's timely. Coriander seeds should be planted in October.'

'You shall be granted your own chamber and still room.'

Olwen smiled. She liked the Dowager Queen and little Eleanora was very sweet. 'Will the children's cousins be at Guildford?'

'Indeed they will. Keep an eye on all of them.' There were tears in the Queen's eyes. She brushed these away with her hand and Olwen felt her eyes on her. 'When you smile, Olwen, you look very attractive. This brings me to another reason I have sent for you today.' Olwen's heart missed a beat. 'Your father granted me care of you, not exactly a wardship, but similar in that I can decide your marriage. I like my servants to be married.'

'Your Grace, I have no dowry.'

'That will be taken care of. Now, leave me. Think on what I have said. On our return from Northampton, I shall have suitors in mind for you.' The Queen gave her a purse. 'This contains gold coins for your recent service to me. I know you are banking with Master Burnell. That is sensible and prudent. Margerie tells me you wish to purchase the lease of a small estate. With the right marriage you may select one of my own and you will be my tenant. We shall discuss this further. Now go. I shall send a small guard with you and two servants to attend to your needs when you travel. You will depart soon.' She looked sorrowful. 'And, I must go and bid my son goodbye before he sets out for Guildford.'

Olwen knew that Henry was so ill doctors and herbalists would not save him. And if they could not, how could she? She stood, bowed her head and curtseyed.

★

185

Olwen was delighted when Eugene, her old companion, was to accompany her on her journeys. The Queen allowed her two maids of her own. She could think of nothing else but the talk of marriage as she was rowed along the river to fetch her seed casket and to collect the maids appointed to her.

Eugene told her he was hoping to find a good position with Queen Eleanor, possibly as custodian of one of her manors. What he had seen during the civil war had horrified him, but whilst King Henry lived he owed him loyalty and remained his squire. With the new regime established, he was more interested in managing one of the royal estates.

'I heard you were married. You left court.'

As they rode from Westminster towards Guildford, she asked the question dominating her thoughts. 'Where is your wife now, Eugene?'

'Matilda died from a tumour, God rest her soul. I loved her well.'

She felt colour rise from her neck to her face and averted her head.

As her face cooled, fanned by the breeze as they rode forward, she asked, 'But why do you not wish to be a knight?'

This time he stared ahead. 'I have no land. I loved King Henry but now he is gone to Heaven,' he crossed himself, 'I am happy to seek other employment. Olwen, I am the youngest son of a youngest son.' He shrugged. 'My father has nothing to give me, but King Henry liked my father, who managed the Tower vineyard, so he did him a great favour and took me into his service as a squire. The rest you now know.'

'I am sorry you lost your wife and child.'

Their horses were nose to nose. She moved hers slightly sideways with a tug of her right rein. 'I am too,' he said in a quiet voice.

As they were thrown closer to allow a woodsman to pass them, his axe slung over his shoulder, Eugene spoke again. 'My wife and I never had a home of our own, just the usual accommodations at court. After King Henry's funeral, I was appointed as a royal messenger and was often away from Westminster carrying letters around the land. My wife served the Dowager Queen in a lowly position, like those girls,' He gestured behind to the following wagon where the two female servants sat on the front seat, one holding the horse's reins and both watching the scenery as the hedgerows sped by. For a moment, Eugene did not speak again. 'My wife was eaten by a cancer. The Dowager was kind to her but even her kindness and my prayers could not save Matilda.'

'It is a sad story.'

'It is.' He grew silent again.

She studied Eugene as they rode, when she thought he was not watching her. He was in his prime – less talkative than he had been ten years earlier. His face was lined and sunburned with a lived-in countenance. His hair was dark. He was of middling height, handsome she supposed, some years older than she, though not many, she assumed.

She looked ahead. The two men-arms accompanying them were almost out of sight.

'Will you remain at the palace?' she asked Eugene.

'I am to ride back to Westminster and await her Grace's decision about my future.'

'Ah,' she said. With an amused twitch of her mouth she added, 'Thank you for escorting me.'

'It is a pleasure.' He smiled back. 'I believe the box you picked up in Westminster contains seeds from the Holy Land. You are still growing things, I see.' His eyes twinkled. It was as if they had picked up a conversation from many years before as if long ago was yesterday. She felt that he enjoyed riding with her.

'How was God's Kingdom?' he asked.

'It seems another lifetime already. I liked it well.' She told him about Acre. She tried to describe sights and sounds; exotic gardens and markets smelling of spice; ships that sailed into port with spices and fabrics; the great Hospitallers' fortress, and the summer heat and the dry landscape outside the fortress. She told him about how Lord Edward had nearly died from an assassin's attack and the long journey home to England that took years. Never once did she mention Guillaume.

'And you are still a maid?' he said, his voice quiet. It was an impertinent question and she considered not answering it. Perhaps all he wanted to know was if she had been married too.

'I have never been inclined to wed,' she replied.

Closer to Guildford, they turned onto a forest path. The wheels of the wagon crunched over last year's dried leaves. Their guards rode ahead watching out for outlaws.

She gripped her reins. Occasional pools of sunlight filtered through the canopy of oak leaves making the velvety air appear like damask, and the pathway ahead mysterious.

'There's nothing to fear in the woods around Guildford Castle. It's the King's forest.' He smiled his reassurance. Her hand strayed to the linen bag she wore across her gown under her mantle, feeling for her seed box.

She did not see the two men appear from the verge with bows held aloft, strung ready to let arrows fly. The strangers appeared from the trees silent as evening bats. Eugene called over his shoulder to her, 'Stay back.' That was when she saw them.

Olwen looked over her shoulder and turned her palfrey about to see what was happening on the wagon. The maid who was driving it seemed to freeze. An arrow flew past. The other maid screamed as it lodged in the cart's cover. Her palfrey became skittish and she put all her strength into controlling it.

The attacker shouted at her and Eugene, 'A warning. Off those horses, the pair of you.' He rapidly waved his bow at the wagon. 'And you lasses, get down from the cart.'

Olwen slid from the saddle but Eugene was quick. He threw his leg over his jennet and seized his sword from its scabbard. Tossing her his reins, he moved in front of her with his sword drawn. Her palfrey neighed loudly. The jennet was calmer but it was hard to control both animals. She glanced around seeking their guards, but they had vanished. The terrified white-faced maids climbed from the wagon. They were weeping. The big gentle carthorse gave a huge neigh and looked about to bolt. In that moment she prayed hard that she could control the palfrey if it did, but the older maid had the presence of mind to hold onto its bridle.

'We are on the King's business,' Eugene said with amazing calm, waving his sword.

'The King's business indeed.' Both rogues stared for a moment. Their arrows were again poised to fly. 'To Langley are ye?'

'Let 'em pass,' the other one said, lowering his bow. 'King's business is no ordinary business. There'll be guards behind them.' Both bandits looked half-starved, as if they had not eaten in days. The tattered garments clinging to their skinny frames were the colour of lichen.

Olwen kept about, peering ahead for their escort. Her heart hammered against her breast.

The first bandit growled, 'Not until we 'ave their horses and purses. Bailiff 'as us poor folks thrown off our farm. Put rents up. My children are hungry.'

The second bandit said, 'King has too much, and us too little methinks. I ain't been paid my due for fighting for 'im. King owes me.' He shouted, 'Put up that there sword. Throw it to me.' He gave his companion a shove. 'You, brother, go get it. Bring it 'ere.'

The brother took a step forward. Eugene threw down his weapon. He whistled a peculiar sound very like a raven's caw, harsh and threatening. A partridge flew up from the trees, straight as an arrow rustling the foliage. Time stilled. Olwen could hear her heart beat. The girls screamed. The carthorse stamped the forest floor and the palfrey let out another neigh. The jennet strained at its reins, almost pulling her over.

Within a heartbeat both men hit the forest floor, clutching at earth, groaning and trying to raise themselves. Their guards edged out of the trees, crossbows raised. They lowered them and bent over the writhing bodies. They pulled swords from their scabbards and set about cutting the outlaws' throats. A gurgling sound, an enormous pool of blood, and a cry. Silence. Even birds stopped rustling in the canopy above.

The sergeant glanced up from his grisly work. 'We've been

tracking these two for a while. They've a hide in the woods amongst a stand of oaks. I'll send a company to fetch the bodies. They'll hang them from the trees to warn others who might get same ideas.' The guards dragged the bodies from the track into the undergrowth.

Eugene took back the jennet's reins and patted the palfrey. It calmed immediately as he spoke quietly. He looked up at her, his eyes full of concern. 'It's over. Olwen, do you think you can you get back on your mount?'

She hoisted herself back into the saddle. Those outlaws had been desperate, but if they had not been killed would the footpads have killed them? She whispered a prayer for their souls. When she opened her eyes Eugene was calming her maids. He tied his jennet to the cart and sat between them, taking control of their frightened horse.

Their small company continued in silence. A short time later, the forest opened out into pasture. A low setting sun cast pink light on the grey stone walls of Guildford Castle.

Eugene called to her, 'Sooner we are over that moat the better.'

Olwen breathed her relief as they clattered across the drawbridge, past guards who waved them through into an outer courtyard.

Soldiers hung around doorways and she noted a long barracks. They moved through another archway into an inner court. Servants crossed between a brewhouse and the kitchen building carrying jugs. She could smell bread baking. Smoke curled into the darkening sky above. They drew up beside the entrance to the hall. An elderly steward, or at least she supposed he must be the steward, bustled out of the door, his long robes flying behind him. He hurried toward Eugene who was giving charge of his jennet to a stable boy.

'Ah, Master Eugene, you have arrived with the herbalist.'

'We have. Good evening, Sir Richard. A moment please.' He turned back to Olwen and waved at the maids to descend.

Eugene helped her from her palfrey and the shaken maids stumbled from the cart.

190

'What is this?' the steward said as they came to join Olwen. 'You all look as if an autumn storm has hit us and shaken you all up.'

'We were attacked in the forest. Our guards will take your sergeant to fetch the bodies. Outlaws. Thrown off their lands, they said. Driven to another trade.'

'By whom?'

'The bailiff. Would that be you?'

Sir Richard looked horrified. He shook his grey locks. 'No, and those footpads may not even be from these parts. Thank Holy St Christopher for protecting you. Come into the hall. Queen Ailenor is there with the children. We have troubles ourselves today. Prince Henry is ailing. The journey from Windsor was too exhausting for him.' He crossed himself. 'He has been near death's door this past week and I doubt doctors can save him. You have had a terrible journey. Let us find you meat and drink. My wife will guide Mistress Olwen and her maids to their chamber. We can talk later.' He turned to Olwen, 'The Dowager Queen will speak with you tomorrow.'

Eugene said, 'I forget my manners, Mistress Olwen. Meet Sir Richard.'

'I knew her name already.'

Olwen curtseyed. The maids followed her lead.

'You are safe now,' the steward said. 'Come, wash your hands and face and join us for supper.'

Bells rang out from a pretty chapel set to the side of the castle. Olwen wondered where the gardens lay. There must be a kitchen garden and an orchard. She wondered what plans Queen Eleanor had for Guildford's gardens. That made her think about the footpad's words concerning the Queen's bailiffs. Were those in charge of the Queen's properties fair?

Olwen's chamber was at the end of the corridor against an outer wall. She gasped at its beauty. A silver moon shone into her chamber through an arched window from a sky glittering with stars. She turned about several times staring at everything. Her bed looked comfortable. The linen appeared fresh and her bedcover was

191

embroidered with acanthus stems. There was a mattress for her maids set into the spacious alcove by the outside wall. Beside it a curtain fell to conceal her garderobe. The floors were covered with rush matting. Several clothing poles stood by the entrance to the chamber and by the end of the bed an oak-wood coffer would serve as a seat.

She asked her maids to unpack her travelling box and shake out her gowns.

'I am seeking my rest, so do it quietly.'

'Mistress, would you like my help to undress?' one asked.

'I can manage, thank you.'

'I can comb your hair,' the other offered.

'I can do that myself as well. Good night to you both. Don't chatter please.'

She stripped down to her linen shift and fell upon the bed. Within moments she was asleep without washing or combing out her hair. It had been a long, trying day.

Olwen quickly settled into the rhythm of life at Guildford. Her maids looked after her linen and clothing; cleaning the chamber; emptying her chamber pot and helping the other servants in the palace. Queen Ailenor frequently borrowed one or the other to sort out embroidery threads or mend clothing. Both were excellent needlewomen. The Dowager introduced them to an embroiderer called Rosalind, a friend apparently staying for a while and a pleasant woman Olwen thought could be in her early fifties. Rosalind took her maids in hand. She tutored them to cut out, stitch, and embroider two new winter gowns for Olwen since Queen Ailenor had kindly given the herbalist linen for new shifts, material for caps, a length of wool for a new mantle, and two pairs of rabbit fur gloves.

Prince Henry died a month later. Olwen had made cordials using borage sweetened with honey. These drinks cooled him but they could not cure him. Never a strong child, his lungs were too weak. Whilst no one was at fault, Olwen blamed herself. Queen Eleanor and King Edward sent gifts to their children as well as fruit and venison to strengthen Henry. They came to see Henry and the other children. They departed the following day for Windsor, but Henry did not improve. Messengers came and went. A few weeks later Henry died.

'My dear,' the Dowager said when Olwen burst into tears after Henry slipped away from them. 'You are not to blame. Henry was never strong. As you see, we have brought many physicians to help him, the best in the land. What you have done is helped him to die without discomfort. Your cordials eased his coughing. Your syrup of honey and poppy juice helped him to sleep.' She placed her hand over Olwen's. 'When God calls his children to him, there is nothing more to be done.'

Eleanora was inconsolable and clung to her grandmother. The other children were hushed and sad. Alphonso, sensing the unhappy atmosphere, cried more than was usual. A funeral bier would carry Henry to London for burial at Westminster. Olwen was to remain at Guildford with Alphonso as well as the other young children of the nursery, including the Breton cousins and a few children of friends. Dowager Ailenor said, 'Your cordials and syrups and simples will be needed as winter approaches.'

'I am happy to remain, my lady.' She looked sorrowfully across the hall at the painting of Lazarus and wished it was possible to raise Henry from death as had been Lazarus. Her reddened eyes moved past the marble columns of the hall to the windows set with coloured glass. They filled with tears all over again.

After much deliberation, the Dowager decided that five-year-old Eleanora should accompany her to London. Olwen was content to stay at the castle. She could not face the King and Queen as well as facing her own grief. It would not be for long, the Dowager told her. After Christmas the royal nursery was to move to the Tower of London.

'You are to travel to the Tower with your maids and join the royal household there,' Sir Richard informed her.

'What about my plants, Sir Richard?'

193

'Mistress Olwen, I have noted how your plants have sprouted. We shall care for them. Take some and leave others.'

'I shall leave you a gift of cumin and instructions on planting outside in pots once the frost has gone.'

'My wife will be delighted. Thank you.'

On a chill January day, wrapped well in her new fur-lined mantle, riding gloves, and warm woollen gown, Olwen set out for London with her maids, the remaining children, and their nurses and guards. She was returning with a selection of plants kept warm with wrappings against the frost.

When they parted company, the steward said, 'There won't be bandits. Those you met before had travelled here from Kent. They had been unfairly put out of their homes and yes, they left widows and children behind.' He shook his head and lowered his voice. 'Queen Eleanor may be building up great lands, acquiring more and more of them, but she should ensure her bailiffs and stewards are honest.' He raised his shoulders. 'Those footpads would have killed for a crust of bread, never mind a purse. You and your precious charges will be well-protected this time.'

On her return to the Tower, Olwen settled into yet another chamber, not as spacious as her chamber at Guildford. This time her maids were to share a dormitory with Princess Eleanora's and Prince Alphonso's maids. Her chamber was a small room within the royal apartments. It was no larger than a nun's cell but it looked out over the river. She would plant her remaining seedlings in the Tower's herbal garden after the winter frost was gone. Meanwhile she placed them in pots around her small chamber, thankful for the sunshine that slid through her glazed window.

When Queen Eleanor gave birth at Windsor to a daughter whom she called Margaret, Olwen wondered if she had been forgotten. She was not forgotten. In June the Queen summoned her to Westminster. With a maid in attendance, Olwen took a wherry upriver

194

to the palace. On her arrival, she was ushered to the Queen's administration office, a chamber lined with shelves of scrolls and a table which held a huge opened sheet of parchment which the Queen was studying. A conch shell had been placed on each corner of the document. From where Olwen stood waiting for the Queen to notice her she realised it appeared to contain the design for a garden.

Eleanor glanced up. Immediately Olwen sank into a deep curtsey, nervous in case the Queen was displeased with her. When she rose again she saw that Queen Eleanor was smiling.

Pointing to a shell, the Queen said, 'Would you like to listen? Here.' She picked it up and gave it to Olwen. As Olwen held it to her ear, the sights and smells of Acre returned to her in a rush. She could hear the sea's flow as a whooshing sound and in her imagination Guillaume was standing waiting for her on the shore.

Eleanor reached out. With reluctance, Olwen released the shell and returned it to her waiting hand.

'It's quite magical, is it not, Olwen, how a shell can carry the sound of the sea and with it many memories,' Queen Eleanor said in a quiet voice. She paced to the window before turning back again. 'Olwen, I have news of the physician.'

'Guillaume? Your Grace, you do mean Master Guillaume?'

Eleanor nodded. 'He has asked the King's permission to join the Hospitallers in establishing a hospital in England. Master Guillaume is a qualified doctor but he is also part of a religious order.' Her voice grew even gentler. 'A heart can heal. There are others who love you.' Eleanor appeared to draw breath. 'Have you thought of the matter of which we spoke last September? There is an offer.'

Olwen's heart sank. She hoped the Queen had forgotten.

'Before you refuse, think hard, Olwen.'

'I had not thought to wed.' She glanced at her feet. The Queen was manipulating her. This was unfair. Why had Guillaume not written to her? Had he forgotten her?

'Master Eugene is to manage an estate for me and I had thought to put another of my properties in your name as a dower gift. You will have servants of your own.' She paused. 'If I needed you, you will join my court from time to time.'

Had Guillaume placed his love for the Hospitallers above her? This was a blow as sharp as a sword thrust. Even if the Queen was pushing her into marriage, though, Eugene was a kind and good man. She was not in love with him but perhaps she could come to love him.

After a lengthy silence, during which the Queen said only, 'Master Eugene has strong affection for you, I believe,' Olwen finally replied, 'I do not know, your Grace.'

'It has been a difficult year. Lady Aveline died. Queen Margaret of Scotland, my lord's sister, died. Princess Beatrice, whom you knew well, died giving birth to her little Eleanor. Henry died. So many of our loved ones have gone to God.' She swallowed. 'This summer I would like you to join my court. Master Eugene will be accompanying us. Perhaps you will find him amiable company.'

There was silence as Olwen absorbed the Queen's words. At last she said, 'Thank you, your Grace.'

'Now, to plants. Have you been successful?'

'I have planted cumin, coriander, and rosemary in a warm dry spot by the wall in the Tower herbal garden. They will produce more seeds.'

'The royal nursery will be housed in Windsor and the Tower for some years. While one nursery is cleansed they will dwell in the other. I have gathered up a lot of children. Now, my new castle at Leeds.' She turned to the waiting scroll. 'As you see, I have plans for the gardens.' She tapped the scroll with the garden plan. 'I want fountains, water features, a nut garden, orchards, vineyards, and a pleasure garden. There will be an aviary for the King's birds and a flower and a herbal garden will contain many new plants. This will take some years but I value your opinion. What do you think?'

As Olwen peered at the design, her eyes widened. The gardens would be extensive. She gasped, 'It is impressive.'

Olwen's thoughts raced on elsewhere. It seemed she and Eugene were destined to make journeys together and perhaps even marry.

England was green and gentle in summer; the hedgerows full of scents and the scuttles of wild creatures. It was not a bad arrangement. Even so, her eyes filled with tears of loss.

Eleanor smiled to herself as Olwen left her presence. She had already spoken to Eugene, who liked the herbalist very much. They were without doubt well suited to each other, and trustworthy too, which was important to her. Mayhap there could be a suitable manor for Olwen and Eugene in the west, somewhere close to Gloucester.

Chapter Sixteen

Oldbury
August 1275

Eleanor glanced around the pleasant manor hall at her new property at Oldbury. She clicked her tongue against her teeth with satisfaction. It had been well prepared for her visit. Walls were painted; tapestries had been hung; the floor was covered with new rushes and camomile. She looked approvingly towards the small raised dais, where a carpet was already laid and the table was draped with a linen cloth ready for supper. She walked about peering at walls and into corners. A chimney and fireplace had recently been installed to the outer wall of the hall. She smiled to herself. This was already a renovated manor.

She raised her hand to stop her ladies, scribe, and steward following and climbed the narrow stairway from the hall up to the main chamber. This she saw was one of three above including a long solar. They would pass several nights at Oldbury while Edward sought Prince Llewelyn who owed him homage for Gwynedd in Wales. The chamber was comfortable, light and sweet-smelling. She descended the stairs and lifting an arras beyond the staircase wandered through. Two further chambers lay beyond the hall, one a spacious antechamber, the other a child's bedchamber judging by the few toys neatly set on a shelf and small garments hanging from a clothing rail. A second cot, possibly for the child's nurse, was situated behind a curtain. There was no sign of either.

Oldbury was surrounded by a moat. She had noted huge golden fields beyond the moat where crops were being harvested. This manor would be just as productive as the manors Edward added to her dower. The estate had an heir, Nicholas Burdon, a little orphaned boy, whom she would take as her ward to join Alphonso, Eleanor, and Margaret in the royal nursery. When the child came of age she would give him another estate in exchange and a good marriage. He would be wealthy one day.

Her gown flew up as she stepped out of the hall into a spacious courtyard. The weather had turned windy but she did not care. She wanted to explore outside buildings and gardens. First, she surveyed the yard and nodded her approval to the steward who followed her around. The courtyard was clean and neat. It contained a dairy, laundry, and kitchen. A second courtyard, leading from the first, housed a mews, kennels, hen runs and a rabbit run. Turning to the steward she said, 'All is in good order but a covered walkway must be built between kitchen and the hall. How servants manage to keep food hot, I have no idea.'

The steward, a mean-looking fussy man with a narrow face, his shifty eyes lowered instead of looking at her, remarked, 'We manage well enough.'

'Not good enough.' She addressed the scribe who walked about beside her with a portable desk hanging from his neck. 'Write it all down.'

Lifting up the little desk, the clerk struggled against the wind to note her instructions on a scrap of parchment using a stick of charcoal.

She had taken an intense dislike to the steward. The Oldbury servants clearly feared him. Ignoring the miserable creature, she marched across the yard closely followed by her ladies, all of them battening down their skirts against the wind and all high-stepping to avoid mud. Turning about she spoke to the steward again. 'Master Christopher, show us the gardens.' She looked at the note-taker, who was beginning to fall behind. 'Scribe, stay close.' Her ladies were still picking their way forward. 'Olwen, you come here,' she called. 'We are going to walk in the gardens.' The progress had brought colour into Olwen's face. Eleanor gave her a reassuring smile. 'I need your advice on planting.'

The steward opened a gate and led them into the herbal garden which was sheltered from the wind. Eleanor grunted at the weeds suffocating the herbal beds. 'Work to be done here.' She turned to Olwen, who was folding back weeds seeking other plants. 'I want these cleared and replanted. You will remain, after I leave, to provide instruction.' Olwen nodded assent. Eleanor followed the pathway through the garden towards the rear wall. She pointed. 'A door here.' She called the clerk forward. 'Note this. A door is needed in the wall. It's to lead into a rose garden. Olwen will supervise all the planting. There must be a fountain and turf seating. Note it all down, scribe.' She turned to Olwen again. 'Master Eugene and the scribe will remain with you and your two servants. This garden should take no longer than a month to plant. The local monasteries will provide all the herbs you need. A rose garden will be built next springtime.'

'Yes, your Grace.'

'You will list what is in the orchards. Next year we shall create a vineyard and a fruit garden as well. What do you suggest?'

'Raspberries, gooseberries, strawberries, plums.'

Eleanor smiled to herself again. This was where she would place Olwen and Eugene if, God willing, the pair would agree to wed before the year closed. She turned to the steward. 'Master Christopher, before supper, I wish to meet the boy. Where is he?'

Master Christopher nodded, looking more humble and less objectionable. 'He is with the priest up at the Church getting learning.' His gaze met her own but with diffidence. She wondered if he guessed that his weeks at Oldbury were numbered. She suspected he had been creaming off produce for sale, the proceeds of which rightfully belonged to the child, but now would come to the crown.

Exiting the garden, she stared once again at the manor house. It was stone-built, tile-roofed, and solid. The boy would be educated and one day she would marry him to an heiress. It was fair exchange for this manor, which she intended to bestow on Eugene and Olwen. She wrinkled her brow in thought. The boy, as part of her extended family, would always be loyal to the crown. Possession of this manor had been a good summer's work.

Nicholas Burdon brought her other recently acquired lands, not only those at Oldbury but lands linking her estates at Woodrow, Didmartin, and Poulshot together. It was a consolidation and she knew the exchange she intended when Nicholas was older would benefit him too. These new demesnes were close to Quenington, the hunting lodge where she and Edward always enjoyed hawking and the chase and where the children as they grew older would join them. She studied the map laid upon the linen-dressed table on the dais. It was pleasing. Her estates in the west now spread all over Somerset, Wiltshire, and into Herefordshire. She peered hard at the tiny drawings of rivers, churches, towns and villages and, significantly, her new properties. Some lay close to land belonging to Gilbert de Clare. The scribe had shaded Gilbert's lands in with red ink. She gave a harrumph. One day, she would acquire those red-inked properties as well.

A door blew closed. Glancing up, she saw a small boy entering the hall with his nurse. She ordered the scribe to roll up her map and the land transfer documents, and turned her attention to the child waiting below the dais.

'Mount the steps, child. Come closer,' she called down.

He climbed to the dais and knelt before her. Nicholas was only four years old, small, confused, sad, lost, and thin. Her heart unusually softened. She thought of Henry, not more than two years older when he died. Nicholas's eyes were huge and brown just like her favourite puppy's eyes. He was, in truth, an extraordinarily beautiful child. She told him to rise, reached into the folds of her mantle, and withdrew a small knight, carved from wood. Stooping down low towards him she took his hands and placed it in them.

'This is for you, Nicholas. The knight's name is Launcelot. When you come to live with my children, they will tell you tales about him. My daughter Eleanora loves to tell stories. She is only a little older than you.'

201

The child's eyes brightened. He clutched the knight close to his beast.

'Thank you, your Grace,' he said, looking up for approval from his nurse who stood beside him.

'Your nurse will live with you in my castle, Nicholas. You will never be lonely again because you will have other children to play with and learn many new things, maybe even how to become a knight yourself one day.'

His face grew animated.

'Would you like to be a knight?'

'I want a sword.'

'Then you shall have one, a wooden one for now. You are to travel to London tomorrow. Will you like this too?'

'Yes.' His nurse nudged him. 'Yes, your Grace,' he repeated. He had been well coached.

'Good. I shall see you again soon.' She nodded to the nurse who took his hand; his other clutched the knight. A moment later the nurse had led Nicholas away.

The outer door was flung open again. This time, a sudden wind blew in and gusted through the hall, lifting chamomile flowers from the floor straw, causing them to scatter. A page with pale hair, wearing a tabard with leopards embroidered on it, slipped in and announced King Edward's arrival. A heartbeat later Edward himself filled the doorway. The first thing she noted as she descended the dais to greet him was Edward's face. It was highly coloured with fury. She hurried forward and reached up to place a hand on his forehead. 'You are overly heated, my lord.' She turned to a group of waiting servants. 'Cool ale to be served by the fireplace.' They scurried off.

Edward threw his cloak over the back of a settle. Her ladies and his lords sensing his mood withdrew, leaving them together by the empty hearth.

'What is wrong?' she said as soon as he was seated in a chair with his long legs sprawling out towards the fireplace, a mug of ale in his hand.

He shook his head, hair flying about his face. There was grey in it these days, not much but it was growing in. His blue eyes darkened, his pupils larger than usual. 'Llewelyn,' Edward spat the Welsh name after he seized and gulped down his cup of ale. He slammed the emptied cup onto the side table by his elbow. 'He refused his homage. He says if he comes to either Chester or Hereford, Gilbert's knights will murder him.' Edward drew a long breath. 'And he claims he is not responsible for the theft of Gilbert's cattle or attacks on villages east of the Severn.'

'Who does he say is raiding?' Eleanor said, keeping her voice even.

'He has no idea. He just refuses to cross the border.'

'You *could* go to him.'

'Are you out of your senses, Eleanor? That brigand! I value my knights' lives too much to risk it, and my own. No, I'll summon him to London in October.'

'And if he refuses?'

'He'll suffer if he does not show. It'll be war.'

'What else?'

He let out a weary sigh. 'My mother has expelled Jews from all her dower lands including Marlborough. She insists the Church demands this and as good Christians we must obey the Archbishop's decrees. There's new pressure from His Holiness to enforce Jews to wear the yellow badge.'

'It's been so for fifty years, Edward. King John paid no attention to it. Henry ignored it.'

'And I don't like it either but I would prefer to help them live by lawful trade, not moneylending.'

'They lend money since Christians may not.' Eleanor immediately thought how she had acquired many of her properties. After the Battle of Evesham nobles borrowed from the Jewish money lenders so they could pay their fines, hopefully without losing lands. Eleanor paid their debts to the moneylenders for a minimal cost, acquiring the estates promised against loans.

'My father availed himself of Jewish loans. The Church won't have it at all. I shall offer the Jews the King's Peace. My bailiffs must treat them fairly or they'll answer to me.' He leaned forward, lowering his voice. 'We have huge debts ourselves. By restricting the Jews to legal trade, I can raise a tax from them legally within Parliament. It'll help cover our debts.' He sighed again. 'It's expensive being a king.'

She placed her hand in his. 'My love, seek a compromise. Allow the Jewish communities to live in our own towns. It works in Castile. Maybe they can help us rebuild our wealth. In Castile we allow them to live in peace. Christians and Jews contribute to the cultural life of our court. Muslims practise their religion.'

He raised an eyebrow. 'As ever you have solutions, my love. I'll allow them to buy property on our behalf. I'll permit them to trade. Robert Burnell is the man to see this business through. If anyone can influence Parliament he can. As to the rest, I don't think our clergy would be so tolerant, nor our nobles. And I doubt it is always quite so easy in Castile.' He rose to his feet. 'I am famished. It's time they served supper.'

She called for the steward and ordered him to have a cold supper set out in the antechamber behind the arras. Edward's knights and her ladies could dine in the hall. Her eyes were drawn to a group of far benches where Edward's squires were playing dice games. They lit on Master Eugene. He had engaged in a game of counters with Olwen. Gathered around them, a group of her women was encouraging Olwen to cast a bet, the forfeit no doubt a ribbon, or maybe a kiss.

Eleanor took Edward's hand. 'Come and see the antechamber.'

'Christ's holy bones, yes. Seems like I'll have you to myself this evening.' He winked.

Edward had forgotten the Welsh prince for now. Her thoughts, too, entered the world of romance. Tonight, after supper, she and Edward would make love, and if God smiled upon them, they would create another child together.

Parliament agreed that Jews could buy houses on behalf of the King, but they could only dwell in the King's towns, no other place. They would not be exiled but they *would* have to wear a yellow felt badge shaped like a mosaic tablet on their outer garment. To Eleanor's relief the Jews were not expelled. Edward, however, was so influenced by his mother, his tolerant attitude might change. Eleanor liked Dowager Ailenor less and less these days. Edward's mother was devoted to the children. She was particularly close to six-year-old Eleanora. A daughter should owe her first loyalty to her mother, not her grandmother. She shrugged. For now it was convenient. She was far, far too busy to pass precious time with small children.

Llewelyn of Wales refused to travel to London in October to render homage to the English King. He would, he wrote, if Robert Burnell and Earl Gilbert himself stood as hostages for his safety. Eleanor tackled Edward about this as they walked around the Tower walk inspecting Edward's recent improvements.

'Earl Gilbert should experience captivity in Wales for a few months,' she remarked.

Edward glared at her. 'I need Gilbert in full possession of his head. You may be in possession of lands close to his but you are not taking possession of *his* territories. I have other ways to bring Llewelyn to heel and Gilbert is part of my plan.'

She kept quiet. This was a battle she could not win. They entered Edward's newly decorated chambers. She looked around the new apartment and cried out with delight. 'My favourite colours. You have had these chambers painted to please me.' She hugged him, her arms encircling his waist. He was so tall she barely reached his shoulders.

He bent down and kissed her. 'The gardens are to be refurbished as well.'

'Olwen? Is she advising?'

'No need. Anyway, I thought you were arranging her marriage.'

'Not until after Edmund marries Blanche of Artois in January. Eugene is to manage a few of my Hereford properties. I intend giving them Oldbury and a neighbouring property for Olwen as a dower gift.'

'You have it all planned, I see.'

205

'Eugene has written to my office asking my permission for his marriage. She has agreed to the marriage.'

'My wife, the matchmaker.'

'I like to see my ladies wed.'

'You conduct a serious court.' He gave her a knowing smile. She knew why. Her ladies loved to play pranks on him, and she was not always serious.

Her memory cast back to the previous Easter Day, when her ladies had burst into her chamber and taken the naked Edward captive until he promised them a ransom of silver mantle brooches for permitting him to sleep with their mistress as Lent ended. There were no conjugal relations during the Lenten time. Such intimacy was forbidden.

She corrected him. 'A playful but sensible court.'

'And I love you for it.'

He led her away from the smell of new paint and workmen's ladders leaning along his new wall. She paused and studied the river. For a moment she considered how many of the vessels departing the London wharfs were carrying wool from her estates to Flanders. She could be looking at considerable profits this year.

'My Lord.' She spun around on her heel to see a page had appeared on the walkway. The youth bowed, handing Edward a letter from which a seal dangled. The boy withdrew. She recognised the seal. It belonged to William of Pembroke. For a moment words were trapped in her throat. What if Joanna was ill or the children were unwell? She waited anxiously while Edward leaned against the wall reading. Although it appeared to be a short letter, he took a long time to read it.

Clutching the letter to his chest he gave a large guffaw. Thrusting it to her he said, 'Read this, Eleanor. We'll have another guest as well as Edmund's Blanche this Christmastide.'

She felt herself grow pale as her eyes sped along the words which William had written over a week earlier. Simon de Montfort's daughter, Eleanor, had been captured in the southern channel on her way from France to Wales, intending to join her betrothed who was none other than Prince Llewelyn himself. Her brother, Amaury de Montfort, was escorting her. One of William's vessels would deliver her to Bristol under guard. It was a cruel thing, as the girl was Edward's full cousin, but they had to face the fact that Edward could use this leverage against Llewelyn.

'I don't care what you do with Amaury,' Eleanor said, giving Edward back the letter. 'But we must treat the Lady Eleanor well. She is your cousin.'

'Amaury is my cousin too, but I cannot ever forgive what the other Montfort brothers did to dear Henry, our cousin too. Lady Eleanor may be an innocent, but she won't be marrying Llewelyn of Wales. My cousin will remain with our children at Windsor. We shall allow her to attend my brother's wedding after Christmas. If Llewelyn cannot behave, we could always marry her to Earl Gilbert.' He grinned wickedly.

Eleanor pursed her lips. 'The thought of Gilbert de Clare as part of *our* family is distasteful. Besides, he is still wed to Alix.' She locked her eyes on his. He never blinked.

'Legally separated. He can always purchase a divorce.'

'Not easily.' Eleanor glanced back at the river. It was not sparkling any more. The sky had filled with clouds and it looked as if it might rain. 'I think we should return to Westminster,' she said, changing the subject from Alix, still a sore. She added quietly, 'Eleanor de Montfort bears my name so we shall call her Ellen whilst she remains at court.'

Ellen was beautiful, sad-faced, and very quiet. Eleanor and Edward welcomed her. Christmas came and went. She remained at their court over Christmas and afterwards Edward sent her to Windsor. Her brother, on the other hand, was imprisoned. Ellen's freedom was to be restricted, and she kept writing requests to Edward asking for Amaury to be brought to her. He declined them all and refused Llewelyn's demands for her to be sent to him. Eleanor had her own concerns. She was into her third trimester. Time to birth another baby for the royal nursery.

★

In April, Eleanor went into seclusion. On the first of May, she gave birth to a little girl at her comfortable property of Kempton in Surrey. Olwen came to her for the birth and remained throughout her lying-in. The new baby slipped from her with ease and praise be to St Margaret, she was healthy.

'Madam, what is her name to be?' Olwen asked her as she gave her a sleeping draft.

'Berengaria,' Eleanor murmured, as smiling she drifted into sleep. She dreamed that she was in Spain again. Her three little girls were no longer babies. Baby Berengaria, too, was grown into a little girl with hair the colour of chestnuts so like her own. In her dream, Joan had returned from Flanders. She was jumping up and down with uncontrolled excitement, her fairy-like golden hair flying around her pretty face. Eleanora, as eldest, was bossing the others around as they played in the courtyard of the palace at Burgos. She was showing her daughters how to wield a sword . . . but their son, Alphonso, was missing. She found herself sobbing in her sleep. Why was Alphonso not present?

Berengaria was installed in the nursery at Windsor, overseen by the Dowager who reclaimed the apartments she once owned when she was queen.

'I am pleased to occupy these spaces again,' Dowager Queen Ailenor said, looking around her reclaimed apartment and clapping her hands. Her bedchamber had beautiful glass windows that could open on hinges and overlooked the rose garden. 'Henry built these chambers for me. He created my garden.' She stood by the opened window and breathed deeply. 'Alba roses. It was Henry's idea.' Tears swam in her eyes. Little Eleanora who accompanied them into the chambers clung to her grandmother.

'Grandmama, don't cry. Would you like to walk in the garden? I'll come.'

'Of course, sweeting. We shall cut a white rose and place it in a cup to set on the table in your own chamber.'

Eleanor whispered to Edward, 'Eleanora is growing up. We must take her with us on next summer's progress. Time she learned to hunt.'

'What did you say?' The Dowager, as ever alert, spun around on her heel. Ailenor remained tall and queenly. As if to insist on her special position within the family, she even used the title of queen when she signed her correspondence.

'I simply remarked how Eleanora might like to learn about hunting this summer.'

'A good idea, Eleanor. I must organise some gentle sport for her. It will do me good too.'

Edward grinned from ear to ear. 'Mother, take great care of Eleanora for us. She is promised to the King of Aragon's son. There'll be a queenship for her one day.'

Ailenor raised her finely etched eyebrows and touched her crispinettes. 'Well, there'll not be a marriage for years yet, if my opinion is of any value. I was married to your father when I was thirteen . . . far too young.' She studied Eleanor with a stern look. 'And you married at only twelve to my son. That was most unwise. It was foolish to allow you to set up house together in Bordeaux without supervision.'

Eleanor felt herself grow pale. How dare Ailenor refer to that time? She remembered only too well the child she had lost when she was only thirteen years old. Composing herself was difficult, but stiffening her back she said quietly, 'I was indeed too young.' She looked sternly at young Eleanora and added, 'However, you, my daughter, will learn to be a princess before you become a wife.'

'Yes, Mama,' Eleanora said earnestly. 'I have no desire to be wed in a hurry.'

Edward grunted. 'We shall see about that.'

The conversation concerning Eleanora's future was dropped.

Several months later, Eleanor was enjoying another summer touring her manors. That autumn, a marriage *did* occur. Olwen married Eugene on a September day of cloudless skies as blue as the Virgin's cloak. The wedding took place in Chichester. First, Edward had created Eugene a knight, so Olwen was now Lady Olwen.

Since Eleanor had founded the order of Chichester Dominicans, she selected a Dominican Bishop to marry the pair. Olwen's father travelled from Canterbury to attend his daughter's wedding. Eleanor had only met the apothecary once before, during the time in Canterbury ten years before when he had placed Olwen's future into her hands. Now he was a widower again. It was apparent to Eleanor that the white-bearded apothecary, who was similar in age to the Dowager herself, was proud of his daughter.

Olwen was happy to see her father and could not bring herself to be sorry at her stepmother's passing. Her father appeared more light-hearted, so perhaps he enjoyed being widowed, though with pragmatism ruling her heart she decided she would never ask because it could open old wounds. Let the wedding be a joyful occasion for them all. She had dressed for her wedding in a becoming blue silk-velvet gown with tight sleeves. Her sleeveless surcoat was edged with purfelle of vair, a fur that was checked bluish grey and creamy white. Eugene's grey tunic was likewise trimmed with the expensive fur. As Olwen walked into the choir area where as a knight's bride she could marry, her pale brown hair fell flowing to her waist. It was no longer tawny in hue but bore a golden sheen in the mellow candlelight. Eleanor's ladies had washed the girl's hair with camomile and brushed it over and over until the sun dried it. On her head, Olwen wore a garland of small white lilies. She was so beautiful on her wedding day Eugene appeared moon-eyed, obviously smitten.

Eleanor and Edward slipped away from the wedding feast, which was held in a large merchant's house, to the Bishop's palace located close to the Cathedral. The following day Eugene and Olwen would ride north to Herefordshire to begin their married life at Oldbury. Eleanor would return to London with Edward for the October Parliament. Edward determined to call Parliament twice yearly. He was intent on regular tours of his kingdom. They rarely stopped in any one place for long because they wanted to be seen by the people. After all, a king and queen were God's earthly representatives. It was convenient for Eleanor because she could use such progresses to

210

visit her manors and hunt deer in her woods. When they mounted their horses and rode out of the merchant's yard, Eleanor noticed a hooded man dressed in a Hospitallers' gown, a cross stitched onto his mantle. His gait was familiar. He was hugging the shadows of buildings and walking with speed towards an inn with a sign with a painted bull.

'Edward,' she leaned over to him. 'That man entering the inn. Is it . . .?'

'Guillaume of Acre? I saw him by the Cathedral earlier. He is far from the hospital in London.' Edward tugged his horse's bridle around to face her palfrey. 'Let well be, Eleanor. He is harmless.'

'What if he still is enamoured with Olwen?'

'He should have returned to England sooner. She'll be happier with Eugene.'

Edward grunted to Eleanor. 'I have no time for love-stricken Hospitallers. Eugene is *my* knight and your steward. Guillaume of Acre has no business here.'

'He saved your life, Edward.'

'That was then. Now is now.'

They rode in silence through the moonlight, the sounds of the wedding celebration, drums, and cymbals signalling dancing, the music fading into the distance as their horses and escorts approached heavily guarded gates of the Bishop's palace. Tomorrow they would move on and she hoped Olwen would never see Guillaume again.

Chapter Seventeen

November 1277

'Llewelyn still refuses to give me homage. He persists it is unsafe for him to travel into England.' Edward tossed the Welsh prince's message onto the fire. It flared up, consumed in a red and yellow flame with a whiff of melting wax. 'It's a poor excuse.'

'What did he write?' Eleanor glanced up from her book of hours, her curiosity piqued. She assumed Llewelyn would want his bride and speed to London to do homage.

Edward growled, 'Gilbert's men are occupying his lands. He says the Earl is a law unto himself.'

'I imagine Gilbert *is* a law unto himself.' She folded her arms. 'You should make him account for his boundaries as I must mine.'

'I need Earl Gilbert's support. You, madam, will behave with decorum towards him. In doing so you honour me as your King as well as your husband.'

'Gilbert is a bully. He is sly as a fox. You cannot believe him.'

'Ah, but I can, and so will Llewelyn obey his overlord, as will you. I am that, and if I say Gilbert occupies those lands to protect his own it is none of your affair. Now be gone from my presence, least I send you away under guard.'

'What? How dare you threaten me! My *overlord*! I am a princess of Castile. I am a princess of blood royal and a queen. And, remember this, Edward, our lands are held in *my* name. Remember that, *sire*.' She flounced from the chamber, knocking over a vase painted with a parrot. It was one which he loved. She did not look back as it crashed to the floor tiles.

'Come back and clear this up!'

His voice resounded through the doorway and along the corridor. She shouted at a page, 'Fetch a broom and sweep up the vase your King has caused to be knocked over.'

The boy fled to do her bidding.

Edward did not speak with her for a week. Not until Christmastide, not until she approached his chamber on Christmas Eve. Until that morning she saw him only in the chapel and even then she turned away from him and kept her ladies around her. Now, this dispute must end. It would spoil their twelve days of festivities. She said, standing tall and determined not to seem contrite, 'You are right, my lord. We may need all the Marcher earls' support if we are to control Wales. I agree since your wisdom surpasses my own. Still,' she deliberately paused and watched him raise his bushy brows, 'Gilbert de Clare should not be allowed to threaten the Welsh prince because we need the prince's support as well.'

Edward tugged at his beard and studied her without smiling. 'We must wait and see. Let us not quarrel over the Christmas season. Let us remain watchful. Now, Eleanor, return to your ladies. I hope you are decorating the Hall in readiness for the Christmas festivities. I shall join you when they drag in the Yule log.'

The quarrel was over. She did direct the decoration of the hall, sing carols, and supervise the placement of the Yule log, feeling easier that she had not condoned Gilbert's actions.

Llewelyn's messengers arrived in the Tower after Christmas. The Prince's half-brothers were colluding with the Marcher earls including Gilbert. Llewelyn was in fear of his life.

Edward declared war on Wales.

'War?' Eleanor said. 'Has it come to that?'

'By St George, I am tired of Llewelyn's excuses. A military campaign will commence in summer.' Edward rapped his knuckles against the wall. She loved this newly decorated chamber but the red

213

and gold decorations seemed suddenly to lose vibrancy. Wars were dangerous. Memory alone was enough to cause her shudders. The civil war was not so long distant.

'Once I've made adequate preparations,' Edward added and crossed to the bed. She felt his kiss upon her head. These new events seemed far more significant than any disagreement they had over Gilbert de Clare. Edward pulled on his boots and moments later was clattering down the stairway.

Later that week, they moved from the Tower to Windsor. As they sat side by side in the royal barge enjoying rare winter sunshine, Edward announced, 'I am calling up my war council.' She drew breath. So that was his reason for their sudden departure from the Tower. And she had assumed they were to enjoy a week's hunting in Windsor Park.

'And hunting,' he said, reading her thought. 'Your dogs will have missed you.'

'Indeed, I shall anticipate that with pleasure,' she replied coolly, thinking how poor Ellen, who was incarcerated at Windsor, would be distraught at the news of a war with Llewelyn.

'Ellen . . .?' she said.

'Ellen must not know anything. Christ's holy bones, Eleanor, who knows how the wench might manage a warning sent to Wales.' He raised an eyebrow. 'Or to her bastard of a brother. After all, you once managed to send a secret messenger to the borders.'

'Twice,' Eleanor corrected him and turned away, holding her breath as their barge coasted through the water surging under London Bridge.

She received regular updates as Edward plotted strategy with old crusading friends Roger Clifford, Otto de Grandison, and John de Vescy. Edmund, too, who owned land in South Wales, rode into Windsor early in February. Within weeks Roger Mortimer, young Henry de Lacy, Earl of Lincoln, and William Beauchamp, Earl of Warwick, had all joined Edward's war council.

By March, they planned to ride to Chester where they would be joined by Earl Gilbert. He, more than anyone, was ready to attack Llewelyn. He was furious at Welsh raids into his own lands.

'He has too many lands,' Eleanor complained. They had managed an afternoon's hunting and their horses were ambling side by side through the drizzle. 'William de Valence should be part of the war council too.'

'William is better employed in Gascony.'

'What about Joanna and the children? Are they in danger if there's war with Wales?' she asked.

'Since they are in Kent, they can stay there. Edmund will see to it there will be no assaults on Pembroke Castle, and Goodridge Castle is a building site again.'

'As long as they are safe.' She peered into the trees. 'Look, Edward, a deer.'

The conversation stopped as Edward turned in the saddle and signalled to his huntsmen to move softly forward.

The day came for the earls' departure. They said their goodbyes in Windsor's great hall before the whole court. Edward announced, 'Preparation is all-important. Chester will be our base. Gather your knights. Guard it well.'

As they knelt to receive Edward's and Eleanor's blessing, Lady Ellen stood amongst the children's household watching, her large eyes swimming tears. Watching her, Eleanor hardened her heart.

The chill air in the hall seeped tension as the earls knelt.

'God is on our side,' Edward drew himself taller than he already was. His eyes were steely. The earls rose from their knees. Edward declared loudly, 'This Welsh prince thinks he is King Arthur himself. God will decide which of us the true King of the Britons is. He will give me homage or I'll have his head on a spike.'

There was not a rustle and even the children fell silent. Lady Ellen mumbled something. She pushed through the ladies of the court and ran to a side door. Two ladies followed. They took her by her arms, supporting her. Words were exchanged with the armed men on duty. Followed by guards, the group of women quietly left the hall. Eleanor, resolved not to pity enemies, looked away.

Edward insisted he was God's representative in his earthly kingdom. God was on the side of a just king and to prove it, Edward and Eleanor planned to make a tour of their favourite East Anglia shrines to pray for God's guidance.

It was March but instead of spring sunshine, it rained incessantly. Eleanor knelt before her portable altar every night and prayed the rain would stop. Roads would be waterlogged and they would never reach Walsingham if this weather continued.

At last, on a drizzling morning, they kissed the children goodbye. Their grandmother would remain at Windsor throughout the summer. The Dowager held tiny Berengaria in her arms and remarked pointedly, 'Eleanor, I fear for this little one. Should you really be leaving her side?'

'Her wet nurse says if she survives her first year we have nothing to fear.'

Ailenor shook her head. 'She is fragile, so tiny.'

'Edward needs my support.'

Edward, always Edward. He came first. He was her husband and her King.

Eleanor remembered her other children who had died before their fifth birthdays. She would pray for her living children at every shrine. It was important. It did not matter how much it rained, she would kneel in the mud and beg the Holy Mother and her saints for their safety.

The Dowager's concern for eight-month-old Berengaria haunted Eleanor throughout their five days of travel. At times she felt angry. Why did Ailenor manage to make her feel guilty? As she rode her palfrey, her hood sheltering her face from the constant showers, a heavy mantle pinned close about her neck, her lips often moved in prayer. Gloved hands strayed to the amber rosary fastened onto her belt as she counted her prayers. The Virgin must understand, because she also had been a mother. Yet Eleanor dared not hope too much.

Too many of her children had died. She could not depend on their survival. She was still afraid to draw too close to her children.

By August, they had crossed England and ridden northwards to Chester. Edward was waiting to attack Llewelyn. The Welsh prince had vanished. Edward's considered planning and timing, thorough attention to detail, his well-trained knights, and the magnificent ships placed strategically around the coastal waters, were all helping Edward's success in Gwynedd just as much as the prayers and offerings they had given to shrines in Norfolk. Llewelyn was running scared.

Eleanor's eyes flicked towards a familiar book placed on a side table in their antechamber in the castle. It was Vegetius. Eleanor bent over the table and picked up the book on strategy she had given Edward years before.

Edward glanced up from lists he was studying as she set down the book. 'We've recruited hundreds of masons. Flint will be a strong castle fortress.' He grinned. 'Speed is of the essence.' He stretched, raising his arms above his head. Her eyes followed his as he looked out through the arched window at a cerulean sky. 'Thanks for fine weather again. Ships can sail with the supplies for Flint.'

She lifted an unfinished circlet from a peg on the wall. It was a summer garland of lilies to place on the statue of the virgin in the castle chapel.

'Leave that, Eleanor. Come and look at this.' He pointed at a map.

She stared down at it and glanced out of the window. Out in the fields the harvest was already being scythed. Tiny figures were moving slowly about the meadows. Women were gleaning, collecting the left over barley stalks into their skirts. Her own properties, too, she could not help thinking, would be productive.

'Eleanor, concentrate.' Edward's sharp tone drew her back to the present.

She stared down at the map. 'Ah, we are here.' She pointed to the miniature castle that represented Chester. Edward took her finger and moved it along a pattern of trees lying between Chester and Flint.

217

'My woodsmen are felling these trees and building a road from Flint to Rhuddlan. The enemy uses forests for concealment so the road needs to be wide enough for a dozen horsemen to ride side by side. Our train will need protection.' He moved his finger around the coast to a village on the western coast. 'Edmund has advanced through those valleys . . .' he tapped the mountains and valleys drawn on the centre, 'and is building a castle at Aberystwyth.' He grinned at her. 'Ships have sailed to him from Bristol with men and materials.'

'Where is Llewelyn?'

He drew her closer. Her hair was braided in two thick plaits. He touched it. 'You do have beautiful hair. It's like squirrel fur.'

She smiled up at him. 'Concentrate, Edward. Where is Llewelyn?'

'You distract me, my love.' He pointed to a mountain sketched on the map's interior. 'Llewelyn is in the mountains they call Snowdonia. We'll just have to move the army from Flint to Rhuddlan, build a wide road, and flush Llewelyn from the forests. Rhuddlan is where I am going to build another new castle.' His blue eyes were shining. 'And a town too. I have plans to build towns around my castles and introduce English settlers. What do you think?'

'May God bless your plans and keep you safe, my lord.' She lifted her amber prayer beads to her lips and kissed them.

'Spoken like a warrior queen,' Edward said as he folded the parchment, tucking the map into his leather scrip. 'I shall carry this with me.' He patted his beloved well-worn satchel. 'My campaign begins after the founding of the new abbey.'

'I'll miss you when you go.' Her eyes filled with tears. War was dangerous.

'We can enjoy a day's together hunting first.'

Her hounds pricked up their ears at the word hunting. One set up a barking. Eleanor laughed as they flocked about her skirts.

'Falconry this time, hounds,' Edward said as he leaned down and fondled their ears.

'So much castle-building,' Eleanor said as she tossed a bone into the rushes and watched the dogs scramble after it. She threw two more she had saved from dinner.

218

Edward watched them rutting after the bones. 'Castles as strong and as beautiful as those we saw in Savoy.' He sank into his chair. 'And a new royal abbey on the borders. We'll ride for Northwich at dawn tomorrow.'

The royal household, cooks, clerks, grooms, huntsmen, cages with hawks, wagons, carts, and an enormous contingent of mounted guards set out as the sun rose. Moving anywhere, even on a short journey, was always a huge operation.

'The abbey will be a statement of power, just like the new castles,' Edward said as they jogged through the countryside. 'God is with us.'

They arrived as bells rang for Sext and the midday sun was high in the sky. Edward reined in his horse. Eleanor followed his lead drawing her palfrey up by a river running through a valley where there was already a tiny abbey. Her eye approved the surrounding arable land, yellow with ripening grain.

'Look around us,' Edward said, sweeping his gloved hand towards the crowd gathered before the old abbey. 'Everyone who matters is here.'

They dismounted. He took her arm and led her into a large field where the high altar for the new abbey church would be built.

'It's a beautiful site,' she said as she looked around her and back towards the river 'High enough to avoid flooding if the river overflows.'

'And,' he said clearly delighted, 'Earl Gilbert is here too.'

She scowled in Gilbert's direction and declined to comment. She had spotted Alix amongst Gilbert's supporters, standing proudly with their two daughters, looking handsome as ever, and certainly richly robed. The girls must be nearing marriageable age, twelve, thirteen? She must not show ungratefulness today. It would neither be dutiful nor gracious. After all, Gilbert brought Edward's war knights and a huge contingent of archers.

She stepped forward when summoned by Robert Burnell and laid two stones, one for herself and one for Alphonso. Burnell had been elected as Bishop of Bath and Wells two years earlier. Turning on her heel, she swelled with pride to see Bishop Burnell summoning the nobles who stepped in an orderly long line towards the altar spot. She watched intently as they all laid foundation stones. This abbey was to be the largest Cistercian abbey in the whole kingdom. She turned to Edward. 'It will be as big and as grand as Westminster.'

Looking down on her with a smile he said, 'It will be magnificent.'

She proudly watched the banners of Gloucester, Cornwall, Surrey, and Warwick flutter in the light August breeze and considered that Edward's leopards overshadowed all others. Bishop Burnell gave a sermon. He spoke in his cultured voice and finished by saying, 'With the founding of this abbey our noble King Edward will bring God's blessing upon the King's just intention to return peace and honourable rule to his Kingdom of Wales.'

'No abbey will be as beautiful,' Edward said loudly for all to hear. 'It is already royal in wealth and honour. We name it Vale Royale.'

Eleanor found she was weeping. She choked back her emotion, though her ladies were all dabbing at their eyes with their veils. Edward was so proud and she was proud of him. His sire had begun the rebuilding of Westminster but Vale Royale was *his*. England's earls bowed their heads and prayed. It was as if they had stepped into a book of legends and onto a richly painted illustration gilded with gold.

Eleanor felt as if she, clad in a green velvet gown edged with gold embroidery, was Guinevere and Edward, decked out in a scarlet robe trimmed with ermine, was Arthur of the Britons. One day, she mused, they, too, might become the stuff of legend.

On her return to Chester, after a tour of her newest borderland properties, Eleanor discovered letters from Edward waiting for her. She tucked her feet under the cushioned window seat, broke his seals and unfolded them all. Working out the order was not so easy but the letters were short. Edward was no scribe. She began to read them aloud from first to the most recent.

Castle of Flint, August 20th,

Eleanor, Queen and Wife, I pray to Our Lady daily that you remain in robust health. The new road has advanced. We move the army forward towards Rhuddlan. May God grant us success.

The second read –

Llewelyn's brothers, Piers and Dafydd, demand their share of spoils. They demand Gwynedd and an end to Llewelyn. Nay, I am intent on deciding this outcome, not them. There has been hard fighting around Rhuddlan. We are building a castle by the Clwyd. My new castles are to be concentric, built entirely of stone. We have more than fifteen thousand men engaged in battle. Stay safe, my love, until I return. Send me word of our children if you have received news from my mother.

She lifted the third piece of folded parchment.

This past week I have lost men in battle. I dismissed others. They have served beyond their forty days' duty. It is overly expensive to retain them. With the help of our fleet we have sent two thousand men over the Menai Strait to the island of Anglesey where we are harvesting crops to supply my army. In so doing, we are starving Llewelyn into submission.

Llewelyn was not beaten yet. He was, she realised, holding out in the mountain lands. Eleanor placed the three letters in a casket and locked it. At least she could sleep well, knowing that if the war was won, it would not be long before Llewelyn surrendered. She could ride homewards to Windsor and wait for Edward there. News from Windsor Castle said their son and daughters were all well. Eleanora was reading a horn book and learning Latin. Alphonso was obsessed with his father's aviary of exotic birds. Queen Ailenor reported that he chattered away to them. This would amuse Edward. Margaret was toddling around after her brother and sister. Berengaria had not sickened after all.

The Dowager wrote, *I intend moving to Marlborough. The children will have the care of their household and that of the custodian of the castle and his wife whom they love. They are a happy family, including young Nicholas Burdon who has settled well.*

Mary, Queen of Heaven, had listened to her prayers. When Eleanor received the letters from Ailenor the messenger reported that the Dowager had already moved to her castle in Marlborough and intended remaining there. Eleanor smiled. The children's household would continue happily without Grandmother Ailenor overseeing it. There was no urgent need to return to London yet but she would send them toys and new woollen mantles lined with satin. It was her desire to wait at Chester for Edward to return, and when he sent her word she would ride along the coast to meet him.

As it was Michaelmas, a feast was to be prepared for that evening. In the morning, Eleanor requested a bath filled with warm water and herbs. Maids arrived with pails of water. The scented steam filled the chamber with the aroma of roses. Wearing a thin linen shift, Eleanor stepped into her bath.

'Lay out my linens and the emerald gown for this evening but I shall wear the brown linen one for now,' she said to Margerie. She called to her maidens who swarmed into her chamber like a hive of bees. 'Bring me rose water and soap and towels too, girls. Make haste.'

They scurried off. When she ordered anything done, there was no hesitation. She knew it was because her temper was hasty when aroused.

'I hope to attend Mass this morning with my husband, if you permit it. It's his name day,' Margerie said, her blue eyes earnest.

'Yes, you may, Margerie. I've a letter to write to Edward this morning. It's a heavenly day and the carts are arriving already with the quarter rents. I'll let the clerks do that job. No need for me to be present.'

Margerie crossed to a chest containing the Queen's best gowns carefully folded between layers of soft linen. She lifted out a green gown edged with gold bands. Fennel scattered to the floor tiles as she shook it out. 'Your Grace, the girls will help you now. I'll return in time to dress you for St Michael's Feast. We'll hang the gown to loosen the creases.' She placed a pair of soft leather shoes and stockings beside it. Finally she selected a pair of golden crispinettes for Eleanor's hair. Eleanor nodded and Margerie turned to look inside a second chest. She withdrew an under-gown of fine linen.

Afterwards, the maids returned with bucket after bucket of warm water. Two of her damsels, huge aprons tied about their waists, began to sponge her back using soft soap scented with roses. They were so gentle she hardly felt their touch. Outside noises grew distant. The maids began washing her hair, gently massaging her head with soap and pouring jugs of rinsing water over it. 'Hurry,' she managed to say. 'No time to waste. I have work to do today.' She waited a few more moments and rose from the scented water refreshed ready to attend to letters concerning her properties and to write to Edward. She had a busy morning planned.

The castle was busy all morning as peasants leading carts with sacks of grain entered the courtyards, and townsmen with fat purses full of coins. She could hear the clanking of carts and animal sounds as well as shouting. Her hair, wrapped in a linen cloth, smelled sweet. It could do no harm to look out. She peered down from the window, kneeling on the cushioned seat, leaning on the broad ledge, absorbing the busy scene below.

Knights returning from the war trotted about the courtyard below watching deliveries and helping to move the storage of barley and wheat. She saw one of her household knights drag a bag of flour from a wagon. It burst open and he was covered with a dusting of white. Others tried to scoop it all back into the sack. The knight marched off leaving them to deal with the mess. Royal bailiffs and reeves, many of whom she knew well, would sit at desks in the hall taking in rents and meticulously ticking off deliveries of grain. Well, they could be one full bag of flour short today. She shook her head, nearly dislodging its wrapping, then went to sit at her own table and wrote to Edward. Her rents would come in all over the kingdom, bags of coin to swell the royal treasury; grain to be sold on and proceeds sent to her coffers.

By mid-afternoon she had sealed her letters with wax, stamped them with her emblem and sent for a messenger to ride along the coast with Edward's letter. She called for her ladies to accompany her and descended a private stair to the garden where she sat on a turf bench allowing her damp hair to dry in the sun. Two maids brushed it until it shone with golden lights. Anna, the most senior lady present, read to them from a book of Arthurian legends. She could smell geese roasting for the feast and realised she was hungry, knowing her damsels must be also. Margerie sought her out to help her dress for the feast.

'What an absurdly lazy hour this has been,' she said as she rose from her bench and passed the belt she was embroidering to a damsel to put into her work basket. 'I should pass more hours seated in the sunshine within a garden.'

'You would soon be restless, your Grace. I doubt you would sit still for long.' Margerie touched her hair. 'It will look well bound in the gold crispinettes.'

'Just plait it into a net at the back of my neck and find a short veil and circlet for my head.' She stood and drew Margerie's arm through her own. 'Still, I do enjoy wearing my green gown.' She threw a glance over her shoulder. 'Ladies, go, Lady Margerie will remain with me . . .' She nodded to a young girl little older than her own Eleanora, a ward whom she hoped would remain her maiden for some years yet before marrying a knight. 'Annette, you can help Margerie dress me today and walk with us to the chapel for Vespers.'

After Vespers, holding herself regally, knowing she needed little adornment in order to impress, Eleanor swept into the royal hall. Her ladies, dressed exquisitely in silks and velvets, were already seated on benches along the lower trestles. Eleanor took her place on the dais beside Bishop Robert, who had ridden in from Anglesey some days earlier. He would be returning to London with her business letters, her collected rents, and plenty of coin for the royal treasury.

The feast proceeded with dishes paraded into the hall on enormous trays balanced on the servitors' shoulders. Pages poured wine. Tasters sampled each dish and goblet. She watched a juggler toss golden balls into the air and catch them. She smiled as mummers took on the roles of St Michael and various attendant angels and paraded around the hall distributing blessings. A devil appeared through an archway carrying a pronged spectre. The angels set upon him and banished him from the hall with threats and loudly recited Biblical verses. Everyone held their sides, they were laughing so much.

Eleanor simply smiled. Her thoughts were elsewhere. She turned to Robert Burnell. 'The King should return soon. Do you think, if the Welsh prince agrees to give homage, Llewelyn will be permitted to marry Lady Ellen?'

Robert discreetly coughed. He lowered his voice. 'Better that Llewelyn is chastened. The King won't make too many concessions yet. Still, better the devil you know. The prince's brothers are even more untrustworthy.'

'My husband used them to help him fight the war.'

'Lest they misuse *him*.'

How true his words were. If only her much older brother, Alfonso, could be aware of deceit when dealing with his own nobles. Recent news from Castile was worrying. Alfonso was making rash decisions about the succession. He could not please the traditionalists who favoured his younger brother, Sancho, as the Castilian heir, as well as his neighbour, Pedro of Aragon, who favoured his nephew as successor to the throne of Castile. The complication was the French King's support for Pedro's nephew. Aragon was strong. France was powerful. Pedro's son was betrothed to Princess Eleanora. Where should her own loyalty lie? She loved Alfonso with all her heart.

'What can we do about the situation in Castile?' she said aloud to loyal Bishop Robert, who always had good sense.

'Nothing. You must watch and wait.' He laid his hand over Eleanor's and she felt his warmth, his devotion and his intelligence. Whilst Robert guided them, sound decisions would be made in England even if foolish ones occurred in Castile. She sighed. *This will be another discussion Edward and I must have when he returns.*

Chapter Eighteen

1278

The war was not over yet as Eleanor had hoped. For weeks messengers rode between Edward's camp at Rhuddlan and Chester. He took Llewelyn's submission at Rhuddlan with grace. In early November, Eleanor set out for Flint to greet her husband, thankful Edward had Llewelyn in his power at last. Llewelyn had submitted at Rhuddlan and accompanied Edward to Flint.

The senatorial Llewelyn was almost as old as the Dowager. His hair and beard were dark streaked with grey and his eyes were sharp as the clearest blue sky, icy and focused. Llewelyn studied a speaker with considerable attention before ever responding to the speaker's words. When he finally spoke, a smile could light up his face and she quickly forgot the winter in his eyes. The Welsh prince was weathered, lined and rugged as the uncut stones piled up about Flint's rocky walls awaiting a mason's attention. Llewelyn's was a furrowed face. She was impressed and hoped he could soon marry Ellen, who seemed so sad.

That evening, wrapped in furs and warmed by braziers inside Edward's campaign tent, Eleanor stretched her gloved hands towards the coals. 'So what next?'

Edward dropped his voice, reminding her Llewelyn was housed in an adjacent tent. The Prince's Welsh retainers might be passing their way as they visited the privies. She leaned towards him to listen. 'The war is over, Eleanor. Llewelyn has agreed to give his homage formally at Westminster in front of our whole court.' He drew breath. 'What he does not know yet is that he will give it on Christmas Day.'

'Perhaps that is kind since all present will be in a jovial mood. We had hoped he would come last Christmas, after all.'

Edward frowned. 'Let us hope the border lords accept this peace. Christ's Day is one of the most religious days of the Church's year. It will remind him and them of the sanctity of his oath.'

'And Ellen? Will he marry her at Christmas?'

'Not yet, not until we can trust him to behave.' Edward folded his long arms.

'Ah, well, let's hope. Welsh lands; does he retain all these lands?'

'Anglesey and Gwynedd, yes. His two treacherous brothers will get parcels of territory but *we* must retain the greater part of Wales for the crown. Llewelyn will pay a great fine, of course.' He wiped a hand across his brow. 'The war has been costly for us.'

'We continue to protect the borderlands. That must please Earl Gilbert. And we add to our own lands, too, which might not be so pleasing to that Earl but we shall have great castles and loyal towns.'

'Tut, tut. Gilbert is best kept sweet, my love.' He glanced towards his bed around which hung a curtain embroidered with English leopards and covered with thick furs. 'Warmer under the covers,' he said softly, taking her hand, drawing her to the bed. She was glad to crawl under the furs. Slowly, he drew off her woollen gown, his large fingers surprisingly nimble as he undid her side lacings, peeling away her clothing until she lay in her linen under-gown. His own shirt and leggings were even quicker to remove.

After making love, they grew warmer and as she was lying in the crook of Edward's arm beneath the bed linen and soft rabbit skins, Edward remarked, 'One thing makes me uneasy about these Welsh princes. They assume they are descended from King Arthur. Their subjects believe in this lie too and claim Arthur as their own.'

'Then they are thieves. King Arthur is buried at Glastonbury Abbey, Guinevere too. The Dowager has visited their grave.'

'Yes, but we need proof of this so everyone knows Arthur is dead and not reincarnated in Wales as Llewelyn or any other upstart princeling.'

She sat up, her eyes widening. 'Let's dig up the grave. We'll show all the world that Arthur was a true, civilised English king and no wild Welshman.'

'But what if there are no bones, Eleanor?'

'Oh, my love, there are indeed bones there.'

'I shall think about it.' Edward gently moved his arm away. 'My dearest, I wish you would not call my mother *the Dowager*. She's Queen Ailenor.'

'And so am I.'

'Don't ever let her or her ladies hear you call her *Dowager*. She would not like it.'

'As if I would. Good night, Edward.'

He kissed her forehead. She smiled into the dark. He would forgive her favoured name for his mother as long as she remained respectful in Ailenor's presence.

'When Lady Ellen smiles she is beautiful,' Eleanor remarked to Edward as they rode towards Glastonbury during the following April. Eleanor's idea had caught Edward's imagination. They would exhume Arthur's bones, or whatever bones were there.

'Ellen resembles her mother, not her sire, I am relieved to say,' he replied.

'And her brother, Amaury? He was not involved in the killing of your nephew. Could it be unfair to hold him responsible?'

Edward never replied. His face was stony. His gloved hands twitched at his stallion's reins. Turning in his saddle, he slowed their cavalcade right down with a wave of his hand. Eleanor reined in her palfrey. Two elegant light brown hunting dogs, granted to them as a gift by Llewelyn before he returned to Wales that year, raced past them. The kennel master running along with them, clutching his cap in one hand and a stick in the other, whistled them back again.

'My lords and ladies,' Edward, rising in his saddle, called back. He pointed towards a hill rising up in the distance. 'Camelot.'

Eleanor was so thrilled by the hill appearing out of a mystical veil of thin mist she forgot their previous words until Edward turned and said, 'Amaury has been released as a wedding favour to his sister. He is on his way to France.'

She glanced back at two girls whose dark heads were thrust out from the long painted carriage peering at the distant grassy hill. 'Does Ellen know?'

'She knows.'

'She's happier. As well she does.'

They rode until they turned into a hawthorn-edged lane. A number of attendants had ridden ahead days before with Lady Margerie and her husband to ensure a manor close to Glastonbury was prepared for their royal visit. Other nobles and servants waiting for the King and Queen's arrival were billeted in small manor houses round about. Tomorrow, their court would continue to the Island of Avalon.

Edward turning again to her said, 'At twilight, we'll open the caskets and everyone can behold the King of the Britons. Any Welshman who speaks of Arthur dwelling in the mountains of Snowdonia will be known for a liar.' He rubbed his leathered hands together. 'My father loved organising such ceremonies. He would have enjoyed it.'

'Edward, I see your true intention. Lady Ellen witnesses all this before she marries her Welsh prince.'

'As indeed her mother once witnessed the graves with my own mother,' Edward said, reminding her, though she needed no reminding. The Dowager had often spoken of the occasion. Ailenor intended riding over from Marlborough to join them for the opening of the burial caskets. The bones would afterwards be removed to the monastery's treasury.

'The Dowager was only thirteen at the time,' Eleanor reminded him.

'Arthur of the Britons was my mother's hero. She never forgot seeing the graves. Neither will my aunt have forgotten.'

'King Arthur is a hero for us all,' Eleanor said firmly. 'Our daughter will remember it all her days.'

Eleanor glanced back again at the long painted carriage rattling along the lane with Eleanora, Ellen and their ladies.

'Look, Eleanor, we've reached the manor,' Edward was saying.

A fissure of excitement raced through Eleanor when they glimpsed the manor through a stand of beech trees. The large slate-roofed house with its serene greenish moat lay before them. She nudged her palfrey, Merlin, with her foot. She would find it hard to sleep that night. She did not care if the bones in the caskets at Glastonbury truly belonged to Arthur and Guinevere or not; it was enough that she wanted to believe in them and important that others did too. She could smell baking bread and roasting meats. Her belly rumbled. After the long day's ride, she was hungry.

As Vespers drew to a close in Glastonbury Abbey, afternoon light faded and a full moon rose. Lit by torches and moonlight the court crossed from the church to the graves. They were led by Glastonbury's tall abbot whose jewelled, embroidered gown crackled as he moved. Monks followed, ghostly in their grey habits. Eleanor shuddered as the abbot and his monks removed the first casket from an opened grave, and then the second. The two caskets were placed on the grass. Neither was rotting or damaged, a miracle indeed.

Edward inclined his head to speak to the Abbot who nodded and instructed two of his monks to carry the caskets into the Abbey church. The court processed back across the swath into the church led by a line of monks bearing torches, two carefully carrying the remains in their boxes as if they were as precious as reliquary. Indeed, Eleanor was sure they must be. After hundreds of years the caskets remained intact.

Courtiers filled the long central aisle, spilling into the Abbey's side chapels. Edward and Eleanor clasped hands as Arthur's skeleton was laid out on a huge table close to the altar. Slowly, Guinevere, too, was reconstructed. There was a collective gasp of awe from those watching the laying out of the bones. Candles flickered. Eleanor grew chill. She drew her thick woollen mantle close. To their side she saw how nine-year-old Eleanora clung to Ellen's hand. Ellen appeared ashen, Eleanora seemed overawed. It occurred to Eleanor that perhaps Ellen felt afraid. Censors swung to and fro,

231

perfuming the air with the scent of frankincense as the Abbot said prayers over the remains. The choir sang Ave Marias, their harmonies floating through the nave into the side chapels. Edward leaned down, lifted an ell of crimson silk from a basket on the floor tiles, and used it to line the emptied casket. He carefully placed the bones into the silk. He folded the silk over them like he was wrapping a gift until they were placed into Arthur's casket except for the skull.

Eleanor drew a deep breath and stepped to the table. She lifted Guinevere's bones, which were smooth, delicate, and truly beautiful. With all the reverence she could summon up she placed them on a second ell of crimson silk within the second casket and folded it over. Both skulls were to remain on display in the abbey for some weeks so anyone visiting the Abbey could see for themselves that Arthur and Guinevere were present at Glastonbury. Not only were Arthur and his queen dead and not dwelling in Snowdonia, the remains of the royal couple were in Avalon. Eleanor gave a satisfied smile as she finished folding the silk over the bones. The King of England and his Queen were witnesses to this fact. If these were not really Arthur and Guinevere's bones, others would consider them so and that was all that mattered.

For weeks, Eleanor toured her Somerset properties before moving south to Winchester. She felt elated and like Guinevere, who was the greatest lady in their books of legends. Edward, himself, appeared as Arthur reincarnated. The knights who accompanied their progress belonged to his magical round table. When Edward suggested an actual magnificent round table for the great hall in Winchester, Eleanor encouraged his idea.

They set out for Westminster, in time for Edward's summer Parliament. No sooner than they had returned to the City than Berengaria grew ill and died of ague. Her funeral held in the Abbey at Westminster was a quiet family affair. The Dowager visited them in Winchester and travelled with them to Westminster. It was she, not Eleanor, who tried to comfort the Lady Ellen, Eleanora, and three-year-old Margaret. The girls wept and wept for the loss of their small sister and cousin who was less than two years old when she died.

Eleanor was relieved when it was all over. She could not cope with grief. She had lost too many children. Had she so displeased God that he punished her and Edward in this way? There was one consolation. Alphonso remained in good health. He was a lively little boy who loved his pony and his menagerie of small animals, especially an aviary he kept in the Tower gardens. He had a favourite bird there, a stork called Longbeak that, to Eleanor's amusement, had its own compound and small pond. It looked down on everyone from its long neck as if they were all lesser creatures.

'Edward, I hope Alphonso can soon travel with our court,' Eleanor said a few days after Berengaria's funeral. She turned a ribbon belonging to the tiny girl around and around in her fingers and placed it in a silver box engraved with intricate crosses. In it, she kept keepsakes relating to the children. She managed a bemused look. 'Though, hopefully, his white mice, Longbeak, and his other creatures will remain at home.'

'We shall see, Eleanor. If anything happened to him . . .'

She placed her hand over his. 'I know, he is our only male heir. But Eleanora is next in line to the throne.'

Edward nodded. 'We need to be careful whom she weds. The Aragon marriage . . .'

'May never happen,' she said with firmness.

Eleanora and Ellen became friends during the spring progress period despite the fact Eleanora was much younger than Ellen, and still a young girl. Yet, Eleanora was mature and had a charming and beguiling way with her so it did not seem odd to Eleanor that Ellen enjoyed reading with her daughter or helping her with Latin. In turn, Eleanora seemed to look up to Ellen as if she was a much older sister. Edward decided on an October wedding for Ellen and Llewelyn. Eleanor promised the girls a new wardrobe for the occasion. They passed days together discussing fabrics for the gowns.

Wales was settling down, castle-building progressed, and the royal debt was lessening. Eleanor's properties were making profits. God had called her youngest daughter into his heavenly kingdom. Nothing could change this. She ended her grieving within the month and threw herself into managing her properties from the office at Westminster. Prayer had not saved their other dead children. Even so, Eleanor added prayers for this little daughter to those for her earlier losses – Katherine, Joan, John, and Henry. She placed flowers on their graves within the Abbey regularly and gave alms to the poor to pray for her children's tiny souls.

Eleanor's property office was always busy. She had established seven departments to administer her lands and they were efficient. When she returned to Westminster that year she consulted with her administrators and met with her group of professional couriers. These riders were ready to jump on fast horses at a moment's notice, carrying messages day and night to bailiffs throughout the land and across the sea to France and Flanders.

She was alerted to possible misconduct on the part of her bailiff in Gloucestershire and Herefordshire because she had forgotten to confirm that Eugene and Olwen were not to pay rent for the manor and lands at Oldbury, just taxes. She had neglected to formalise this generous gift in her account books. Her bailiff, suspiciously a friend to Gilbert de Clare's bailiff, questioned the legality of this grant in a letter to her.

She threw the letter at one of her clerks in a temper and shouted, 'How dare he question my knight's right! How dare he write to me that Sir Eugene owes two years' rent and it has only just come to his attention.' Her clerks cowered. Spittle landed on their tunics as she looked from one to one, repeating herself. 'You have done nothing. Nothing! The letter is dated March.'

'Your Grace, I was waiting for your instruction,' a trembling clerk said with diffidence.

'No excuse. How can I instruct if not alerted?'

She marched to an empty desk, sat at it and called for parchment and quill. When these arrived with a quaking clerk, she dipped the

234

pen into ink and began to write in her neat script. Every few moments she paused and glared at the clerks who stood watching her tantrum with opened mouths. 'If you want something done properly you do it yourself,' she hissed at them. They began to shift about on their feet. She put down her pen. 'Now make three copies,' she snapped. 'This issue concerns my own knight and my lady. I shall personally keep a copy of the grant.' Looking up she saw the tall Otto de Grandison entering the long chamber. 'Otto,' she called to the studious-looking knight, her tone still sharp. 'Find John de Vescy. You will both witness this grant.'

Otto hurried to her side and read the new charter. He took the pen and added his signature. 'I see this concerns Eugene and Olwen. I thought you had made the grant official last year.'

'Apparently not.'

'I shall fetch John. He's . . .' He coughed. 'I mean . . .'

'He's where?'

'In the rose garden by the merman fountain reading poetry to your ladies Joanna and Isabel, Marie St Amand, and Ermintrude de Sackville.' He coughed again.

'Lady Isabel Beaumont,' she said thoughtfully. 'Well, well.' She had wondered if Isabel would be a suitable match for the handsome, flashing-eyed knight. This alliance was satisfactory. Eleanor's mood immediately improved. She dipped the pen into the ink pot. 'Bring both Lady Isabel and Sir John here. I shall have their signatures on this.'

Once the land grant was witnessed and Lady Isabel and John Vescy, who appeared blushing and bashful, had left the chamber to return to the garden, Eleanor wrote a personal letter to Olwen and Eugene, inviting them to Worcester for Ellen's wedding.

It was fortunate that a fast courier was available that day to ride to Gloucester where Earl Gilbert was dwelling, with another letter and sealed copy of her charter. 'He must stop this bailiff's harassment of my knight,' she muttered to herself. 'Gilbert's lands border my own. A bailiff would know the boundary.'

★

235

Gilbert sent his response by return, saying he acknowledged the property indeed belonged to the Queen and was granted to her knight, Sir Eugene.

Once she had Gilbert's letter in her hand she sought Edward out. Discovering him by a cage with two squawking parrots he had brought years ago from Sicily, she thrust Gilbert's note into his hand. 'Earl Gilbert has been playing with Lady Fortune. He has greedy eyes on my Gloucestershire holdings.'

One parrot squawked 'greedy, greedy . . .' The other joined in, 'Eyes, eyes, eyes,' imitating her voice and Spanish accent perfectly. She glared at the creature.

'I think you read too much into this business,' Edward replied, folding the letter again, bits of Gilbert's seal dropping from it onto the pavement, sprinkling it with blood-like crumbs of wax. 'He has more than enough lands of his own around Gloucester and Hereford.'

She shrugged. 'You always take his side.'

'No, Eleanor, you persist in holding a grudge against my earl. You are set on revenge for his behaviour long ago.'

The second parrot shrieked, 'REVENGE.'

She covered her ears with her hands saying, 'Those birds!'

'Come away,' Edward said to her and took her arm. 'A cup of wine and a dish of sugared plums will calm your nerves.'

They moved away from the cage, Edward bending his head as they entered the palace by a side door.

'Thank heaven for silence,' she said, her hands dropping from her ears. 'Have you heard anything of Master Guillaume?' she asked, changing the subject.

'What an odd question of a sudden. As it happens, I have. He is one of the Hospitallers who will set up a new hospital somewhere. I cannot recollect if it is to be Gloucester, Hereford, or Worcester. I can find out.'

'Do, I have invited Eugene and Olwen to Ellen's wedding. Hopefully he'll be nowhere near it.'

'Unless I call him to attend me.'

Eleanor glared petulantly. Edward laughed. 'My love, we have other doctors.'

By May, she was sitting at her desk again, this time under Winter's image, wrinkling her brow as she began a letter to her mother in Flanders. This concerned her daughter Joan who had lived in Montreuil for five long years. That spring, messengers had crossed the Narrow Sea with bad news. Jeanne was unwell. It was time to bring Joan home. They were planning a betrothal for their second daughter so it was good timing, but there could be other benefits. Once Ellen was married, Eleanora would be bereft. Joan, as a new sister at court, would be a suitable distraction – and in a distant land, anything could happen to Joan now her grandmother was ailing.

Creasing her brow in thought she considered how she would form this letter. *I should go myself, fetch her and see Mama one last time.* She began to write that she would travel to Montreuil but dropped her pen again, realising she could not. There was not enough time. There was the October wedding. Using a fine knife she erased the words she had begun and began again. Jeanne might rally. Even so, Joan must come home, accompanied by a governess, maids, and a knight, at least one knight.

It was time now to tell Eleanora her sister was returning to them. Eleanor summoned her daughter into the gardens at the Tower on a sunny afternoon at the beginning of June. The flowers were creating a vivid tapestry of colour. The world felt perfect. They trailed through the walled Paradise garden, straw hats tied under their chins, breathing in the scent of lilies. They slipped into the rose garden to gather rose petals into a small basket Eleanora carried for this purpose. As the morning grew hotter, they sat on the turf bench in a confidential manner. It was as if they were novices in a cloister garden about to whisper secrets. Eleanor rarely spent time with her daughter. She was far too busy. Eleanora was laughing her delight at the occasion.

'I can dry these for a potpourri,' Eleanora said as she sifted her fingers through the petals.

Eleanor nodded. 'That would be lovely, my child.' She immediately came to the point. 'You know you have a sister who lives in Flanders.'

Eleanora glanced up from her basket, her hazel eyes bright with excitement. 'My sister is coming to England. Is that what you want to tell me, my lady mother?'

'Yes, you read my thoughts. I want you to welcome her home and share your books and games with her.'

'Of course, Mama, and I shall stitch a purse and a new belt for her. She can have my best doll, Gina.' She sniffed. 'I am too old for Gina now. I have ten summers and a betrothed as well,' she said with pride. 'I shall give her my glass animals too. The orange cat is very realistic.'

Eleanor smiled to see her daughter's nut-brown eyes, so like her own, sparkle with enthusiasm. 'That is very thoughtful of you, Eleanora. I am sure Joan will like those very much.'

'Will she have a betrothed like me?'

Eleanor considered for a moment. They were trying to make a match for Joan with the sovereign of the Romans, King Rudolf's eldest boy. Perhaps, it was best not to say anything until the match was accomplished. Instead she remarked, 'You have weddings much on your mind, my daughter.'

'Well, Mama, we all do. I'm helping Ellen get ready for her wedding.' She tilted her head. 'I am to attend her at her procession . . . like a sister.'

'Please include Joan in the preparations when she arrives.'

'We shall. I can't wait to have my sister here.' She leaned down and plucked a lavender stalk from a bush growing by the seat, held it to her nose and inhaled the scent. 'Margaret is only three. It's hard to talk to a three year old, but a girl of six whole years is very different.'

'You *are* growing up.' Eleanor smiled down at this daughter who resembled her more and more as she grew older. If Alphonso died, this child would be heir to the throne. She was learning decorum very well already. She seemed older than her years. 'I too am pleased that Joan is returning to us all.'

'I never want to leave our family,' Eleanora declared.

'That won't be for many years yet,' Eleanor replied. 'I shall be most loath to let you go when that day comes.' She sighed. 'I was sent into marriage far too young. You'll be older than my twelve years when you marry the Prince of Aragon, I promise.'

Eleanora hugged her mother. 'Thank you, thank you, my lady Mother. Grandmama says the same. She married Grandfather when she was only thirteen. I am happy as I am.' Her eyes shone with tears of relief.

Joan arrived a week later with many attendants. She was a blue-eyed, fair-haired child who was made a great fuss of by the children's household staff. Joan was immediately indulged by the Dowager, petted by her father, and, at once, presented with gifts. The children lined up when she arrived at the Tower to give her a miniature knight from Alphonso's new castle, a wooden puppet with strings from Margaret's collection, and the doll, Gina, from Eleanora. Joan settled into her family with ease, but a calculating, determined look in her daughter's young eyes sent a warning to Eleanor. The child was indulged. Such indulgence must not continue.

'An enchanting child,' Edward said as he watched Joan dance with Eleanora during his June birthday celebrations. He glanced up at the goshawk that sat on its perch watching his daughters through beady eyes. 'She has mesmerised your birthday gift to me, Eleanor. It's as well the bird is chained to its perch, else it would be swooping after them.'

'Nonsense,' Eleanor said, laughing. 'The hawk likes movement. You should hood his eyes.' Her eyes moved from the supercilious bird back to Joan. 'Our daughter *does* dance well. The other children love her already.' She looked straight at Edward. 'I hope your mother does not spoil her, for I fear Joan was overly indulged by mine.'

The hawk swivelled his neck towards her and ruffled its feathers as if it agreed.

★

In October, the court moved to Worcester for Ellen's wedding, which was to be on the thirteenth day of the month, the feast day of St Edward. She was married in the Cathedral on a day of autumn sunshine. Eleanor noted Olwen amongst the guests. During the celebrations that followed, Eleanor sought her out.

'Your Grace,' Olwen tried to extricate herself from the bench where she sat and curtseyed to Eleanor but Eleanor stayed her and said, 'No need for ceremony now. It was a beautiful wedding. What did you think?'

'It was. As you requested, your Grace, I supervised the herbal and flower decorations myself.' Her eyes flicked around the hall where garlands hung along the walls. Eleanor's eyes followed. They had been made with evergreens, woven through with ribbons and late roses. Olwen said, 'It's difficult to find the best flowers in October, but I think the castle hall looks fitting for a royal wedding feast.'

'Indeed it does. It was but a step from the Cathedral too, and we are fortunate to have fine weather.' Eleanor breathed deeply. 'What a relief to escape the intensity of all that incense. I thought the censor would never stop swaying. Why don't we walk about the hall. I have something else to ask of you.' She took Olwen's arm.

'They'll be pushing the trestles back for the dancing.'

'You must see how Eleanora and Joan dance. Come, I know this castle well and there's a place where no one will disturb us.' She led Olwen to a quiet corner and lifted the arras. 'This leads into a private chamber.' Eleanor led Olwen into a room softly lit by wax candles. A small fire glowed in the hearth. There was a lemony smell from it and Eleanor nodded to see Olwen breathe it in.

'I bring Spain wherever I go.' She indicated the hearth. 'Please sit.'

They sank into cushioned low chairs by the fire. As words began to tumble from their mouths it seemed to Eleanor as if no time had passed since they were last together.

Olwen looked well this evening, her figure shown to its best advantage in a pink velvet gown with tight sleeves and darker pink

240

silk ties. She was still slender for all she was past thirty. It occurred to Eleanor that Olwen's was the sort of beauty that looked better as she matured and wondered how she had ever considered her herbalist plain of face.

'I am sorry for Berengaria's death,' Olwen said after a while had passed.

'I give thanks to our Lord for my daughter's short life,' Eleanor said quietly and moved the sad subject on. 'I am sorry for the trouble you had with the bailiff. Some bailiffs are not entirely honest or fair. I am constantly riding over my lands checking up on them. I should have paid you a visit, but I had thought everything was settled.' She lowered her voice. 'I suspect Earl Gilbert decided he had a right to your manor. If you recollect, I purchased Oldbury in return for taking the heir into my household, and providing Nicholas with another better estate and a home with my children. Earl Gilbert ought to have known this fact and realised I had granted Oldbury to you and to Eugene.'

'I am not sure Earl Gilbert is at fault. He has always been pleasant to us, your Grace. But then his bailiff came sniffing around. Still I am glad all is settled on us now. Is the heir, Nicholas, happy?'

'He and Alphonso are companions. They have a menagerie of small creatures between them.' She clasped her hands together. 'It was a successful arrangement. One day, Nicholas will marry well.'

'It is good to hear Alphonso is well.'

Did she sense tears in Olwen's voice? Olwen had no living child even though two years had passed since her marriage. 'You should have a copy of the charter granting you the manor. If there are no children from your marriage you will inherit Oldbury and its lands should your husband die. You also are granted a dower property.'

'Thank you, yes. We have the charter. My dower is a fine farm given over mostly to sheep. We have already profited from the wool. We can pay our taxes.' She smiled. 'We have even introduced the Spanish sheep you suggested. Their wool is so soft.' Eleanor noted how Olwen's eyes remained troubled. 'I think my husband may never have an heir. I have used herbs. I have tried to be passionate,

241

because as you know a baby should be conceived thus, but there may be no child and I fear the fault is with me.'

Eleanor lightly touched the woman's hand. 'Doctors in Salerno question that belief, so I have heard. Do you love Eugene?'

Olwen lowered her troubled eyes. 'With the will that God has given me to love.'

'There may be a child yet. If there is not, that is God's will too.' Eleanor changed the subject, drawing their conversation towards the question she wanted to ask Olwen. That Olwen did not have children to care for might enthuse her for the project she was about to propose. 'I have a request to ask of you.'

'Yes, your Grace.'

'Edward is building castles in Wales. I am of a mind to have a Spanish garden designed at Rhuddlan, one with fountains, arcades, and orchards. I am also of a mind to have fig trees. There must be rosemary and basil if you can get both to grow.' She took Olwen's hands in her own. 'Olwen, would you come to Rhuddlan to grow them once the garden is ready for planting? It could be a while yet. I am sure we can find someone to look after your manor so Eugene could come too. I have need of another household knight at Rhuddlan.'

Olwen said, her eyes genuinely smiling now. 'I shall think about it and ask Eugene. We have a small business selling herbs and other plants to other farms as far off as Gloucester. I have grown wallflowers such as you introduced from Spain, your Grace. They thrive in my walled garden.'

The queen placed Olwen's hands back in the woman's lap. 'I shall write to you when the castle building has progressed enough for the garden.' She rose. 'Now, let's join the dancing. I promised Edward my ladies and I would dance a Spanish dance tonight. The wedded pair will be bedded soon. I think Ellen has been dreaming of this day for a very long time. And let us pray to Our Lady that this marriage brings peace to Wales.'

'Amen to that, your Grace.'

Eleanor took her herbalist's hand again and led her back through the arras into the hall where viols and recorders accompanied the dancing. 'Look at Joan.' She pointed towards the fairy child who never stopped moving gracefully. 'She dances well at all of seven years old, just.' She saw Eugene note his wife and smile over as he turned in the circle dance. 'Go to him, Olwen. Don't forget my request.' She gave Olwen a gentle push towards the circling dancers.

Eleanor stood very still by the pillar and breathed in candle-perfumed air mingled with the scent of marzipan. If only time could pause right here, right in this moment. It was one of those scenes she wanted to remember all her days. If only her daughters never had to leave their court. Her hand passed over her stomach. She was sure she felt new life fluttering there yet again.

Part Four
Wales

1282–1290

Chapter Nineteen

Olwen
Wales, 1282

After the wedding, another year passed peacefully at Oldbury and Olwen did not conceive as she had hoped.

'It matters not,' Eugene said. 'The world is enough for me with you, my life's love.'

It was true, they were happy. Their family was their servants and the friends who came to celebrate feast days which she loved to make into festivals.

After a few more years slipped by them she stopped thinking about children. Their business was growing and the manor farm was productive. She was content at Oldbury with its calm moat, stone buildings, and the gardens where she was busy in every season. They were respected throughout the neighbourhood. As Eugene would often say their world was enough. She heard nothing further about Rhuddlan, though she knew the King was castle-building.

One day in March a letter stamped with Queen Eleanor's own seal, her image, arrived with a messenger who came trotting over the moat. The Queen had remembered her and sent them a generous purse as well.

Olwen sent the messenger to the kitchen. Her hand shaking, she broke the seal and opened the letter.

'What does it say?' Eugene could hardly contain his excitement.

'She asks if we can place a steward to look after our manor.' Olwen looked up. 'The queen finally wants us to travel to Rhuddlan – I am to give advice on planting the new castle gardens, and you,

Eugene, are to establish a guard for her older children's apartments. Queen Eleanor, King Edward, Eleanora, Alphonso, and Joan will spend the summer months there.'

Eugene frowned, but said, 'I do like the idea of being present at court again if only for a few months.'

'And I like the idea of planting another royal garden, but let us think on this before sending the messenger back tomorrow.'

That afternoon, followed by Eugene, as they excitedly inspected their plant and seed collection, they discussed and decided they must accept the summons.

'March is a perfect month to plant herbs,' she said. 'I'll bring rosemary, chervil and the alexanders. The alexanders will thrive well, positioned so close to the sea, better than here. Besides, I may discover new plants and herbs in Wales. When we return we'll be all the richer in knowledge.'

His eyes shone. 'Amen to that. By the rood, a new adventure, my love.'

A week passed in preparation. On the day they were to depart, Eugene slid his newly polished sword into his scabbard and hung his arms of honour, yellow and red stripes on a white ground, underneath his best saddle.

They packed plants into a wagon.

They left a trusted land steward and his wife in charge of Oldbury. Their servants waved them goodbye. Trotting over Oldbury's wooden bridge they set out on the long journey north towards Chester with Olwen's favourite maid, Belle, and Eugene's squire, Piers.

The week preceding Easter was the most religious week of the Church year and roads were busy with travellers as well as groups of pilgrims visiting shrines. It meant many delays on the roads towards Hawarden Castle. A host of pilgrims travelling to Chester for Holy Week crowded their route. No sooner had Olwen and Eugene passed through one group of them than another appeared as if from nowhere. A band of lepers, desperate for a cure, claimed they were travelling to a hospital outside Chester. Eugene dropped coins into the cups hanging from their necks. They thanked him, crossed themselves and lifted their eyes to a squalling sky in prayer. The tinkling of bells on their leper staffs grew fainter and distant as the lepers moved off but by Nones the road towards Chester was again blocked, this time by a band of knights. Olwen noted they flew Earl Gilbert's pennants. They nodded to Eugene, since he was also a knight.

'It reminds me—' Eugene began to say.

Olwen finished his sentence, 'Of Canterbury and that journey.' They smiled at each other, remembering the secrets they carried that time nearly twenty years before.

'I was a squire like Piers.' He glanced back at the long-legged, red-headed young man who sat on the wagon seat beside the black-haired, buxom Belle.

Soon after the knights had ridden off in the opposite direction, one of the cart's wheels worked loose and tumbled to the ground. Piers cursed. 'By St David's balls . . .'

Eugene reined back and growled, 'Mind your tongue, boy.'

Piers leapt from the cart and helped Belle clamber down from the slanting bench where she had sat patiently as the country hedgerows sped past. She wiped her hand on her gown as he let it go, knelt against the tilting cart, and lifted up the canvas cover. Belle peered underneath the canvas at their cargo of plants and herbs. Olwen slid from her palfrey and joined her. Eugene dismounted his jennet. Grumbling, he hurried to help Piers.

'The plants are safe, my lady,' Belle said, glancing up.

'Praise God for that.'

Olwen and Belle sat on their cloaks eating bread, drinking water, and watching travellers pass.

'I wonder will Queen Eleanor bring her youngest daughter to Rhuddlan Castle in summer,' Belle remarked, finishing her bread and sweeping away the crumbs from her lap.

'I think not. Mary is still small, as is Princess Margaret. Only the oldest children will join the progress.'

249

After a bit Belle said, 'The Queen is always travelling. They say she will not let King Edward out of her sight.'

'Who says this, Belle?' Olwen was alert at once. Belle came from a respectable family. She was surprised to hear Belle gossip so.

'My papa says some call her a *she-wolf*.'

'Belle, never please let me hear you say this again. It's idle gossip, and it's untrue. The Queen is fair and kind.'

'Papa says she is the richest landowner in England. He says many of the nobles she purchased land from distrust her.' She shook her head. 'Well, she's a woman so I suppose they would.'

'Don't repeat that either, Belle. I would not like to complain about you to your parents, now would I?'

'No, my lady.' Belle had the grace to look chastened. She began plucking daisies from the verge, making a chain which she offered Olwen, her eyes downcast. 'I am sorry for my words,' she said simply.

Olwen accepted the daisy chain and hung it around the cart-horse's neck. 'There,' she said as the horse neighed at her.

It was true Queen Eleanor was obsessed with property and true too she had upset some of the nobility, but ordinary folk spoke well of Queen Eleanor. The nobles resented how she took control of wealthy wards, and rich orphaned heirs and heiresses. The heir to Oldbury was only one of many lucrative wards living in the royal nursery. Yet, the wards must be pleased to dwell with a family appointed by God to rule the land. How could anyone ever say anything bad about Queen Eleanor? Those men jealous of her abilities, no doubt.

'It'll be nightfall by the time we stop at Hawarden,' Eugene said, glancing over at them as he finished securing the cart's wheel back onto its axle. 'I hope Earl Roger can provide our supper. I'm famished.' He wiped his hands on a cloth. 'Piers, put the wrench back under the canvas.'

I'm hungry too, thought Olwen. She and Belle had nibbled on the remains of a small loaf but it had been a long day of travel.

As the sun dipped low in the sky, the small travelling group crossed the drawbridge to the castle of Hawarden. A monkish boatman was rowing a small boat across the moat towards the castle walls. Olwen wondered where he was going since skiff and boatman vanished, swallowed up by a wall where it curved away out of sight. Perhaps there was a postern gate he had navigated through. She looked away to see orchards spread out to the west from the banks of the moat. Sheep grazed on distant hilly fields and a cluster of cottages nestled in a clearing close to the woodland opposite the castle. It was a placid enough scene but there was a sense of unease in the air.

Chapel bells began ringing for Vespers.

'Supper,' Eugene said, 'always follows Vespers.' He leapt from his jennet and banged on the gatehouse door.

'Who's there?' shouted the gatekeeper.

'Lady Olwen and Sir Eugene of Oldbury Manor on the Queen's business.'

'Prove it, master.' He slid back a grille set in the door and poked his head through the opening. Olwen recoiled from the choleric face that seemed to leer out at them. A fat wart spouting hairs protruded from his chin. There's an ugly man I'd not wish to meet alone on a black night, she thought to herself.

'Here.' Eugene withdrew a letter from his jerkin and thrust it towards the grille, pointing to the seal. 'Queen Eleanor's seal,' he said. A hand shot out to receive it.

The gatekeeper peered at it. 'Can't read. Seal looks real enough.' The grille closed with a clang. Slowly, the gate screamed open. Piers flicked the tired horse with his stick and the cart rumbled into the castle bailey. Eugene remounted and they nudged their horses forward and followed, past sentries who stared after them with suspicion in their eyes.

'A poorly armed band. They look sullen and lazy,' Eugene noted.

Too tired to reply, Olwen shrugged.

Hawarden was a motte and bailey castle with a keep and a protective wall against which nestled a hall, kitchens, barracks, a forge, workshops, and a herbal garden next to the chapel. The bells stopped clanging.

Steep steps cut into the motte led from the bailey up to the high keep. They climbed down from their mounts. Eugene and Piers hurried with the three horses and the cart to the stables, saying they would pay a stable boy to guard their wagon for the night.

'Olwen, go on into the hall and see if you can find the steward. Here, take the Queen's letter.' He thrust it into her hands. 'You'll need it to prove who we are.'

Since the hall door was ajar, Olwen and Belle hurried into the hall. They stood inside the doorway. Olwen wondered at the servants hurrying about, all busy. Whom should she speak with? She had not long to decide. The steward – he must be so, a slight man clad in a plain brown gown – bustled forward from where trestles were being laid for supper. He had authority in his appearance.

'Who are you?' he asked her, his tone sharp.

'Lady Olwen of Oldbury, Queen Eleanor's herbalist.' She thrust the letter towards him.

'I see,' he muttered and accepted Queen Eleanor's letter. He turned it over. 'The Queen's seal.' Glancing up he said, 'Do you need accommodation, or do you wish to see Lord Clifford?'

'If Lord Clifford is busy we are happy with a chamber for the night.'

He scrutinised Queen Eleanor's letter and nodded. 'You are welcome to Hawarden Castle,' he said. 'Lord Clifford dines in the keep. He'll speak with you in the morning if you make your way up. I'll advise him you are passing through Hawarden on the Queen's business.'

'We only intend stopping overnight. We are on our way to Rhuddlan.'

'Very well. You may need an escort. There has been unrest around Flint.'

Olwen frowned. She thought Wales had settled down. Queen Eleanor would never knowingly send them into danger.'

'We shall speak with your lord in the morning.' She kept her voice calm. The sense of disquiet she had felt earlier still bothered her.

'I'll have maids make up pallets with fresh linen for you behind the hall. How many?'

'My maid, my husband, and his squire.'

The steward bustled off waving toward the trestle. 'Eat,' he called back over his shoulder.

She was famished and wasted no time approaching the table. Castle staff and maids shifted along a bench to make room for them. No one engaged Olwen in conversation. Servants and artisans who had glanced her way lost interest and returned to their own conversations. Yet she was a high-ranking guest who ought to be dining up in the keep with the lord and his personal retainers.

Moments passed. Eugene hurried into the hall bringing a chill breeze through the opened door. A servant ran to close it behind him. The company ignored him too.

Eugene scanned the board as he squeezed in between Olwen and Belle. He said in a quiet voice, 'Piers is eating in the kitchen. Says he'll sleep in the cart tonight.' Laughing he added, tapping his nose, 'He might know a maid here.'

Belle mumbled, 'No doubt.'

'Where are we to lay our heads?' Eugene asked.

'The steward said we could have the chamber behind the hall. There are pallets and linen, enough for us all. Lord Clifford will see us on the morrow. There's been trouble on the road to Rhuddlan and we might need guards.'

Eugene's brow darkened. 'That bodes badly. Let's pray it's not serious.'

Olwen dozed off to the sound of midnight Angelus bells. A few hours later she awoke confused and frightened. She stretched her hand out for Eugene who was snoring and sat up, allowing her eyes to adjust to torchlight that edged through closed shutters in spits. Belle lay sound asleep on her pallet by the door leading from the chamber out into the yard. They were all safe and present, yet something felt wrong. She wrinkled her nose. She could smell burning. For a moment she wondered if a rush light had fallen onto the damp floor straw. She peered far into the darkness but nothing was alight in their chamber. She rose and felt her way towards the door to the hall. Tugging the door open a crack she suppressed a cough and drew her hand over her mouth. The hall was filling up with a greyish fug. She could just about make out a group of shadows moving silently past the central hearth towards the outer doors. She stepped further into the hall. Looking towards the nearest of the sleeping alcoves, she stuffed a fist into her mouth and stifled a scream. She could make out two bodies lying prone. Blood was seeping onto pallets and garments. She stepped in a little further. Small fires were catching on the floor straw.

She withdrew, slammed the door shut, stumbled over to their pallet and began to shake Eugene's shoulders. 'Wake up. Oh, wake up, do.'

Eugene started, 'What the . . .?' He sat up blinking.

'We're under attack!' Choking back her terror, she pointed to the chamber door. 'All dead in there.'

'Who? What? Where?'

'The hall.'

Belle was sitting up, her mouth opening in a scream. Olwen hurried to her, almost tripping in her haste. She placed a hand over Belle's mouth. 'Hush. Get dressed at once. We have to go.' She thrust Belle's clothing towards her. 'Now!'

They could hear a cacophony in the yard – the suddenness of yelling and horses neighing. The noise grew louder and louder.

Eugene pulled on his trousers and belt, strapped his scabbard to his waist, and tugged on his boots. 'Get yours on too,' he said pointing to his feet, his tone insistent. He threw his mantle over his shoulders. 'We must get out. Now!'

She could hear beams crashing down and the crackling of fire from the hall. Flames had taken hold. There was no one left to put them out. Reading her mind, Eugene said, 'I'll go in there. There'll be no one to save but I'm going to look. You get yourself and Belle out, and please Christ, there is no one to stop you. Hurry.'

She grabbed Belle's wrist, opened the door a crack, slowly wider, and pulled the terrified maid outside with her. The first thing she noticed as she tilted her chin towards the sky, gulping in air, was how the moon beamed down on them like a heavenly lantern. Unlike the heavens, the yard was in a state of madness. Stallions, palfreys, and jennets cantered wildly about outside the smouldering wooden buildings. Stable hands raced about trying to catch them. She and Belle stood frozen not knowing what to do or where to run. A heartbeat later, Eugene exited the chamber they had escaped, smoky tears rolling down his face. 'All dead inside as far as I dared go. Smoke everywhere. Flames licking tapestries. Destruction. Terrible.' He looked towards the keep set high on its castle mound. Belle, too frightened to utter a word, was as if struck dumb. Figures were scrambling up the steps set into the castle hill. Arrows fired down from the battlements missed some and sliced into others. A rebel army, if that was what they were, struggled up, moving steadily on towards the keep.

Olwen clung to Eugene's arm. Belle tugged her veil over her mouth. The yard was permeated by smoke.

'Where's Piers?' Eugene shouted. 'We must get away before the hall collapses.'

'I know a way,' she gasped.

But Eugene was not listening. He shouted above the noise, 'The gatehouse is on fire too.' He spun her around in a semicircle so she saw how trapped they were. 'Christ,' he said. 'Stables and barracks burning as well.'

A crowd was racing towards the burning gatehouse. Some caught loose horses and climbed onto them. A falcon screeched. Another hunting bird flew through the smoke.

Eugene croaked, 'Cart and the horses are lost to us. Piers . . . Christ's bollocks, where's Piers?'

Olwen tugged at his sleeve. 'We can get out of the postern gate. I know where it is. Piers must fare as best he can.'

Eugene looked into her eyes. His were half-crazed. 'Do you? You must go. God protect you, but I cannot abandon Piers. He's my cousin's son. A bastard.'

Her eyes widened at this information she had not known before.

'Never mind that now. Quick, tell me. Where's the postern gate?'

'I saw a boat earlier. It disappeared through the castle wall. It's behind the chapel.'

'Go and cross the moat. I'll swim it with Piers once I find him.' He pulled her so close she smelled singed fabric from his tunic. He kissed her and gave her a push. 'Go, my love. God be with you.'

Dragging Belle with her, stumbling through the chaos, Olwen ran for the chapel. Dogs barked at their heels. She kicked one away and raced on, weaving through people running for the drawbridge, hoping to dash through the burning gatehouse. They hurtled forward, avoiding leaping, neighing horses none of which were their own. The chapel loomed up. She pushed at the garden gate but it refused to budge.

The maid grimaced as her eyes followed Olwen's eyes to the garden wall.

'Yes, Belle, we are climbing over.'

'But I dislike heights.'

'Do not look down. I shall give you a start and I'll be behind you.'

Olwen interlocked her hands for Belle to place her foot. Belle began to slowly climb, grasping at grooves and jutting out stones, never heeding their sharp edges.

'There, not so difficult.' Olwen coughed. 'The smoke. It's everywhere now.'

They sat for a moment on the top. 'Jump, Belle.' They dropped down, Belle first, then Olwen jumped, landing into herbal beds with no more than scrapes. She stood up and helped Belle to her feet. She surveyed the garden. No one was hiding in the bushes, though a cat spat from a leafy cabbage behind which it had taken refuge. Ignoring it, they hurried over herb beds, trampling them, until they reached a door set into the outer wall.

Olwen said, 'It'll be a source of water for the garden, from the moat.' She pushed. It did not give. It was locked with a small padlock.

'I can pick that one,' said Belle, grasping the dangling lock and finding her tongue at last. 'My cloak pin.'

'You can what?'

256

'I can open that lock.' She bent down, eyes screwed up, peering at it.

'Hurry.' Olwen's voice urged.

Belle stood up and whipped the pin out of her rough woollen cloak and set to work. Behind them the sound of fleeing people grew louder. They were coming closer, towards the garden.

Olwen turned to peer back, but a cloud blotted the moon. It was too dark. 'The drawbridge must be on fire too. They've thought of the postern. Hurry, Belle, please. We are lucky. This door will take us out too.'

'It's done, my lady. Look!'

The lock tumbled to the ground. Olwen dragged the small door open. Bending low, they slipped through the arched opening. The moon was visible again causing a wavering sheen over dark water. Olwen glanced up. Fire lit up the sky. The Hawarden keep was burning. An army of men was descending like giant crawling insects. She could clearly see the Clifford arms embroidered on a pennant slowly moving down the hill. Insect-like humans vanished into smoke as they descended lower. She turned to the water lapping at the bank below her feet. The postern gate lay to their right. Soon the bank would be filled with escaping victims and their attackers. 'Quick,' she hissed and pointed to a skiff floating out from the incline's edge. 'Pull in that rowboat. They have not thought to burn the boats.'

'Aye, mistress, that would have revealed their presence before they entered the castle is why.' Belle leaned down, caught hold of a rope, and pulled the rowboat in. 'My lady, get you in. Can you row?'

Olwen nodded. 'Of course I can row. Hurry.'

Within moments, they reached the other side. Olwen tied the boat to an overhanging willow branch. Climbing out, they scrambled up the bank not caring about scratches and their ripped clothing. She glanced back over her shoulder. A small crowd was exiting the postern tunnel. To her relief, she was sure she could make out Eugene's scarlet cloak amongst them. Piers too because he was taller than most men and resembled Red Gilbert with his russet hair. Eugene was leaning on Piers.

'Belle, look back. I think Eugene is coming. He's injured. I'm sure he is.'

'Piers too?'

'I think so. He's helping Eugene.'

'We've lost them plants now.'

'I fear so; cart and horses gone too. Have gratitude, Belle, we are spared. But we're not safe yet.'

Belle muttered, 'True enough.'

They hid amongst the trees close to a stream. Eugene's arm had taken a slash. He needed treatment but it was not yet safe to leave the security of the woods. They sat leaning against a huge oak trunk separate from other refugees. Piers and Eugene related in hushed tones what had happened. The maid Piers had slept with in her kitchen nook ran off the moment the rebel band appeared. Piers was knocked senseless and came to to find himself trapped under a fallen table. That was how Eugene found him.

'I pulled him out. A sword came slashing at my arm as if from nowhere. I tried to draw my own sword. The attacker was nowhere to be seen.'

'He was a castle man,' Piers said. 'He made off through the smoke with the cook's silver server.'

'All for the sake of a dish,' Olwen said shaking her head, peering at the gash on Eugene's forearm. 'If I had honey, I could put it on the wound. It's a nasty one. We'll get you to a hospital when we reach Chester.'

'*When*,' Eugene groaned.

She washed and bandaged the cut with a strip of cloth ripped from her underskirt. She created a sling and prayed he would not have to lose his sword arm. The wound was deep. They kept to themselves all of the next day though they could hear movement close by. The oak they were leaning against had a hollowed-out trunk where they could conceal themselves. Piers and Belle dragged bracken and branches over to hide the opening.

They remained inside the ancient tree until they were sure none of the army attacking the castle were in pursuit of those who had escaped. Chester was less than ten miles distant from Hawarden. Tired and feverish, all that day Eugene leaned against a beech tree trunk. Olwen covered him with her mantle and crawled close to him to keep warm too. They were hungry and filthy, tired and too frightened to try and make a fire. A stream provided water. As evening descended the wood grew strangely quiet except for the rustle of creatures, those above and below the trees.

Using moonlight to guide him, Piers ventured to the edge of a village. On his return he reported, 'Most of the servants who have survived are returning to their families in villages around Hawarden. We'll have to walk to Chester tomorrow. The enemy seems to have vanished as stealthily as they appeared.' He opened a small sack. 'They gave me stale bread and cheese.'

'Anything. I'm famished,' Belle said as she bit into her share.

'Eugene's wound will fester if it's not treated,' Olwen said, after sharing out the food.

'I'll be fine to walk. We'll find an inn there,' Eugene said, struggling up. 'Piers knows the road. Part of it runs through these woods.' He collapsed again. 'Maybe after I rest a while.'

It began to rain, softly at first. Soon heavier. They were all shivering now. Belle suggested trying to get a fire going.

Olwen said, 'No it'll alert outlaws to us. We best hide within the tree.'

'It won't stay lit with such a downpour,' Piers said peering into sheeting rain.

They waited through what was left of the night sheltering within the oak tree. They continued to huddle together. Eugene grew increasingly hot to her touch. No one dared complain about hunger. They were fortunate to be alive.

As soon as dawn broke they set out. The rain had stopped but trees dripped and soon their boots were soaking. Once they reached the road, Piers purchased a loaf of hard barley bread and dried apple slices from a traveller fleeing east from one of the settlements close to Rhuddlan. They paused to eat the sparse breakfast by the roadside. A constant stream of passing carts was heading along the Chester road. All were terrified of Welsh marauders. Olwen said they were too many to travel together in one crowded wagon. She was tempted to send Eugene ahead on a cart, but he refused and continued to walk leaning on Piers.

They joined a band of soldiers. The archers had miraculously escaped from the castle and like them had hidden in the forest. What had actually occurred around Hawarden soon grew clearer.

'The fuckers outnumbered us,' one soldier told Olwen. 'Rebels armed to the jaws. They broke into my lord's chamber and took him. We were no defence. The bastards would have slaughtered him before our eyes had we resisted. That was that. They made off with our lord and his pennants.' He shook his straggling hair. 'Lady Fortune smiled though. His lady was not at home. A pox on the fucking bastards.' He spat. 'We'll be riding against those sons of whores once the King gives orders. It'll be war again.'

'God protect Lord Clifford,' Eugene said crossing himself. 'Was it Dafydd or Llewellyn?'

'Hedge-whore Dafydd's men. He wants the settlers out of Wales. And, by our good sainted Mary, who knows what else. He's a friggin' castle burner, I do know that. A sly bastard, that Dafydd. Llewelyn, unlike the brother, deserves a warrior's respect.'

'Llewelyn's wed to the King's niece,' Olwen said.

'Aye, and he's far away in his sea palace in the west. No love between those brothers. There'll be war again, by Christ.' He drew breath. 'Who knows where loyalties lie in a war.'

Eugene struggled on with the help of a fallen oak branch for support. He still felt hot to Olwen's touch. They marched on until, at last, the spires of Chester rose up in the distance. Ragged and exhausted, only possessing the clothes they stood up in but with Queen Eleanor's letter well concealed under Eugene's cloak along with his purse, they arrived as the bells rang for Nones.

News of the sack of Hawarden Castle and Lord Clifford's abduction had already reached Chester. Piers knew the city well and found them an inn. They were welcomed at the Swan as if they were heroes returning from an ancient battle. Wishing them Godspeed, their ragged soldier escort carried on wearily towards the castle.

Eugene was too ill to negotiate chambers for them that night so Olwen drove a bargain for the best chamber to be had and a closet for Piers, though he said he would give Belle the closet and sleep on a pallet outside the door.

'Safer,' he said gruffly as he looked Belle's way with longing.

'As long as you stay away from the kitchen maids this time,' Olwen said. She went back down the corridor to the kitchen where she insisted on clean linen for their bed and fennel scattered amongst the floor straw.

The innkeeper's wife, a pleasant woman called Mistress Lilian, took one look at Eugene's arm and confirmed Olwen's suspicion. 'That's bad,' she said as she helped Olwen clean the wound and apply a nettle poultice to it.' Peering at it, she added, 'Take him to the Hospital of St John. There's a new apothecary there can save limbs. I wouldn't depend on my nettle and honey poultices, my dearie. He has a fever.' Casting her eyes over their bedraggled, mud-stained clothing she added, 'You'll find fresh clothing in the market place. Nothing fancy but clean and, if not, my maids will brush any dirty outer garments. They'll wash the linen.' She sniffed. 'Same with those you are wearing.'

Belle took directions and slid coins into her own belt purse. Followed by a maid from the inn to guide her, she hurried to the market to seek out fresh clothing and linens.

Eugene closed his eyes. Olwen was sure the downpour that had drenched him had caused a fever. The innkeeper lent them a horse, cart, and a lad to drive it. Eugene lay on a blanket in the wagon's bed and they set out, carefully negotiating the streets, bumping along cobbles, avoiding riders on horses, pedestrians, street sellers, pigs, cats, dogs, and offal until the boy said, 'We're here, me lady.'

'Praise Mary,' she muttered to no one in particular.

Piers hurried to lift Eugene from the cart, complaining, 'The journey knocked the stuffing out of me, never mind the master.'

The lad waited with the cart whilst Piers and Olwen helped Eugene stumble to a door set into a long street wall. Piers pulled on the bell rope. A monk appeared and simply said, 'Follow me.' He led them into a cloistered courtyard. Church bells chimed the hour of Vespers as they awkwardly helped Eugene to a stone bench and sat him down. He leaned against the wall closing his eyes as if the world was too unbearable to look upon. In truth he appeared distracted and in pain.

Olwen glanced around. Others seated about the courtyard were also waiting to be attended. A very old man stared ahead, unseeing, as if he was blind. Another had ugly swellings on his face. Yet another was doubled over with pain. He was moaning. Eugene collapsed, his head leaning on his wife's shoulder.

Olwen said softly to Eugene, 'The apothecary will help you. If he has half my father's skill he'll save your arm.'

She was not convinced by her own words.

An attendant monk led them into a chamber where she noted various instruments laid out on a bench. The floor was tiled and clean. Charts hung on the wall, one showing a man with Latin notes written neatly against his various body parts. Another displayed signs of the cosmos placed around a naked man. The chamber was sparsely furnished but a narrow bed stood against one wall. As Olwen turned towards the couch hoping to help Eugene to it, she started. The apothecary, clad in a long white gown, a red cross stitched at his shoulder, was staring at her. He stood absolutely still as if he was a statue in the cloister. She held his eyes for a heartbeat but although she knew him, neither said a word of recognition to the other. He said in a quiet voice, 'Welcome to the Hospital of St John. I am Guillaume, apothecary, surgeon, and doctor. May I examine your husband?'

Her neck flushed and hot tears began to gather behind her eyes. *He knew Eugene to be her husband.*

Blinking her tears back, she nodded. They helped Eugene to sit on the bed. Guillaume should not be here. She blinked. He really was no statue but a living person.

She leaned down and focused her concern on Eugene.

Glancing up, she said, her voice halting, 'My husband has a fever. There's a sword bite on his arm. We were attacked at Hawarden . . . my own medicines, herbs and plants were lost . . .'

'We heard of the attack and Lord Roger's abduction.' His eyes looked saddened. 'You are fortunate to survive, my lady. Others were not so blessed.'

She said in as calm a voice as she could manage, 'The Queen expects us at Rhuddlan with plants for her garden.'

'And there now are no plants.' He was gently removing Eugene's filthy shirt. He passed Eugene's sword and scabbard to Piers who was watching closely. He turned back to Olwen. 'Your husband is of rank?'

'A knight and a landowner.'

'I see.' Guillaume commenced on an examination of the wound. He was clearly absorbed, fascinated. When he touched the flesh around the slash, Eugene cried out. Otherwise he spoke not. Guillaume glanced up at Olwen. 'You have it well cleansed, my lady.'

He felt Eugene's forehead. Her husband's eyes had closed again. She knew the signs. If Eugene did not die of his wound, he could die of a fever. She did not want him to die. She loved him deeply in that moment when she thought she might lose him. He was her anchor.

Guillaume was saying, 'We have a bed in the hospital. It is clean and it is quiet. There is fresh linen. Patients must be clad in cleansed gowns. We cannot permit fleas or other biting things.' He paused. 'It's not the plague, praise God, but the fever must break and his wound be treated for fear of infection. With God's mercy, I can save his arm.'

She nodded. 'When may I return?'

'On the morrow, lady.'

He bowed his head. 'My Lady Olwen.' He spoke her name gently but this time when he looked up she saw something else in his eyes, a softening like velvet, and a feeling akin to longing. 'God bless you, Olwen,' he whispered.

She felt her heart still and it was with a sense of regret that she said, 'Thank you for your care of my husband, Master Guillaume.'

Her heart beat too quickly. She looked away for fear of Piers' sharp blue eyes noticing.

News filtered into Chester. Aberystwyth Castle had fallen to Dafydd. The new town around the castle was destroyed and its English inhabitants were massacred. Rhuddlan was besieged. Again the new town was razed to the ground. Belle returned daily with further horrors. Gossip flew into markets and inns as if carried on wings. Babies skewered on the points of swords. Inhabitants of these new towns burned alive in their homes. Women raped and killed. Olwen was relieved that God had watched over them, allowing their escape to Chester and she was thankful Eugene's life was spared.

Olwen visited the hospital daily though she was not permitted into the patients' hall. As time passed, Eugene's fever lessened and he grew stronger. Finally, he was sitting up. On one occasion, when she glanced through the door into the long hall she noticed him in an animated discussion with three apothecaries. None of these was Guillaume.

The day arrived when Eugene was recovered enough to leave the hospital. All she wanted now was to make their way home to Oldbury, give prayers of thanks, and donate a generous offering to their Parish Church of St Lawrence. Eugene would grow well in the quiet of their country manor. There, she could soothe him with possets and strengthen him with her own special curdles.

On the day she came to escort Eugene to the inn the usual collection of unwell and injured waited in the sheltered cloister. Her heart jumped. Guillaume swept out of the hospital door in his dark gown with the Hospitallers' cross stitched upon the shoulder. He asked if he could speak with her privately.

She turned to Belle and indicated the parcel of clothing she was carrying. 'Send the clothing to Sir Eugene with Brother James there.' They were not a knight's garb but the garments had been washed and were in excellent condition, far better than those they'd arrived in some weeks earlier. Belle did as she was asked and after delivering the bundle sat ready to wait on a stone bench between two pillars.

'I would like to speak to you concerning your husband's recovery.' Guillaume lifted the latch of a gate leading into the monastery garden. In the far corner there was a dovecot with a multitude of little windows in and out of which doves flitted. He indicated a wooden seat by the pond milky with frog spawn. She felt her heart quiver at a distant memory, a recollection of another garden below a cerulean sky far away in an arid land. This memory was not damp with spring smells of mint, thyme and April rain. It came flowing into her thought with scents of roses and purple-blue lavender, a garden where fountains splashed and water channels threaded through herbal beds. She glanced up at clouds brooding above. It would rain soon.

'I must speak.' Guillaume sat so close, she could feel his breath on her face. Her eyes filled with tears.

He folded his hands. How long, elegant, and fine his fingers were as they steepled. 'Olwen,' he began, 'You know I had to learn what I could in Salerno.' She raised her eyes to meet his. 'Your king gave me an opportunity to study medicine and it was my heart's desire to do so. As my knowledge once saved your king, it has helped your husband to recovery. Eugene will grow strong. He will fight again like the knight he is. There is to be war in Wales.' She started as he said this. 'He will take up his knightly duty and wants to fight for the King because his life is spared. Your husband is a good man.' Guillaume's voice grew into a whisper like a soft breeze passing between them. 'And without doubt a loyal husband.'

A tear slid down Olwen's cheek. He reached over and touched it with his middle finger. She quivered at his touch. 'Olwen, it cannot be, and I am sorrowful too.' His whisper melted into the air.

'Guillaume, you were supposed to return to me after those years in Salerno. I waited and waited. How I longed for you to come back to me but you never came.'

'I was not ready to love,' he reminded her. 'It was for such a purpose as treating your husband that I became a doctor.'

'Thank you for saving Eugene's arm. He *is* a good husband.' She turned away. A blackbird hopped through the herbal beds seeking worms. A pair of white doves flew into the dovecot.

'You do not love him?' Guillaume said.

'No, Guillaume, I do not love him but I care deeply for him.'

He drew a long breath. 'And I have never taken vows even though I wear the robes of the Hospitallers. I delay my vows over and over. They accept this in the hospital because I am one of their most educated doctors. I am a surgeon and I am an apothecary. I do not wish to belong to an order I may not leave . . . maybe it's because I want the freedom to choose my own pathway.'

'You have found another to marry?'

'No, I shall never find another such as you. I have lived a chaste life.'

'You doubt God?'

'God sees all . . . but God allows us to make mistakes. I believe He allows us to choose.'

'You, Guillaume, are troubled, I see.' A salty tear coursed down her cheek.

'When I returned to England and heard you were to marry, I slipped into the church on the day of your wedding. When I saw you my heart cracked into pieces. You were a beautiful bride. I was angered. You should have been my bride but you chose to marry your knight.' He smiled down at her. *Were those tears in his eyes too?* 'Your knight is healed and though I wish it different, you will continue to have a joyful life together. There is much I would say but it's best I do not.'

Olwen looked away. Her eyes lit on a rose bush which in summer would be filled with damask roses to become queen of the garden. She had not made her own choice. Queen Eleanor had chosen for her and she had agreed.

'Have you children?' Guillaume said.

'God has not willed it.'

'I hope you do not believe this is to do with woman's corruption, as the Church would preach.'

266

'No, I do not believe such a thing. Nor does my husband.'

He nodded and placing his hand over hers for a moment he said, 'I am glad we have spoken. Now let us find Eugene. May God bless your journey to your estates and may he watch over you both.'

Olwen smiled through her tears. 'God bless *your* journey too, Guillaume.'

Chapter Twenty

Worcester
May 1282

Edward paced the chamber and came to a stop by the door. 'Eleanor, return with the children to Windsor. We are at war and you are with child,' Edward said, his lisp pronounced today and his left eye drooping. He was tired.

Eleanor bristled. With his huge cavalry, crossbow marksmen, and infantry troops pouring into Wales, she would be safe. Of course she would. She always travelled with him. He was not leaving her behind this time.

She felt her throat flush. Her temper was rising. She looked at her book, tempted to fling it at him, but a book of prayers was too precious, its pages illuminated in gold, its cover studded with precious stones. Her hands strayed over the cover. As if they possessed a will of their own they lifted a silver plate from the table instead. A heartbeat later it was sailing through the air towards Edward. Reaching out just in time, he caught it in a mid-spin.

'No you don't, Eleanor. Go to Woodstock or any of your manors as would any sensible wife at such time,' he shouted at her. His face grew angry. 'Just not Wales.'

She sank into the cushioned chair by her desk and cradled her head with her hands. Her velvet cap tumbled to the floor tiles. Her hair fell loose from its coils. She glared up at him as he calmly replaced the dish on the far end of her table, out of reach. He was not smiling as he sometimes would when she threw a tantrum to get her way.

'Well?' he said, his tone firm. 'Will you do as I ask?'

'This child should be born in Wales. The Rhuddlan siege is lifted. I want to have our child at Rhuddlan and show the Welsh they have a new prince. Alphonso and Margaret can travel back to Woodstock.' She crossed her arms and scowled. 'Eleanora, Joan, and I will not be riding to Woodstock. Llewelyn shall see us as a family, you as his King and I as his Queen, and this new child a prince or princess of Wales.'

Edward stroked his beard and faced her. 'How am I supposed to get you to Rhuddlan? The coast road is under attack.'

'Very well. I shall wait here in Worcester for the rest of May. If it is still dangerous in June, I shall retire to Woodstock in July for my lying-in.' A compromise was fair to her mind.

Her women stitching an embroidery at the far end of the long chamber each caught her eye. Had they heard? Of course they had. Soon husbands would know about the *she-wolf* who dared challenge her husband and King.

Margerie hurried over with a box of pins to pin up her hair again. With an impatient flick of her hand Eleanor dismissed her. Margerie retreated behind the embroidery frame where she was stitching an altar cloth with Ermintrude and Isabel. Eleanor waited until the women returned to their sewing before turning again to Edward. 'The younger children and their nurses can go to your mother at Langley. After all, Alphonso likes it there. He has his much-loved menagerie to devote his time to all summer.'

Eleanor smiled to herself. She had an idea. She, her daughters, and their entourage could travel by sea from Chester to Rhuddlan. At least eighteen ships had been summoned to Chester from the Cinque Ports of Kent, and more ships were sailing from Gascony. She shook her shoulders, pursed her mouth, and picked up her book of prayers. Deep in thought, she merely glanced at the pages as she turned them.

She would wait until the children had departed for Langley before she shared this suggestion with Edward. She had her household knights to protect her. He could not take them from her.

269

'So be it,' Edward was saying, his drooping left eye adding a disconcerting note to his look. In such respect he resembled the third Henry. 'I am for Chester tomorrow.'

He stalked from the chamber without kissing her goodbye and giving her his blessing. She called for Margerie to now come and pin up her fallen hair. Edward had not invited her to accompany him to Chester where his mean-faced justiciar, Reginald de Grey, a hard, balding, squeaky-voiced man with the coldest eyes Eleanor had ever beheld, was waiting for him.

As a few days passed, their sense of harmony partially resumed. Edward left for Chester saying, 'I shall send for you.'

Eleanor saw Margaret and Alphonso off to Windsor and Langley but kept Eleanora and Joan with her. The younger children were excited at the thought of a reunion with their grandmother and their tiny sister Mary, who was devoted to the Dowager. I'll have Eleanora and Joan to myself, Eleanor mused. Eleanora, now a maturing thirteen-year-old princess, was more interesting now she was older and was learning queenship from her mother's example. Hopefully, in time, the daughter who resembled her most, would travel to Aragon to marry her prince.

'Mama, not yet,' Eleanora would say every time the topic of her betrothal was discussed. 'Tell Papa I am not ready. I still have much to learn. I don't want to leave you both, nor Grandmama, my sisters or my brother or even his creatures.' She made her dark eyes so pleading, Eleanor softened.

The Dowager supported her every time she spoke to Edward of the dangers facing a very young bride. 'It happened to us both, Edward,' the Dowager had once said with meaning. 'Make the Aragon boy wait.'

The delay suited Edward anyway, as Eleanora understood, because the French king remained furious at Aragon's support for the Sicilian rebels who hated Charles of Anjou's control of their island. Edward had enough to concern him in Wales. He wanted England's peace to continue with France and so Eleanora remained betrothed but unmarried.

'I am glad *my* betrothed, Hartman, died,' Joan said to Eleanora as they embroidered little gowns for the new baby. 'And I am not going away anytime soon.'

Eleanor glanced over at them from her desk where she was studying property deeds. Hartman had died in a boating accident. 'You should never be glad anyone is dead and certainly not your betrothed, Joan.'

Joan is wilful. She determined to be firm with this daughter.

'Mama, I shall pray for dear Hartman's soul.' Joan bent her head over her stitching.

'Make sure you do pray for that young man's precious soul.'

After the younger children set out across country to spend summer at King's Langley, messengers stopped at Eleanor's castle on their way to Chester. They carried news of a monstrous defeat in the south of Wales. William of Pembroke and Joanna arrived the following day and elaborated on what had occurred. Gilbert de Clare commanded a large southern troop which successfully attacked a fortress in the mountains known as Carreg Cennen. His army was returning south when an enormous rebel contingent attacked them. Earl Gilbert escaped with his life but many knights, horsemen, and foot-soldiers lost their lives that day, Joanna and William's eldest son, Will, amongst them. Joanna was heartbroken. Earl William was incandescent with rage and Eleanor found herself wishing Gilbert dead.

Joanna and William shared a private supper with Eleanor and her daughters. As it was a warm evening, all the window shutters were opened on to the garden. The scent of roses and peonies drifted through the chamber. After they had been served wine, cold meats, bread and cheese, and a gooseberry tart, Countess Joanna, who had picked at her food, said, 'It feels too normal here.' A tear ran down her cheek. She wiped it away with the back of her hand. 'It's not only our son's death that breaks my heart. Many of his dearest companions were slaughtered. Our lives are never more filled with tragedy than during a war.' She dabbed her eyes with her napkin. 'He was our joy, our eldest son. I cannot forgive Gilbert for his carelessness, for his lack of foresight, for his stupidity. Gilbert was a devil all those years ago and he's still that. He must answer for this . . . murder.' She spoke the last word in a near whisper. Eleanor reached for her old friend's hand and clasped it in her own.

'Where is Earl Gilbert now?'

'On his way to Chester, I hope, to answer to Edward for his mistakes, his impulsive behaviour, his arrogance,' William said, his tone furious. 'And to answer personally to me for our son's unnecessary death.'

Joan, never long silent, spoke up. 'I don't think you can blame Earl Gilbert for a surprise attack on his army. He *did* capture a castle.'

Eleanor was about to open her mouth to chastise Joan for speaking out like this. It was a privilege for her daughters to dine with their great-uncle and aunt. Eleanora pinched Joan and her sister squeaked. Joan was not to be stopped. She raced on. '*I* like Earl Gilbert. He's always fun when he's at court. He's very good with Alphonso's creatures. He tells us stories.'

'What?' Eleanor was speechless. William glared. Joanna's face paled. She looked as if she would faint.

'Joan,' Eleanor managed to say to her daughter. 'How *could* you like that monster? Besides, you are far too young to understand the world of adults.'

Eleanora covered her face with her napkin.

Eleanor glared at them both and impatiently rang a little bell by her side three times. Margerie hurried from the chamber's far shadows.

'Take my daughters away. They need lessons in behaviour. They must remain on their knees in the chapel thinking about how a princess *should* behave.'

The girls' faces dropped.

'No argument, on your knees until the midnight bells sound,' Eleanor said with firmness.

They stood and curtseyed. Eleanora had the grace to weep as Margerie swept them away. Joan, defiant, marched off, her head held high.

Supper resumed with a void of fruit. William made a point in a quiet voice. 'Many knights lost their lives that day, not just our boy.' She sensed William was holding something back. She was sure of it.

Eleanor tried to remember whom she knew under Gilbert's command.

'My knight, Eugene?' she managed to say. 'Was he killed too?'

William nodded. 'He died during the attack. I am sorry for Lady Olwen's loss. I remember her as courageous after the Battle of Evesham. I recollect the messages she carried to the priory at Hereford, braving roads filled with that damned Montfort's troops.' He paused. 'Including Gilbert de Clare at the time. I remember Olwen's wedding to Eugene, a loyal and brave soldier.'

Eleanor felt her heart sink further. It was bad enough to lose the younger William de Valence – but Eugene, too, who had begged to fight even though he had taken a slash to his arm at Hawarden. She said in a whisper, her throat feeling as if a stone had lodged in it, 'Earl Gilbert has much to answer for. Olwen and Eugene were caught up in the attack on Hawarden in March. I had sent for them to attend me at Rhuddlan but they returned to Oldbury. Eugene was injured though he recovered in Chester.' She paused. 'Olwen must still be on her manor. I wonder, has Gilbert sent her a messenger. Oldbury is south of us.'

William shook his head. 'Gilbert de Clare thinks only of himself.'

Eleanor glanced down at the floor rushes. 'The castle here needs cleansing. I shall accompany you to Chester. I'll send for Olwen to join me. I'll send an escort. Besides . . . ' she looked from William to Joanna, 'my time is near. This child *will* be born at Rhuddlan.'

'But only if it is safe,' William said.

Joanna repeated, 'Gilbert is never to be trusted again.' She rose from the table having hardly touched a morsel. 'I would like to pray for our son's soul. He was laid to rest a week ago in Dorchester Abbey. I shall join my errant goddaughter in the chapel.'

Eleanor rose too. 'We must all observe a vigil tonight for William's soul.'

William of Valence threw his napkin on his platter. 'Amen,' was all he said as he followed Eleanor, Joanna and their ladies to the castle chapel. They discovered Joan and Eleanora kneeling before the statue of the Virgin, their hands folded in prayer. Eleanor noted how innocent they appeared as they both glanced up from prayer with reddened eyes from weeping. She hoped they felt chastened.

A week later, Eleanor stood by Edward's side in the great hall of Chester Castle. Gilbert de Clare knelt before them, his eyes swimming tears. He made a humble obeisance, spoke his apologies, and seemed near to weeping aloud as he looked at the King. His reddened eyes moved to William of Valence by Edward's other side. For once Gilbert looked contrite. Even so, Eleanor hardened her heart. This man, now on his knees, had been that devil Montfort's helper.

Edward made him remain on his knees before he finally spoke, 'You cannot command again, Earl Gilbert. You have made too many widows. You lost hundreds of fine men including my uncle's beloved eldest son.' He gestured to his side. William's eyes bored into Gilbert and never spoke. The pennants belonging to the knights who had perished were proudly held aloft by standard-bearers. There were so many gathered in the hall that doors were opened and windows left unshuttered to allow a cooling breeze to blow through the banners. Eleanor had entered the final trimester of her pregnancy. She longed to sit but determined to remain standing whilst she contemplated Gilbert with utter distain.

Gilbert lowered his head. 'Forgive me, Sire. I did not summon up the attack on us. I could not have foreseen it.'

Edward raised his eyes heavenwards and lifted his arms in a gesture of frustration. 'You have scouts and you knew better than to expose your troops to a marauding army.' Looking down again, he added, 'Too sure of yourself, eh?'

Gilbert was silenced.

'Earl William will take over your command.' At this Gilbert looked up, his face reddened with anger, his eyes dry. Had he really expected forgiveness?

'You are dismissed.' Edward's voice rang out. 'When – *if* I decide to recall you, you will learn from those more astute than yourself.' Edward glanced around until his eyes lit on Lady Olwen, the herbalist and landowner who had so recently lost her husband during Gilbert de Clare's fiasco. He lifted a long finger and pointed to her, 'Look there. See whom your miscalculation has widowed. Lady Olwen's husband is only one of the knights who died because of your mistakes. Sir Eugene was a brave knight.' He moved his finger to the striped banner that was Eugene's. 'You will make recompense to her and to all families who lost husbands, sons, and brothers under your command. Go to Abergavenny. Pray for forgiveness. The Earl of Pembroke takes over the southern command.'

When Gilbert rose and swept out of the great hall, his face was red as his hair. Eleanor was relieved to be rid of him. Edward announced to his court that he would be advancing towards Rhuddlan once repairs to the castle walls had been completed. He touched Eleanor's hand. 'My Queen, our daughters, and their households will sail to Rhuddlan with my forty ships, right up the Clwyd to the castle walls. Now, my lords, I will speak with my Earls Grey, Grandison, Latimer, and Lestrange in my private chamber.' A cheer echoed throughout the hall as Edward departed followed by his commanders.

Eleanor, awkwardly heavy, descended from the dais. She approached her ladies and on reaching them she enclosed Olwen's hands in her own. 'I am saddened by your loss. Thank you for coming to me again. It may take some time but you will see for yourself how my lord treats with rebels who defy our law and that of God and I promise you, those who have destroyed our loved ones' lives will suffer.'

Olwen was maybe four-and-thirty years old now, and still handsome. She could remarry. Her green eyes were expressive and her expression serene despite her recent troubles.

She said calmly, 'My Lady, the lord giveth and he taketh away, and I shall remember my husband for all time. Earl Gilbert sent my husband's body to me some weeks past.' *At least he did that*, thought Eleanor. Olwen spoke again, her gentle voice filled with sadness. 'My life has been turned upside down. I was lighting a candle to Eugene's memory . . . I was praying for his soul in the Chapel of St Lawrence when your messengers arrived . . . Guy de Fiennes led them. It was kind of you to send him, and here I am.'

'Your estates?'

'In safe hands. My stewards and their wives are able, sensible, and trustworthy. My business has gardeners to care for it.'

'You could be with me for some years,' Eleanor said. 'I like my ladies to remain close to me.'

'I have no children, I have no husband, but I do have lands and two manor houses. As long as I may spend some months each year on them I am content to serve you.'

'I ride about my many properties, and as do I, so may you return to your manors. I am happy for you to spend a part of your year at Oldbury and the other part at court. May God bless us all, Lady Olwen. I am grateful to have you with me.'

The Lady Olwen knelt to receive her blessing.

The next day Eleanor, her daughters, ladies, and household boarded ships to sail to Rhuddlan Castle. After her arrival in Chester, Edward had at first remained doubtful about her remove to Rhuddlan, but since he had determined thence was to be his base, guarded by thousands of soldiers, it was now deemed safe. He gave way to her wishes. Eleanor would birth their child there.

Eleanor determined to make Rhuddlan a handsome turreted castle, comfortable, with well-designed furniture, and exquisite herbal, flower, and pleasure gardens with water channels and a fountain. Olwen would help create them and she, Eleanor, like Queen Guinevere, would gather a court of loyal knights and lovely ladies within the castle, where they would discuss literature and religion, debate, and hunt. Wales was a magical country filled with majestic mountains, deep forests, possessing access to seas with great white cresting waves. Gwynedd was scattered with newly constructed and renovated castles possessing the latest in comfort. It sparkled with legend, song, and poetry. Eleanor smiled to herself. She wanted to be there.

Her daughters were as excited as she when they boarded Edward's flagship, the *Eagle*. They were sailing into a war zone. How thrilling was that. Eleanora caught her veil and circlet in two hands as the wind attempted to tear it from her hair. Laughing, she clutched it as they sailed away from the port. Joan hugged her friend and governess, Eveline, and confided, though Eleanor overhead - Joan was not guarded at all in her speech – 'Edeline, Earl Gilbert will be forgiven, you'll see. He'll be back in favour soon enough.'

Edeline placed a finger on her lip and frowned at her charge. Eleanor spun around and glared at her daughter. 'I heard those words, Joan. Guard your tongue. Respect your father's decisions. We shall wed you to a man who will chastise you on the slightest provocation, one who will throw you over his knees and paddle your nether regions until you cry for mercy. Meanwhile, go below and pray for forgiveness.' She turned to black-eyed Edeline. 'Take my daughter away.'

With a dark look of anger on her face, Joan allowed herself to be ushered to the stairway. Eleanora looked away and replaced her circlet and veil. Surrounded by a cloak of silence, Eleanor continued to watch the port grow smaller and smaller until it was like a painted picture in a book. Edward would be riding the coastal road westwards, determined to occupy Anglesey. If she strained her eyes hard enough could she catch sight of his royal standard but land was too far distant.

Eleanor shook her head at the rolling sea below thinking how

Joan was a tiresome child, one who had much to learn about discretion. Of even more concern was Llewelyn's recent support for his brother Dafydd. His lovely young wife, Ellen, had died that summer after childbirth and, though their baby daughter survived, the Welsh prince had decided he no longer owed Edward his loyalty.

Chapter Twenty-One

Rhuddlan Castle
August 1282

Elizabeth had such a sweet face. She mewed like a kitten. Eleanor held the baby close in her arms, reluctant for the first time ever to hand her newborn to a wet nurse to suckle. Queens, she reminded herself, did not nurse their own children.

Lady Olwen helped her sip a sleeping draught of honey and camomile. Eleanor found herself drifting towards sleep with Olwen's reassuring voice saying the baby was healthy. It was best the wet nurse put the baby to her breast. She felt Olwen take the child from her arms. As she allowed sleep to possess her mind, Eleanor's closing eyes looked on Lady Mary's girdle which hung by her bedpost. Her dreams became filled with visions of Mary suckling Jesus. When she awoke from her dream she was convinced the Virgin must have had a wet nurse too. Or had she? Perhaps she could debate this with the Archbishop or with her Dominican friars.

Days passed growing into a month. How she longed to enter the world again. Too long. For a whole month she had been cosseted within her stuffy chambers with no man permitted entry. Elizabeth had been born in August. It was time she organised her churching. Edward had not returned from the war. He was everywhere but Rhuddlan. He was fighting along the coastal route or he was in the country's interior moving through deep valleys, marching by rivers searching for Llewelyn's army. Llewelyn had firmly joined in alliance with his brother, and had declared war on the English.

Eleanor, unlike the demoiselle, had survived all her childbirths even though she lost so many babies, too many of them. She was fortunate whereas Ellen, beautiful Ellen, had died in July giving birth to a daughter. It was why Llewelyn, she reminded herself, who had stayed on their side since his homage, now supported Dafydd and his rebels and why after Ellen's death, Llewelyn considered the English treaty void. Anglesey was occupied by Edward's forces, the island harvest taken in to feed Edward's troops. Luke de Tany, Otto de Grandison, and William Latimer were busily building a pontoon bridge between the island and the mainland. Edward wrote he would not be back in time for her churching.

She must be active. She *must* be churched. Eleanor gathered her ladies around her. 'I am going ahead with my churching. You, Lady Margerie, will organise the service of thanksgiving. You, Lady Isabel, will send for minstrels to play at the celebration. Lady Olwen, you will see there are roses and ivy to decorate the high table and we must have lilies for the chapel. Lady Anna . . .' Eleanor's eyes searched the room. 'Lady Anna de Fiennes . . . I see she is not present today. Is the lady unwell?'

'Your Grace, she is with Princess Eleanora,' Lady Ermintrude dropped her voice. 'The princess has her courses.'

'Ah, well, Lady Anna can liaise with the kitchens after I have discussed the menu with her.' Eleanor turned on her heel. 'Margerie, you and Lady Ermintrude will see to my robing and as keeper of my jewels – my sapphire and pearl coronet.'

'Who will stand as godparents?' asked Margerie.

'Otto de Grandison is on Anglesey and John de Vescy is in Gascony. They can be named as they were named at Elizabeth's christening. Lady Anna must have the honour of holding Elizabeth as a godparent.'

Eleanor smiled to herself. Blue-eyed Joanna de Fiennes was very popular amongst her women. She had been affectionately named Anna, since they all knew so many Joannas and Joans. Anna would spend a full day selecting a gown to wear as she carried little Elizabeth into the chapel's nave. It was such an honour. She glanced at her friend Ermintrude, fearing she would feel overlooked, but Ermintrude, ever generous, was smiling.

'These are all fair decisions, Eleanor,' she said. 'And how exciting it is to have a feast exclusively for ladies this time.'

Eleanor took her friend's arm. 'It will be a very special occasion.'

Before the churching ceremony a ship flying pennants with red crosses on a white background docked by the castle's wharf. When Eleanor heard of the vessel's arrival, she broke with protocol. Followed by her daughters and ladies, she sped to a chamber with a view of the wharf. A sanctimony of clergy was disembarking. There was no mistaking the central figure's distinctive gown, its hem trimmed with a jewel-spangled offrey, his long tunic covered with a sarsinet soutane, and his rich cloak pushed back by a sharp wind. His long head topped with its tonsure ring of light sandy hair was staring straight towards her window. She drew back a little into the shadows. 'I believe that's Archbishop Pecham himself. If he hopes to see Edward, he'll have to wait. Look, Margerie, Ermintrude, look, his retinue is endless.' A line of monks and clerics had emerged from the ship followed by servants carrying baggage. 'By St Cecilia, he's here to stay.' Her hand flew to her mouth. 'Oh no, he'll be here for my churching. I'll have to allow him to officiate.' Her face fell. 'It will be a more sober occasion than we had hoped.'

'No dancing, Mama,' Joan said pertly. 'All those sober, long-faced monks!'

'We'll have to attend all the offices now they are here,' complained Eleanora with a gasp of protest.

Eleanor's ladies let out a collective sigh.

She turned away from the long deep-set windows. 'No, we will not. He'll have come to see Edward so we'll send him—'

Eleanora interrupted, 'Where, Mama? We don't know exactly where Papa is.'

'We'll send him with an escort to Anglesey.' She looked at Ermintrude. 'Go to the steward. Make sure the Archbishop is well-accommodated.' She lowered her voice. 'Plenty of Gascon wine. That will distract him.' She added, 'Tell him I will speak with him before Vespers. Fortunately, I am officially still in seclusion. He must come to the door of my chamber and speak through the grille. Now, ladies, let us all hurry back before someone down there recognises their queen gawping through a window.'

It pleased Eleanor that the Archbishop could be kept at arm's length until after her churching. Pecham was like a slimy water creature with his pale skin, sandy tonsure, and narrow eyes. He was obsequious and at the same time was inclined to attack her tolerance towards moneylenders, from whom she purchased debts turning them into land gains. There were lesser nobles who had named her a she-wolf queen, unnatural and avaricious, and a lover of Jewry. She paid no attention to such rumours. So what if a few discontented peers bore her a grudge, even though she had just rescued them from debt! She smiled to herself. On occasion, she had liked to divert Archbishop Pecham into intellectual discussions because in debate she more than held her own. She studied scriptures and sermons and she was certainly his match. Still, until her churching, she was in pious seclusion.

As the sun began to set, following the small feast held for her Churching, Eleanor walked in the garden with the Archbishop. Her green and gold silk quintise gown edged with pearls for purity made a swishing noise as they strolled through rose bushes transported by sea from England and set into planters under Lady Olwen's supervision.

'I am surprised we have any roses left,' she remarked. 'We used so many to decorate the trestle tables for the feast.'

The Archbishop smiled a thin smile. 'Despite war all around us, your garden is a haven and a delight.' He lifted a long, heavily ringed hand in a gesture towards the wall. 'Are those hollyhock-roses? Since your Castilian gardeners introduced them, we see them everywhere. They clearly have decided to stay.'

'Does the rosemary bush still thrive in the Canterbury herbal garden?' she asked. 'I had it brought there from St Guthlac's Priory near enough twenty years ago.'

'Ah, the rosemary. It smells divine, the herb flavours our plate and tickles our palates, especially when paired with spring lamb. We have found its oil refreshing. Just a little on the wrist.'

'I favour rose oil myself,' she said, curving her mouth into a smile. 'Rosemary is too sharp and acrid for my liking.'

Glancing into the hall she saw a swirl of colour. Her ladies and daughters were dancing to the strains of harps played by the Welsh musicians. Joan moved faster than her sister, her yellow silken gown floating in the air as she turned in the dance. Eleanor caught the girl's eye and looked away. She indicated a turf bench by a fence of ton barrels. The Archbishop fastidiously gathered up his heavy, jewel-encrusted gown – a pair of skinny ankles emerging from his crimson velvet slippers, how could he think those shoes suitable for such a wild territory as Wales? He sank onto the turf. When they were seated, she asked, 'Archbishop, why are you here so far from Canterbury?'

'I wondered if you would ask.' He stiffened his back and seemed to grow taller even though seated. 'I have received a long list of complaints on behalf of your Welsh subjects from Prince Llewelyn, God bless his deceased wife's soul. There needs to be compromise and peace. I intend to seek it.'

She made an impatient clicking sound with her tongue. 'I wish you success in that. Llewelyn's behaviour is that of a traitor. King Edward will return soon. Tell me, what are these complaints?'

The Archbishop folded his long hands in his lap. He narrowed his eyes. 'Edward's knights permit the burning of churches, theft of relics, killing of monks and nuns, slaughter of women and infants. This must be investigated and righted. There is the great matter of Welsh law. It's been ignored since the English settlers arrived . . . and there are other matters of discontent.'

'I see. Edward's camp is at Llangernyw on the Conwy. Anglesey is occupied by us too. You could venture either way, Archbishop.'

He unfolded his hands. 'No, I shall await Edward's return here at his headquarters.'

Eleanor sighed. The Archbishop was meddling, and she would have to tolerate his presence for another two weeks. She must keep him too occupied to discuss her own dealings. He must not enquire into her properties, her land-dealings, and her business with the Jewry. Nor must he complain about her favourite debt collector, who lived far away in London. For a heartbeat, she studied his pious face. He played chess and in that game, too, she could easily distract and outwit him.

Three days later two envoys' decapitated heads were delivered in a cart to the castle along with injured guards who had ridden with the envoys. Eleanor thought this must make the Archbishop reconsider his plea for peace with the Welsh princes.

'Really, you still seek reconciliation, after this murder?' she said. 'Even an archbishop's envoys are not respected by such worthless people.'

'It is why there must be peace. God rest my envoys' souls.'

September eased into October. Autumn brought with it rainy weather punctuated by occasional sunny days. Eleanor was running out of ideas to keep the Archbishop busy. He liked to hunt and she longed to take her dogs out into the woods for a day's sport. Surrounded by a band of household knights as well as a foot guard with crossbows, they rode out of Rhuddlan heavily protected. Her huntsmen carried bows and quivers filled with arrows, and axes strapped to their belts. She ordered her daughters to ride close to her. You never knew what enemies lurked in the woods. The Archbishop and his party rode warily to the hunter's horn because of the danger of attack. When the huntsmen brought down a stag, Joan clapped with excitement at the kill but Eleanora turned away, saying it was sad to kill God's creatures.

'You will enjoy this venison so stop complaining,' Eleanor said as a second stag was trussed and made ready for their return to the castle.

'Yes, 'tis true, but, Mama, it's hard to see the slaughter.'

A smooth voice spoke from her side. 'Just as stags are slaughtered, so are good Christian men senselessly killed in war? At least the stag provides us with nourishment.' The Archbishop twitched his reins and his horse, a dark jennet, snorted as if in assent. Dogs raced about barking. One of her favourites barked right at Archbishop Pecham, turning its head to and fro in a disdainful manner.

Oh dear, *good Christian men*, thought Eleanor. My dogs sense my mood with this cleric. 'And *women*,' she said aloud, smiling. 'Our settlements were attacked by the Welsh. Women and children have been murdered in their beds. Our dearest friend, Roger Clifford, is Dafydd's hostage. We pray for his safety. And, Archbishop, do you really think it acceptable to kill the Jewry?' There, it was out.

'They killed Christ. If they do not convert they do not deserve to live.'

'I see,' she said and pursed her lips. Eleanor did not see. In Castile religions had existed together in harmony. Unlike the Dowager and even Edward himself, she was content to be a tolerant and *Christian* queen.

When they reached the castle, Edward and his commanders had arrived that very afternoon. They had not been expected for several more days. Servants and retainers bustled around. Ovens were fired up to bake extra bread. Bed linen was carried in enormous wicker baskets up and down narrow stairways. Water was heated for Edward's bath. Lavender-scented soap appeared. His bedchamber had been swept and old rushing replaced with fresh sweet-smelling floor matting. Everyone had to be accommodated and domestic arrangements had to operate as smoothly. It was as if Rhuddlan was the great palace of Westminster itself.

That night, they shared a bed for the first time in months. Edward insisted that Elizabeth was brought to them the next morning. He cradled the baby in one arm with his other arm thrown around Eleanor's shoulders. Looking down at his newest daughter he sighed.

'She is beautiful, like her mother.' He kissed the baby's dark downy head. 'Elizabeth of Rhuddlan,' he murmured. 'How I adore our princesses. If anything were to happen to Alphonso I want Eleanora to be Queen of England after I die.'

She caught herself clicking her tongue, a habit she was acquiring when displeased, somewhat too like the Dowager, she realised. 'I agree, but the English nobles will not accept a Queen of England married to Alphonso of Aragon. They are hard-headed.'

'Pecham informs me the Pope has not sanctioned her proposed marriage. The French king is against Eleanora's union..'

'The Aragon marriage will keep Gascony safe, as does the alliance. We can wait.' Eleanor drew breath. 'You *do* know why the Archbishop is here, Edward, my love?'

He nodded. 'The Archbishop is here to berate me over Wales.'

'Are you going to permit Pecham to send an emissary to Llewelyn?'

'I can't stop him. After all, he is Archbishop of Canterbury. How I wish Robert Burnell was the Archbishop instead of this penny-pinching, sanctimonious man.' He stroked his beard. At length he said, 'Pecham can seek a surrender . . . nothing less. Says he is going into the valleys himself, in person, to see Llewelyn. I don't approve of it, but I cannot stop him. My men *could* track him to the enemy's lair and find the wretched prince.'

Eleanor wondered if Edward would dare to place Archbishop Pecham in danger.

Archbishop Pecham travelled into Snowdonia and returned to Rhuddlan on the sixth day of November. Llewelyn had refused outright surrender.

A war council convened in the castle hall at Rhuddlan. Eleanor joined it.

The Archbishop wearing his sarsinet robe along with a tight-lipped face sat at the table. His back was stiff, his shoulders set, and his hands were folded to clearly display his jewelled rings. A huge gold cross hung from his neck. 'The Prince says terms must be guaranteed before he surrenders,' he informed Edward's war council. 'Safe conduct and negotiation.' The Archbishop drew himself up, attempting to meet the even taller Edward's eyes.

'If he gives up the fight in Wales, perhaps he could have an earldom in England,' suggested one advisor.

Edward shook his mane of greying hair. 'No!'

That was not a bad suggestion, Eleanor thought, but remained silent.

The meeting's outcome was indecisive.

On the following day just before Vespers, messengers galloped into the outer bailey. Eleanor hastily changed her simple woollen gown for a silk one with narrow sleeves and a heavy burgundy damask over-gown. She wore a short veil under a queenly circlet studded with rubies. Her hair was plaited into two latticed golden crispinettes at her ears. Sweeping her hand along her rich gown she considered herself ready to meet this new delegation.

She received a shock when she stepped into the hall. Edward's councillors wore faces displaying disbelief. The women present were weeping, as were some of the men. She stared around the hall, utterly dismayed. Archbishop Pecham was paler than usual, if that was indeed possible. The messengers who were conversing with Edward turned and bowed low as she approached the dais table. They had looks of anguish on their exhausted faces. She looked from them to Edward. He had tears in his eyes.

Edward took her hand and drew her to the empty chair beside his own. He sent the messengers away to find their needed refreshment and rest. As they departed, she noted patches of sweat on their cloaks. They had ridden hard. 'What has happened?' she said to Edward in a voice hardly audible, even to herself.

'It's the pontoon bridge at Anglesey. Luke de Tany led a force over it. He knew Llewelyn was at the castle nearby to speak with the Archbishop. Once Pecham left, they tried to capture Llewelyn, thinking the war would end once we had the traitor in our power.'

287

'Foolish knights seeking glory.' The Archbishop's voice was raised. He sounded furious. 'While I was in conversation with the prince! Until Llewelyn reached the mountains he should have had the safe conduct promised him.'

Edward's look was thunderous. 'I never granted Llewelyn safe conduct. Our army was attacked and cut down. Llewelyn watched and waited. He had spies. He knew when Tany was crossing over from the island. Tany's forces were outflanked by rebels swooping down from the mountains. Our troops could not escape because the tide turned, cutting them off from the boat bridge. The enemy's numbers were too great. Our knights and soldiers tried to swim for it and, not able to reach safety, they drowned.'

'Who died?' Eleanor said, her voice rising with anxiety. Otto was there, she knew. William Latimer too. And they had all crusaded together, old companions in arms.

'Sixteen knights, Luke de Tany, two of Robert Burnell's nephews . . .' he said quietly.

'Otto de Grandison – and what about William Latimer? By sainted Mary! No.'

Edward shook his head. 'It's heart-breaking, Eleanor. I know not if William Latimer survived. Otto survived the attack and has taken over command. He sent for surgeons from Chester. There can be no peace now.' He turned to Archbishop Pecham. 'Lead us in Vespers today, Archbishop.' There were tears in Edward's eyes. 'We must pray for the souls of the departed.'

As Eleanor walked to the chapel, she puzzled as to how Luke de Tany could have taken it on himself to conduct such a foolhardy mission. And Otto was usually not so impatient. Could Edward have sent that command himself? Was her husband as careless of life as Gilbert of Gloucester had been months earlier?'

News filtered into Rhuddlan over the coming days. Otto had bravely swum to the Anglesey shore. Their much-loved knight, William Latimer, had survived because his horse had swum him to safety. A letter arrived from Llewelyn for Archbishop Pecham.

Pecham reported its contents to Edward before dinner. '*The people of Snowdonia do not wish to do homage to a stranger, of whom language, manners and laws they are entirely ignorant . . .*'

'And they consider themselves descended from Brutus,' Edward remarked with a cynical sneer. 'We'll disprove that myth. These lands belong to us, not them.' Eleanor wondered if the war would ever end. She thought of her neglected estates. She had not seen Mary, Margaret, and Alphonso for near enough a year.

As weeks passed Eleanor became absorbed by baby Elizabeth. She passed hours with the baby's cradle by her side as she wrote letters to her bailiffs and land stewards in England. She read and discussed legends with her daughters. She played chess with her ladies.

Occasionally they rode into the nearby forest with sparrow-hawks on their wrists and returned with small birds for the table. Edward was frequently in discussion with his commanders who visited Rhuddlan during that November. The Archbishop grudgingly agreed to support Edward to raise more tax for the war, but with a caveat: his support would be granted only if Edward was harsher on the Jewry.

'He's obsessive,' Edward would complain to her. 'Overstayed his welcome. I'll not be sorry when Pecham returns to Canterbury.'

At last Edward's wish was granted. The Archbishop and his retinue sailed away on a wintry November day, their embroidered crosses and extravagant gowns arraying them with a semblance of power and wealth. Pecham had to be in Canterbury in good time for Christmas. On the day of the departure, Eleanor smiled as she received his blessing. Her daughters behaved with decorum when they said goodbye and heaved a sigh of relief when his ship moved gracefully along the river towards the sea.

The war resumed following Pecham's departure. After Edward departed to command and fight, Eleanor devoted her time to educating her daughters. Winter blew in with cold crisp air, bracing breezes and blazing log fires. Autumn rain dashed against tightly closed shutters.

When the weather permitted, Eleanor walked in her gardens

with Olwen, discussing designs for other gardens for the stronghold castles she and Edward planned for Wales. She pored over Olwen's herbal book asking her to explain the plants she had sketched with Latin names.

'The Pope requires another Crusade,' Eleanor confided to Olwen one wintry afternoon. 'He would like Edward to lead it. According to Archbishop Pecham, Pope Martin has raised a Crusade tax. Would you crusade again, Olwen? Discover more treasures such as these growing in Palestine?' Eleanor touched the drawing of the small greenish fruit from *chrozophora tinctoria* with her index finger. It provided a vivid blue ink. 'You draw very well.'

'Thank you. I would have to think about it, your Grace.'

'I would, without a moment's thought.' Eleanor glanced up from the drawing. 'Where the King goes, so must I.'

'But the Welsh war . . .'

'Will soon be over, Olwen.'

Master Guillaume abruptly flashed into Eleanor's thoughts. Had it been wrong for her to insist Olwen married Eugene? Olwen had been happy in her marriage, broken by her loss, and now, at last, she had begun to smile again. She enjoyed the company of the other ladies at Eleanor's small court. Olwen was popular.

'Your Grace,' Olwen was pointing out of the window into the garden. 'A Christmas rose.'

Eleanor glanced from the window. 'I believe you are correct, Lady Olwen, and in time for Christmas.' She reached her arms high and stretched. 'I must go and peep at Elizabeth. Why don't you fetch your cloak? We'll go into the garden and look closely at that rose? I'll meet you there.'

Olwen curtseyed, closed her herbal and tucked it into its leather case.

One of the knights she assumed was with Edward, the well-seasoned Bertrand, was kneeling in the opened doorway to the chamber. He called softly, 'Your Grace.' She stared at his crinkled face, puzzled by his presence. Her hand flew to her breast.

'Not the King?'

'No, no, not the King, your Grace. Good news. Prince Llewelyn was killed some days since, near Builth.'

'The Marcher lands,' Eleanor muttered. 'Killed there.' Time seemed to still as she absorbed the significance of Llewelyn's death. Remembering the kneeling knight, she said, 'Rise, Bertrand. Tell me what occurred.'

Coming awkwardly to his feet, the knight stepped further into the chamber. As if it was an afterthought, he pulled the door closed. 'A battle occurred between the younger Earl Mortimer's men and the rebels. The Prince was killed at Cilmeri on the eleventh day of the month. His army is broken, dead or prisoners or in hiding.' He drew a rasping breath and continued. 'The King has ordered Llewelyn's head sent to Anglesey so his troops there can see he is really dead, then he is sending it to London. Llewelyn's head will be skewered on a spike on the great bridge in London.'

'Where *is* my husband?'

'On his way back from the south. He was safe when we parted company.'

'Perhaps this is to be an end to it all.' Turning to Olwen who stood by her chair still clutching her herbal case she said, 'God has blessed us this Christmastide.'

'Amen,' Olwen replied.

Chapter Twenty-Two

Olwen
March 1283

As coastal rains hammered the castle walls throughout long wintry evenings, the Queen's court played. They invented silly jokes and told riddles to amuse themselves. Welsh minstrels played haunting melodies. The ladies embroidered. They read and played chess and backgammon. They danced during firelit nights and slept late into bitterly cold mornings. At last spring was approaching, heralded in by warbling garden birds and softer breezes blowing from the south.

Olwen was restless and longed to be outside. Looking up from a book she was sharing with Anna and Isabel, a sigh escaped her lips. 'The siege of Troy is thrilling but we have read it so many times.' She leapt up from her window seat and stared out at the garden. 'I need to be out there.' She rubbed a circle in the pale glass with her sleeve. 'Buds are bursting into flower on the haw-thorn hedging.'

'Windy today,' Isabel replied, glancing up from a page filled with figures pouring out of a wooden horse. 'I had to take a message across to the bakehouse earlier.'

Isabel nodded at Anna and they laid the tale aside. Both joined Olwen to look out down into the garden. Narcissi budded. Prim-roses peeped up along the ton-barrel fencing. The frost had melted.

Olwen thought for a few moments. She turned to the women. 'I have to design a garden for the new castle at Conwy. My heart is not in it. I keep thinking of Eugene, how only a year ago we were full of hope. Eugene's life was saved after Hawarden fell, only for him to lose it a few months later in the war here.' Her thoughts turned to the Hospitaller who had saved him.

She had seen Guillaume briefly at the Christmas Feast in Rhuddlan. He had given her his sincere condolences and said he prayed daily for Eugene's soul. Such a good man as Eugene would be in Heaven already. Those words had made her chest feel as if a stone had settled in it. She missed Eugene so much that even Guillaume's presence could not lighten her heart at Christmas. She was surprised at how much she had grown to love Eugene and at how much she missed him by her side - their conversation as they worked together in their gardens, his support for her as she had grown herbs and plants to sell, and his loyal, comfortable, and gentle manner. She missed waking up each day with him beside her.

The apothecary returned to Chester after Christ's Day. Before he departed he gave her a New Year's gift of a rosary made of amber beads. Closing her hand over it, he reminded her how feeling these smooth beads as she was counting out her prayers could be soothing for the soul as well as the fingers that held them.

Lady Anna took her hand. 'You will find a way to create the garden. We are to travel with you to Conwy.'

Lady Isabel took her other hand. 'The Queen likes her comforts but as it's a building site, there'll not be much comfort at Conwy. We are the advance household. We'll have to do the best we can to make Queen Eleanor's accommodation pleasant. You won't be on your own.'

'The Abbey still stands. We'll be housed there while they finish building the Queen's house,' Anna reminded her. 'Now, Olwen, are we walking in the garden today, or not?'

'Yes,' Olwen found herself brighter. 'Yes we are.' These two great ladies had befriended her and she was grateful for their friendship. She laughed as she sniffed and wrinkled her nose. 'No wonder the Queen wants to move. The castle here needs cleansing.'

They descended the stairway down from the bower. As they entered the corridor leading to the garden, they passed three lords, namely Johnny Fere, Hugh de Cantilope, and Henry de Lacy. Rushlight lit up their faces creating a halo-like glow about their caps. Their heads inclined inwards. They were so deep in conversation they never glanced up as the ladies passed.

'The magic circle,' Isabel remarked.

'You are part of it,' Anna said. 'Your own John is a great favourite.'

'My husband is in Gascony. He's not part of any circle,' Isabel replied archly.

'They could be discussing the next campaign,' Olwen said, her hand fumbling as she opened the lock that secured the garden door. 'Everyone knows they have to capture Dafydd now.' She pushed open the door and waited for the other two to pass through. 'His bandits were responsible for Hawarden's fall, so sooner the better.'

'Edward wants Dafydd's head and unconditional surrender, even though Dafydd sent Roger Clifford to the King with peace proposals,' Anna said as they swept into the garden.

Olwen pulled her cloak closer against the nipping air. 'Poor Lord Clifford. At least he is no longer a hostage. That was a terrible night,' she said with a shudder.

Anna's touch was reassuring. 'It's over, over, over, thank Heaven. It must have been a nightmare.' She knelt down and parting the damp grass, discovered a clump of snowdrops. 'Look, how beautiful,' she exclaimed.

'So pure, tiny white trumpets amongst green foliage.' The fragile flowers reminded her of how the earth renewed itself. Castles fell and were rebuilt. Survivors could often rebuild their lives again. With hope and prayer, the human spirit could be resistant to destructive elements that tried to stifle it.

'Conwy is the new base for operations,' Isabel was saying brightly. 'It belonged to Llewelyn. Just think, you are planting a garden beside Llewelyn's old hall. I wonder if Ellen ever lived there.'

294

'Ellen was so beautiful,' said Anna with a catch in her voice. 'She was unhappy at Edward's court. The day she wed Llewelyn was the first time we saw her with a genuine smile on her face.'

Isabel seemed to think for a heartbeat. 'Dafydd must have the baby now its parents are dead. I wonder what will happen to the child when Edward captures Dafydd.'

'Gwendolyn, they called her. If we are to go to Conwy it means the war must be almost over,' Olwen murmured as she examined the flower beds. 'Nettles. Young nettles. I shall use these in a tonic. We could all do with one. I'll see if the gardener can gather them. Excuse me.'

She left the women discussing the war and set off through the outer gate in search of the gardener. She found him in the small orchard examining a mulberry tree. Olwen was a great favourite with the old man whose kindly face was like a wizened apple. She had no trouble persuading him to help her. Like a faithful old hound, he followed her into Queen Eleanor's garden, carrying a trowel for nettle digging and a wooden pail.

'Success,' she said to Isabel and Anna. 'A tonic for us all.'

It was early morning. Their ship was full of baggage. This included a great bed with hangings for Queen Eleanor, as well as linens and carpets and tapestries. Soon they were sailing beneath a hazy blue sky along the coast, destined for Conwy. The wind was for them and by sunset, they were disembarking. When Olwen glimpsed the recently constructed timber Queen's House set amongst the building site that was to be a castle bailey, her heart sank. She could never plant a garden in time for Queen Eleanor's visit.

The accommodation granted them was a guest house in the Abbey. Olwen began to work alongside a team of Abbey gardeners with only a short pause for the Easter period. She sourced turfs for the lawn and plants for the flower and herbal garden sending the ship they had sailed on from Rhuddlan to Chester for these. The Abbey's gardeners provided periwinkles for borders, wallflowers, roses and herbs for the planting of the neat beds by the walls.

Meanwhile, with aid given by the steward who travelled with them from Rhuddlan, and a small army of servants, Anna and Isabel organised the Queen's accommodation. They directed tapestries to be hung and a richly patterned carpet laid in Eleanor's great chamber. The chambers smelled fresh and clean and of new pine that had come from the mountains. Only a small group of intimate courtiers would lodge with the Queen. The others would dwell in the old palace hall.

'It's an honour,' the bent old abbot of Conwy said. Olwen detected tears in his rheumy eyes. 'But it's a sorrow too. The King wants our Abbey pulled down when he demolishes Llewelyn's Deganwy. He promises to rebuild our Aberconwy up the valley. Forgive my tears, Lady Olwen, I weep because I cannot not live long enough to see its completion. Just as King Edward wants to destroy the Welsh palace and build his new fortress, he wishes to remove all trace of Prince Llewelyn's most beloved abbey.'

Olwen bowed her head. It was indeed sad. Looking up again, she carefully diverted this difficult issue by requesting more rose bushes for the garden. 'And angelica please, Lord Abbot, if you can spare it.'

The Abbot gave her a ghost of a smile. 'I suppose it's a comfort to think that this ancient abbey garden will be renewed.'

'And perhaps it is a comfort to know that the garden will be an enclave of peace,' she said with a smile. 'Come and see it and the Queen's house. The door from her great bedchamber opens to a stairway leading to the garden. A hall with an indoor kitchen stretches the length and breadth of the house. It's airy, bright, and clean. The bedchambers all have privies built out over a small rushing stream that flushes effluence into the castle moat.'

'You are kindly, my dear. Change is the way of the world. Nothing stays the same, not even an ancient seat of kings. But your kindness, love, and hope are enduring personal qualities.'

'The people have King Edward to guide their future.'

'Indeed, and I pray he will be a fair and just king and that his

Welsh subjects do not suffer under his rule. I *shall* visit your Queen's house, and bless it.'

She glanced at a wheelbarrow where a monk gardener was waiting patiently for her. 'Thank you, lord Abbot, for the mint, peas, onions and strawberry plants.'

'Only ask,' the Abbot said, his eyes still tearful. She thanked him again, signalled to the monk gardener, and followed him, his wheelbarrow filled with plants from beautiful Aberconwy's garden.

Eleanor, Edward, and the princesses arrived at Conwy with tiny Elizabeth and her nurses. They came by ship with a great number of attendants and servants.

'We'll be relegated to pallets in the new bower now,' muttered Isabel as they waited on the dock for Eleanor to disembark. 'The Abbey and old Hall will be filled to overflowing. They won't stay long though. The royal household will soon move on or return to Rhuddlan, you'll see. The Queen is a restless soul and the King is still campaigning.'

'I hope she likes her garden,' said Olwen, relieved it was ready in time. They had made the garden so quickly, in only three months.

Eleanor exclaimed with delight when she walked down the stairway from her chambers into the walled garden. 'You have created a miracle, Lady Olwen. How did you manage all this?' She strolled amongst the herbal beds and admired her new lawn and flowers. 'Roses, pinks, honeysuckle, and pansies. Ah, the scent!'

'With the blessing of good weather and the Abbot's help, your Grace.'

'Heather too. It's such a pretty plant. Thank you.' The Queen spun around. 'How can I reward you?'

'I have a request.' Olwen drew breath. 'I wish to return to my own manor this summer. I have been absent too long. Planting this garden has reminded me of my own neglected garden.'

'Granted.' Eleanor touched Olwen's arm. 'I shall send an escort with you. The Marches are restless.' She folded her hands. 'God willing, Dafydd will soon be in chains and the war over.'

Olwen inclined her head and murmured her thanks.

By June, as the Queen predicted, Dafydd had been captured at the foot of Mount Snowdon and was brought as a prisoner to Conwy. Dafydd's daughters and Llewelyn's little girl, Gwendolyn, were sent far away to a nunnery in Lincolnshire. The royal party moved on from Conwy to Dolwyddan Castle and Olwen's return home had conveniently been forgotten.

Some weeks into June, Eleanor sought Olwen out in the bower hall where she was writing a note to her steward at Oldbury. *I hope to return, and remain for the winter at Oldbury . . .* she penned. A tear dribbled down her cheek onto the writing desk, splashing the parchment. She blotted it and glancing up saw Queen Eleanor standing by the window bench watching her.

'Olwen,' she said. 'I saw your words. If you must return to Oldbury, wait a few more weeks and travel with us to Chester. Besides, a Roman sarcophagus has just been discovered. It contains Magnus Maximus whose line gave us the first kings of the Britons. There'll be another great castle built at Caernarfon to celebrate our discovery.'

Olwen's heart sank. Was she to be retained to design another garden? The Queen ran on, her voice a noisy hum in Olwen's ears. 'It will be the King's great centre of administration. We have a master builder arriving from Savoy. Meantime, we are going to reinter the Roman prince in the Abbey here. There'll be a celebration with a feast and song and storytelling and jousting and dancing.' Eleanor's voice rang with an excitement Olwen could not share, 'You enjoy the minstrels. I've seen how your face glows when they sing old Welsh tales. And you must have a new gown, Olwen. You are still pretty.' Her eyes seemed to skim over her person from head to toe. 'There may be a knight amongst our followers who seeks your hand.'

Olwen let out a gasp. 'I do not seek marriage, your Grace,' she said quickly. Queen Eleanor could be very manipulative.

'You said that before and you were happy with Sir Eugene. He would not want you to mourn him for ever.'

'I *do* mourn my husband. Never a day passes but I say a prayer for him and light a candle.'

'I have observed this.' Eleanor paused. 'As does Eugene, who dwells in God's heavenly kingdom.' The Queen touched her cheek with long cool fingers. Olwen could not refuse the Queen but she would never marry again to please her. She had her widow's rights, owned estates, and it was enough.

Yet, occasionally, Guillaume returned to her dreams. On her knees in the chapel, she asked God forgiveness for such thoughts of desire. It was a relationship that could never be.

On the day of Magnus Maximus' reburial, Olwen wore a new gown with tight sleeves embroidered with golden flowers. It was made of crisp silk by the Queen's own seamstress and it rustled when she moved. She was only five-and-thirty but sometimes she felt she had lived a lifetime. Anna brushed her hair for her until its tawny shade shone with golden lights. Belle, devoted to her all that long year, coiled her hair into a crispinette at her neck and gave her a gossamer veil to wear under a plain silver circlet from Queen Eleanor's own collection.

'If only Papa lived to see me now.' Olwen's elderly father had died in Canterbury during February. She heard of his death in a message from her step-uncles who sent a curt note to Rhuddlan with the captain of a Kentish ship. They enclosed a ring, gold with a large garnet, her father had willed to her. At least they had done that. She regretted she had not seen her papa in many years. His younger brothers inherited the apothecary business. How high she had risen, the curt letter had remarked, suggesting she had no need of them or an inheritance. It was true and she did not intend to contest the decision. Yet, how she regretted her father had not come to live with her and Eugene at Oldbury as she had suggested on her wedding day.

The feast was everything Olwen had imagined it might be. She tasted dishes such as swan and lampreys seethed in exotic spiced sauces. She ate larks' tongues, regretting the poor larks who lost them. She enjoyed fruit Eleanor had imported at great expense – delicious scented oranges from Spain and figs from Gascony. She was reminded of her time in Acre. A subtlety resembling the castle planned for Caernarfon, with a turreted tower and three further turrets with three looming eagles perched on them – a marchpane castle resembling a Roman fortress – crowned their board.

'They're the symbol of the Roman legions, the eagles I mean,' whispered Isabel.

'How do the pastry cooks create such a masterpiece?'

'With colouring and marchpane and sugar. How do you create your gardens? With great talent and knowledge of plants, no doubt, just as the pastry cooks can make that castle with their own special ability and training.'

They nibbled a piece of the three-sided tower when it was passed along the King's table. They noticed that the King preserved the eagles. He was wrapping them in his napkin.

'He might intend sending those to Alphonso in London.'

'But they could melt.'

'Maybe he'll just eat them later instead.'

They laughed and were taken unawares when Otto de Grandison ambled over. The minstrels began to play dancing tunes. He bowed and asked Olwen if he could partner her in a dance. Otto was such a dark-eyed, handsome, important lord Olwen could not decline. His companions – the King's brother Edmund of Lancaster and Cornwall, Gilbert of Gloucester, and William of Pembroke – were all watching, three pairs of eyes that made her feel nervous.

'Lady Olwen, you dance like a princess tonight,' the charming Otto said with a smile hovering about his mouth. 'May I be your prince for this one afternoon? You see, they have challenged me,' he threw a glance over his shoulder at his friends, 'to find a princess . . . but, naturally, I am pleased to be so challenged,' he added quickly, as he led her into the space cleared for dancing. She smiled back at the handsome Lord Otto. He had never married. Some gossips at court said it was because he was devoted to Queen Eleanor. If this was the truth Olwen considered she had nothing to fear from the Frenchman.

The sun dipped. Stars flickered in the night sky. When sconces were lit outside, the court moved from the old pillared hall to dance in the courtyard. Olwen decided this was one of the most magical nights of her life. Lord Otto was easy to converse with. He was interested in mysterious plants, castles and the legends they both knew so well. They had known each other for years, and for all that long evening she enjoyed his undivided attention, although, like a princess in a story it was but a moment, elusive as a dragonfly circling a garden pond. The Queen smiled her approval at them. Even so, Olwen knew this great lord's heart truly belonged to Queen Eleanor. Just as King Arthur's knights were devoted to Lady Guinevere, Otto was the Queen's most dedicated servant.

When Olwen rode into Oldbury that August her people were celebrating the feast of St Peter ad Vincula. She was glad not to be accompanying Eleanor and Edward on their tour of the Queen's newly acquired properties. By the time the royal party reached the borders it would be October. Olwen could not wait that long, nor did she particularly want to attend the trial and execution of Dafydd of Wales in Shrewsbury.

'I have heard they are planning a ghastly punishment for him,' Anna had whispered to her a few days before she left court on a ship to Chester.

'They'll chop off his head,' Isabel added, 'and . . .' She paused. Olwen had been drawing flowers for her new notebook – a record of the garden at Rhuddlan, where they had returned after Caernarfon – when her friends, arms linked, approached the bower's long work table. She dropped her goose quill. Ink pooled onto the table, narrowly avoiding the precious sheets of parchment.

'And?' Olwen repeated as she blotted up the mess with a linen cloth.

Isabel looked about the bower before replying. Clearly she did

301

not want the princesses to hear what she was about to say. Olwen followed her friend's eyes. Joan was stitching a piece of embroidery and her head was bent over it as she concentrated. Eleanora was reading a book. Other ladies were busy with an altar cloth they were embroidering for the chapel at Rhuddlan. Only Joan's governess, Lady Edeline, glanced over, eyes narrowed and thin lips pursed.

'That Edeline woman,' Isabel muttered under her breath. 'She's always snooping.'

'Never mind her. What is the King planning for the Welsh prince?'

Isabel leaned closer to Olwen's ear. 'He will be dragged by horses to the scaffold, then strangled by a half drop so he'll see his bowels removed and burned before his eyes. It's shocking. And he'll be cut down and beheaded.' Olwen felt her eyes widen.

A moment later she was running for the garderobe.

'What ails Lady Olwen?' Edeline had called over from the embroidery frame and Joan jerked her head up from the belt she was stitching.

Olwen heard Isabel's response. 'She ate a bad herring at breakfast.'

'At last,' Belle was saying as they rode alongside familiar golden fields with ripening barley. 'Home at last.'

'And I can claim my own bedchamber,' Olwen said. For a moment they rode on in silence. She was saddened as she remembered how before she set out for Rhuddlan she had ordered a stone coffin for Eugene. 'I want to stop at St Lawrence to give thanks for our safe return. Come with me, Belle.'

With a signal of her hand, she halted her escort and bade them wait. She climbed from her palfrey, tied its reins to a post, and made her way through a gate in a hedgerow filled with the scent of wild roses. Belle followed. They entered the Church and crossed themselves in the Nave, curtseying to the altar. Eugene's remains had been laid to rest in a side chapel dedicated to the Lady Mary so Olwen approached the sepulchre and touched the face of the knight she had ordered carved on Eugene's stone coffin. Her hands traced the carving. Although he did not look like Eugene, he did appear peaceful with his hands folded in prayer and a sword placed by his side. Olwen knelt by the tomb where she quietly prayed for Eugene's soul, and touching the blue velvet alms purse she wore on her girdle, determined to send alms to the Cathedral in Gloucester for relief of the city's poor.

Chapter Twenty-Three

1283–1284

Eleanor, Edward and their small court rode into the courtyard of Hope Castle on their way towards Chester. She did not care for the small castle. Their chambers lacked the usual comforts of her manors or the great castles inside the Welsh borders and the food they ate tasted plain.

'A few days here should be enough,' she said glancing sideways at Edward.

'Your new properties lie between Flint and Whitechurch,' Edward replied rolling up a parchment map and placing it on his table. He looked down at her. 'As you wish, my dear.'

North Wales was finally at peace. They enjoyed taking stock of their new properties, watching harvests being brought in, inspecting mills, and manor houses and ensuring responsible stewards were left in charge of those manors once owned by rebellious Welsh lords. On the second day, they turned their horses' noses towards the sea. The sun hung like a saffron globe in a cornflower blue sky. A gentle breeze bent the seagrass rustling through branches, setting beech leaves into an unexpected swirling dance.

'It's magical; it could be one of Heaven's gardens,' Eleanor sighed as the breeze made her skirts billow.

'It is,' Edward said. 'Peace at last.'

Manor after manor welcomed them and, by the time they rode through an autumn-scented dusk back to the castle, Eleanor longed for a supper and sleep. She bade Edward good night as soon as they ate and fell into bed exhausted.

★

A banging on her chamber door disturbed her sleep which reached so deep she was not even dreaming. 'Your Grace, wake up, at once. The castle is on fire. The kitchen . . . The King . . .' Margerie's shouts broke into Eleanor's heavy slumber.

Eleanor started. She pulled on her boots, grabbed her robe and raced down the stairway followed by Margerie, and Edward who was sleeping in an adjoining chamber. Her frightened damsels appeared from chambers adjacent to the stairways. Knights raced behind them, hurrying them down staircases which spiralled endlessly through the castle's belly. Eleanor's ladies snatched up cloaks and purses. Smoke caught at throats. Men drew cloaks over faces, women lifted veils to their mouths. At last, guards were pulling open an outer door. They fell out of it gasping for air. Servants were already running across the swath through smoke and cinders.

Eleanor stopped running. She gasped, 'Our daughters!' She tugged at Edward's sleeve. 'I can't see our girls.'

'They were on a lower floor. They'll be outside already. Gilbert is fetching them.'

'You trust him, that man who was responsible for Countess Joanna's son's death and others!' she gasped.

'Silence, Eleanor. Save your breath. You are foolish. This is different.'

Edward pulled her along behind him. She seethed at his defence of Gilbert. Her arm ached. Her throat was dry. Her heart beat with urgency. Chapel bells rang a frantic warning.

'The girls will be safe,' Edward said, more calmly than before.

Lord Otto was waiting for them by the smoke-filled entrance.

'Are we under attack?' Edward said.

'No, thankfully. It's a fire. I think it began in the bakehouse.' Lord Otto ushered them through the door.

'Joan and Eleanora?' Edward said. 'Where are my daughters?'

'Gilbert has them safe. Hurry.' Otto gestured towards the roof. 'It might come crashing down.'

★

305

Once Eleanor and Edward reached the outer courtyard their household gathered around them. She searched through her ladies calling frantically, 'Gilbert, Joan, Eleanora. Where are you?'

'Mama,' came Joan's plaintive voice as she raced over the short narrow bridge between the two courtyards. 'We're safe.' Eleanora followed. Close on their heels, their damsels ran, led by Edeline, Joan's hatchet-faced governess.

'I've saved them, Your Grace,' she shouted. 'I woke them up.'

'I heard Gilbert de Clare saved you all,' Eleanor said sharply, irritated by the woman's arrogant tone. Gilbert was bad enough, but the governess was self-important and above her station. Eleanor took the princesses into her own arms and folded her cloak around them. 'Thank God, your Papa was right. You are safe.'

'Earl Gilbert did save us,' Joan said. 'He came for us.'

'I know, and thank Christ he did,' Eleanor said, her opinion of Gilbert improving for the moment. She saw the Earl's red head bobbing up and down through the smoke as he ran back into the inner bailey. He had organised a chain of servants with buckets the whole way to the kitchen well. 'He surprises me,' Eleanor muttered and began to cough. The bailey was filling up with people escaping the keep and castle buildings. Women clutched veils to their faces, men jostled each other to collect buckets and join the lines stretching to the wells and the moat.

'He said he had to rescue others,' Joan said. 'He saved my kitten as well.' Joan was clutching a tiny grey tabby cat, no more than a kitten. 'I am keeping it, Mama. It can ride on my saddle in a cage, if we can find one. I'm calling it Misty.'

'Bless you, my sweet,' Eleanor said. 'And God bless your kitten too.'

Rows and rows of servants tried to save the castle by making a chain from the well to the bakehouse and the kitchens where the fire burned fiercely with red, yellow and bluish flames. Gilbert de Clare was in the thick of it, running back and fore. They could hear him shouting encouragement: 'It's nearly out! No lives must be lost!'

Edward said, through a renewed batch of coughs, 'I fear . . . those asleep in the kitchen . . . may have suffered burns. Some may have died. The old kitchen is gone.' He spat grey bile. 'The keep is lost but at least . . . the sumpter horses and wagons were safely guarded in the stables . . . well away from the fire.' He turned to their daughters who both clung to Eleanor's cloak. 'Can you ride?' he spluttered.

'Papa, we need to get as far away from here as possible,' Joan said in an urgent tone. The smoke was still choking them all. She coughed but still held on to Misty. 'My cat is coming. We must get away.'

'Indeed we do, poppet.'

Earl Gilbert appeared by their side with a cage for the kitten. 'The horses are safe. Go ahead, Sire. I'll catch you up. I'm returning to help.'

'Someone will be made responsible for this night,' Edward said as knights appeared through the smoke with their horses.

Eleanor mused some days later how no culprit was discovered, but this fire did appear to have been an accident. Yet, they could all have forfeited their lives and she could have lost Edward and the girls. She had to admit she was grateful to Gilbert de Clare. She remarked to Margerie, as she supervised the repacking of their coffers for the next part of their journey towards Shrewsbury, 'I come near to forgiving him for his support of Montfort.'

Margerie, now showing grey hair under the light coif she wore in the Queen's chambers, looked up holding aloft a rescued gown. She murmured in her gentle tone, 'If we forgive others who have wronged us, we will be forgiven for the times we may have wronged others, your Grace.'

'I shall pray for guidance from the Madonna,' was Eleanor's response. Gilbert was not easy to like but perhaps she would forgive his behaviour during the barons' uprising, maybe even his changing sides from the King to the rebels and back again. Maybe she would stop seeing him as self-seeking and arrogant and a pursuer of women. Time had passed and time could be healing.

Eleanor would never forget witnessing the horrific execution of Dafydd ap Gruffudd. She would remember it as long as she lived. Yes, Dafydd deserved his brutal punishment and if his execution was a warning to others who would play the traitor so be it, but the sight of his quartering haunted her sense of humanity. Edward insisted Dafydd had committed four crimes – homicide, treason, other crimes such as kidnapping during the holy season of Eastertide, and by plotting King Edward's death, regicide. Dafydd was just as guilty of that act as the assassin who had plotted in Acre years earlier to poison Edward.

'By Christ, we'll put the bastard's head on a spike alongside his brother's on Tower Bridge – crowned with ivy.' Edward growled on the morning of the prince's execution. Edward's wrath was evident all the way through the grisly death. 'So dies another traitor,' he said angrily, as, after watching the execution, they stood to leave.

'No citizen will forgive you for such a death,' Eleanor said. 'No humane person will forget. Thank Jesu, the girls were not here to watch this.' Those placed close to her turned and stared at her. Tears coursed down her cheeks. This was too cruel.

Edward did not speak to her until they had left Shrewsbury far behind. She did not care a whit but sat high and proud on her mare, her face immobile. Finally he drew his mount beside hers and as they rode towards Hereford Castle he said, 'Never display complaint about my decisions again. N–n–never in front of city dignitaries, ever.'

'Dafydd's punishment was God's justice but that justice was hard to witness,' she retorted. 'A quick beheading would have been kinder.' She considered asking to take Ellen's child, tiny Gwendolyn, into the new royal nursery at Langley but did not dare. Edward would never agree. Gwendolyn would remain beyond English cloister walls, alone and forgotten. She galloped ahead for a while, then dismounted and sat on a bank tearing daisies into pieces and cursing Edward. A minute later, she saw one of her household knights galloping towards her, and she rose, reluctantly, and threw her left leg up and over her horse's back, glad she was not using a side saddle. She waited for the knight to reach her and when he did, did not speak but turned about to rejoin the main party with a frown on her face. Edward had drawn back to converse with Lord Otto. Margerie rode forward from the other ladies to join her mistress. They rode on in sombre silence.

November 1283

Eleanor rode back to Rhuddlan under leaden November skies, the sea rolling along the coast in changing curves of grey. This landscape possessed as fascinating and grand a romantic beauty as the Welsh estates she had gained that autumn. Even so, her heart remained heavy. She rarely gained significant weight during the middle trimester of pregnancy but this time she felt constant hunger and was only comfortable when seated by a blazing fire in her antechamber, cushions to her back. The quarrel about Dafydd's cruel execution passed and Edward came to her daily after Vespers. He was solicitous towards her, making sure he plumped up her cushions himself, and always remained to share a simple supper.

When Edward was angry at Welsh awkwardness, she was too exhausted to discuss new troubles with him. 'By Christ, the Welsh will observe English law,' he ranted, banging a spoon on the table, shaking the soup tureen so a mess spilled onto the linen cloth. She dabbed at the spillage with her napkin. 'Tomorrow I am riding on to Caernarfon to inspect the building works. I'll summon lawmakers to me.' At last he looked with concern into her tired eyes. 'I'll return in a few days. Rest, my dearest, while I am away.' He threw his napkin from his shoulder, stood, and drew up to his full height. 'I find I am not hungry.' Folding his long arms across his chest he said in an exasperated tone, 'By Christ, it's been a busy few months.'

Eleanor struggled to her feet. 'I want to have the child at Caernarfon, Edward. The new tower will be comfortable by spring.' She swept breadcrumbs from his gown and took his hand. 'I am summoning masons to design a garden after the Spanish style.'

'That will be interesting. You mean like Leeds and Langley?' His tone had quietened.

'Yes, like both those gardens, with fountains and arcades and statues. And I want to move there for our child's birth.'

She sat down again, leaned into the satin cushions, and sipped her ale. She lifted a ginger cake from a silver plate. Ginger settled the stomach. If only Olwen were still with her, she would know what simples to brew to help her sleep.

Reading her mind, Edward leaned over her chair. 'Will you ask Lady Olwen to return to work on the gardens again?'

'I want grander gardens than at Rhuddlan and Conwy and I promised her time on her estates. I intend to honour that.' She looked up at him. 'Another thing I have to tell you. I've decided to commission a psalter for Alphonso's wedding. It will take some years to complete.' She became thoughtful as he stroked her neck. 'I want illustrations depicting his beloved birds. It must be perfect, a special psalter.'

'That, my sweet Eleanor, is a task God who is Lord over all earth's creatures would approve. Have your gardens, but Caernarfon must have an aviary as well, as grand as that at Charing, an eyrie for special birds.'

'King Arthur himself would be jealous of your plans,' she said, and standing up on tiptoe she turned to kiss him goodnight. He bowed to her as if he were making an obeisance to receive her kiss.

Once her pregnancy settled into its second stage her energy returned. After Christmastide they toured the North, crossing the Pennines in a snow storm to reach York. Their court retraced their journey west and south to their own castles and estates and, in March, a number of close friends and courtiers accompanied Eleanor to Quenington near Woodstock. The children, shepherded by the Dowager, joined their parents for a much-needed family reunion. Ailenor, lively as ever, was full of the usual advice Eleanor resented and ignored. Eleanor rode out into the woods to watch Alphonso fly his new bird. Ailenor complained he could catch a chill. Mary was subdued. Within a year she would enter Amesbury Abbey as a child novice. Ailenor, who objected to early marriage for Eleanora and Joan, approved this different form of marriage for little Mary and planned to join her in seclusion once apartments fit for a dowager queen were built for her use at Amesbury.

'We must never dwell in poverty,' the Dowager promised her granddaughter.

Mary nodded. 'I'll be an Abbess one day.'

Eleanor snapped closed her Book of Hours. 'Mary must return to court for Christmases.'

'Oh, we shall see we do,' the Dowager said with insouciance.

Well, wasn't it typical that Ailenor would never forgo her comforts even if she ought to exchange silken quintises for a nun's robes and wimple. Eleanor smiled to herself knowing the Dowager would never show up at court in a nun's garb.

After the two-week holiday the older girls returned with their grandmother and siblings to Langley. Only little Elizabeth remained with Eleanor.

The new baby was due and although Caernarfon Castle was a wreck of a building site, the castle only half-built, Eleanor made sure her tower rooms were prepared with all her desired comforts. Led by Lord Otto and an elderly cleric, the court processed behind through the courtyard to the Tower. Accompanied by Edward, watching Margerie's gown dancing ahead as her lady held up a lantern to guide attendants and midwives, they reached the Castle's Eagle Tower. Eleanor paused on the lower stairway and turned to bid the court farewell. She received the Bishop's blessing and kissed Edward goodbye.

Edward knelt and kissed her hand. 'My dearest love, they will bring me reports every day, morning and night. I shall pray for our child's safe delivery.' Edward lightly touched her belly. The cleric, a Bishop, nodded his approval, his white beard wagging.

She peered over her great, cumbersome belly. 'Pray for a healthy son, my lord.' Turning to the Bishop, she shrugged her shoulders. 'I would kneel if I could. Farewell.'

'God bless you,' he repeated, shook his crucifix and mumbled a prayer.

Helped by Anna and Isabel, her head held high, she slowly mounted the stairway.

She glanced approvingly around her chamber at her comfortable bed, the birthing stool, rich hangings and a view of the garden below, once the hideous dark-coloured window coverings were removed. She stood in the candlelight and sighed. At least, here in the Tower she would be away from the hammering, sawing and shouts of workmen who were building all about them.

'Remove the window tapestries. I need light to work.'

'Work, your Grace. You ought to rest and pray,' Lady Ermintrude said in a scolding tone.

'Do not repeat the Dowager's advice, Ermintrude. I endured enough of that last month.'

'I shall remove the curtains for now,' Margerie said in a diplomatic voice, though Eleanor caught her winking at Ermintrude.

'I insist, ladies. We must have light.' Her voice had risen considerably, and a fit of anger which could harm her child threatened, but it was her final word on the matter.

Eleanor passed her days checking accounts carried up to her eyrie. She made lists of creatures for Alphonso's psalter and, since she was a fine artist herself, she sketched pictures of birds for it.

Glancing over Eleanor's shoulder Margerie remarked, 'The scribes will not lack direction.'

'No, they will not. Alphonso will be delighted.' Glancing up from her work, she added, 'At Quenington, his falcon flew higher than his father's. He'll miss his papa.' She frowned. 'Still, the Dowager is with them. They love her more than us, I fear.'

'Nonsense, Madam, the girls look up to you. Elizabeth prattles about you constantly.'

Eleanor sighed. 'She is a comfort and a pleasure. The others I have preferred grown up, but Elizabeth - either I have changed or Elizabeth is the most engaging of children.'

'Both,' the loyal waiting woman said, weaving her needle soothingly to and fro as she worked on a dainty baby smock she was embroidering.

On the twenty-fifth day of April birthing pains assaulted Eleanor with a vengeance. She clasped Our Lady's girdle, especially brought to Caernarfon from Westminster, and she breathed deeply – one two, one two, in and out - as her ladies chanted with her breaths. Her chamber was darkened. It was too hot. Nearly delirious, she shouted at them between excruciating pains to stop feeding charcoal to the braziers. Eleanor was not one to hold back. She wailed and moaned and dragged herself about the chamber until she could bear it no longer and took herself to the birthing stool. When the candle clock had burned down too many notches, the midwife told her to push. She pushed, feeling rent in two. Yet, with it finally came relief.

'A boy,' the midwife called out as she caught the child in her cupped hands. 'He's healthy; fingers and toes all present,' the midwife reported as she laid the baby on Eleanor's breast. Once the placenta was taken away to be burned and the cord cut, the midwives washed the baby, swaddled him, and carried him outside to his father.

'By the rood, Eleanor, this child is another Edward,' Edward called through the opened door. 'His name is Edward, do you hear, Eleanor? No more Johns or Henrys. He is Edward for his father.'

She felt too feeble to reply. Ermintrude de Sackville ran out to reassure him his son would be baptised Edward.

Returning to Eleanor's chamber, the midwives put Edward to the wet nurse's breast. Eleanor was relieved to allow her attendants to gently wash her, bind her breasts and ease a soft, clean night rail over her shoulders. Ermintrude and Margerie called for Gertrude, the new herbalist. The girl fussed around Eleanor's bed offering possets and rose-scented cloths to cool her forehead.

'Let me rest. Stop fussing, girl.'

Eleanor drifted into sleep.

Happiness was not destined to last. Terrible news had come from Spain. Alfonso, her beloved much older brother, had died a leper's death in Castile. Her heart was breaking.

'Let our lady grieve,' Margerie whispered to her ladies and they discreetly drew back to the wall bench in the garden. A small rose bush was in bud amongst the sage, thyme, borage, and balm. She plucked a rosebud, remembering gardens in Castile where Alfonso had occasionally read to her when they were children. She thought how he was reputed to be the most intelligent, educated mind in all of Europe, and recollected how playfully her brother Enrique had taught her to fight with a sword in their palace's sun-baked courtyard, and Papa's encouragement of learning.

'Teach her to be an educated princess, Alfonso.'

'She must know how to defend a throne,' Enrique had piped up.

'Using her intellect,' her father replied. 'Teach her Latin and counting.'

As those beloved voices entered her head, tears coursed down her cheeks. She must stop this weeping, be strong and pray for Alfonso, a brother she loved with all her heart as she would a father.

Edward tried to cheer her. 'The Lord giveth and the Lord taketh away, my dearest Eleanor. This year he has given us the greatest of all gifts, a healthy son.' As he drew her into his arms, she leaned against his chest feeling how his physicality increased her own strength.

He spoke into her hair. 'This will cheer you. We'll celebrate my birthday beside a lake hidden deep within the mountains to mark our conquest of Wales.' His voice raised a decibel as he held her from him and added, 'By the rood, those treacherous Welsh lords will never again claim Arthur of the Britons as their own.'

'Amen to that,' she said, liking his idea.

He drew her to a window seat and sat her down. Taking her hand, he said, 'We'll have a spectacle with tournaments, dancing, jesters, ballad-singers, music-makers. We'll have a knightly round table and feast on roasted swan.' She felt her interest in the world of legend return, and her eyes widening. Alfonso was momentarily forgotten. Dear Edward! God had granted her a husband who knew how to make her happy. 'Oh and a wild boar to be captured and spitted.' He looked down at her with observant eyes. 'I have already sent an invitation to William and Joanna at Pembroke.' He held her hands. 'When did you last see Countess Joanna? Eh?'

She smiled through her tears. 'Some time since, I fear.'

Lacy hawthorn and wild flowers painted verges green, white, golden and blue. As they rode deep into the mountains towards Lyn Cwn Dulyn south of Caernarfon, her heart sang like a thrush's song. The mountain lake was dark and glassy like onyx. She heard it possessed mystical qualities. A nightingale sang. An owl hooted. She felt lighter, as if all sorrow had vanished, as if she and Edward were a king and queen of legend where time's passage was not guided by a wax candle marked out in hours.

The lake was all Edward had promised. Stars hung like lanterns in the night sky. Musicians played, singers carolled, and balladeers sang of romance. A silvered full moon glowed for a week. The tournament held on the second day was light-hearted. Edward's knights, all weary of war, behaved perfectly, in a chivalrous manner. The courageous lover of the tournament, Earl William of Pembroke, competed although his wife tried hard to stop him.

'You are too old, William.'

'I have not given up the tourney entirely. It will be my last.'

'I shall hold you to that,' Joanna replied with firmness.

Eleanor and Joanna walked with their ladies by the lake. 'How are your children?' Eleanor asked Joanna.

'They are growing up, all of them.' Joanna bit her lip. Eleanor noted tears welling up in her friend's eyes and embraced her.

'You miss William?'

'I do. I pray for his soul every day.'

She released Joanna and said, 'Childhood is precious. You have memories of William to cherish. In Spain I had a treasured childhood. I loved my brothers and now I am sad we have lost Alfonso.' Admitting this deep sorrow, her heart lightened and her memories of Alfonso grew less painful.

Joanna said, 'I manage our household affairs and I enjoy the company of my younger children. I am fortunate in that. You, Eleanor, have many duties to attend to. How do you find time to be with your children?'

'I try. I never enjoyed the children when they were tiny because I feared illness would take them from me. I lost so many, Katherine and John and Henry and all the other babies, even the first baby, a girl-child I had given birth to in Gascony. Edward and I were left alone to rule. It was our first year of marriage and I was only thirteen years old. My heart was broken then and many times since.' She brightened. 'I like the company of our daughters now they are older. I enjoy little Elizabeth, so I think I am changing. I almost feel maternal at last, and I am less fearful for their future.'

'And I grieve for William when you have had much sorrow, Eleanor.'

'That was a terrible loss, of a brilliant young man.'

All too soon the magic was broken and knights departed with their ladies to their estates. Joanna promised to visit her at Christmastide.

'It will be Bristol this year,' Eleanor said, glad she would see Joanna again in December.

'We hope to be there,' Joanna promised.

After they returned to Rhuddlan, Edward spoke of having a very special round table made for the hall in Winchester Castle.

'And I shall improve the garden at Winchester,' Eleanor said, clapping her hands. 'So my ladies and I shall discuss matters of the day there while you plan wars with knights around your great table.' Elizabeth was impatiently tugging at her skirt.

'Mama, a story,' she insisted. 'You promised.'

Eleanor gently removed the child's hands. 'I'm coming, cherub.'

316

'Women talk whilst men act,' Edward called to her retreating back.

She spun around. 'I *do* know how to wield a sword; as Earl Gilbert of Gloucester can assure you when you next see him.'

'I hope it won't be necessary again,' he said. 'Have you packed your coffers yet?'

'My ladies are busy as bees in the hive.'

Their next circuit was to be The Marches.

As riders came closer, Eleanor made out three golden leopards on a red field. Royal pennants, and another banner blowing in the breeze showed red chevrons on a gold ground. The second belonged to Gilbert de Clare.

'What do they want? ' she said, twisting her head around to face Edward. She was riding again in the saddle like a man, wearing a practical gown divided in two, her legs flung over both sides of her palfrey's withers.

Edward turned to Bishop Robert Burnell who rode on his other side. 'Go forward, Robert, and greet them.' She heard him exhale. 'By Christos, there's a band of them. The Abbot and a party of monks as well as Earl Gilbert. Something's amiss.'

Nothing *must* be wrong, Eleanor frowned and gripped her reins more tightly.

Robert Burnell's face was ashen. He cantered up followed by royal messengers. She recognised the Abbot of Vale Royal Abbey, several clerics, and Gilbert with a band of his knights. Her heart beat faster. Long faces. Bad news. Everyone one of them dismounted. Robert knelt in front of her. The others, including Gilbert, knelt behind the Abbot and Bishop Robert. All their heads were bowed. It must be Ailenor, the Dowager. It must.

Edward said. 'Rise, for Christ's sake. Your faces look as if you are attending a funeral. Is it my mother?'

'No,' Burnell said in a quiet voice. He rose and indicated Gilbert who stood beside a messenger who held out a letter with Queen Ailenor's seal.

Gilbert said, 'Wait, Edward. You might be wise to dismount and we should withdraw a while. Bishop Burnell, if you could help her Grace. Abbot, come with us.'

After they dismounted, Gilbert led them into a stand of beech trees followed by the visibly upset messenger. Edward accepted the letter and turned away from them. He broke the seal and, leaning against a thick tree trunk, slowly read his mother's words. Eleanor's breath caught in her chest. His hand began to shake. Trembling, he passed her the letter. Ailenor's seal was broken in two, its rose petals scattering flakes of wax on his gown.

'No,' she said, her voice choking as she read. 'This cannot be true.' She glanced in turn at Robert Burnell, the Abbot, and Earl Gilbert. They were all solemn-faced, tears welling up in their eyes. She looked again at Edward. Tears coursed down Edward's cheeks.

'Alphonso died after a short illness,' Gilbert said to those gathered with them. 'I am sorry. There is not enough time to reach Westminster. The council has sent you a letter.' The Abbot withdrew another folded letter and passed this to Edward. 'The Council in London will arrange the funeral.'

Edward did not cut this seal. Instead he said to the abbot, 'How far to Vale Royal?'

'Not far, not more than a few leagues, your Grace. Earl Gilbert rode to us first. He thought you might be with us already. All is prepared for your arrival. We decided it was best to ride out to meet you in case you changed course today.'

'No change and no delay, Abbot. We shall grieve at Vale Royal and decide there what is to be done,' Edward said, his voice breaking as if into a thousand pieces.

Eleanor was too shocked to weep or speak. This was worse than the news she had received about her brother's death that spring. It was August now and the pain of that loss had only just lessened. But to lose a boy, an heir to the throne, a beautiful ten-year-old son who adored his father, was cruel beyond bearing.

They left the clearing in silence. Birds sang. The trees rustled leaves like little bells. She heard every minute crackle and crunch as

318

they returned to their waiting horses. Moments seemed stretched in time. Once they faced their long cavalcade, Edward had collected himself. He said, his voice almost a whisper. 'Our son Alphonso is with God. We continue to Vale Royal where this night we shall keep a vigil for his soul's safe passage to God's Kingdom.'

As one, the party knelt by the roadside as Bishop Burnell led them in prayer. As Eleanor prayed, her fingers sliding over the onyx rosary beads she wore on her girdle, she saw images of Alphonso laughing. She saw him fly his sparrow hawk into the sky. If only, if only we had passed more of those blessed days together. For a moment Eleanor felt overcome by grief for lost time, for a beautiful life taken; and she knew guilt.

She refused to travel to the Abbey in the long coach carrying her ladies. Her back stiff, her heart broken as if shards of glass pierced it, she remounted her horse and sat erect beside Edward as they rode the final miles through the woods to Vale Royal. Alphonso would be under a cold slab before they could return to Westminster. She would never see his laughing eyes again, never hear him sing or talk to his birds.

Chapter Twenty-Four

Olwen
1284–1285

Prince Alphonso is dead.

Olwen rolled closed the note that had been delivered by one of
the fast messengers riding between Caernarfon and Hereford. The
messenger leapt back on his horse, and a moment later was a shadow
on the landscape. Lady Anne, her old friend who was with the
Queen, had persuaded this rider to carry her letter to Oldbury since
he was delivering messages to Hereford Castle.

This death will be hard for them all to bear, Olwen thought. She
tucked the letter into her satchel and hurried from the still room. It
was almost midday and the yard was busy because she was restock-
ing ready for winter. Two carts had just rattled over the drawbridge
after the messenger cantered off past them. Alan, her steward, stood
waiting in the yard with a wax tablet on which he was to list goods
as they were unloaded. The priest of St Lawrence watched carefully
as the steward checked everything. There would be no mass said at
Sext today in St Lawrence's Church. Prayers for Prince Alphonso's
soul must wait until Vespers.

Sadness and shock heightened Olwen's senses. She gagged at the
stink of herrings being unloaded. Her kitchen maids would be busy
salting them all afternoon. The second cart contained a sack of rice
flour, smaller sacks of pepper, cloves, liquorice, salt, currants, and
dates, a jar of soap, a box with ginger, cinnamon, saffron, nutmeg
and a flat tablet of red sugar, as well as jars of treacle, figs, raisins, and
ground curry spice.

320

There was no time to pray for Alphonso this afternoon. She must stay with the priest and her steward to supervise the unloading, as well as a delivery of wine which they expected later. She could hear the hens squawking in their run. So normal, yet the day was not normal. An old sow was grunting in its pen to the side of the courtyard. The poor creature would be fetched away for slaughtering within days. Tears came to her eyes as an image of Alphonso and his pet pig, Narcissus, slipped into her thought. Narcissus had been a very proud pig and Alphonso would never permit her to be taken away. He was even more protective once his pet pig gave birth to a litter of piglets. When all but one were stolen away one night, the little prince was inconsolable.

A magpie strutted along the yard wall in the direction of the stables. It paused by the gate to the outer yard and took flight as a yard boy raised a broom and shooed it away. One for sorrow.

They held a vigil that evening in the Church of St Lawrence. With tears flowing, her household and tenants prayed for the departed Prince. Olwen gathered flowers and laid them before statues of both St Lawrence and St Francis, lover of animals and birds. Solemnly as if it were a pagan ritual, she hung a garland of herbs and flowers about the wooden St Francis's neck. Yew and sharp-scented rosemary and autumn roses. After everyone else had departed she knelt by Eugene's tomb and whispered her memories of the little prince to him.

A month later, Olwen set out for Gloucester with six members of her household guard and Belle. She had deliveries to fulfil and purchases to make. In their wagon, she had packed bags of seeds from her gardens, fruit trees for the Abbey in the town as well as herbal powders and salves to be delivered to the leper hospital of St Margaret by the Westgate Bridge.

Once her deliveries were made there was almost a whole day left to explore Gloucester. Olwen asked Piers, who had returned to her service and was now captain of her guards, to accompany them to the church of St Nicholas. She prayed for Eugene and Alphonso's souls before a statue of the Virgin before visiting the market.

A crowd had gathered around the market cross where a Dominican friar was preaching Crusade. His black cloak flapped open in the breeze revealing his white robe. Olwen thought for a moment of how Queen Eleanor patronised the Dominicans, granting them monasteries and convents in London. They had a school in Oxford and they welcomed women of intellect into their fold.

They lingered close to the edge of the crowd. Piers, who had been a child at the time of the previous Crusade, stood watching, his face bright with enthusiasm.

A shout rose from the gathering, 'You have lost us, Friar.' The interruption came from a fat burgher. His cloak opened as he walked his mount forward to show fur lining, probably cat. He sat on a horse with a decorated saddle and bridle, his leather gloved hands clutching the horse's reins.

The merchant called out, 'Ye have lost us merchants of Gloucester. Just paid up for Wales. Now you expect us to fund another war. Jerusalem is a long way from here.'

A goodwife heckled, 'Shame on you, Master Edmund. Shame. Shame. Jerusalem is God's Kingdom,'

'If it is,' the merchant countered, 'God's taking a long time reclaiming it.' He leaned down and flicked his riding whip at the servant carrying his linen-wrapped parcels and rode on.

The Dominican called after him, 'God forgives the sins of all who fight to free his Kingdom from the infidel.'

Olwen wanted to call out her support for the Crusade and describe Outremer to anyone who would listen. It was the adventure of a lifetime. But, glancing about the gathering, she could see the burgher's was not the only cynical face amongst those listening. Besides, she would not go on the Crusade again so how could she encourage others? As a widow, she had regained the independence she once desired. She preferred to contribute to a Crusade rather than go on one.

'Come, we'll leave well alone,' she said, but as she passed the

Friar, she bowed her head, opened her purse and dropped three silver coins into his collection box.

'Ribbons, velvets, silk, linen . . . all the colours of a rainbow.'

'Ginger cakes to whet your appetite. Angelica sugared to tickle your tongue.'

'Pies and sausages.'

'Cloth . . . woollens and worsteds.'

'Furs - squirrel, vair.'

'Wooden arks for your sons.'

'Poppets for your daughters.'

'Spices.'

'Tooth-pulling.'

'Tapestries.'

Merchants' calls continued along rows of booths. Olwen bought curry spice because her grocer had forgotten that in his delivery earlier that month. Examining a wooden tray of cloak pins fashioned like animal heads, she purchased gifts for her maids and a special one for herself, a rose crafted from silver. She could not resist a hand mirror of battered-down metal with a silver handle. Glimpsing into it she saw that her face had more lines than some years before. A brown curl had escaped from her wimple so she hastily tucked it neatly back. Belle pranced ahead. She caught up with the maid, who was purchasing a tunic belt with a brass buckle. Olwen wondered if she intended this for her father. He had been content to leave his daughter in Olwen's care when Olwen had served Queen Eleanor. Now, he was demanding the girl's return to her father's house at Christmas. Olwen suspected he had found Belle a husband.

Belle nudged her. 'Look who it is.' The words were whispered. Piers was buying dyed candles from the chandler for her since she had spotted green ones similar to those Queen Eleanor kept in her chamber and she had sent him to bargain the price down.

'Who?'

'Lady Olwen, is it you?' a soft voice said.

She whirled around. 'Master Guillaume, what, by the Madonna's halo, are you doing in Gloucester?'

Her eyes followed his person from head to toe. He was wearing a physician's long gown, a broad hat, and a cloak. Over his arm he carried a basket. 'I could ask you similar.'

'Selling fruit trees, pearmains, Blandurel apples, Janetter pears. Seeds to the Abbey and herbs for the Leper Hospital. And you?'

'I am at Saint Bartholomew's teaching medicine to the monks. Today,' he lifted up his basket, 'I am purchasing herbs for simples. I need more sage than we produced this year and a clump of camomile.'

She peeped into his basket and whiffed at the herbs. The sage smelled sharply of lemons, reminding her of Acre. 'Healthy plants considering the time of year.' The Dominican Friar's voice continued in the background, slipping through the busy noisy crowds. How strange to see Guillaume today.

'Will you join the new Crusade?'

'I have seen enough war to last me a lifetime. I hesitate to crusade again. But,' he lowered his voice, 'it may not happen. The kingdoms of Europe are poised to war with each other. Haven't you heard, you who are close to Queen Eleanor?'

She shook her head. 'I am on my own manor, not with the Queen.'

'Well, Pedro of Aragon has seized Sicily from Charles of Anjou. Pedro's son is betrothed to Princess Eleanora and the Pope won't allow their marriage.' He chuckled. 'Pope Martin is French, so since the French side with Anjou there's no chance of any of them uniting under a crusader flag flown by King Edward, not if there's war in Sicily.' He drew breath and said. 'And you? Would you crusade again?'

'I have two manors. I grow plants in my garden and fruit trees in my orchards. I'd be sad to leave England now.'

'I would like to visit your manor,' Guillaume said, his brown eyes dreamy.

'You'll be very welcome. Come at Christmastide,' she said, noting how Guillaume's face brightened.

'I would like that very much.' He politely bowed to her and to Belle.

324

'Master Guillaume, are you not a Hospitaller anymore?' Belle queried. She was so bold, Olwen found herself frowning. It was true, though. He was not wearing the Hospitaller cross.

'No, Mistress Belle. We have parted company. I am a doctor and surgeon and must now take my leave. The monks await my services.' He bowed again, and added, smiling, 'Christmas on the Eve.'

Olwen's watchful eyes followed him making his way through the market until his back vanished and he was lost to her again.

On Christmas Eve, snow fluttered down from leaden skies. Its light frosting seemed to weave a magical, glittering coat over her apple trees. Excited, Olwen oversaw the Yule log dragged into her Hall along with a flurry of snow. Guillaume had promised. He would make this a happier Christmas than the last one. Once the log was lit in her enormous fireplace that afternoon, it would burn through whole twelve days of Christmas until Epiphany. Cooks were busy. For Christ's Day the Oldbury kitchen promised a rich winter pottage, a side of boar, capons in wine sauce, pheasant, goose, pies, herrings, rice dyed yellow and flavoured with curry spice, and winter greens in a sauce made with her precious imported lemons. They would enjoy such treats as syllabubs and fruit tarts. Her servants would all eat in the Hall and she had hired mummers and three young local musicians for the whole twelve evenings of celebrations. Relishing the feasting after days of fasting on a diet of herrings, root vegetables, and endless peas, her stomach turned over and rumbled loudly.

A message arrived with the Gloucester vintner. Olwen sought the privacy of her still room. Shivering in the cold wintry air, she broke the seal, opened, read, folded it again and tucked it into her belt purse, her eyes brimming tears.

Lady Olwen, I cannot visit because I am summoned to the King's Christmas Court at Bristol Castle. King Edward is unwell with stiffness in his muscles. I will miss you sorely and shall pray daily for your good health.

He never wrote if he could visit on his return to Gloucester, or even if he was returning to Gloucester. Her heart beat faster with a deep sense of realisation. She could never stop loving Guillaume. Yet again, this passion would come to nothing. She pulled open the still-room door and walked back to the vintner's wagon to check her wine had been unloaded, her boots angrily crunching snow as she stepped on it. Whilst she was independent, her heart was not. It answered its own calls and hurt cut deeply into her breast. She might not see Guillaume again for a long time.

Chapter Twenty-Five

September 1285

Mary, at only seven years old, was to enter Amesbury Abbey.

The mellow September day chosen for this child gift to Amesbury was golden with leaves turning on trees. Eleanor glanced around the nave. Lozenges of red, blue, and green light slanted through coloured glass and the tiled floor pooled softer light glowing from a hundred beeswax candles. Mary herself resembled an angel, dressed in a pure white gown and wearing a circlet of minute roses on her head, her tiny figure seemingly surrounded by a golden halo. Elli of Brittany was to be veiled with Mary as well as thirteen other girls chosen from the nobility. Mary would not be lonely and this thought comforted Eleanor.

'One day you might be Abbess. Think of that, Mary,' Eleanor whispered to her daughter. 'Abbess of a great nunnery. Think of how important you will be.'

'I am happy just to be with Grandmother,' Mary said. 'Besides, we are to have our own chambers.' Mary narrowed her almond-shaped eyes. 'But, I expect to come to Winchester next month to see Papa's round table. You promised me Christmases too,' she added. Seven years old and Mary already knows her mind. Eleanor smiled to herself at this thought.

Elli of Brittany eyed Mary with a puzzled look, one Eleanor did not miss. *Our niece is displeased with Mary.* Ignoring the older girl's cold glance, Eleanor said to her daughter, 'If appropriate for the Abbess to permit it, you may come to Winchester next month.'

'Our Abbess must agree, or else I shall not take vows,' Mary muttered below her breath. Eleanor's keen ears caught her words and she suspected the Abbess did too. The ceremony would begin in a moment. Eleanor, at once, took the Abbess to one side and said Mary must join her family as often as she wished. The Abbess nodded. After all, the Abbess would not wish to lose the patronage a king's daughter would bring to Amesbury.

So Mary became a novice nun.

In October, the family gathered around Edward's new round table in Winchester's great hall. Forty-four knights joined the celebration. Glancing around, Eleanor's eye caught Gilbert de Clare studying Joan with a speculative look that she disliked. Looking away from the glances Earl Gilbert was giving Joan, and worse Joan's fluttering eyelashes, Eleanor remarked to Edward, 'Why so many knights?'

'We need fighting men. The number of knights has fallen since the Welsh war.'

'I see,' she said, looking at Gilbert again, who was speaking with a servitor. Gilbert shook his head. Doubtless he was asking for Malmsey. Eleanor knew he had a penchant for the expensive Greek wine. He was stroking his fox-like beard thoughtfully and his attention turned to Edward who smiled at him. She felt a presentiment. It was as if a wordless conspiratorial moment had passed between them. She lifted her jewel-studded goblet and sipped. She'd discover their plot, if, indeed, a plot it was.

A few days after the ceremony, Eleanor sat in the bower with her daughters, rain rattling against the new window glass. All was peaceful except that Joan seemed to seek out excuses to go down into the hall where Edward and his earls sat around the new table in council. Her first excuse was to request tisanes of ginger and honey. Later she muttered something about particular threads she had left behind. Finally, she wanted to retrieve her pup, Posy, from the adjacent kitchens. Besides, she desired a plate of wafers.

'Send a servant down,' Eleanor said snappily after she had refused permission.

'I want to see them all seated at the great table. It's a glorious sight, Mama.'

'I expect Earl Gilbert is there,' Princess Eleanora remarked with a sly look. 'He won't get his divorce, you know. If the Pope won't allow me to marry Alfonso of Aragon, he certainly won't let you marry an old goat like Gilbert de Clare and, anyway, he won't permit his divorce from Lady Alix.'

Eleanor froze. What was this about a marriage with Gilbert de Clare?

'Ancient. He's as old as Papa,' quipped Margaret. She fluffed out the tassels she had been working on for a little velvet bag. 'There, that's done,' she added.

'Earl Gilbert is still a handsome man,' Joan said and sat up pertly on her stool. Eleanor felt herself scrutinising her daughter. Joan brazenly looked back at her and said, 'He is richer than you, Mama, with all your lands.'

'I am not so sure, Joan, about that. Still, I won't gainsay a marriage with him, though the Pope might.' She remained calm, even though she was determined this match would not occur. She had forgiven Gilbert somewhat but not entirely, not for those young men's deaths in Wales, not for the loss of William of Valence, and it did not mean he could worm his way into the family. She might forgive him but could she ever trust him? Besides, what about Alix? Alix was living a quiet life away from court, she had heard, and there were his two daughters. Would he disinherit his girls? He craved a son. This was what he wanted, no doubt, a son by Joan, a king's daughter.

Joan piped up, 'He sends me gifts.'

Eleanor raised her eyebrows. 'You have not accepted any, I hope.'

Joan fished out a brooch from her belt purse. 'It's set with pearls and it's gold.' She waved the gift boldly in Eleanor's face. 'Of course I accepted it.'

'You will return that and any other token Earl Gilbert gives you.'

'I hoped to wear it on my cloak at the hunt tomorrow.'

'There will not be a hunt tomorrow in this weather. If there is, you will not be attending, impudent girl.' Eleanor felt her temper rise. She reached out and slapped Joan across her face.

Joan dropped the purse but clutching her brooch, she ran to the window. She rubbed a circle in the window glass with her sleeve and turned back to her mother and sisters, a red imprint in her left cheek where her mother had struck her. Eleanor glared at her daughter's crestfallen face. 'Well?' she said instead. 'Not hunting weather, I fear.'

One of her hounds stretched and shook his crimson velvet collar. He had heard the word 'hunt'. He barked at the window. They all looked startled. Joan returned to her stool.

'The brooch please, Joan.'

Joan handed over the brooch with a scowl.

'This will be returned to the Earl.' Eleanor put it into her alms purse. She called Margerie over. 'Go with Joan to her chamber and retrieve any other baubles Earl Gilbert has given her and bring them to me.' She frowned at Joan. 'Do not return until I have everything. Jewellery, letters, anything.'

Joan tossed her head and marched from the chamber without another word. The girls resumed sewing and for a time the bower hall grew very quiet. Lady Elizabeth, who was sitting on a stool, lifted up the scrap of linen on which Mary was teaching her to make neat stitches and broke the silence. 'Look, Mama,' she said. 'It's for my poppet, Cassandra.'

'Very well stitched,' Eleanor said examining the small neat gold stitches. She gave the linen scrap back to Elizabeth and asked Eleanora to pour them cups of hippocras. Eleanora watered down her younger sisters' cups and proffered a full glass to her mother. Eleanor gestured around the bower to the other ladies and damsels, who were hushed and engrossed in their various sewing activities. 'Offer the jug and wafers around, Eleanora,' she said pleasantly. 'Perhaps tomorrow, instead of the hunt we can have minstrels and dancing in the hall.'

'Can Joan join us?' Margaret said. 'She dances better than any of us.'

'If she behaves, I suppose she must,' Eleanor said. 'I'll ask your father.'

Eventually, Marjorie returned with a linen bag. Eleanor peered into it. There was a plain gold ring and a bracelet along with two small scrolls tied with velvet ribbons. Joan never appeared again all that afternoon.

Before supper, Eleanor discovered Edward in his bedchamber looking through a scroll. He poured a glass of Gascon wine and offered it to her. She shook her head. She had already enjoyed two cups of hippocras that afternoon, one too many. 'I have come with a suggestion,' she said. He raised his eyebrows. She explained. 'The storm seems to have set in. The girls would like minstrels and dancing tomorrow instead.'

'Ask the steward to organise it.' Edward carried on reading more scrolls. These, she noticed, glancing over his shoulder, were to do with new laws he intended for Wales now he had completed his conquest.

She had Joan's linen sack containing two verses of Gilbert's poetry – very bad poetry, she considered – the bracelet, a ring and the offending brooch. She poured the contents onto the table beside his chess board.

He looked up again. 'What are these?'

'Gilbert!'

'What?'

'He's wooing Joan.'

'Is he indeed? She'd best not raise her hopes. There won't be a marriage for years. Pope Martin is exceptionally awkward.'

'You *know*?' A very disturbing realisation dawned on her. *She* did not completely know Edward's mind. 'You have permitted this? Nay, you *suggested* it without consulting me?' She swept her hand towards the pile of trinkets. 'He's an oaf. He can't even write a good poem and he's too old.'

'Not grey yet and no older than you, Eleanor. He has the figure of a strong man. Besides, I have a plan.'

331

Eleanor felt her mouth open, close and open again. 'What plan?'

'He can wed her if he signs over all his lands to her on his death, and he makes *her* children, our grandchildren, assuming they have a son, his heirs. If they only breed daughters the girls share his lands with their mother.'

Eleanor felt her posture stiffen. 'Alix? What about her?' She remained wary of Edward's beguiling half-cousin and was glad Alix was never with the Dowager at court, though she knew they were sometimes together at Marlborough.

'Alix is already well provided for, as are their daughters.'

She raised her eyebrows. If Gilbert died and he and Joan had no children, Joan could acquire Gilbert's great wealth, and if they had a son, that son would inherit the Clare earldom. If there were daughters, they and Joan would be the wealthiest women in the kingdom. A just revenge on arrogant Gilbert after all these years. Eleanor realised she might be inclined to agree this distasteful match after all.

She managed a thin smile. 'Tell Gilbert not to give Joan any more gifts until the Pope annuls his marriage to Alix.'

'As you wish, my love, but don't you see how bringing Gilbert into our family makes sense.'

She wrinkled her nose as if there was a bad smell in the room. 'I'll tolerate it. He'll control Joan's wilfulness.' She would, but Gilbert de Clare remained a tension between herself and Edward she endured beyond any reasonable point.

'He's better than the pup we've betrothed Margaret to. By Christos, the Brabant lad is bedding every pretty maid he gets his paws on,' Edward said stroking his beard. 'I intend asking Pembroke to bring him to heel.'

'How dare that boy insult our daughter,' Eleanor sat down with an angry bump on a cushion by Edward's feet. 'Why ask Uncle William?'

'William will give young Brabant a spell of fighting in Gascony.'

'I see. Sooner he's sent to William the better.'

★

Not a moment was to be wasted. If a betrothal between Joan and Gilbert was to take place it was best everyone at court who mattered was aware of their intent. Joan, to Eleanor's chagrin, had her way after all. They summoned her to a serious discussion that very night. Joan demanded all her gifts returned to her. Edward shook his head and said a firm, 'No'. However, the family celebrated the proposed betrothal at a discreet dinner on the following afternoon. Jan of Brabant wore a subdued expression on his face but Eleanor was delighted to see William of Pembroke sitting beside the gangly pop-injay of a youth. Earl Gilbert was attentive to everyone in the royal family.

'Dear charming Gilbert. He's clearly delighted. I hope when they marry he keeps his own court at Cardiff Castle,' Eleanor said quietly into Edward's ear.

'Most likely at his London property. He's an asset to us. Remember this.'

Their long silent duel over Gilbert de Clare was closed.

Musicians with harps, glitterns, and a viole were all ready to play. A hurdy-gurdy player struck up a dancing tune. Eleanor's daughters glanced at each other with excitement in their eyes. Mary had dressed in a burgundy gown, unadorned except for a small pearl cross hanging from a chain on her chest. Although her hair was pinned up, she wore no adornment in it. Joan wore a yellow velvet dress, the flowing sleeves trimmed with vair and a coronet set with garnets and pearls graced her flowing golden hair.

Why did Joan want this ageing suitor? Perhaps, like Edward, Joan recognised in Gilbert a good investment. He did look a decade younger than he was, she thought grudgingly. Tonight Gilbert's beard was trimmed. She tried to suppress another glance his way but could not. He was clad in a long flattering gown of indigo silk banded with a gold and burgundy border; soft leather boots encased his neat feet. His hair was cropped short. He looked much younger than Edward, and very trim.

She turned her eyes away. He was still Red Gilbert de Clare.

A gust of wind blew into the hall. With it, an envoi clad in French livery – golden fleur on a blue ground and golden lions on red, burst into their presence. Music paused. Musicians lowered instruments. The envoi slowly approached the dais. As he came closer, Edward waved a long-fingered hand at the players and nodded. They began to strike up their tune again. The messenger knelt and presented the King with a scroll. Eleanor edged closer to her husband as he broke the seal and began to read. Edward crossed himself. He called a page to his side.

'Take the emissary to the kitchens. He must eat.' He turned to Eleanor.

'King Philip of France has died. Philip the younger is now King.'

'But he is still a child. How did the King of France die?'

'As . . . as . . . did his sire, Louis . . . of dysentery. It was on campaign against Pedro,' Edward said looking down at the Latin again. 'Young Philip is more likely to agree peace with Aragon and . . . this, this should bode well for Eleanora's marriage.' He rolled up the scroll. 'I will announce it just before Vespers,' he said, composed again. 'Let them enjoy an afternoon of dancing first.' His smile was sardonic.

Eleanor fingered her rosary and whispered, 'God bless his soul.'

'Amen.'

She turned her attention to their daughters who had taken the floor. They twirled to a carol, oblivious to the King of France's demise.

Owls hooted out in the orchards and a strange blue moon shone from the heavens. The Angelus bells cut into the night. By torchlight, the English court silently processed to the Cathedral. Within the Nave, they bowed their heads. As candles cast a soft light on the mourners, the Bishop of Winchester led prayers for the dead king's soul. Apart from the occasional cough, a respectful stillness held. Throughout the next day, bells tolled from Winchester's churches. *God speed King Philip's passage to the heavenly kingdom. God bless the boy who was the new Philip of France.*

Chapter Twenty-Six

Olwen
1286

Olwen opened a small casket which contained her personal correspondence and lifted out three small scrolls and three flat folded letters scribed on parchment. She read them all again, one by one. She was a foolish woman, always longing for more. If she was sensible, she would be happy that Guillaume found time to write to her at all. He guarded the King's health and when he was not with the constantly travelling court, he was at St Bartholomew's Hospital caring for sick pilgrims. He had written letters to her, delivered by fast messengers touring Queen Eleanor's properties. He related snippets of news. She peered at his latest letter. It was shorter than the others, simply saying:

My dear Lady Olwen, I hope to come to Oldbury in the last week of April in the fourteenth year of the reign of the first Edward.

Olwen regretted there was not more to puzzle over. There was no word here either of how long he would stay. She sighed as she ran her middle finger over his signature, as if it would bring him closer. She glanced through her opened casement at the moon - it was silver and full, a lovers' moon - and placed his letters into a casket, locked it, and pushed the little chest deep into her clothing cupboard.

The jangling of his bridle bells echoed across the cobbles.

Olwen, on her way through the courtyard from the garden, dropped her basket, herbs scattering by her feet.

'So you are here! What a surprise. Give your horse to the stable boy,' she said, looking up at Guillaume. A youth ran forward and lifted the jennet's reins from Guillaume's hands. 'Come inside and we'll find you food and drink.' She studied at him with a question in her eyes. 'What brings you today?'

He smiled. 'A truly rare opportunity to see you, my lady. May I stay a few days?'

He had never time to linger before. Why now? It had been six months since April. She placed a finger on her chin, tapped it. She would make him wait for her reply. Eventually she said, 'You are not exactly a frequent visitor. Two Christmases promised. Two gone by without you. Brief stops only.' She bent and gathered up her herbs. Looking up she smiled. 'But since you have arrived for more than an hour or two this time, you may indeed stay. Come inside and tell me all about Queen Eleanor and court.'

'I can explain my absence.'

'As you did other long-ago absences, but I forgive you,' she said quietly.

Food was cleared from the trestles and her new maid, Amy, hurried off to order a chamber readied for Master Guillaume. They were alone at last. She pulled out the chessboard and set it on a low table.

'You are too clever for me,' Guillaume said as they began to play.

'I had a good mistress to teach me. It is difficult to win a game against the Queen.'

'That's true.'

They moved pieces across the board, pondering over a pawn or a knight. When Guillaume slid his bishop over the squares, they paused and exchanged news. To her surprise he was winning this time. He had improved his skill at court.

He looked up from the board. 'Where is Belle? You have a new maid.'

'Belle was married last Christmastide. She's with her husband on his family's manor in Oxfordshire.' She sat back and stared at his handsome green woollen tunic and the grey mantle pinned with a silver brooch on his shoulder. 'More like a courtier than a physician.'

She could not resist adding, 'But has Queen Eleanor found you a wife yet?' It was a tease and, after all, they were old friends. Yet, as the years fell away that evening, she felt as if they were back in Acre, shedding time like an old cloak.

He studied her. His eyes, no longer exhausted from travel, softened in the firelight. For a moment, his hands hovered over a knight as he then moved the piece into place to protect his Bishop. This time, she captured it with one deft movement. He shook his head and seemed to stare at the board as if contemplating a counter move. At length he said, 'No, the Queen has not meddled with my life as she clearly has other lives.' He looked up and held her eyes again. She could not look away. 'There is one lady I would wish to wed if the lady in question would agree.' He glanced down at the pieces she had taken and lay like lost things on her side of the table. 'This lady has captured not only my knight, but for many long years she has owned my heart.' He looked up. 'Until now events determined to part us, duty and loyalty both. I am saddened by that. Dare I hope for forgiveness?'

A restless wind blew against the shutters rattling them. Her heart beat faster. She drew a long intake of breath to steady it. Releasing her breath slowly, she lowered her eyes and said so softly the words almost disappeared into the spitting logs. 'Once I could not. Now I find I must.'

He leaned across the board, scattering the chess pieces. He took her hands in his. His touch was gentle. How she had longed . . . but was it too late . . . now the moment was here she knew not what to make of it.

'Could we marry, do you think, Olwen? I would be with you always if we were wed. I want this. Don't you?'

She withdrew her hands and folded them in her lap. There were tears in his eyes. 'Guillaume, I have nearly forty years. We are both older. Perhaps we are caught on other pathways.'

She hesitated and rationalised but Lady Fortune was casting her fate and after all life was like the moon's waxing and waning, as short as a heartbeat. An owl hooted far away in the fields. Another answered it. 'I *will* marry you, Guillaume,' she said at last. 'But only if we pass much of the year at Oldbury. That is my condition.'

He leaned over the chessboard again, in his obvious excitement, knocking it to the floor. The pieces lay scattered on the woven rushes. 'Yes, I am happy to, Olwen, but you may have to wait just a little longer because I am committed to one final duty. I must accompany the King to Paris. Queen Eleanor will welcome you back at court so would you travel with me to France?'

She shook her head. 'No, Guillaume. I prefer to remain here until you return.'

'Could we be betrothed before witnesses before I leave for Paris?'

After so many separations there had to be something binding them together. She felt it too. 'Betrothal is as binding as marriage,' she said, looking into his eyes trying to make sense of what she was about to say and do. 'Tomorrow I shall summon Friar Christopher from St Lawrence. My steward and his wife will witness our betrothal but it may take a few days to draw up the appropriate documents.'

'I have a week. My duty to King Edward is to be the end of my service. We shall dwell here when we are married. I'll take a merchant's house in Gloucester close to the hospitals as well . . . if you agree.'

'The dower property from my marriage with Eugene must remain in my name.'

'It is yours and this manor too.' His pleasure and excitement were both evident as he added, 'I will help you with the gardens.'

'As well you do, for I am in need of such aid.'

He withdrew a sapphire ring from his purse pouch.

'You were so sure I would say yes.' Her eyes widened.

'I was most unsure but I brought this with me just in case and because I prayed you would agree.' He slipped it onto her middle finger on her right hand. She was surprised at how well it fitted. 'God has answered my prayer,' he whispered into her hair through which strands of silver, like those on his own head, gleamed in the candlelight.

The hour was late. As the Angelus bells rang midnight they clasped hands.

'May I share your chamber tonight? We can wait longer if you prefer.'

She stood, took his hand, and led him up the narrow stairway into her bedchamber. She drew him to her bed. 'This is your answer. You realise I am unlikely to give you a child?' she murmured.

'What? It matters not, my love.'

'I never stopped loving you,' she said, melting as he took her in his arms and kissed her, desiring more.

He slowly unlaced her gown and she removed his tunic.

'And I never stopped loving thee,' he said as he lifted her onto the bed. Lying beside her, he smothered her face with kisses. He whispered into her hair, 'We have years to make up, and with God's grace, many years still left to us.'

She sent for a lawyer who rode to the manor from Gloucester. Papers were drawn up and the priest was summoned to Oldbury. Over the following days, the kitchen was busy with preparations.

The hall was filled with spring garlands and her whole household stood before the dais to witness the ceremony.

'I take you as my betrothed, Olwen of Oldbury.'

'And I thee, Guillaume of Acre.'

The priest spoke a brief prayer of blessing and her hall resounded with cheers. Her steward witnessed the signing of their betrothal documents. She lifted her hand to add her signature to the parchment, the sapphire ring prominent on her middle finger.

A betrothal feast followed. Trestles were laden with fresh salmon, eggs, tarts, pastries, salad from the garden, peas, a brace of pheasants, wild boar, and venison.

Their betrothal was binding. Trees shook and rustled as the wind blew through them. They tumbled into Olwen's bed each night knowing no one could spread unwanted gossip. Later they sat wrapped in mantles within her window alcove where they sipped hippocras, ate honey cakes, and watched the waxing moon.

'Tell me more about court,' she said one evening.

'Princess Joan is to wed Earl Gilbert de Clare. He waits for an annulment of his marriage to Alix of Lusignan'

'I heard it from Isabel de Vescy. The Queen loathes him.'

'You have heard that Princess Mary joined her grandmother at Amesbury Abbey.'

'That too. You wrote it to me yourself.'

'And that Queen Eleanor has acquired many more properties. The Archbishop complains she is guilty of conferring with the Jews.'

'I believe he would. I hear he preaches against them.'

'Pope Martin is dead. Charles of Anjou died this year too, and since Pedro of Aragon is also dead, Edward is determined to negotiate peace between Aragon and France.'

'He still hopes Lady Eleanora will wed Alfonso of Aragon.'

Guillaume nodded. 'He's a king.'

'Anything else?'

He took her hand. 'Alfonso of Aragon has taken Charles of Anjou's son prisoner. To keep the French happy, Edward must negotiate his release.'

'How is Queen Eleanor really?'

'Busy. You know, as usual, with her lands. Little Edward is betrothed to little Margaret of Norway, another child, granddaughter of the dead Scottish king, and his heir.'

'Is this all?'

He scratched his head and looked thoughtful.

'There is something you are not telling me, what is it, Guillaume?'

'The royal family took several boat trips along the river. Queen Eleanor has suffered bouts of illness and I have wondered if she has caught quatrain fever in the summer from biting insects. I've heard they carry it. I have been treating her, and they lit a mensural, a wax candle as tall as she, two months since.'

Olwen sat straight up. '*Should* I return to court?'

'I'll be home with you soon and we can be wed.'

She lifted her face and kissed him. 'I'll send Queen Eleanor a box of healing salves and tinctures and a cream of lemon balm to keep

340

biting things away.' She thought for a heartbeat and said in a quiet voice. 'Guillaume, when must you leave?'

'We have three more moons,' he said staring through the opened shutters at the night sky. He pointed up. 'Look, you can see the Great Bear up there watching over us. I shall look at it when I'm in France and think of you here watching the same sky.'

She glanced up at the stars. 'We saw those stars in Acre. Time stills and it is as if all time is one time.' She turned back to him. She was puzzled. 'Who will look after the kingdom when the King is away?'

'Edmund of Cornwall. He will take good care of the realm.'

'May God bless him,' she said, and crossed herself.

Chapter Twenty-Seven

Eleanor
1286–1289

Pinnacles gleamed from palaces on the sunny afternoon of their arrival. Parisian roofs glowed red. The city was bustling with the calls of street sellers, peels of bells, rattling of carts over cobbles and different accented yet familiar French. Eleanor's excitement mounted. Citizens downed tools to stare at pennants bearing the golden leopards of England and banners of the many nobles accompanying the royal party. The long procession of riders moved slowly forward, led by Eleanor and Edward mounted on white horses with plaited and ribboned manes, gleaming ornaments stamped onto bridles. Several dozen knights of their households rode on equally elegant mounts. Marching mail-coated guards followed. Long, decorated carriages stamped with royal arms rolled carefully forward, carrying Eleanor's ladies. Finally, taking up the rear, grunting pack horses and sumpter carts filled with goods, chests, and various coffers plodded along. In this manner, the royal procession rumbled, clip-clopped and rattled over cobbled thoroughfares.

Eleanor had felt unwell during the crossing from Dover to Wisent though she had concealed her aches and pains when they had met Philip of France and his fourteen-year-old wife Jeanne of Navarre at Amiens the previous week. She would be better now they were in this city of cathedrals and palaces encircled by a wide river and not travelling.

Their monastery lodging at the Abbey of St Germain-des-Pres lay on the river's left bank looking over gardens. Their apartment spread out over several floors. She smiled to see such comfort. Carpets had been set down in Eleanor's enormous chamber for her to walk upon. Her walls were painted red and green to please her, and her bed was hung with curtains on which were embroidered the golden and red leopard arms of England. Her English maids enjoyed a spacious dormitory above, amongst the attic rafters. Her ladies were accommodated in a long bower hung with tapestries, and Edward slept close by in a chamber beside her own. She approved the luxurious antechamber that lay between their airy rooms. Turning to Margerie, she said, 'It will all do very well. I am better already.'

Their court would remain in Paris long enough for a new treaty to be signed confirming Edward's territories on Gascony's borders. Edward also intended brokering another treaty to end the ridiculous French war with Aragon. This would prevent the French encircling Gascony's southern borders. However, their visit would not exclusively concern treaties and diplomacy. Eleanor longed to see Paris's shrines and magnificent cathedrals.

They had been living in the secluded monastery for several weeks before the invitation to an important banquet arrived. Eleanor asked her ladies to choose a gown for her to wear and sat by a window overlooking gardens where nasturtiums spilled from earthenware pots and white and purple lilies grew along the walls. Anna and Isabel lifted up a favourite gown of burgundy silk decorated with gold embroidery for her approval. She nodded enjoying the rustle of its stiff silk. She had worn that gown at Rhuddlan years ago and it still fitted her well despite her recent illness.

Eleanor's thoughts turned to the garden at Rhuddlan she once planned with Lady Olwen. With a jolt she realised she had not made a visit to Oldbury since she gifted the manor to the herbalist years before. Lady Olwen always paid her taxes on time. She asked for nothing further than to live in peace on her manor and grow plants. Her lands were rich in barley and oats. She sold plants to monasteries and salves in Gloucester's market.

So why had Lady Olwen betrothed herself to Master Guillaume?

It was true Olwen had admired the apothecary, but he had spent years learning medicine in Salerno. Master Guillaume had departed the Hospitallers without taking his oaths and Edward kept him close, trusting the apothecary's medical knowledge. And, Master Guillaume had helped her recover from her recent marsh fevers when they struck her low. So they have come together at last, he and Lady Olwen.

'I could do with Olwen by my side,' she said aloud.

'Who did you say, your Grace?' The young Lady Isabel glanced up from linen she was folding, allowing sprigs of lavender to drop onto the carpet.

Eleanor glanced around. 'Lady Olwen, of course. She has betrothed herself to Master Guillaume. Have you and Anna heard of this? Am I last to know?'

Isabel's cheeks reddened. 'I have heard something of the sort.'

There was a hint of pique in Eleanor's voice as she said, 'Pity she has not returned to my service.'

'She might, your Grace, if you send for her.'

'I doubt she would arrive before we leave Paris.'

Eleanor picked up the lapidary she was reading. Glancing from it to Isabel, she said, 'Do you know, Isabel, I have a desire for strawberries. Could you, do you think, send to our kitchens for a dish?'

'Yes, Madam.'

Eleanor had just eaten a second strawberry when Edward entered the chamber. She wrinkled up her nose. He had been riding through the meadows chasing birds in the company of his brother Edmund, and now he smelled of horse and hawks. Her ladies closed the coffer lids and sank into curtsies. Edward waited for them to leave before he fell into a chair and stretched out his legs. He glanced over at the elegant gown laid out on the bed. 'Remember we have to manage the truce with Aragon and the French. We want Philip to help us pressure Pope Honorius to grant us a dispensation for the Aragon marriage. The banquet is an opportunity for us to advance our interests.'

Eleanor never spoke.

'My dear, are you unwell again?' he said with concern in his voice. 'Are you able to attend the banquet at the Palais?'

She moved behind him and stroked his greying hair. 'I am just a little tired. I'll rest for an hour.'

He reached around and caught hold of her hand and held it for a moment. 'I promise you, after this banquet we'll be private again. We'll visit St Denis, see Christ's Crown of Thorns in Sainte-Chappelle, and you can meet the goldsmiths and purchase gifts. Our daughters will not lack jewels and fabrics from Paris.'

'We must get the homage for Gascony over and done with as well, and that for my territory of Ponthieu over and done with too.' She sighed, feeling weary of it. 'And the truce with Aragon, of course.'

'I am sending Otto to Rome.'

'Otto won't change this Pope's opinion, Edward. Alfonso of Aragon, himself, must make peace with Pope Honorius.'

Edward sighed. 'Eleanor, wise as an owl.' He raised himself up. 'I'll bathe and dress.' He took her in his arms and kissed her. 'We'll perform homage to France for our lands. After that's done we'll indulge ourselves . . . by Christ we shall, we'll enjoy this wonderful city.'

With the death of Pedro of Aragon and that of Pope Martin, Edward had seen it more important than ever to mediate with the French to save Eleanora's marriage and prevent Gascony from being encircled by French-held territories. Before they had departed England, after a long wait Edward had ensured an agreement for the marriage between little Edward and the infant Margaret of Norway. At last they had departed on the thirteenth of May and this important feast was to be held on the celebration of the Trinity. The new French King Philip was only nineteen years old and very handsome. His new wife Jeanne of Navarre was not beautiful but she was doughty. Eleanor had liked her on their first meeting in Amiens, since she was intelligent and appeared wise. Perhaps she would help influence Philip to agree the treaty between Aragon and Sicily, a treaty that would persuade Pope Honorius to allow the dispensation for Eleanora's marriage to Alfonso of Aragon at long last, but Eleanor was tired. Her health had been poor for almost a year. She who had never suffered ill health before was ill off and on. She was appreciative of the medicines prepared by Guillaume and today she felt stronger than usual.

The banquet was a success and the talks were hopeful. They did homage to the young King Philip for their territories. Edward and Eleanor began to visit churches and called merchants to St-Germain with jewels and fabrics which they intended sending home to the princesses including a gift from King Philip, a magnificent crown set with sapphires, emeralds and rubies.

Eleanor travelled west of Paris for a few days with her own small retinue to consult with the Viscount of Fronsac concerning property they both claimed bordering Gascon territories. She was successful in her negotiations and a compromise was reached over which lands the Viscount could hold. On her return to Paris, Edward praised her and she glowed in his approval. She truly was a Queen, one who understood property and who had worked hard for years to add to their own estates. Those in England were vast and she had held the title to Ponthieu as well since her mother had died.

But on her return to St-Germain Edward was restless. There could be no hunting as the weather was thundery and lightning threatened in the distance for two whole days. It was magnificent to watch so together on the second afternoon following dinner she and Edward sat in a window embrasure. A yellow light hung about the river. 'It's still distant,' she said. 'What a spectacle it makes.' Edward turned to her, stood and stretched. 'I hope it will pass soon.' Clearly his thoughts were elsewhere. 'We must travel into Gascony, Eleanor. It has been too long.' he said.

'To Bordeaux and our Palais des Ombres. I think it's time to leave Paris.'

'Then we shall soon.' Edward lifted her hand and kissed it. 'My beloved wife and Queen,' he said. He called over a page and ordered hippocras and almond cakes to be served.

Their attendants were playing board games or conversing in small groups about the great chamber. The day was chill and a fire warmed the chamber. As the day grew darker and thunder rolled outside over the gardens, Eleanor still watching remarked, 'Edward, the lightning, it's—' She had no more time to speak because a bolt flew like an arrow between them, shattering glass. She jumped to her feet and fell to the floor clutching her head. It struck the two pages who were approaching them with refreshments on a tray.

'By Christos,' Edward yelled as he stared down at the writhing bodies. 'They are dead.'

Her ladies rushed towards her, sewing and embroidery hoops dropped. Shaking, Eleanor struggled to her feet. Her ladies wrung their hands. Someone found a broom to sweep up the shattered window glass. Edward dragged her away repeating over and over, 'But Lord God has spared us.'

A crowd gathered about the dead pages. Others ushered the King and Queen from the hall up the stairway to Edward's privy chamber which only possessed a high oriel window. They knelt by his portable altar and desperately clasping hands prayed for the departed souls of their pages and thanked God for preserving their lives.

The Sicilian conflict was insoluble. As September approached, Otto returned from Rome with bad news. The Pope still laid a veto against Eleanora's Aragon marriage.

Edward stormed about the palace, grunting and stammering, his eyelid drooping as he raged. Eleanor could not calm him. 'The Pope is unreasonable,' he ranted to her. 'You have seen as much here as you need to see in a lifetime. We are leaving for Gascony now. Tell your ladies to repack the coffers.' He waved his hand at the oak chests lined up against the wall and swept out through the arched door into his own chamber. She heard him barking orders to his servants to do likewise.

She turned to her ladies who were seated by the widow looking fearful. 'I suppose he will have us on the road by daybreak. We had best hurry. What we can't take with us can follow. I'm going to take my most expensive jewels now. We won't trust those to fate.'

She released a key from her girdle, pulled away a tapestry covering and opened up the strong chest concealed under it. This was where she secured her valuables. She turned the key in the padlock. She lifted up the crown of sapphires, rubies, and emeralds, admiring it as her ladies hurried to pack her coffers ready to load onto sumpter wagons.

'I'll send this to Eleanora along with the new velvets, furs, and silks. Perhaps this will compensate for delays with her marriage.'

'It is a beautiful and a generous gift,' Margerie said.

'I must make sure there's enough presents for Joan and Margaret too.'

She fished around the glittering pile of jewels on her bed, selecting jewels for their other daughters. 'And a silver chain with a topaz for Elizabeth. It's tiny and she's still small, and like all little girls she adores glowing stones!'

By Vespers that day all was ready. Edward dined with her alone in the antechamber. He was so relaxed now they were departing Paris the next day he was grinning at her. She saw his mouth twitch and raised her brow. 'Have you a revelation or a secret perhaps?'

'No but I have a gift for you, my dear,' he said. 'I purchased it yesterday and thought it could wait for your name day in November. Yet, when I am away from you negotiating a treaty between the French and Aragon,' – *so he was still hopeful of this* – 'you might enjoy it?'

He did have a secret and was bursting to reveal it.

He signalled to his page. The boy scurried through the archway from the antechamber. He whispered in the lad's ear. The boy rushed off again and returned a heartbeat later with a second page. Between them, they carried a large cedar box. Carefully, they set it on Eleanor's side of the table. The sharp scent of cedar wood reminded her of Spain. She leaned over and opened the lid. Her eyes widened as she lifted out a knight fashioned from jasper, another and another just the same, a queen and king, bishops and pages.

She touched the pieces again and again, loving the carvings so smooth and cool in her hands as she picked them up. She gasped her delight. 'It is the most wondrous chess set I have ever beheld.' Crossing to the arras, she called to her ladies who had just closed the last chest for travel, 'Come and see.' Her ladies crowded into the chamber jostling each other and laughing. Edward lifted Eleanor off her feet as if she were a pillow of feathers and swung her around. 'Put me down at once,' she screeched. 'I can't bear it.'

'You ungrateful harpy,' he teased and put her on to her feet again.

'Oh no, Edward, I am enchanted. Thank you,' she said and closed the box. Looking up at him she said with firmness. 'But a word. I *shall* be accompanying you to Aragon.'

The year turned. On the very last day of January, seated at her table in her chamber in the St Macaire Priory in Gascony, Eleanor composed a letter to her eldest daughter. She sighed as she dipped her pen into ink. There was no good news to give Eleanora and that saddened her:

I send you greetings, my dearest daughter, and pray that you, your sisters, and little Edward have passed a joyous Christmastide. We enjoyed the season here in the Priory of St Macaire, with the hall lit with hundreds of red, gold, and green candles, feasting, dancing; jesters and mummers all present. We received many gifts from the Gascon nobles. That malcontent, Gascon de Bearn, presented to me an elegant white hound. I have named him Aragon. Unfortunately, I suffered another bout of illness after departing Paris. The herbalist, Olwen, crossed the winter sea in November to join our court. You must remember her well. Master Guillaume, our doctor, and Lady Olwen were wed in this Abbey on St Celia's Day. We call Olwen the Ladies' Apothecary, if I dare name a woman who is so clever with medicines such in our world of men. Master Guillaume says my problem is a renewal of the four day fever carried by biting insects. We are too close to riverbanks which these devil creatures inhabit. Lady Olwen makes a salve with oils and lemons. It deters the creatures if we smear it on our skin.

How Joan would have enjoyed our Christmas revels here. I expect Earl Gilbert has corresponded with her. Gilbert will have informed Joan, who likes to dance, how we had one hundred and twenty minstrels to play for us throughout the Christmas season.

Your father is planning a Wolf Hunt. Perhaps I shall send you a skin for a winter mantle and Edward might like a paw. We shall travel to Aragon soon. Our destination will be Oloron. Be assured God will grant your queenship of that noble country before the year's end. Pray to Our Lady for our success regarding this matter of your marriage.

Your devoted mother Eleanor, Regina, on the last day of January, in the fifteenth year of the reign of the first King Edward.

The day of the wolf hunt was as brilliant a morning as the crystal encasing the abbey's precious reliquary, a splinter of the true cross. Eleanor's boots crunched snow as she crossed the courtyard belonging to Blanquefort Castle, its bleached stone blending into the snowy landscape.

Locals avoided the woods because of the wolves inhabiting them. The hunting party set out from the fortress early, determined to make the most of the day's short window of light. Eleanor rode her grey mare, staying close to Edward who was seated erect on his great hunter. Half a dozen gamekeepers, wolfhounds on leather leads, raced in front of their horses. John de Vescy, Lord Otto, and Gilbert of Gloucester directly followed behind. Of course, Gilbert, she noted, had already made the acquaintance of the wolfhounds, stroking their shaggy coats and talking to them in a low voice, gently promising the creatures, heaven only knew. She held her reins firmly in thickly gloved hands, ignored him and stared ahead. He may win her friendship at long last, but never her trust.

Riding further into the forest, she caught glimpses of blue sky through bare branches. They dismounted in a clearing and she slid to the ground onto a sprinkling of snow. Olwen and Lady Isabel climbed from their mounts helped by squires. Knights erected a tent and built a fire. Hunters with spears gathered close by. When a cart with a huge cage drew up, Edward folded his arms and shouted in her direction, 'Stay back.' Eleanor and her group of ladies drew into the shelter of beech trunks. Skeletal branches were shedding snow and she swept it from her mantle with her hand.

'Now,' shouted Edward.

The cage door was opened. The hunters stood by, reining in barking dogs as the bait, two stags tempted by sudden freedom, shied at first. A heartbeat later they galloped into the trees fast as arrows. The keepers knelt and allowed the dogs the scent left on rags within the cage, but although they strained their handlers kept them on leads.

'Eleanor, stay with your knights, grooms, ladies and the horses. We're for following the hunt.' He pointed up at the pale winter sun. 'If it begins to set and we have not yet returned, ride back to the fortress. The moment you feel cold you must break camp. Do you hear?'

'But . . .' she said as another lump of snow plopped onto her hood.

'It might thaw.' Edward reached over to sweep snow from her cloak.

Spears and hatchets were safely tucked into the belts of the hunters' fur-lined tunics. The men smelled pungent as they passed her. It was as if the grey leathery cloaks they all wore were made of patched-together oblongs of wolf skins. After all, they most likely were. Three sharp blasts of the horn sounded. The master of the hunt would let the hounds follow the deer scent deep into the forest but keep their dogs on long leashes. They would only be released at the end.

The sun rose higher. She listened to the noise of the hunt, close at first and later distant. She caught the odd oath such as *'Christ's Holy Blood'* and *'By the Rood'*, an expletive she thought to be Edward's. The horn's call occasionally rang again far into the echoing forest. Hours passed. Olwen passed her a cup of wine laced with cinnamon and she sipped it wrapped in her furs, seated on a stool by their fire. Despite the blaze, she began to shiver. Olwen gave her a second cup laced with ginger. She continued to shiver.

351

'Your Grace,' Olwen said quietly. 'We ought to return. You are catching chill.'

Guillaume added his own concern but Eleanor refused to move. 'No, just a little longer,' she said, trying to stop her teeths' chatter with stubborn determination.

As the sun slid down behind the trees, Edward returned at last with Earl Gilbert behind him. 'Success, my Queen. Two pelts, white and grey. Paws for our son.' He turned around. 'You did well, Gilbert.' He slapped Gilbert's back. 'By the rood, your spear caught that grey wolf right between his ribs.'

'But yours, my liege, caught it between the eyes.'

'Still, I think you can claim the grey wolf's pelt.'

'And you, the white skin.'

'Joan will like a wolf's head adorning the hall at Cardiff Castle,' Edward teased.

'She'll prefer the pelt cleaned and scraped,' Gilbert sparred. 'A grey lining for a crimson mantle.'

'Better a rug hanging on a chamber wall any day.' Edward bowed to Eleanor. 'The white pelt. Do you fancy a cloak lined with wolf?'

She wrinkled her nose. 'There are many hunting lodges here in Gascony. I think a floor covering will please me well enough.' She sneezed.

He looked at her with concern. 'Time to call it a day.'

'I want to see the dogs return.' Glancing over her shoulder, she saw Guillaume and Olwen exchange worried glances.

They watched the returning huntsmen arrive, their grey cloaks splattered with blood, come into the clearing, the hounds back on their leashes. The hunters bore the wolves laced with ropes on to poles. She sneezed again. Her ladies fussed about and at last she gave in when Guillaume insisted. 'Edward, I do feel unwell.' Her throat ached and her head throbbed.

The joy in Edward's eyes, the exhilaration after a successful hunt, had turned to concern. 'Eleanor, go back now.'

She felt Olwen take her arm. Squires brought her mare forward.

Wearily, too exhausted to speak, she mounted and said, 'It's nothing rest and a warm chamber won't cure.'

Edward mounted his jennet and rode back to the fortress at her side, leaving his retainers and huntsmen to close up the camp. Once they reached the outside stairway she allowed Edward to lift her from her mare, carry her up the steps into her apartment where he gently laid her on the bed. Braziers warmed her chamber. Slowly she began to thaw. She closed her eyes as her ladies unlaced her clothing and slipped a warmed night rail over her head.

She heard Edward say to them, 'Send for Master Guillaume. If it's a return of the quatrain fever, he has ways to aid her recovery. Lady Olwen, should she be bled?'

'No, my Lord, it would only weaken Queen Eleanor further. Just my husband's medicines for now.'

'As you wish, Olwen, but send for me if she worsens.'

Chapter Twenty-Eight

Olwen
1286–1289

Queen Eleanor was near to death when the court moved to Bordeaux, to the Palace of Shadows. Shortly after their arrival in Bordeaux, a mensural candle as tall as the Queen herself was lit in the Chapel of St Thomas as an intercession to aid her recovery. Olwen prostrated herself in front of it and prayed for the Queen's recovery, fingering her beads, her eyes swimming with tears as she prayed to St Jude to bring Eleanor hope and recovery.

Guillaume attended the Queen daily. Olwen brewed soothing tisanes of willow bark and ginger to ease her fevers and gentle her inflamed throat, and slowly the Queen's health improved.

'Your Grace, please sleep,' Olwen would say. 'You must get strong again.'

Eleanor refused. It was as if resting would steal her life away. In between writing letters to her stewards in England, she amused herself by asking Olwen to design a new herbarium with for the palace at Mauleon.

'We shall pass a month there, close to the sea,' Queen Eleanor announced as she chose plants from Olwen's herbal. Olwen tapped a page of her book. She said, 'Very well, Madam, and flowers to be planted amongst the thyme and camomile. Gillyflowers . . .'

'Acanthus by the walls and Star-of-Bethlehem,' the Queen said as she turned the notebook's pages carefully, fingering the parchment, scrutinising Olwen's drawings. 'A Christmas rose, white lilies, Madonna's

354

pins.' She lay looking exhausted against her cushion. 'Let it be a Marian garden, Olwen. Can we manage it?'

'If the nearby monasteries can help with plants.'

'They shall, for I shall insist.' Eleanor had that determined look on her face which suggested she would always get what she wanted. Olwen smiled to herself. At least, Eleanor's recovery was imminent.

On Palm Sunday, the Queen was well enough to order yew, box, and willow to decorate the Church of St Thomas, where her mensural had melted to nothing, having burned day and night for two months.

'I am well again, quite recovered,' she declared to her ladies. 'And I'm weary of a diet of fish stews and herbs. After Whitsun we are travelling south to Oloron for summer.' She sighed. 'So close to Spain. How I long to revisit memories of avenues littered with oranges and lemons; to see pomegranates fall from trees and indulge my desire for figs. And the wine. Oh, such rich wine.'

'Your Grace, plenty of these fruits are carried to you wherever you dwell,' Margerie declared.

'It's not the same.'

On Easter Day's night, Guillaume rushed into the chamber he and Olwen shared in the Castle of Mauleon. 'I need medicines and balms.'

'What's happened?' She sat up half asleep, rubbing her eyes.

'The far tower has collapsed. The one that stands on its own. The King was in conference with his knights discussing when and where they would take the cross for the new Crusade.'

'No!' She was wide awake now.

'A storm blew in. I heard the tower crumble. Did you not hear it too?'

She sat straight up in their bed, shocked out of her drowsiness. She could hear rain lashing the shutters. 'I thought it was just thunder.'

'Lightning. The King's knights rushed into the hall covered with debris and soot. We grabbed what we could – scissors, bandages, salves, cloths, wooden splints. When we reached the nobles, John de Vescy was helping King Edward from under a fallen corpse.'

Olwen grasped her hands.

Guillaume hurried his words. 'The King is alive. Vescy is bruised. Lord Otto has a broken arm. Earl Gilbert unhurt; a ginger cat with nine lives, that one. William of Pembroke laid out on his couch – shock and bruises. I have sent him a draught of poppy and honey. Now, I need arnica balm for their bruises.'

She threw off her bedcovers and stood beside him. 'It's there,' she said, pointing to a shelf.

'Ah, here it is.' He lifted down a jar.

'By Lady Mary, does Queen Eleanor know?'

'She's by Edward's side.'

Olwen began to dress hastily. 'I must go to her. What else, husband? Was anyone killed?'

'The floor collapsed. Knights died; others are buried under collapsed stones. Your gardeners are digging them out.' He made the sign of the cross. 'King Edward has a broken collarbone. A doctor is setting it with splints. They need the arnica. We'll gather up more splints too and help others.' He looked straight at her. 'The King takes his survival as a sign God has spared him to Crusade.'

'He would.' Olwen filled a basket with pots of salves and after a moment's thought added stones with healing qualities. 'I'll accompany you to the tower.'

They hurried, stumbling with two baskets with arnica, splints, and lengths of linen, through endless corridors to the royal apartments in the western part of the building far from the site of the disaster. Torches flickered as they passed. Rain pounded against shutters and splashed into the passageways. Consternation flew like wild fires chasing through hallways. A milling of panicked people persistently blocked their movement as Guillaume shouted to be allowed through. Men stomped down staircases making noise loud enough to compete with the downpour outside.

'The thunder is further off now. The fortress is safe,' Guillaume gasped and to any who asked, added, 'No fire, just the tower fallen down.'

Eleanor bustled about within the King's chamber. Edward was sitting up in a great chair in his dusty shirt and braies with a furred rug covering his knees.

'No worse than a little battle injury. Lady Olwen, take the Queen away and give her whatever will settle her. Her fussing is unsettling.' He turned to Guillaume. 'Go back to the tower and see to the others.'

Guillaume handed his apprentice a small pot of arnica. 'Make sure it's rubbed into the King's bruises. I shall return later.' He patted his satchel, which contained another jar of arnica and various healing salves.

Olwen spent the rest of the long night with the Queen. 'As well we are leaving soon,' Eleanor said. 'I think the gardens can take care of themselves now, Olwen. Does this not remind you?'

'Of Acre? I think the King will recover better now than then,' Olwen replied.

'He has had a fortunate escape once again. Thanks to your husband his collarbone will set intact.'

Olwen smiled. 'All will be well.' It was not so well for the new garden. Such a storm would have caused much destruction.

The court moved south as soon as Edward was comfortably able to sit a horse. Olwen rode close to the King and Queen, sad to leave the garden where the plants had been flattened by the terrible storm. As they moved in a long cavalcade towards the border with Aragon, Olwen watched the landscape change from a carpet of wild spring flowers into grass paths that wound across marshland. It was a strange world inhabited by peasants who looked equally pale, reedy, and watery. Serfs stared in amazement at the passing horsemen, ogling the royal sumpter carts and carriages from which richly dressed ladies looked out from heavily curtained windows. Marsh fishers stood to point fingers at pennants fluttering in the soft, damp breezes. The royal party made slow progress because they paused for several days at a time to visit shrines, and for the King and Queen to show themselves to their peoples of southern Gascony.

After weeks of leisurely travel the courtly cavalcade reached the foothills of the mountains separating Gascony from Aragon. Snow-capped peaks with long thin pines lining their lower slopes, gleamed in the sunlight high above the travellers. Olwen stared up awed by the grandness of the mountains. This was surely a place inhabited by creatures belonging to a bestiary. Dragons might dwell in secret caves. Wizards might live in the towers of castles that guarded the lower slopes of the Pyrenees.

It was July when they rode into Oloron, a town with a pinnacle-capped castle on a hill. Yellow tile-roofed houses clustered below it. The castle had prepared for their arrival. Carpets had been laid over floor tiles, walls were repainted and thick arrases embroidered with hunting scenes had been hung throughout the royal apartments.

Within days of their arrival, the King and his advisors locked themselves in conference deciding what to say to the visiting King of Aragon.

'They have to release Charles of Anjou. He was captured in battle by Aragon,' Guillaume reported to Olwen in the spacious room they shared close to the royal chambers.

'For the marriage to proceed?' Olwen said.

'Otherwise France will continue backing Anjou over Sicily. And there'll be no wedding for Eleanora.'

Later, from a long window in the solar, Olwen spied on the Aragon party entering the castle courtyard.

'The tall, regal, black-eyed man wearing chain mail is Alfonso of Aragon,' whispered Lady Isabel. The other ladies pushed closer to see.

He was accompanied by many horsemen with thick dark moustaches and pointy beards. So this, Olwen mused, was the elusive young man who was Princess Eleanora's betrothed.

★

Queen Eleanor orchestrated lavish feasts. King Edward organised tournaments. Olwen began to enjoy the holiday atmosphere that cocooned them from the outside world. Edward did not ride in the tourneys. Guillaume forbade it. The King's neck remained stiff so Edward watched and cheered on their English and Gascon knights and they, to Olwen's delight, proved unbeatable.

Occasionally, as the month passed, Lady Isabel confided to her the news she learned from her husband.

'They have agreed Princess Eleanora's dowry,' Lady Isabel reported as they sat companionably in the bower apart from all the other ladies, sorting silk embroidery threads into smaller skeins. Olwen laid a skein of crimson silk on the windowsill and remarked, 'It looks as if the marriage really can proceed.'

'Apparently. But Pope Honorius is still very difficult.'

A week later Isabel confided a treaty had been agreed. 'Charles of Anjou will be released from prison if he provides hostages and a huge amount of gold to line Aragon's coffers.'

'Are you quite well?' she said to Olwen her eyes narrowing.

'Isabel, I have news of my own,' Olwen said, putting aside her herbal. She was drawing a rush-leafed narcissus that grew higher up in the mountains. She shyly glanced up at Isabel.

'Are *you* with child, Lady Olwen?'

'I thought I was too old, Isabel, and as you well know I'm not nineteen any more, unlike yourself, but I believe I am with child.'

'It's your first?'

Olwen nodded.

'Does Guillaume know?'

'He does, and he wants me to remain here at Oloron until the child is born.'

'You could stay here, but you can safely return to St Sever with us if you travel in one of the carriages. When are you due?'

'I think November or early December.'

'Plenty of time. Stay with us, the Queen's ladies. We'll treat you like precious glass.'

Olwen, who never cried, wept and Isabel hugged her close. In the warmth of sensible Lady Isabel's embrace, Olwen knew she had good friends amongst Queen Eleanor's ladies. She would not remain in Oloron.

They retraced the route back towards St Sever in September and passed the rest of the month resting. When October arrived, Olwen felt enormous and Queen Eleanor paid for midwives. She insisted that Olwen had a spacious chamber of her own within the Dominican Nunnery of St Sever. Eleanor's ladies stitched tiny garments for the child and pampered Olwen who had so often helped them recover from their own aches and pains.

Olwen withdrew into seclusion as October drew to its close. Clutching an eagle stone well-known to ease childbirth, she gave birth to a girl child on the fourth day of November. They called her Marian Rose. Marian looked just like her doting father with a down of dark hair. Within a month Olwen was churched.

'I am perfectly well,' she said to Guillaume. 'Stop fussing.' He would hardly allow her to move from her chamber.

At length he calmed down and settled into fatherhood and Olwen was relieved not to be treated like an invalid.

By the time the court planned to move north to Bordeaux she was able to travel with them. This late child would be her first and last baby. Her labour had been easy and Marian Rose was a healthy baby, but Olwen declared to Guillaume she never wanted to experience such pain ever again. As they made the tiring journey back to Bordeaux, she longed for her estates. By the time they reached Bordeaux, she was so homesick for Oldbury she wondered if she should return home alone with Marian.

Then Queen Eleanor fell ill again after Christmastide and Olwen lingered on at court. Guillaume said the Queen was suffering a reoccurrence of quatrain fever.

'Marsh fever again but this time I have a new treatment to try.'

'Do you?' Olwen glanced up from nursing the baby. 'Barley water helps. Willow bark helps so what new cure are you thinking of?' She shifted Marian into her other arm. Laying her over her shoulder she patted her back. Marian burped loudly.

'Thank God, our daughter is healthy,' Guillaume remarked. 'Greedy too.' His eyes were filled with adoration.

'The cure?' Olwen said.

'I mix plantain roots with wine and water. If the Queen takes this every day and sleeps with her head raised, I believe it could help.'

'Salty and bitter,' Olwen said laying the sleeping Marian into her cradle. She glanced up. 'Use honey as well.'

'The Queen is convinced if she wears a necklace of rock crystal it might ease her fevers.'

'It won't do her any harm if she believes in it,' Olwen said. Her own belief in stones had diminished since she considered any power they contained lay in the eyes of the beholder.

Queen Eleanor recovered in time for her ladies and knights and herself to accompany King Edward back to Oloron in the summer. Olwen remained in Bordeaux, thinking soon they would be returning home. Then Pope Honorius died. The King was waiting on the appointment of a new pope who he hoped would permit the marriage between Princess Eleanora and King Alfonso. The Church, Olwen mused with cynicism, always controls the future of kings. Later, she chastised herself for such heretical thoughts.

All summer long, she received letters from Guillaume who travelled with King Edward's court.

From Master Guillaume of Oldbury to his wife Lady Olwen of Oldbury

My dearest wife, he wrote to her, *the Queen is again unwell. We have retreated to St Sever. The King remains in Oloron negotiating with Aragon as to which hostages he should retain to ensure Charles of Anjou keeps peace; that Alfonso's rule in Sicily is preserved and yet another huge amount of money is paid to Aragon. Lady Isabel is distraught. John de Vescy is to be given over as a hostage as well as Lord*

Otto. We are purchasing many medicines for the Queen. This time it is more than quatrain fever. This time there is some other ailment that I believe resides in her belly, and it's not a child.

He asked about her own health and that of Marian Rose. The Queen and her ladies would return to Bordeaux soon. She closed the letter and put it away. When could they return to England? Should she go home without him?

Queen Eleanor's health did improve. Reunited in Bordeaux, Isabel and Olwen hugged and retreated behind a heavy arras into an alcove where they could pretend to play merills. This time it was Olwen's turn to comfort Isabel.

'John is in Provence,' Isabel said. 'I fear for him. He was released. Charles of Anjou sends his own hostages to Aragon. There's a new Pope.' She looked tearful. 'It's not over yet because the Pope supports France's claim to Sicily.'

'Do you think Charles of Anjou will not abide by the treaty?'

'I fear not. There's much to-ing and fro-ing to no avail.'

'I am sure John will return to you safely.'

'I pray for him every day.' Isabel's blue eyes were weeping. Olwen dabbed them with a linen cloth. Her dearest friend was depressed. She took Isabel's hands in her own and together they wept for John and for their desire to return to England. 'I'll make us both a restorative cup with English mead,' she whispered. 'I know where we can discover some. Come with me to the kitchens.'

Another Christmas passed in the Palace of Shadows. Another springtime followed moving from castle to castle around Bordeaux. Otto returned to Edward. In February, John de Vescy died in Montpellier. Lady Isabel wept every day because she had loved John with all her heart. When his bones were released for burial, Isabel sailed to England with the coffin, hoping to discover solace amongst her own family, the Beaumonts. 'I shall forever remain a widow,' she stubbornly confided in the other ladies who tried to comfort her.

★

The new Pope, Nicholas, a Franciscan, had been elected in February, and he was known to be pious and peace loving, but to Edward's disappointment he crowned the second Charles as King of Naples and Sicily. Encouraged by his support, France spent the Crusade's Papal twentieth on a new war against Alfonso of Aragon. Edward was incandescent.

'It's hopeless,' he stormed, and for days everyone including the Queen stayed out of his way. His knights returned to Bordeaux in a fury, feeling they had been betrayed. And Eleanora's marriage was not to be. There would be no new crusade in the Holy Land either. Alfonso of Aragon was excommunicated.

'Time to return to England,' he announced to the court in Bordeaux.

'My lord,' Eleanor said with pragmatism in her voice. 'We have done what we can. There will be another prince for Eleanora, or at least a count.'

'We have secured Gascony,' Edward said. 'And, I haven't seen my mother for three years.'

'We have not seen Edward and our daughters either. Your mother is happy in Amesbury. She has Mary as her companion.'

'Amen,' Edward replied. 'Let us go home.'

At length, the King and Queen prepared to depart for England.

'I am glad of it,' Olwen said to Guillaume as she packed their newly purchased silks and velvets into a strong oaken coffer ready for travelling. Lovingly, she set lavender between the layers of beautiful fabrics. 'How I long for England. I long for Oldbury. I long for our own bedchamber.'

Marian Rose looked solemnly at her parents and said, 'England.'

'That's a big word for a tiny child to say.' Guillaume lifted up his daughter and hugged her. 'Yes, England. We're all going to sail over the sea on a big ship. We are returning home.'

Chapter Twenty-Nine

Eleanor
1289–1290

Eleanor felt much better for being at Leeds Castle in Kent, a castle she admired all over again after three years away from England. She called it Gloriette. Her older daughters welcomed her wearing dresses of cloth of gold, trimmed with green velvet. When Elizabeth and Margaret stepped forward, she admired their equally luxurious gowns of rose scarlet. Ah, so no nun's garb for Mary but a gown of cornflower-blue linen. Edward held Mary's hand. He was now a golden princeling.

'You all look so beautiful,' Eleanor said, appraising her daughters. She leaned down and kissed Edward. 'How you have grown, my little prince.'

Edward said, his wide eyes narrowing, 'Are you my Madam Mother?'

'Edward, of course this beautiful lady is your mother,' the Dowager admonished.

As ever, Ailenor beamed all around. Mary had travelled from Amesbury with her to meet Eleanor and Eleanor was touched by the former queen's consideration. After all, she had left her quiet convent to take such good care of the children at Kings Langley during her own long absence. 'Thank you, dearest Mother,' she said with a broad smile. 'It is a perfect reunion.' Her eyes were moist.

Following a week with her family, Eleanor grew anxious about her properties and began to plan another journey. There was too much to do. Her health could fail her again at any moment. The unfortunate treaty forged for Aragon's benefit had emptied Edward's treasury. Her properties could replenish the royal coffers but rumours soon reached her ears. The Earls on the Welsh Marches had seized lands not their own. She made up her mind. They could not wait. She broached moving on from Leeds Castle.

'We must see to our affairs, Edward,' she said in a whisper. 'My own lands—'

'Yes, yes.' He looked around the hall where they were conversing by a window. Her eyes followed his. Courtiers appeared involved in their own conversations.

'Let's discuss this somewhere more private.' Edward ushered her out of a side door into gardens.

'The masons have done well here,' he remarked as they walked along a shady colonnade. 'They came from Aragon, if I recollect?'

'Yes. Gloriette is magnificent.'

Edward led her to a seat shaded by a large mulberry tree. 'We won't be overheard here.' After a few moments he said, 'You tire easily but we can tour your properties and visit shrines to pray for your health. I know this is what you want, but we must be present in London too. London has suffered lawlessness during our absence. I am appointing a new mayor. We will remove the plagues of knife crime and theft. Yes, you looked surprised but I . . . I am decided. The City will come under my control. Merchants and minor nobles alike will put up with my decisions or their goods will fill my coffers.' There was concern on his long face.

'Edward, then it is settled. I must visit my properties before winter sets in,' she said. 'Let's visit Walsingham. I am sure Our Lady will grant me better health if we attend her shrine and pray there.' She reached out for him. 'My love, I believe I may have not long on this earth. Let us make use of the time granted me.'

Edward took her hand. His blue eyes had filled with emotion. 'Do not say this. God will spare you, my lovely Queen. We shall visit Walsingham before Christmastide, if it so pleases you. Now, no more talk of illness. Did I hear you say earlier you would enjoy a game of chess?'

'I can still beat you at chess.' A smile concealed her own concerns though darkening shadows were encroaching on her happiness. Yet somehow these melted away like a dissolving mist when Edward took her hand into his firm grasp. He was a warlord, a strong and decisive King, but he could be as gentle as a tame greyhound. As if sensing her thought her newest beloved hound, Elysium, stretched and licked her free hand. She patted the animal's head with affection.

'And we have weddings to arrange,' she said. 'There's both Joan and Margaret. I want them wed soon.'

'Scotland for Edward.'

'That too,' she said, her eyes clouding over again. She knew she would not live to see Edward grow up.

The court progress took several weeks of preparation but soon enough they were moving into East Anglia with their usual grand processions of knights, sumpter horses, wagons carrying furniture, her travelling altar, and her maids. When she was travelling forward, Eleanor could shake off the ominous feeling she had felt at Leeds Castle. She toured her East Anglia properties and she felt well for a time. They prayed at all the usual shrines she loved. Christmas passed with the court at Westminster, and still she remained in good health. God answered her prayers. Her daughters' wedding plans were set in place for April and July.

They visited Quenington in February for a family holiday with only their closest retainers to attend them. It was here, as she began to relax, her ague returned. She felt she had entered the land of frost and, though there was no frost in reality, no fire could warm her through. Fevers revisited her so that she could not eat and grew thin.

Edward sent for his doctor, a young man who was Portuguese and well-versed in the medicine of Arab lands.

'Send for Guillaume and Lady Olwen,' Eleanor begged. He had made her well before. 'After all, Oldbury is not far distant.'

Olwen and Guillaume rode to Quenington from Oldbury. Olwen had brought with her not only healing syrups but baskets of dried garden fruits and a barrel of nuts from her hazel trees. On the last day of Olwen's visit, Eleanor called the herbalist to her bower chamber and sent all her ladies, except Margerie, away.

She waited by her desk for Lady Olwen to enter, fully dressed and her desk piled with scrolls demanding her attention.

'I am so afraid,' she said, after Olwen rose from a deep curtsey and was seated opposite her armed chair on a wide velvet-padded stool. Eleanor drew a shallow breath. To breathe deeply hurt her chest. 'Death might take me too soon. Even so, Olwen, I am determined not to die.' She crossed herself and touched the beads on her rosary. 'They are creating images of gold of me, you know . . . for intercession. Everyone assumes I'm dying.' She sat back and gestured towards her desk. 'But I have work to do.'

Olwen said, '*They*, my lady? By *they* do you mean the clergy?'

Eleanor nodded. 'Others too . . . including the King.' Her speech was hoarse.

Olwen leaned forward and the herbalist's eyes seemed a little misted over. 'My lady,' she began in a quiet voice. It was calming. 'My lady, we cannot turn time around, but we *can* pray for you and we can make you comfortable. The syrups have helped before.' She smiled her gentle smile. 'Medicinal waters are beneficial. We shall send for these.'

Eleanor fingered her rosary beads, her hand resting on a pear-shaped heart at the beads' end. 'I wish to see my children settled, Olwen. Joan is to marry Earl Gilbert in April. Margaret is to wed John this summer. Will I live long enough?' She found herself leaning forward again, grasping Olwen's hands. 'Tell me truth. Can I survive that long?'

'Yes, you *will* live to see them happily wed.' Olwen's firm, calming reply comforted Eleanor. She took heart from Olwen's strength.

'I should have made sure you and Guillaume married years ago,' she said quietly as she let go Olwen's hand, stood up and moved restlessly around the desk. She picked up a bookmark with angels embroidered on it in gold threads and absently studied them. She had forced too many of her ladies into marriages,

367

arranging them herself, because ever since Edward's supposed affair she had preferred married women within her entourage. She had pushed Olwen towards Eugene when she should have summoned Guillaume back from Salerno. She sighed. It was all so many years ago.

Olwen was speaking and so she turned her attention towards that quiet, reverential voice. 'Your Grace, I loved Eugene and I love Guillaume too. I always loved Guillaume. He broke my heart when he never came to me from Salerno.' Her voice became an almost imperceptible whisper. 'But, I think it is possible to love more than one person. My marriage with Sir Eugene was most generously arranged by yourself. Love grew between us and now, God has granted me Guillaume, the love of my heart and my body. We have Marian Rose too who is a joy to us.'

'In time, Marian should join the court as one of my daughter's ladies. Your words reassure me.' Eleanor found herself wanting to confide further in this woman who, although she was not of noble birth, possessed great nobility. 'Olwen, I have always loved one man only, the King. I pray he does not forget me when I am in Heaven, but also that I may see my lord and our children celebrate life, if God grants me such charity.'

Olwen inclined her head. 'Amen.'

Eleanor lifted the bookmark again, and held it in her fluttering hands. 'Come to Westminster. See Joan married to Earl Gilbert.' She smiled. 'The time for dislike of Gilbert is long over. *To all there is a season*. He is welcome into our family, he whom I once loathed, that man who dragged me into custody in Canterbury.'

'I remember that year well. It was the year I grew up.' Olwen's mouth widened into a grin. 'We shall attend Joan's wedding to Earl Gilbert. I never was fond of him either but Joan will be a spirited match for him.'

'So they would have us believe.' Eleanor found herself smiling.

Horses were returning from the hunt, snorting and rattling over the cobbled courtyard. Eleanor dismissed Lady Olwen saying, 'The wardrobe master will grant you accommodation at Westminster.'

Olwen curtseyed and began to depart until Eleanor realised she had forgotten something and called her back.

'I am granting Guillaume a merchant's house in Gloucester. Lady Isabel once mentioned he would like such a house for you both near the hospitals.'

She heard Olwen's gasp. 'How thoughtful of Lady Isabel. Your Grace, I thank you for such generosity.'

'Your smile is enough thanks. It is no less than Master Guillaume is due for his vigilant care of me in Gascony.'

After Lady Olwen departed, quietly as a mouse slipping through a cornfield, Eleanor allowed Margerie to help her onto her day bed. Edward would come to her soon. There was so much to do and she must conserve her strength to see it done.

The shadow of Lady Alix had haunted her ever since she had discovered the lady's passion for Edward. Now Alix's husband had finally been granted a divorce by the Pope, on grounds of consanguinity, he was to marry their daughter.

The royal family returned to Westminster to prepare for Joan's wedding. After the wedding banquet Gilbert and Joan decided they might dwell for a time in his luxurious manor house at Clerkenwell which lay north of the City walls.

Eleanor felt her health improved. In an effort to rest prior to the wedding, she sat quietly with her ladies in the Paradise Garden at Westminster, reading a book of hours and enjoying birds singing in the aviary beyond the garden wall. The sun was gentling the spring flowers. Peonies, marigolds and narcissi gave off a soft, fragrant scent and the Rose Alba with its shaggy branches, the centre piece of this small walled garden, grew straight and proud as any queen. *It's delicate just like the love I have borne Edward all these years. If only Joan finds such love in her marriage with Earl Gilbert.*

The court hummed with excitement as the days leading up to Joan's wedding sped by. Excitement gathered in chambers and halls,

369

darting about like a swallow flitting in and out of its nest, peeping from under the palace eaves. Eleanor sensed it everywhere and was grateful it allowed her to forget her illness. Her ladies reported to her how a sense of anticipation passed from courtier to courtier, to cooks in the kitchens, how it lingered amongst gossiping maids and hovered around the seamstresses, embroiderers who were working on gowns Edward had promised Joan.

Eleanor heard how Earl Gilbert doted on his princess and daily gave thanks for this blessing. Gilbert had, as agreed, signed his lands over to Edward to be redistributed to both himself and Joan jointly after their wedding. We have harmony at last, Eleanor mused, and gave a tinkling laugh of amusement at this thought.

The morning of the wedding arrived.

'Mama, I need the privy,' Joan said, jumping impatiently up, beside herself with nerves. Her ladies were about to dress her flowing locks with pearls.

'Go,' Eleanor said. 'But once you are dressed you'll have to wait it out so do not drink another cup.' Her eyes lit on a silver vessel with watered wine sitting on the table tucked amongst pots of make-up 'And I advise you to use those paints lightly. The Abbey will be hot and you don't want them running down your face.'

Joan looked horrified but nodded. She disappeared behind the garderobe door. They decided she was to wear the gold gown she had worn to greet her parents on their return from Gascony. It would be ridiculous to have a new cloth of gold wedding gown when this one had only had one brief wearing. Besides there was no time. Joan had bathed. Her hair was washed with perfumed soap and had been gently brushed dry until it gleamed and fell in loose golden curls to her waist. A crown gleaming with rubies and emeralds, and a belt studded with pearls sat waiting on a cushion.

Once Joan reappeared from the garderobe, Eleanor glanced at the candle clock. 'When it burns down another notch we must all be ready.' Glancing out of the long, glazed windows. There had been a brief April shower. She noted how the spring sun had caused the gardens to sparkle.

A cacophony of bells sounded beyond the palace walls.

'Not long now, ladies. I must be robed at once. When I return, Joan, you must be ready.' Eleanor swept from the room with Margerie and Isabel tripping behind to her chamber where the figure of Winter still watched from above the hooded mantelpiece. She turned away from it. Her ladies enclosed her greying hair in a crispinette net in one of her favourite fashions, nestling at her neck. She would wear her own glittering crown. For a moment, she felt sad for Eleanora whose younger sister would be the first of the royal princesses to marry. Yet, Eleanora had never wanted to leave them for Aragon and that was a comfort.

Eleanor and the princesses met Edward in Westminster's hall. Six-year-old Edward held eight-year-old Elizabeth's hand. He walked stiffly in his new surcoat. The family were joined by a small procession of lords and ladies. It was a small wedding. As they swept out into the spring sunshine to cross the courtyard to the Abbey, heralds blew trumpets. Bells rang out. Bishops, clad in fabulous vestments opulently bordered with gold and silver and jewels, greeted them. Earl Gilbert stood by the west door. His long, sweeping cloth of gold surcoat gleamed. His fashionable pointed shoes glittered jewels as he moved forward to watch them approach. Eleanor placed her hand on Edward's arm. For a fleeting moment Gilbert looked down at her and their eyes met in understanding. This would be a good marriage.

Ah, she thought as Earl Gilbert's face broke into a smile. The tiger has been tamed once and for all.

Lady Margaret's wedding followed on the eighth of July. In contrast, this wedding was a very grand affair since Margaret would be Countess of Brabant and Brabant was an important ally. It was sad that Margaret was not as enthusiastic as Joan about her marriage. Her betrothed, Jan, had behaved well ever since he had honed his knightly skills with William of Pembroke in Gascony, but it was clear that Margaret and Jan would only ever tolerate each other. Fifteen-year-old Margaret despised Jan for his gambling, whoring and extravagance. Jan, in turn, was getting a true courtly young lady in Margaret who was always beautifully dressed, her manner perfect, and her embroidery and weaving skills better than any of Eleanor's other daughters could ever hope to aspire to. Margaret hunted with passion as did Jan, but Jan, well, Jan . . . Eleanor sighed. Jan thought himself a model knight but he was puffed-up and conceited.

Eleanor smiled with serenity at a host of guests, welcoming them to the great feast following the wedding, even though she had little energy for it all. The pageantry, the celebrations, and greeting the Duke of Brabant with his great entourage, made it a frenetic time so close after Joan's pleasant, quieter wedding. Overseeing table linens for the feast, and now so many nobles and entertainers arriving from many distant lands, was demanding and this new excitement exhausted Eleanor. She wondered, could she see the day through without a collapse. During the ceremony, she glanced over at the Duke of Brabant, dressed in a cape of black vair with rows of white triangles. He was such a peacock and it made her dip her head to conceal her laughter, so she bit her cheek until the irreverent feeling passed.

And where was Joan? Olwen and Guillaume had attended both nuptials. Joan made excuses and did not come to her sister's wedding. She was unwell. Gilbert, however, was present with a hundred knights and sixty ladies. The truth was that Joan felt jealous of the enormous wedding her younger sister was enjoying, and without doubt that was the real reason she was not present. Furious, Eleanor decided to gift Joan's seven new gowns to Margaret, and her promised new belt of pearls to Eleanora.

Later, during the wedding feast, Eleanora said as the subtlety, a huge ship, was served up, 'Mama, you have sat through all the courses. You look exhausted. Let Margerie and the ladies escort you to your chamber and I will take your place beside Papa. Otherwise, you will collapse. I'll send Lady Olwen to you.'

'Where's Joanna?'

'Which Joanna? Oh, Uncle William of Pembroke's wife? She has departed already. She said to bid you goodnight and remind you to write. You were surrounded by all those guests from Brabant when she departed. She could not get near you. They must leave for Pembroke at daybreak. Uncle William has a very short time to see to his affairs there, she said, before returning to Gascony.'

Eleanor glanced along the hall. Musicians had struck up dancing tunes. 'In that event I shall retire. Take my place and explain to Papa. It's been a long day.'

She glanced over at Margaret. Jan was popping a piece of marzipan into his wife's mouth and she was laughing. Perhaps their marriage would work out after all. Eleanor shook her head. She was saddened not to bid Joanna of Pembroke Godspeed. Her old friend had slipped away from the feast without saying goodbye. There were too many revellers, so much splendour and pomp. She knew it as she looked back at the harpers, trumpeters, lutenists, pages, jewels and glittering robes. Her daughter's magnificent wedding would be the talk of all the courts of Europe. Joan was right to be envious.

After the wedding the court planned to ride towards Nottingham and then to Clipstone. The ladies were sewing in a bower hall at Westminster.

'Will you stay with us?' Lady Margerie asked Olwen. 'The Queen . . .'

Lady Margerie looked tired too. She had aged, her face was wrinkled now. We have all aged, Eleanor thought as she looked from Margerie to Olwen. 'We would like your company,' Eleanor added, looking up from perusing a small book of poetry.

The Queen's eyes were overly bright and it seemed as if Eleanor did not have long to live. Olwen wondered at the Queen's determination to accompany the King north.

That morning Olwen had remarked to Guillaume, 'The Queen should recover what health she could at Windsor, not going on another progress, or visiting her properties,'

'Queen Eleanor is never happy far from Edward's side. She'll carry on until the very end,' Guillaume had said as he took his wife's hand.

It was true. Eleanor was always working, joining in the dinner hour conversations, praying at shrines.

Olwen did not hesitate. She sat her sketch board aside. 'I shall come with you this autumn, as will Guillaume. Marian is perfectly happy at Oldbury with her nurse.'

'Thank you, Lady Olwen,' Eleanor replied, with a smile playing about her lips, and returned to her book. She had been listening.

She is still beautiful when she smiles, thought Olwen, still a most gracious queen.

'I'll send word to Oldbury, Olwen,' Guillaume said. 'Would you like to accompany me into the City today? I am of a mind to visit St Bartholomew's Hospital. I can purchase medicines to take with us. What do you think? You may have purchases of your own to make in the market.'

'We need new linen for smocks. There's just enough time to have them stitched before the court sets out. We'll bring Piers and Ursula with us.' Ursula was a new maid whom she knew had her eye on Piers. It was time he settled, and golden-haired, quiet-spoken Ursula had caught his eye.

'They can carry for you and guard you.' Guillaume smiled at her and winked. He had noted the budding romance too.

Chapter Thirty

November 1290

Clipstone, 30th September in the year of our Lord 1290

My Dearest Lady Joanna,

Illness is never far distant. We visited shrines in Norfolk once again. And now Edward has decided to hold Parliament at Clipstone, not Westminster. I find I am too unwell to travel that distance to Westminster. The manor here is spacious. There is room in the stables for two hundred horses. Joan has arrived with her groom, a lady attendant, and a guard.

I was pleased you attended Margaret's wedding but saddened you left for Pembroke so quickly after. We had no time to talk. Joan was displeased because her sister's wedding was grander than her own. This may make you smile. As compensation, Joan took from Westminster her trousseau of hundreds of silver dishes, four enormous canopied beds, and mattresses stuffed with feathers, velvet bed curtains and cushions, table linens, and a new carriage. It took six carts to carry it all to Clerkenwell. She forthwith sent a messenger to say she was indisposed and could not attend her sister's wedding. It did not prevent Gilbert from attending at the head of one hundred knights and sixty ladies. Little Edward, only six years old, sat at the head of his own troop of knights. Eleanora looked beautiful in a gown with six hundred silver buttons. Jan of Brabant was handsome clad in black vair like his sire. He changed his wedding outfits four times. Did you notice?

Edward intends visiting Scotland. The tiny princess of Scotland who was to be betrothed to our son died on her way from Norway. She was to be Scotland's Queen. Unless my husband controls Scotland that country will be as unruly as Wales was once. As for our boy, we shall have to find him another princess.

Joan has been forgiven. She came to me because I am most unwell. They all have. It is a comfort to me to have my daughters with me here at Clipstone and to see little Edward's happy face. He loves to build things. I wonder is he taking after his grandfather, King Henry, but will he make as great a king one day as his father or is Edward destined to be a dreamer like his grandsire?

And now I am so very tired. Dear friend, pray for my soul. Life is short and our mark on it but the lightest touch of a painter's brush. God bless you, Joanna, Lady of Pembroke.

Eleanor the Queen.

Eleanor felt every jolt as her carriage slowly moved towards its destination, Lincoln. She lay back against her cushions and a sheaf of papers slid from her lap onto the floor. She had wanted to ride, but Edward said, 'No, how can you ride from Clipstone to Lincoln? You are too ill.'

'In Lincoln I would have the care I need.'

Perhaps she could recover, for after all, she had become well again before. Perhaps in Lincoln I can find medicines to make me well again, Eleanor thought every time the carriage shook. She tried to suppress her moans of pain but she could not. How could she have ridden indeed – but oh, how she longed to ride, her white hunting hounds racing along beside her mare. She closed her eyes and imagined forest tracks. She summoned up golden autumn leaves and the crackling of twigs as her palfrey trotted through them. She felt herself rise high in the saddle, her head low to avoid the odd branch that threatened to whip against her. Then she jumped a low, woven fence and cried out.

'Your Grace, drink this.' Margerie was helping her up, leaning her back against the pillows. Supporting her with one arm Olwen helped her to sip a cordial. It tasted of lavender, honey, and mint. 'It has angelica oil and lemon balm to soothe,' Olwen said in a gentle voice. 'A spoonful of poppy to stop the pains.'

After a few sips Eleanor raised a hand. 'No more,' she whispered.

She dozed, this time pain seeping from her. The carriage stopped. She caught hold of Margaret's voice, and Eleanora's and Edward's too, though they spoke in whispers. Even so, she heard snatches.

'Mama is too ill to continue to Lincoln tonight,' Eleanora was saying. 'She can't go on.'

Margaret was insistent. 'Papa, she needs the comfort of a warm bed and her priest. Her breath is too shallow. Lady Olwen persuades her to sip a pain-relieving cordial and after that a sleeping potion, but she hardly takes a drop.'

She heard the curtain fall, the carriage door close. She heard Edward's loud shout, 'We are only three miles from Harby, ride ahead, Simon. Take three squires with you. Tell the master of Harby to make a chamber ready for the Queen.'

So they were to stay that night at Harby. Where was this place, Harby? She heard herself moan. Another pain sliced through her stomach. Cold fingers were tightening and squeezing her organs. Pain was everywhere, driving through her heart as if she was thrust by a sword. Was it her brother's sword that drove into her heart, the same sword she once practised with in the sun-baked courtyards of Burgos? No, her mind was playing games with her. She could smell rose oil burning in the censer by her couch. Who was she? She was Eleanor, Queen of England, Countess of Ponthieu, and Duchess of Aquitaine, who travelled in a carriage to a place called Harby. She opened her eyes. For a moment she could see faces, Olwen, Margerie, Eleanora, and Margaret. Reaching out to Eleanora she grasped her daughter's hand and said, 'Where are the others? My other children?'

'Mama, Joan returned from Clipstone to her manor at Clerkenwell. Mary is with Grandmother in Amesbury. The little children have returned to King's Langley. We are travelling to Lincoln, but we shall first spend this night in the manor of Harby.'

She took another sip of Olwen's cordial and found it eased her pain but only for a short moment or two. They were rattling over cobble stones. The carriage stopped again with a bump. She felt a draught pass through the heavy curtains. The carriage door opened. There was Edward's dear reassuring face. He was smiling down at her. 'My love,' he was saying, 'I have sent for more medicines for you. We shall rest here at Harby awhile. I am going to lift you. Soon, my love, you will be lying under soft covers in a warmed bed and not on a couch within this draughty carriage.'

She reached up and managed to clasp her hands loosely about his neck. He scooped her up. She felt light as a feather. The persistent agony seared through her body again and she bit her lip against it. Soon there would be no discomfort. An angel would greet her and take her by the hand to where she would wait for Edward to join her in paradise. She was ready. During the short few weeks they spent at Clipstone, she had put everything in order. She redistributed land where necessary. She asked for justice to be done where her bailiffs had mistreated tenants and lined their own treasure chests. She gave her beloved daughters keepsakes by which they would always remember her. Elizabeth would own the beautiful psalter of birds she had long ago commissioned for Alphonso and a crown with pearls, emeralds, and rubies. She had given them all, her lovely daughters, gifts of books and jewellery; belts studded with precious stones; gloves, and ivory boxes for precious trinkets. She gave away the magnificent jasper chess set Edward had granted her as a birth-day gift some years before. That is for Elizabeth as well, she had said to Edward.

To Edward, her husband and her King, love of her life, her prince who had everything, she gave her heart. She leaned her head against his chest and tried not to cry out. She concentrated on the damp leafy November smell clinging to his mantle. He smelled of oak woods, of the outdoors, of horse, of sleek hunting hounds and of the rain that dripped from his beard onto her head, reminding her of how she had loved him from the day they met in Burgos, so many years since. She could hear the jangling of bridle bells, the sounds of horses snorting, stable boys' calling. She caught anxiety that haunted other voices, the doors opening, closing, and a sense of bustling. There was a rush of warm air and she was carried up a stairway. Her eyes opened wide. Edward was lowering her into a bed smelling of lavender and fresh linen. A Bishop was administering to her. Her daughters hovered about her bedside.

'Sleep peacefully, my heart's love,' Edward said as she drifted towards sleep, hovering above pain, beyond it and simply outside of it. She opened her eyes one last time. Edward was smiling down at her. His perceptive blue eyes were brim-filled with tears. 'God bless you, Eleanor, love of my heart. May God's angels guard your sleep.'

She felt a smile hover on her lips. 'I go happy into God's grace. Never forget, I have loved you always, Edward,' she whispered. She felt his hand covering her own. Somewhere outside in the November evening, Angelus bells were ringing, and a branch rattled on the window glass as if summoning her away.

Epilogue

Olwen
November 1294

During the last days of her life our Queen said goodbye to all of us. We do not know truly, but Guillaume thinks she died from a malady of the heart, one we do not understand and could not treat. Queen Eleanor's arteries had tightened and her veins were almost vanished. The King was distraught.

Guillaume and I travelled to Lincoln with the solemn funeral procession that included all who knew the Queen during her final days on this earth. There, in Lincoln, the Dominicans eviscerated, embalmed, and filled our Queen's earthly body with barley ready for the long progress to Westminster. After her body was received by the Archbishop and the Bishops in attendance, it was carried into the choir on the shoulders of priests. I said my own final farewell along with Lady Isabel, Lady Margerie, and her other ladies. Queen Eleanor's viscera were destined to be placed in the Cathedral within an elaborate coffin.

On the fourth day of December the funeral procession proceeded south. The Queen lay in an open bier dressed with elegance in coronation robes. She wore a crown and carried a sceptre. King Edward rode at a distance behind the Queen's chaplain who bore a cross propped up on his saddle. We stopped overnight at Grantham, Stamford, Geddington, Hardingstone, Stony Stratford, Woburn, Dunstable, and St Albans where Guillaume and I left the procession to journey west and home to Marian Rose.

Months later I received a letter from Isabel de Vescy and learned the cortege had moved on to Waltham, and Holy Trinity by Aldgate, and how by the fourteenth day of December rested at Charing before finally proceeding to Westminster Abbey. Every place where the bier rested was sprinkled with holy water. Lady Isabel said Bishop Robert Burnell announced that memorial crosses were to be erected to the Queen's memory everywhere the coffin rested on the long slow funeral procession south. I hope one day I might travel to see them. Queen Eleanor's body was buried in Westminster Abbey in a magnificent coffin and so she was laid to rest opposite old King Henry. Isabel wrote, 'The King often speaks of "my wife whom living we dearly cherished, and whom we cannot cease to love now she is dead."'

King Edward loved his Queen with all his heart.

Our lives resume their old easy rhythm here at Oldbury. The seasons slip by and it is now four years since our Queen was taken into Heaven. I remain both happy and sorrowful and though many of her features have faded into memory, I remember my Queen as owning a thoughtful countenance though, on occasion, we knew her to have a fiery temper when her hazel eyes darkened and she shouted at us. She was a lover of gardens as I am myself. It was this love that took me into Queen Eleanor's orbit and raised me from a humble, uneducated girl into a lady with two manors and who has known two loving husbands. As I enter the final third of my life I believe it is because of Queen Eleanor that I know great joy and happiness here with my husband and our daughter.

I have heard that within the Lady Chapel at the Grey Friars Church in the City an image of an angel holds a heart representing the Queen's own heart, and the embroidered cloth hanging above this is as precious as the wall hangings Eleanor once loved. For the rest of my days I shall pray for my Queen's soul, and so, now, after these tumbling years following her passing we are founding a chantry in a garden planted with damask roses. It is to be dedicated to Queen Eleanor's memory.

Farewell, my beautiful Queen Eleanor, who will be forever missed by those of us who knew and loved you well.

Author's Note

Eleanor of Castile died aged forty-nine on the evening of 28 November 1290. She had been ill off and on for several years. Some historians suggest recurring malaria but it is conjecture as to what took her life in the end. She certainly was exceptionally unwell throughout the final autumn progress. Parliament would have been held in London that October but since Eleanor was clearly too ill for them to return to London it was held at Clipstone and attendees were farmed out and accommodated round about. Of course, she is remembered for the Eleanor crosses erected from Harby to West-minster at every stop made by her funeral cortege.

Eleanor of Castile was a remarkable queen and woman. She grew up during the Spanish Reconquista. Her father, Ferdinand, was a military hero. Alfonso X, her much older brother, was cultured and exceptionally clever. Eleanor was educated and she was, without doubt, a 'bluestocking'. She married Edward at only twelve years old and gave birth to around sixteen children. Most of them died young. She was not strongly maternal in the way Ailenor of Provence was. She seemed to have preferred children once they had grown. I think this could have been because so many of her children died so young, as babies or by the age of seven, and she may have been frightened to invest too much closeness in them. However, another aspect of Eleanor's character was how she stayed close to Edward all through their marriage apart from the enforced separation during the year of Simon de Montfort's rule. She was also obsessed by duty all her life.

Eleanor was a businesswoman. She gathered up properties. Many minor noblemen disliked her for this and saw her as avaricious, thus the term 'she-wolf', one not used in her life time. However, as I see her, she could be exceptionally determined and fierce. I suspected this was in her character but also because of the relative poverty and confinement she endured during the Barons' Insurrection. It is conjecture, but I think Eleanor determined never to be poor again nor threatened financially by the nobility. Edward set her up to acquire property in her own name in case there ever was another insurrection and his property and castles were threatened. It gave her, without doubt, a sense of independence, knowledge of property law, and a raison d'etre. She built up a property empire, collecting minor estates and joining these together to make great land possessions in her own name. Moreover, she owned properties on the continent as well as in England. Her mother was Jeanne of Ponthieu, and since Eleanor was her heir, she collected estates there as well. England still had Gascony where persistent troubles bubbled up, particularly in the south. Eleanor owned property there too. France always had its eye on Gascony and this led to protection of Gascon borders through marriage negotiation with Aragon. Castile was already on side through her own marriage to Edward.

The Crusade was my favourite section to research and write. I am always amazed by the idea of female crusaders and the support these crusading queens gave to their husbands. I could not cover everything I wanted to include because there was too much and, after all, I was writing a novel. A novel is all about characters, scenes, and story. However, I do believe Eleanor was no-nonsense, intelligent, devoted to Edward, and really tough. She lived in turbulent if extremely cultured times. The thirteenth century is often called The Magnificent Thirteenth Century for this reason. It was a period of great Cathedral improvement and one of magnificent castles. English was gradually creeping into every day court language and some documents were scribed in English. It was a period of crusades, conquests and gorgeous manuscripts with wonderful stories such as the much-loved Arthurian legends.

Eleanor was, in time, as were Edward I, Henry III, and Ailenor of Provence, obsessed with Arthurian legends. Eleanor and Edward used these legends as a political ploy in order to impress and psychologically upstage any attempts at Welsh ownership of the heroic King Arthur and his knights. As for the bones exhumed at Glastonbury by Eleanor and Edward, well, I am not at all sure Eleanor herself was convinced about them but it made a very good publicity stunt. You can see Edward's Winchester 'Round Table' to this day on the wall of the Great Hall. If you visit you can also see a replica of Eleanor's garden at Winchester just outside the Great Hall.

Eleanor loved gardens and introduced water technology from Spain. Leeds Castle gardens at the time were a major example of how this technology was used. Eleanor introduced plants from Spain such as wallflowers and it was also during her reign that Paradise Gardens became fashionable at castles and were included in more than a few manor houses.

I found Eleanor's story fascinating and kept to the historical record throughout. However, I invented Olwen the gardener–herbalist, Master Guillaume, and Sir Eugene. I used these three characters to interact with Eleanor's true story, create the period atmosphere, and deepen the Queen's narrative. They saw what she often did not. All the other characters in this book are real historical persons. I, importantly, introduced Olwen to give the story a sense of life beyond the constantly travelling court. I hope Olwen's story highlights these aspects of the thirteenth century: the love of gardens, the knowledge of plants, and the import of certain plants during the crusading period. Of course, the actual events Olwen was involved with are indeed historically true, including the fall of Hawarden Castle to Welsh insurgents. The castle ruins are there to this day, as is the wonderful, much later Gladstone Library at Hawarden.

To facilitate the introduction of an important invented character, I played a little with the recorded history of 1264/65. It is recorded that William of Pembroke and other exiled lords returned to England in March 1265. However, I allowed Earl William to sneak back and forwards secretly from the continent to Wales during the early autumn of 1264. He may have done so and he certainly at some point was in Ireland where he had lands but the record suggests much time that year was spent in Gascony. Ailenor of Provence was in France trying to raise an army to bring down the rebel government led by Simon de Montfort. She returned to England after the Battle of Evesham. I also placed Olwen at this battle but please accept Olwen, Eugene, and Guillaume as invented personalities because I am, after all, writing Historical Fiction. I have also had to select material or the novel would be incredibly long. Forgive any omissions. The thirteenth century is a busy century and Eleanor of Castile led an extraordinary life.

The only real licence I took was with the property of Oldbury. That did belong to Eleanor and its 'wardship' story is historically true. However, it came into Eleanor's possession later than in my story. I moved that event by a few years to make the narrative work.

I had great fun with Earl Gilbert de Clare, known as Red Gilbert, who was one of my favourite characters and probably England's wealthiest landowner. It is recorded that Alix of Lusignan, his wife, hated him and was 'close' to Lord Edward during the Barons' Insurrection. Eleanor may have suspected an affair between her husband and Alix but the truth is, we do not know. The novel pretty well began with Gilbert and Eleanor's mutual dislike and ended there with what must have been forgiveness.

I hope you enjoyed the book as much as I enjoyed researching and writing it. Thank you for reading it. If you can, please do leave a review. Take a look at my website for articles and subscribe to my newsletter for updates, events and giveaways. The newsletter subscription page is on my website below:

carolcmcgrath.co.uk

If you would like to investigate Eleanor further or are interested in medieval gardens, a strong theme within the novel, here are a few books I recommend:

The Two Eleanors of Henry III by Darren Baker, published by Pen & Sword
Eleanor of Castile by Sara Cockerill (Amberley Press)

Edward I, A Great and Terrible King by Marc Morris (Pegasus)

Joanna de Valence by Linda E. Mitchell (Palgrave Macmillan)

Medieval English Gardens by Teresa McLean (Dover Publications Inc.)

The Subversive Stitch by Rozsika Parker (I.B. Tauris)

The Morville Hours by Katherine Swift (Bloomsbury)

The Time Traveller's Guide to Medieval England by Ian Mortimer (Vintage Books)

Everyday Life in Medieval London by Toni Mount (Amberley)

Medieval Women by Henrietta Leyser (Weidenfeld & Nicolson)

Acknowledgements

I would like to thank my editor Greg Rees for the amazing work he has put into editing this book. Greg, you are a very sharp and thorough editor as well as a delight to work with. Thanks also go to Rosanna Hildyard and Eleanor Dryden at Headline who both read an early draft and have been encouraging and supportive. Thanks also to The Vestas, Sue, Gail, and Denise, my critique group who read many chapters of *The Damask Rose*. Most of all I would like to thank Sara Cockerill, historian, who beta read this book and commented on its historical accuracy. Thank you, Sara. Your biography of Eleanor of Castile was an absolutely engaging and wonderful book. It inspired me to write *The Damask Rose*. Finally to my family, thank you, Patrick, Tara, and Ty, for your ongoing support when I am buried under research and busy writing. And to you, my loyal readers, thank you, because without you this book would remain a manuscript.

If you enjoyed *The Damask Rose*
be sure not to miss the first gripping novel in
the *She Wolves* trilogy . . .

They called her the She-Wolf from Provence.
She'd shape the destiny of England . . .

1236. Ailenor of Provence is only thirteen when she meets her
husband, Henry III of England. Foreign and friendless, she is
determined to please him. But as their love blossoms, England's
barons grow increasingly resentful.

Rosalind, an embroideress, catches the queen's attention and earns
her trust. But the young servant is unprepared for the dangerous
ramifications of winning royal favour.

Caught in a web of treachery and deceit, Ailenor must learn to be
ruthless. To protect those close to her, the She-Wolf from Provence
would do anything . . .

Available in paperback and ebook now!

ACCENT

For the latest news, updates and exclusive content from Carol McGrath, sign up to her newsletter at: www.CarolCMcGrath.co.uk

You can also find Carol McGrath on social media . . .

Like her on Facebook: facebook.com/CarolMcGrathAuthor1

Follow her on Twitter: @carolmcgrath

And follow Headline Accent: @AccentPress

ACCENT